J. Margot Critch graduated from Memorial with a BA in Religious Studies and Folklore. She currently lives in St John's, Newfoundland, with her own romance hero, Brian, and their little fur buddies. A self-professed Parrothead, when she isn't writing steamy contemporary romance and romantic suspense, she spends her time listening to Jimmy Buffett music and watching the ocean, all the while trying to decide if it's too early to make margaritas.

USA Today bestselling, *RITA®*-nominated, and critically-acclaimed author **Caitlin Crews** has written more than 130 books and counting. She has a Master's and PhD in English Literature, thinks everyone should read more category romance, and is always available to discuss her beloved alpha heroes. Just ask. She lives in the Pacific Northwest with her comic book artist husband, is always planning her next trip, and will never, ever, read all the books in her to-be-read pile. Thank goodness.

A former job-hopper, **Jessica Lemmon** resides in Ohio with her husband and rescue dog. When she's not writing super-sexy heroes, she can be found cooking, drawing, drinking coffee (okay, wine), and eating potato chips. She firmly believes God gifts us with talents for a purpose, and with His help, you can create the life you want. Learn more about her books at jessicalemmon.com

Sins and Seduction

Sins and Seduction:

Her Every
Fantasy

J. MARGOT CRITCH

CAITLIN CREWS

JESSICA LEMMON

MILLS & BOON

First Published in Great Britain 2023
by Mills & Boon, an imprint of HarperCollins*Publishers* Ltd,
1 London Bridge Street, London, SE1 9GF

www.harpercollins.co.uk

HarperCollins*Publishers*
Macken House, 39/40 Mayor Street Upper,
Dublin 1, D01 C9W8, Ireland

Sins And Seduction: Her Every Fantasy © 2023 Harlequin Enterprises ULC.

Taming Reid © 2020 Juanita Margot Critch
Untamed Billionaire's Innocent Bride © 2019 Caitlin Crews
Best Friends, Secret Lovers © 2019 Jessica Lemmon

ISBN: 978-0-263-31876-0

This book is produced from independently certified FSC™ paper
to ensure responsible forest management.

For more information visit: www.harpercollins.co.uk/green

Printed and Bound in the UK using 100% Renewable electricity at
CPI Group (UK) Ltd, Croydon, CR0 4YY

TAMING REID

J. MARGOT CRITCH

For my author besties, Janice and Candace. Thank you for all your love, support, advice, plotting sessions and late-night conversations over wine. You're the best!

CHAPTER ONE

REID REXFORD RAISED the glass to his lips and tasted the amber liquid it held. Up until that moment, the *tres leches* cake had been the best thing he'd tasted that night, but his cleaned plate lay forgotten on the table next to the unlabeled bottle of rum that Gemma had brought. They were preferred customers at the Cuban restaurant owned by his close friend, Arlo. And for a good deal on Rexford Rum for his restaurant, Arlo gave them a great table every time they came in and allowed them to do such things as open their own bottle of Gemma's newest concoction at their table.

Reid took another small sip, and this time held it in his mouth, rolling the rum around, savoring the intricacies and the layers of the flavor on his tongue. It was smooth, delicious. He tasted it again, as his brother Quin did the same, this time taking a moment to inhale over the rim of the glass, pulling the scent into his lungs—it was dark, sweet, but spicy, with notes of cardamom, cinnamon, and something else he couldn't yet place. It was absolutely exquisite. He winked at his sister. She had really outdone herself this time.

"Well?" Gemma asked, her eyes wide with anticipation for their opinions. "How does it taste?"

He shrugged casually. "It's pretty good," he said, putting the glass down. A clatter from the kitchen briefly muted their conversation.

Reid looked at Quin, who drank from his glass again and also put on a casual demeanor in an attempt to needle their younger sister.

Gemma's smile dropped. And Reid knew her well enough to tell that their nonchalance clearly annoyed her. "Come on, guys," she said. "This is one of the best batches I've ever made, and you both know it. What do you mean, it's just *good*?"

Reid laughed, and put a hand on her shoulder, shaking her lightly. He knew how important the quality of her rum—and his opinion of it—was to her as she'd meticulously worked on the recipe for months, perfecting the proper blend of spices, making sure it would be just right before it had even been mixed, distilled and barrel-aged. The bottle they were tasting was a product of her love and dedication that had been more than five years in the making. "We're messing with you, Gem. It's delicious! You're right— one of your best yet."

She smacked his shoulder, took the glass from his fingers and sipped it herself. His sister's satisfied smile spoke volumes to Reid. Gemma, a perfectionist, who was rarely fully satisfied with the finished product, was proud of her newest rum.

"How'd you make it?" Quin asked, pouring a little more from the bottle into his glass.

"The short answer is I cut the cane sugar with honey and then added more later in the process, and I used those cognac barrels I picked up in France last year. Plus a few more special touches here and there." She winked.

"Honey?" Reid started calculating cost per bottle formulas in his head as he swirled the glass in his hand, watching as the legs of the liquid—thick and rich—trailed down the sides. "Sounds expensive," he noted with a frown, recalling the recent high price of honey.

"Probably," she said, with a shrug. "But you're the numbers guy, I'm just the cook." She wasn't just the cook; she was their master distiller. She'd trained for years—since before she was even legally allowed to drink rum—to be as good as she was, and Reid was more than proud of her. It might have been his business savvy that had elevated Rexford Rum Distillery, and Quin's marketing expertise and networking that had had made the exclusive luxury brand popular and well-known, but it was Gemma's rum that had put them on the map, making them a premium spirit to be found in the collection of every rich and powerful man and woman in the country. "But, if it helps," she continued, "it's specialized enough, given the fact we only had six cognac barrels, that it's a very small batch. We can raise the price even more. Put it in a funky bottle, make it a luxury item. Drive up demand. You know our customers; they'll want it if they think the next guy can't get it. Quin will put the perfect spin on it in marketing, and we'll make oodles of money."

"Solid plan," Quin said, draining his own glass in celebration with a smile on his face.

Reid knew they were both correct. "All right, email me the ingredients and quantities you used, and I'll start crunching some numbers tomorrow."

"I'm taking tomorrow off, so I'll get it to you first thing on Monday morning." When he looked at her, she raised her hands. "Dude, I work enough hours during the week that I can take a Friday off every once in a while. You should do the same."

"Fine." He turned to Quin, always in business mode, even when they were supposed to be having a quiet, leisurely dinner together. "We'll get started on a marketing plan, and we can launch in the summer."

"On Monday," Quin clarified.

"So, you're all taking Friday off, then?"

"Yup. Thursday night is the new Friday night."

"Fine. On Monday," Reid agreed, knowing he wouldn't win the battle.

He turned back to Gemma, already formulating a game plan. "How will the batch have aged by summer?"

"It'll be perfect." She plucked her phone from her small purse and smiled when she looked at the screen. "I'll send you that list first thing in the morning, but for now, I'm out of here."

"You have plans?" Reid asked.

"Yeah, I have a date. Unlike you, I do have a life outside of rum, you know. I haven't given up on all of my wild ways," she said with a wink.

The allusion to their past lives made Reid cringe. In their younger years, the three of them had spent a lot of time at nightclubs, at parties, while their parents worked at making Rexford Rum, the business that had been in their family for generations, a well-known brand. But overnight, their lives had changed with the death of their mother, and their father had stepped back from business. It was then that Reid and his siblings had realized it was up to them to keep the business going if they wanted Rexford Rum to stay alive. He'd had the most complete turnaround, abandoning his raucous lifestyle, settling down, getting married—as well as that had worked out for him—while his brother and sister, as devoted to the business as they were, still managed to find lots of time to have some fun.

"And you know what, I'm wondering why you guys don't have anything lined up for yourselves tonight."

"Who says I don't?" Quin shrugged a shoulder. "The night is still pretty young for me, lots of time to round up some female company."

"You're such a romantic," Gemma said, rolling her eyes.

Reid felt his sister's gaze settle on him. "How about you, big brother? Any hot plans tonight?"

"Gemma—" He'd planned on crashing on the couch with a drink and watching the game, but the unlabeled bottle of rum on the table had changed that. The thought of heading down to the office and planning the new release and cost calculations had his fingers tapping on the table. When it came to passion, the distillery had replaced everything else in his life.

"I know, *you're busy*," she countered, using the words he'd said many times against her. She pursed her lips as she studied him and tilted her head to the side. "When was the last time you were on a date?"

When the urge struck him, which, honestly, wasn't often, Reid had no problem finding women, those who, like him, weren't interested in a drawn-out affair, but an actual *date*? Where he sat across from a woman, and they talked and got to know each other? He poured another finger of rum into the short glass and brought it to his lips. "You know when," he said, grimacing behind his glass, before he took a large swallow.

He could feel his sister's exasperation at him. "That was over two years ago," Gemma told him— like he didn't know—shaking her head. "Carolina did a number on you. But you can't be alone your entire life because of one mistake."

He looked at her. "That *one mistake* almost cost

us everything. I'm not going to let it happen again. So could you just get off my back already?"

"That doesn't mean you shouldn't see any women ever again," she told him. When he said nothing, she kept going. "Two years, Reid. What happened wasn't your fault. Since that whole thing with Carolina, we're all a lot more careful with our information. She's the one who got into our databases. She's the one who turned the information over to our competitors. You made a mistake in trusting the wrong person. We all did. It's time to move on."

"I'm not interested," he insisted. "I've got enough going on with the business. I've completely ruled out any type of relationship. Where would I find the time to devote to another person?"

Gemma's sigh was one of impatience. He knew because he often heard it in his direction when they argued about that very subject. "Fine," she said, standing. "I'm out of here. I'm busy, too, Reid, but I find a little time for a social life."

"Have a good night," Reid told her, dismissing her, not wanting to discuss his social life—or lack thereof—any further. "Be safe."

"You know I will."

"Don't forget, we have a party to prepare for next week," Reid told her. "There's still lots to do." Every year, they threw a party for their employees, industry insiders, and preferred customers. This year, however, they'd decided to go bigger. They'd spent the entire year planning a huge party at a hip beachside rooftop bar in South Beach. They'd shelled out huge cash for one of the country's most popular DJs, and in addition to their regular guest list, they invited celebrities and members of the press. More Quin and Gemma's doing, the party wasn't his kind of scene, but he was hoping to make some serious connections and it would help put Rexford Rum on the map.

"I haven't forgotten, *Dad*," she said, rolling her eyes, earning herself a glare from Reid. She raised her hands in surrender. "Believe me, no one is forgetting about work, or the party." She kissed him on the cheek. "Love you guys. Bye."

"Make good choices," Quin called out to her, and that earned him a middle finger over her shoulder as she made her way outside. When she was gone, Quin pointed a finger at him. "Speaking of the party, we've been meaning to talk to you about this—at least try to look like you're having fun. You don't want to be mistaken for one of the bouncers with that serious look you normally have on your face."

"Fine, I'll smile more. Will that make you happy? But sorry, I won't have time to schmooze with celebrities. Some of us will have to make sure things are running smoothly."

"That's why we hired a very capable event planning company," he told him. "Who we're paying very well to make sure everything is okay. I know it isn't normally your scene but promise me you'll have fun. It's going to be great for us."

"Fine, I'll have fun at the party. I just hope the cost will be worth it to the business."

Quin sighed and poured himself some more rum. "It will be. We went through the projections ourselves. With the press coverage and the online buzz we've already created…dude, it's going to be amazing."

Despite his reservations, Reid smiled at his brother. He'd been a hard sell when it came to the party. He thought the it was an egregious expense, one that could put the distillery at risk—not only financially, but its failure could hurt their brand. They had some of the best event planners in Miami working on it, but he wasn't sure he could put the faith in it like Quin and Gemma did. "I hope so. I hate to think we bankrupted the company for an excuse to invite a certain professional wrestler-turned-actor to our party."

"Already RSVP'd," Quin said with a wink, reminding Reid that despite his opinion of the event, the Rexford party was looking like the hottest ticket in Miami. He knocked back the remainder of the rum. "And on that note, I'm out of here, too."

"Yeah?"

"A friend of mine has Heat tickets. Courtside."

Reid nodded in approval. "Nice. Close enough you can yell at the coach again?"

"If only he'd listen to me." Quin shook his head.

"Have fun. Don't get arrested. We have too much to do in the next couple of days and I don't have time to bail you out."

"You can count on me, bro." They bumped fists, and then Quin was gone as well, leaving Reid alone at the table with a mostly full rum bottle and the bill. "Typical," he said to the closed folio, which held the bill. But it didn't matter to him. What good was money if he couldn't use it to treat his siblings at their favorite restaurant?

He nodded to the server, who quickly came over to collect his credit card, and she smiled as she leaned over the table, giving him a peek at her ample cleavage. They made eye contact, and she said, "Thank you, Mr. Rexford," in a sultry, breathy whisper. He sat back, away from her—his body language putting a barrier between them. She picked up on his cues and straightened, immediately reverting back to being his waitress. He handed her the rum bottle. "Can you see that Arlo gets the rest of this?"

"Of course, I'll put it in his office."

"Thank you."

He watched closely as she walked away. While the waitress was gorgeous, and they would definitely have a great night together, it wouldn't do. She was his regular server at his favorite restaurant, and even though Reid could barely remember her name, she was much too close to him, and knew exactly who he was. But as his eyes followed the sway of the server's hips, his attention caught on the cloud of red hair of the woman sitting at the bar.

The curve of the woman's spine and her smooth skin tempted him, as did the completely open back of her black dress, cut just above what looked to be an ample ass. The woman laughed at something the bartender said. Her laugh was loud and vivacious, and rang out in the quiet, dark space of the restaurant. But neither her volume nor the looks it garnered from the other patrons seemed to embarrass her. He could feel the energy emanating off her, bouncing against the cellar walls, hitting him square in the chest. It sounded stupid, corny, but the small restaurant felt brighter with her in it.

He couldn't help but watch her as she brought her glass to her lips and sipped. Her eyes closed, and her full lips turned upward in a delicate smile and she said something else to the bartender. She was easily the sexiest woman in the room.

He smiled and stood. Checked his watch. He could go talk to her and still get home early enough to put together a plan for the newest rum. Maybe the night wouldn't be such a bust, after all.

Lila Campbell really liked the small, underground cellar vibe of the restaurant. She'd gotten word that the Cuban restaurant was one of Miami's best-kept secrets, and the somewhat hard-to-find restaurant hadn't disappointed. Her dinner had been delicious, and the follow-up cocktail was divine. She was now working on a dessert of in-house-made vanilla bean ice cream drizzled with a thick spiced rum sauce that was so decadent, she'd have to spend extra time at the gym working it off.

Holding her phone above her, she took a picture of herself bringing a spoonful to her mouth. She checked it—*definitely cute*—and it was good to post. Some people hated selfies, thought they were shallow, but Lila didn't care. She thought back to when she was younger. Maybe she would have been one of those women who judged others like that, but she knew it would have been her own insecurities at play. Taking a picture that she felt was good enough to post was hard for her, but it was getting easier. Sure, she still saw the nasty comments some trolls left on her posts, but she just had to shrug and move on.

"I gotta ask you." The pretty bartender, Amanda, leaned closer. "Are you that girl from Instagram?"

"Which one?" she asked. "There are a few girls on Instagram."

"Lila, is it?"

"Well, my name is Lila."

"I knew it." Amanda nodded at her drink. "That one's on the house. Yours is one of my favorite accounts."

"I'm glad to hear it. Come here," she crooked her finger at her, and when she leaned in, Lila snapped a picture of both of them. "I'll post that one later. Thanks for everything."

Arlo's would get a stellar review on her blog, and she knew that her word would ensure they had month-long waiting lists for at least a year. It had happened before, and she took a moment to revel in the online power she had. The staff was friendly, and the drinks and food were delicious. As she sipped her rum and Coke, she again hummed appreciatively at the flavor of—she checked the label on the bottle behind the bar—Rexford Rum, which was not cheap, but a local favorite, the bartender had told her.

Tilting her head to the side, she thought something about the name was familiar. And then she remembered. She'd managed to secure an invitation to their upcoming party next Saturday when their marketing manager had reached out to her about attending in exchange for a few posts. The buzz was that it would be attended by athletes and celebrities. The address she'd been given was for the rooftop of a swanky beachside hotel, and it promised to be a good time. She was looking forward to the party but being seen there would also boost her own reputation. Which would help her gain more negotiating clout for when she met with the GO! Channel.

She'd been in talks with the network for months, to take her well-known online persona and translate it to television. She could imagine it now, traveling around the world, the steady paycheck that would give her more stability, and let her put down some roots in Los Angeles. She never thought she wanted to settle in one place, but as she got older, she saw the value in having a home to call her own.

As she brought her spoon to her lips again, she froze, feeling someone come up behind her. Lila straightened her spine, turning on her best thousand-yard stare, which she used whenever men approached her when she traveled alone. She was ready for every cheesy pickup line. She'd heard them all. With her cocktail in hand, Lila turned, took a sip, hoping to look cool and indifferent, but instead her eyes roamed up the man's body to his face, and she gulped down her drink in one mouthful. He put his hand on the back of the empty stool beside her. She watched, transfixed by his long, strong fingers as they flexed on the wooden frame of the back. "Is anybody sitting here?"

She shook her head, unable to speak. It had been a long, *long* time since a man's looks—his presence— had left her so completely dumbfounded.

"Good," he said with a smile.

"Your usual, sir?" the bartender asked him.

"Please," he answered, without taking his dark brown eyes from her. "And get another one for the lady."

Usually, the presumption of a man buying her a drink would have driven Lila insane. She hated overbearing men, and normally, she would have asked him to leave, but there was something about the man next to her that intrigued her. Whether it was his extreme confidence, his impeccable looks, or the scent of his cologne, she was rooted in place. And it had been so, so long since she'd been in the company of a gorgeous man. Amanda looked at her in confirmation and she nodded, willing to get to know the stranger.

He took the seat next to her, and in a short time,

the bartender put a tumbler with a couple of fingers of dark liquor next to her new drink.

He picked up his glass with long, confident fingers and used it to gesture to her own glass. "What did I just order for you?"

"Cuba Libre."

He drank from his glass and nodded. "Good drink."

"Yeah," she agreed. "I'm told it's Rexford Rum, based here in Miami. I have to say, it's pretty good."

"Just pretty good?" He smiled. "I've heard it's the best."

"Well, I don't know about that," she teased, sipping from her glass, not taking her eyes from his as he did the same. She felt a spark that sizzled between them and stuck out her hand. "Hi, I'm Lila."

"Lila," he repeated, letting the last syllable roll off his tongue. She wanted to keep hearing him say her name. "That's a pretty name."

"Thanks, I've had it all my life." He smiled at her joke, and drank from his glass, but said nothing. "Do you have a name there, hun?"

He seemed to hesitate, but then change his mind. "Reid."

"What can I do for you, Reid?"

"I was just at my table, but then I saw you sitting here. And I'm curious why a gorgeous woman like yourself is sitting here all by herself," he told her.

She bristled at his comment. "What's wrong with me sitting alone? We're well into the twenty-first century." Reid opened his mouth to speak, but Lila didn't give him a chance. "Maybe I just like my own company. Maybe I *choose* to be here alone. Isn't that a good enough reason?"

He blinked quickly, probably not used to having women speak to him like that. "Do you want me to leave? If you're enjoying your own company, I don't want to intrude."

Lila thought of telling him to leave, thought of leaving herself. Lila didn't normally like to invite male attention, especially when she was on assignment, because it was hard enough for women traveling alone, without bringing men into the mix. But there was something about Reid—and she couldn't back away. "No," she said, putting her fingers on his wrist. "You can stay."

"Good."

She wasn't sure why she'd touched him, but it had proven to be a mistake, as Reid took her hand in his, turned it over, and brought it to his mouth. He placed his lips to the inside of her wrist. His warm, dry lips on her almost caused her to stop breathing. Who was this man—this stranger she'd found in a small South Beach restaurant—lighting a trail of desire from her pulse point all the way to her own South Beach?

It was stupid, risky. This guy was a complete stranger. He could be anyone. But when the tip of his tongue flicked against her skin, she realized that it didn't matter who he was.

Reid's lips closed over her skin again and his dark

eyes connected with hers. Lila was transfixed by him, as the rest of the small restaurant fell away. Just the two of them existed in that moment—and she didn't even know his last name. Maybe privacy and anonymity were for the better. She had built up her blog and her reputation to where they were, and she knew that one public misstep could ruin her, especially with everything she had coming up. She had to be on her best behavior. Any rumor or scandal could end her. But none of that seemed to matter when Reid looked at her.

But thankfully, her sanity won out. "Wait," she said, her words more sighed than spoken.

He backed away immediately, releasing her from his touch. "What is it?"

She took a deep breath and gulped down the rest of her drink. "I don't even know who you are. Who are you? What's your last name?" He didn't say anything. "No last name, Reid? Or do you just go by your first—like Sting or Bono?"

"Oh, I have a last name—I'm just not keen on sharing it."

Lila shook her head, and then laughed at the seriousness of his voice. The fact that the man wouldn't give her his last name was a real red flag for her. "You sound so fucking dramatic. What, are you in the mob or witness protection, or a serial killer, or something?"

"That did sound dramatic, didn't it?" he asked with a lopsided smile. She nodded. "I'm just a private person. I promise, I'm not in the mob or witness protection, or a serial killer."

"You know, if you were any of those things, wouldn't you insist that you weren't?"

"That's a good point. I guess you'll have to trust me." He looked around and waved to the bartender. "Amanda, can you come here for a second?"

She stopped wiping down the counter and joined them.

"Amanda, you can vouch for me, right? I'm a good guy?"

The bartender smiled. "He's a preferred regular customer, close friends with the boss, and a good tipper."

"Thanks Amanda."

"No problem, Mr. Rexford," she said and went back to her task behind the bar."

Lila and Reid both shared a laugh at his name having been revealed. "So, I guess you have a name, after all."

"I guess I do."

"I always consider service staff to be the best judges of character." She leaned in closer to him. "And I have to say hearing a guy is a good tipper is a major turn-on for me."

"That's the first time a woman has ever told me that."

"You should date more socially conscious women, I guess."

"Yeah, I guess so," he said with a smile.

Amanda came back and nodded at their now-empty glasses. "Another round?"

Reid looked at her. She wasn't sure what to say. Another round would keep them talking at the bar. But refusing another drink would free up the rest of their evening, whatever they hoped to do with it. Reid took her hand again. "Tell me, beautiful, do you want another drink?" he asked, his thumb tracing light but red-hot circles over the inside of her wrist. There was no way he could miss her thundering pulse beneath her skin. "What do you want?"

Lila tried to find her voice, but it was nearly impossible. *What do I want?* "I want you to keep touching me."

"Do you want to get out of here?"

Lila's mind raced through the lusty fog he'd created in her brain. She felt a connection with the man sitting next to her, but she wasn't sure if she was ready to go somewhere with a complete stranger—no matter how good of a time she knew they would have together. Never in her life had she had a one-night stand with a strange man. She may have possessed a sense of adventure, but she wasn't reckless. With as much as she traveled, Lila knew the world could be a dangerous place. As a woman, and a solo traveler, she had to look after herself—another reason she was glad to have the legitimacy of a potential network deal ahead of her. But as the stranger's deep brown eyes bored into hers, she could barely think straight. The promise that was held in the strange man's touch, his rich scent and his deep voice, were almost too much to bear. "What do you have in mind?"

Amanda backed away discreetly, giving them some much-needed privacy.

Reid leaned in next to her, pushed her hair away from her ear and got closer so that his lips brushed the outer shell of her ear. She shivered at the contact. "I'm not going to pretend here. You're gorgeous, and I'm interested," he whispered. "We have a connection, and I want you underneath me, on top of me, bent over a table. I know we could have fun together, at least for one night. So, yeah, we could put off the inevitable for a couple of hours, get another drink or two, talk, get to know each other, but I don't see why we should."

"Especially since we already know enough about each other?" She teased, trying to lighten the mood. Part of her—the reasonable part—wanted to say no to him. Every ounce of self-preservation begged her to refuse him. But instead, she put her hand on his rock-hard thigh.

He put his hand over hers and it was then she saw the way his pants were tented, showing her that he did indeed want her as much as she wanted him.

"I think we know enough about each other," he told her. "Don't you?"

She nodded. This was it. She was going to do something she had never done before—a one-night stand with a strange man. "My hotel is near here."

Reid signaled Amanda, and before she could stop

him, he'd taken out his wallet and laid down several bills to pay for her meal and drinks. More than enough to cover the total and still have enough left over for a sizable tip—just as she'd expected. Soon they were out the door, and in the alley where the restaurant entrance was located.

They walked up the street and she inhaled. There was normally something so sweet and sensual about the smell of Miami—the scent of midnight jasmine, the sand, the sea, the smell of the food and coffee. Glamorous people wearing expensive perfume and cologne. Even at night, this close to the beach, she could almost smell the suntan lotion, coconut and shea, and the fruit-flavored cocktails. Citrus. Rum. Reid. It might have all been in her head, but walking next to Reid, his hand at her lower back, his fingertips curling over the skin exposed by the risqué cut of her backless dress, she knew she wasn't imagining it—there was something else in the air. The night, the city itself, breathed sex. It filled the air and covered them like a blanket.

She looked up at Reid. He hadn't said a word since leaving the restaurant.

"Where are you staying?" he asked.

When the small white stone boutique hotel came into view, she said a quick prayer to the nookie gods, thanking them for the short walk. "Right here," she told him.

"Thank God," Reid murmured in a little prayer of his own. It shocked her when his arm snaked around hers and he whipped her around and pushed her against the outer wall of the building. His head lowered, and before she could catch her breath, his lips crashed onto hers. Reid's kiss was hard, demanding, and it was exactly what she wanted. Correction: what she needed. Her lips parted and he took full advantage, his tongue was warm, wet and searching, stroking against her own.

Her arms encircled Reid's neck and she pulled him closer. He moaned and pressed her into the exterior wall of the hotel. One of his thighs found its way between her legs, and he pressed it against her already wet panties. His touch was almost enough to make her fall to the sidewalk, but thankfully, he was the one holding her up.

With a groan, he pulled away from her, his eyes smoldered. "I'd better get you inside, before I fuck you right here." He took her hand, and all but dragged her through the hotel lobby to the elevator. When the doors closed on them, he pulled her to him. Kissing her again. The man had a devilish mouth. And she had no choice but to submit to his sinful lips. He smoothed his hands down her arms, and found her breasts, squeezing them. She thrust her chest toward him, leaning into his touch, willing Reid's fingers to go further. His fingertips curled underneath the thin material of the low neckline of her dress. She wanted Reid to never stop touching her. But the elevator came to a halt, and she barely noticed when the doors slid open in front of them.

"Lead the way." His whisper was gruff in her ear, and she pulled him down the hall. At her door, her hands trembled so that she could barely use her key card. He chuckled, took the card from her fingers, and slid it easily into the door. It was slightly embarrassing that she was far more aroused than he was. Men rarely affected her in such a way. But there was something about Reid. He made her brain so foggy with need that she couldn't think straight.

They walked into her room. But instead of stripping the clothes from her body like she wanted Reid to, he took a step back, deliberately putting several feet between them. "Do you want this?"

"I wouldn't have brought you here if I didn't."

He took a step forward. Closer, but still out of her reach. "Lila, I want to hear you say the words. That you want this."

Lila looked over the man in front of her. She didn't have to look at the large bulge of his cock to see how much he wanted her. His strong body was rigid, tense. His shoulders heaved with heavy, desperate breaths. His whole body demonstrated his desire. But he still stood before her, seeking explicit consent from her, and she smiled, charmed by it.

It was her call. Despite his powerful presence, and the effect he had on her, she was in complete control. Lila took a step toward him, bringing her breasts flush with his broad chest. She wasn't wearing a bra—as if the low cut of the back of her dress would have allowed it—and her sensitized nipples sent shocks of electricity throughout her body, as they brushed against his chest. He reached down and grazed her fingertips along the ridge of the bulge. He shuddered underneath her touch, and she grinned.

Lifting up on her toes, she leaned over and brought her lips to the edge of his ear. She snaked her tongue out and traced the outside. "Reid, I want you. And I want this." She paused. "I want you to fuck me."

He let go of the breath he was holding. He put his fingers on her jaw and drew her face upward to his. The hunger in his eyes was unmistakable. "This can only be one night. You know that, right?"

"Sounds good to me." She was in Miami for a little over a week, and she already had a full itinerary. Where would she fit in more time with Reid, even if she wanted to? And plus, if she already felt like falling completely apart at his touch after only a few minutes, how would she survive another encounter? "I know. That's what's best for both of us. I don't expect anything else from you, as long as you do the same."

His smile was easy and charming. And she was struck again with how attractive he was. The chiseled jaw, high cheek bones, straight nose and dark brown eyes all joined forces to create one irresistible man. And while she knew nothing about him except his name, he was everything she would have asked for in a one-night stand. "It's a deal," he said, putting out his hand.

Lila let out a laugh that was more like a breath

at his formal gesture, and she took his hand in hers. When their palms clasped together, Lila felt as if they shared one pulse as electricity traveled between them, strong enough to power the entire city.

In the quiet room, they looked at each other, neither's eyes wavering. But Reid's friendly smile then turned wolfish, as if he knew that she was his, and he would spend his night feasting on her.

Without releasing her, he pulled on her hand, causing her to crash against his firm chest.

"Now, where were we?" he murmured.

"I think, outside the hotel, you promised to fuck me," she reminded him.

"Oh yeah, that's right," he said, his fingers curling over her waist and venturing lower. He kissed her, and just the feeling of his lips against her made her moan.

Already she was growing accustomed to Reid's touch, and she knew that until her dying day, she would crave his fingers and lips. Through the anticipation that clouded her brain as his hands roamed underneath her dress, she reminded herself of their agreement.

Just for one night.

CHAPTER TWO

REID DROPPED TO his knees in front of Lila, and with his hands on her round, lush ass, he pressed his face to the lower part of her abdomen and inhaled her scent, opening his mouth against her, and the silky material of her dress, pulling her essence more deeply into his lungs. He wasn't sure what had possessed him to go home with her. He didn't even know why he approached her or why he came on so strong. It wasn't like him; he normally didn't lose control over women. But despite himself, something about Lila had drawn him in. She was vivacious, gorgeous, and when he kissed her—tasting his own rum on her tongue—it did something to him. He didn't have a chance when it came to her. He was a goner.

He should be at home, or at the office, making sure the last-minute things for the party were finalized and that no crises were about to occur, but that didn't seem to matter to him when he was about to bury himself fully within a woman he needed more than he did his next breath. He looked up at her and saw she was watching him, her green eyes not leaving his, her chest heaving. "What are you waiting for?" she breathed, pushing her fingers through his hair.

"Just taking a moment to enjoy it," he told her.

"There will be lots of moments to enjoy tonight, won't there?"

"You know there will."

"Well, get to it then," she told him.

"Yes, ma'am." He smoothed his hands up her thighs, underneath her dress, his palms gliding over some of the smoothest, silkiest skin he'd ever touched. His journey paused when his reached the lace edge of her panties. Stopping just short of ripping the delicate undergarment in two pieces, he instead hooked his fingers underneath the fabric and pulled the peach lace down her thighs, dropping it to the floor. She stepped out of her panties gingerly and he pushed up her dress so that the tight skirt sat above her hips, exposing her center to him fully.

Lila was delectable, a masterpiece, a treat to be admired and enjoyed by every sense. His mouth watered with a hunger for her, his appetite voracious like he'd never experienced before, and he needed to taste her.

He slid his hand down the entire length of her leg, exploring, lightly tickling the back of her knee, squeezing her well-formed calf, wrapping his fingers around her ankle and draping her leg over his shoulder. He leaned forward, burying his face between her creamy thighs. He gripped her ass, bringing her closer to him. His fingers dug into the firm flesh of her behind, as his tongue spread her lips and he flicked the sweet little bud of her clit with the tip. She moaned, arching into his mouth, and twisted her fingers in his hair, and pulled. Hard. But with Lila surrounding him, unable to hear or feel anything but her, the pain barely registered.

Lila was so responsive, so delicious, and with every stroke of his tongue, pinch of his lips, every slide of his fingers, her moans grew louder, and he could feel the tension build in her body. Her thigh muscles clenched against the side of his head, muffling her cries. She was perfect and he could listen to her desperate sounds forever. His own body ached with the need to be inside her. But he stayed his course. Even though his dick threatened to burst through the material of his pants, he wouldn't stop until he made her come first.

When he hit the right spot, the tremor of her body became a full-fledged earthquake that made her shake. With his lips surrounding her clit, he sucked, prodded with his tongue, bringing her down from her climax, and riding out every aftershock of pleasure with her.

When her grip on his head loosened, Reid stood while unbuckling his pants. But her own fingers joined his, and she beat him in withdrawing his dick. She stroked his length. But he was so goddamn close to erupting that even though he hated to, he had to push her away.

He was so far gone that he almost forgot his golden rule. "Condoms?" he asked her, his tongue thick with passion. Of course, he didn't carry one with him. He wasn't his brother. He couldn't remember the last time he'd had the need, as he wasn't usually one for spontaneous encounters.

"Right." On wobbly legs she walked over to the bed and dug into the cosmetic case that sat at the foot. She pulled out a small foil square and he nearly shuddered with relief.

He crossed the room in a matter of seconds and instead of laying her on the bed, he picked her up and sat her on the small desk next to her laptop. He stood between her parted thighs as she ripped open the packet and rolled the condom over him. Her touch was torture, but he would soon find his sweet relief. He didn't even have time for either of them to undress. He needed to be buried deep inside her. He lifted Lila, tilting her hips to the right angle. When she wrapped her legs around his ass, he held her against the wall as he entered her.

She was hot, wet. *Heaven.* And as he pumped his hips, thrusting into her, he brought both of them higher and higher. If he thought eating from her was amazing, being buried deep inside of her sweet heat was pure bliss.

Lila, her arms wrapped tightly around his shoulders, sought out his mouth with her own. He kissed her lips, and the flavor of her that coated his tongue mingled with the taste of her mouth. He swallowed the moan that came from her throat as it met his own.

Sliding against her slickness, Reid knew he wouldn't last much longer. He broke away from her mouth, and trailed his lips in a line across her jaw and down her throat. And judging by her moans and sighs in his ear, he knew she wouldn't either. Reid gritted his teeth and vowed to hang on until she came again. Her body tightened against him, and her breaths became pants. He increased the speed of his thrusts, and she clenched around him. That was all he needed. He let go, his toes curled in his shoes, and he came with a groan and buried his face in the crook of her neck. The comedown was bliss-ful, and as his balls emptied, she milked him of ev-erything he had.

Taking a breath, he released her, helping her get her footing on the floor. As she straightened her dress, Reid pulled off the condom and tossed it in a nearby trash can. He caught his breath as she reached into the small fridge in the bar area, pulling out two bottles of water. He finally looked around and saw that they were in a huge, luxuriously appointed hotel room. Large windows with panoramic views of the famed South Beach and Atlantic Ocean.

"Sparkling or still?" she asked, holding the two bottles aloft.

"Still's good." He took the bottle from her. "Nice room."

"Yeah." She took a swallow of the water. The red flush still colored her cheeks. "I travel a lot for work. I normally stay at more modest places, but what the hell? I'm in Miami. I got a great deal. I might as well treat myself, right?"

He didn't know a lot about treating himself lately, but he nodded. "What do you do?"

Her lips pursed. "I thought we weren't exchanging information?"

"You're right," he said, taking another drink. He needed to hydrate but with every swallow, her taste vanished from his mouth, and he craved it, wanting nothing more than to get it back. Asking her the question had been a mistake, since they'd agreed on anonymity. If he asked her about who she was, then it would lead to her asking about him. No matter what, his privacy was the most important thing to him, and he was committed to not putting himself out there ever again.

"You know, I don't ever do this," she said, her back to him, as she used her fingers to brush through her red hair, checking out her reflection in the mirror. He could see the small red marks he'd made on her neck, and the rash from his five o'clock shadow marred her creamy skin.

He caught her eyes in her reflection in the mirror as he straightened his own clothing. The finality of them straightening up disappointed him. Despite their agreement for it to be one night only, he wanted more time with her. "Do what?" he asked.

"Meet strangers, immediately have sex with them."

Reid shrugged. "You don't have to explain yourself. I don't care what you do—or have done—with anyone else." He went to her, cupped her jaw and trailed his fingers down her delicate throat, soothing the redness he'd caused. "The only thing that matters is that we're here together. And I've got you tonight."

Lila was quiet. She stood back from him, pulling her jaw away from his fingers. "Well, Reid. This has been a lot of fun. Thanks."

He frowned. "Are you kicking me out?"

"No, but you said it would just be once."

"I didn't say that."

"But you said—"

"I said it was one *night*." He looked casually at his watch. It was only nine thirty, and he made a dramatic show of removing his watch from his wrist, laying it on the nearby nightstand. "The night isn't over yet."

CHAPTER THREE

THE SUN WAS higher in the sky than usual when Reid woke the next morning. He sat on the edge of his bed and wiped his palm over his face. He was exhausted, worn, and could barely find the energy to stand. *That's what you get for not staying on schedule.* He was thirty-five years old. Too old to be out so late with strange women. As tired as he was, he couldn't regret spending the night with Lila, no matter how out of character it was for him.

Eventually he mustered the strength to stand and pulled on a pair of gray sweatpants. After only managing to get a couple hours of sleep, he was tired, irritable, and even though he'd been with Lila until the early morning hours, he was nowhere near physically sated. He wanted her again. Lila's image took up real estate front and center of his mind, and he didn't know if he'd ever be able to forget her. Every time he closed his eyes, she was there. He could hear her voice, smell her on his skin, taste her on his lips, and when his head finally hit his pillow a few hours ago, he realized just how empty his California king bed was. Jesus, he was in trouble. His determination to stick to his plan of having just a one-night stand was wavering. No matter how much he tried to forget her, Lila had completely consumed him. And the next morning, she still did.

In his bathroom, he propped himself up by placing his hands on the bathroom counter, and in the mirror, he caught sight of the day-old stubble that colored his jaw and the dark, tired circles under his red-rimmed eyes. Thank God his siblings had decided to take the day off. Now he could just hide out in his office. And no one would see him in his current condition, and know he'd been up for most of the night.

The need for coffee was strong. So strong that when he inhaled, he could already smell the aroma of it already brewing in the kitchen. He sighed. One—or both—of his siblings had apparently let themselves into his house and made coffee. Even though they had their own homes, both Quin and Gemma had keys to his and often let themselves in. But because he normally woke up before either of them, it was the first time he hadn't already been dressed and ready for their visit. He would undoubtedly face some sort of inquisition this morning about why he wasn't yet awake.

He straightened and groaned with the movement. He was in shape, but his body was sore from the previous night's exertion. His night with Lila had left him seriously discombobulated and had already completely thrown off his morning routine. He had to get back to what he knew—his office, work, his family. He started to mentally tick through his to-do list for the day, and he blanked, not able to remember a fucking thing. He wondered how he could possibly have clarity when all he could think about was the red-haired woman with whom he'd spent the night.

Still wearing only his sweatpants, Reid walked into the large kitchen of his house, and as always, it was made bright and warm by the morning sun through the windows and glass door. He squinted against the harsh light and saw Gemma and Quin getting breakfast ready. Both sets of eyes looked at him, and it was as if they'd known what he'd done the night before.

"Well, if it isn't Sleeping Beauty," Gemma said over her shoulder, standing at the stove over a pan of sizzling bacon. Quin was sitting at the table, drinking coffee, scrolling through the tablet in his hand.

Reid grunted in response and made a beeline for the coffee maker. He poured himself a mug and looked in the frying pans on the stove, which his sister would no doubt leave dirty in the sink for him to take care of. Egg white omelet, bacon and sliced fruit, most likely from the trees in Gemma's garden. Snagging a strawberry from the cutting board, he ignored their curious stares.

"How was your date?" Reid asked his sister, sitting on a barstool at the kitchen island and hoping to take their attention off him and his rumpled state.

"Not bad. He was nice, but boring. Cute, but no real connection there, you know?" She shrugged, not too broken up about it.

"Sorry, Gem."

"It's fine. I'm still young and pretty." She plated bacon and eggs, and brought them over to the table, putting one in front of him. She looked over his rumpled, tired appearance. "Which is more than I can say for you. Here's the real question, though. What did you get up to last night?"

"Nothing. I stayed at the restaurant for another drink and then I left." He averted his eyes, pretending to be interested in the swaying palm trees that surrounded the pool and Jacuzzi that made his backyard a personal tropical oasis.

"Does it feel like Reid isn't telling us something?" Quin asked Gemma, dragging Reid's attention back to his siblings.

"Yeah, I think so. You slept in, too."

He put up his hands. "So, I slept late. A guy can't sleep in?" He briefly considered taking their keys back. He couldn't put up with his siblings before his coffee had a chance to work.

"He can, but it isn't common. Especially on a workday. What time did you get home last night?"

Reid sipped his coffee. He wasn't about to reveal to his brother and sister that it had been sometime after four a.m. before he'd left Lila, retrieved his car and made it home. "Not too late. I'm a grown man—older than both of you. Why do I have to answer for myself?"

"Defensive," Quin noted.

"You look like hell," she pointed out. "Did you get any sleep?"

"What are you guys doing here, anyway?" he asked.

"Way to thank me for making you a delicious breakfast." She took a bite of her bacon.

"Sorry. It's just that you both said you were taking today off."

"We talked about that. And believe it or not, we felt bad about it. You must be rubbing off on us."

"And we thought we'd make breakfast, and all go in together. Just like old times," Quin told him.

"So far, *I'm* making breakfast and Quin is reading the sports scores," Gemma added.

"And I'm keeping up-to-date on current events."

"Plus, you were right. With the party coming up, and launching the new rum, it's not a great time to be taking days off." "Yeah, sounds good. Just let me shower and we can all ride in together." As he ate and drank his coffee, Reid began to feel more awake. Thinking about the distillery helped him focus his mind. "Don't forget to send me the recipe listing for the honey batches."

"That was the plan."

"You know I don't mind you guys coming over, but you could think about calling first."

"Why? In case you have a woman here?" Quin scoffed. "Like you'd let anyone near your house."

Reid considered flipping off his younger brother, but Quin was right. That was exactly why he met women at their homes...or hotels. Again, the image of Lila was enough to make his temperature spike.

"I tried calling you before we came over," Gemma told him. "Twice. It went right to voice mail."

Behind his coffee mug, Reid frowned, trying to remember when he'd last seen his phone. He'd been in Lila's bed, his face again buried between the creamy smooth skin of her thighs when it had rung—it had been a European distributor who had no concept of time zones. For the first time since taking the reins at the distillery, he'd ignored his phone, but when it rang again, he'd disengaged from Lila, frustrated, he plucked the device from his pants, turned it off and put it on her hotel nightstand.

Where it probably still sat. "Shit," he muttered.

"What's wrong?" Quin asked.

He shook his head. "Nothing, my phone must have died. I guess I forgot to charge it." He had to figure out some way to get in touch with Lila to retrieve his phone. The only way he could think was to go back to her hotel room and hope she was still there. He looked up from his plate and realized that his brother and sister were watching him. "What?" he asked.

"Everything okay?" Gemma asked.

"I'm fine. I'm just tired. I didn't get a lot of sleep."

"Maybe that'll teach you to stop screwing around and focus on your job," Quin joked as he raised his coffee mug to his lips. Gemma snorted into her own coffee. Both of them knew that Reid was the most serious of the three of them. It wasn't often he was the one to miss work or be anything other than in complete control.

Reid gave in to his earlier impulse and flipped his brother off and finished up his breakfast. He tried to put his missing phone out of his mind and appear to be invested in the conversation. "All right, I'm focused. You guys want to talk work, let's do it. Are all of the press invites ready for the party next week?"

"The press invites and more," Quin said. "All the usual suspects." He rattled off some local and national news sources. "Everyone wants an invite to a liquor launch party. I've also extended some invites to bloggers and online influencers, some local, some further out."

Reid rolled his eyes. Everyone was a celebrity in today's shallow influencer culture. And that was not the sort of image that he wanted to portray with Rexford Rum. "Why?"

"Because everyone uses the internet, grandpa. If influencers are talking about us, it'll only increase sales and open us up to new markets."

He couldn't argue with that. But he wasn't sure if it was the right way to go about it. Reid had had this argument with Quin before. His younger brother wanted to make Rexford mainstream and more accessible, while Reid wanted to focus on boosting its luxury brand status. "We discussed keeping Rexford a luxury brand. Not a party one." Reid recalled their wilder days, and he wasn't interested in revisiting them, or being known as the brand chosen by those young adults who partied hard on spring break.

Quin shrugged. "Can't it be both? You don't know the disposable income or the follower counts that some of these young people have, and if they're on Instagram sipping our rum, we could go global. That's what we want, isn't it?"

Reid knew he wasn't going to win the argument, and he knew it wouldn't be the end of the discussion. But shirtless in his kitchen, with Lila's scent clinging to his skin, he wasn't about to try. "Fine. We'll discuss it later. I'm going to go shower."

"So, we're all driving in together?" Gemma asked, clearing the plates from the table.

"No," Reid said too quickly, earning him strange looks from his siblings. He'd left his cell phone with a complete stranger. That meant if Lila had the know-how, she could break into his phone and be privy to all sorts of information about him and the company. He had to catch up with her before that could happen. But that would mean seeing her again, and he now knew he couldn't trust himself around the woman, as his body heated in response to the idea of seeing her.

Even as his heart thundered in his chest, and his

blood rushed south, he had to hurry. "I changed my mind. I'll take my own car. I've got something to do before I head in. I'll see you at the distillery."

Lila turned off the water and walked out of the glass shower stall, drying herself with the fluffy white hotel towel. She towel-dried her hair and glanced at her reflection in the mirror, noting her clear skin, her bright eyes and the indulgent smile that perched on her lips. A night of spectacular sex could certainly do that to a girl.

Brushing her teeth, she thought about her night with Reid. It had been incredible. She never hooked up with men when she was working. But she was glad she'd made an exception for Reid. Shivering with the memories of how he'd kissed and touched her, she pulled on the hotel bathrobe and let the thick terry cloth cover her body before she walked out into her luxury suite. It was time to get to work and write her review for the restaurant she'd visited the night before. Where she'd met Reid. She hadn't gotten a chance to make any notes after eating and would have to write her review from memory. But when she racked her brain, trying to remember anything about her dinner and drinks, or the atmosphere of the restaurant, all she could remember was Reid.

She sat in front of her laptop for a while, the blank page of her Word document waiting for her to begin. Lila sighed. She lacked inspiration. The blog post she'd agreed to write eluded her, but she was certain she could write a thirty-thousand-word thesis on the way Reid had made her feel the night before.

Bored and suddenly lacking motivation, she pulled up her blog and looked through her old posts. Parties, adventures and cultural events filled her archives. From Oktoberfest, to Coachella, to Carnival, to that unfortunate day she'd spent on Grand Exuma for the Fyre Festival, she had attended some of the best parties and most amazing events and festivals on the planet. She looked around her hotel room and sighed again. On paper, her life was incredible, full of fun. She was lucky to live the life she did. But as she looked around her room, Lila couldn't help but note the sameness. She may have treated herself to a beachfront luxury hotel in Miami, but when you looked closely, every hotel was the same. The same beds, the same mass-produced art, the same TVs, the same desks, the same citrus-scented shampoo in the bathroom.

That was why she needed to secure that deal with the GO! Channel, one of the world's most prominent travel networks. For months, she'd been pitching her own television show to air weekly with added online content, website access, the whole nine yards.

She loved to travel, but without an actual home to call her own, she was beginning to tire of life on the road. The television deal would give her the best of both worlds. She could travel, but she could also put down some roots in LA and give her a home base. It would give her a schedule, and the fame and financial stability so that her day-to-day life wouldn't be such a grind of posting for likes and clicks, and searching for new income streams.

"All right Lila, get to work, or get a real job," she chided herself. She turned back to her blank document, but the white space continued to taunt her. When she tried to remember anything about Arlo's, she could only see Reid. But she had to focus. She had to finish that one review before she moved on to her next Miami experience—she checked her open appointment book: a scooter tour, a couple of beachside food trucks, parasailing, and then Saturday night, the Rexford party. She had a lot of fun lined up for the next couple of days, and she couldn't seem to motivate herself to do any of it. At least there would be rum at the party. Maybe she'd get another Cuba Libre. Her mouth watered, remembering the taste of the cocktail she'd had the night before. But first, she had work to do. *Write the words; drink the rum.* Unable to focus, though, her eyes shifted to the bed, with the sheets that she and Reid had rumpled. She'd readily agreed to just one night with him. But now she wished that she'd asked for more, or given him her number, or something. Even though it was unlikely he'd call or anything—he'd made it perfectly clear that he was not interested in more than one night. But having had that night with him, there was no doubt she wanted another.

And that was when she saw a cell phone on the nightstand. It was black, whereas hers was pink. It must have been Reid's. She picked it up and turned it on, wondering how she would ever get it back to him. There was no emergency contact number on the lock screen, but the picture displayed was of Reid, with a man and a woman who both shared similar facial features—the same brown eyes and high cheekbones. Probably his siblings. They were standing, smiling proudly, next to a sign that said Rexford Rum Distillery.

Lila blinked and tilted her head as she took in the image. It all clicked into place. Reid. Rexford. She'd spent the night with one of the men who owned the facility she'd been set to tour? She returned to her computer and searched his name, and there he was, a picture of Reid in all his handsome, sexy glory. That second round she'd craved with him was now entirely possible. She would see him at the party.

She was still gripping the phone when a knock on the door startled her. She hadn't ordered room service and she couldn't imagine why anyone would be coming to her room. She put the phone on the bedside table. She walked to the door, checked the peephole, and saw the familiar profile of Reid Rexford. Pulling open the door, she gave him her sultriest smile. "Reid," she purred in a way she'd never done before. He'd apparently turned her into some kind of wanton sex kitten. "What brings you by?"

She raised her arm and leaned against the door in what she imagined—hoped—was a seductive pose.

She saw his eyes roam up and down her body. The robe concealed most of it but thankfully hung loosely at her chest, gaping to give him a peek at her cleavage. His eyes flickered with a flash of heat that she recognized as desire. But a muscle in his cheek ticked as he set his sensual lips in a frown. "I think you have my cell phone," he told her in a no-nonsense baritone.

Rejected. Putting on her best sex kitten impression had barely affected him. Had she played her cards right, he should have ripped the robe from her body and carried her to the bed for another round. But instead he only wanted his cell phone?

"I do," she said over her shoulder, turning away. "Come on in."

He started to take a step forward, but instead remained in the doorway. "I'd better not."

Lila turned her head and struggled not to grin when she saw that his eyes were fixed on the king-size bed, and the sheets he'd helped rumple. Lila sauntered to where his cell phone lay on her nightstand and held it up to him. She shifted so that the loosely tied robe slid off her shoulder, still cinched at her waist, but gaping even further, showing off the rest of her chest and the tops of her breasts. She looked at him from across the room. "You going to come and get it?"

Reid stood and watched her for several beats, not

moving from the door. He huffed out a breath and stretched his neck, not taking his eyes from her. She thought he might leave outright without his phone, that she'd pushed him, but her fears proved to be unfounded when he took a step inside the room. He shut the door behind him and turned the lock. "I'm going to get it."

CHAPTER FOUR

LILA'S BREATH STOPPED short as Reid stalked toward her. His gait was sure and his gaze unwavering. She'd prodded him, poked him, and now Reid was delivering. He stopped in front of her, but he didn't reach for his phone like she thought he might. Instead he pushed the fluffy robe from her chest. The cool air of the hotel room hit her skin, causing small goose bumps to rise, and pebbling her nipples. She felt her pulse pounding in her throat as he stared at her bared breasts.

"What happened to one night only?" she reminded him.

He stepped even closer, so that the tips of her breasts skated against the material of his shirt. She knew that underneath that was the dark curly hair she'd slid her hands over. Her palms itched to do it again. "If you don't want me here, I'll just take my phone and leave."

She shook her head. "That was your rule, remember? Not mine."

She heard what might have been a growl emanate from deep within his chest and his mouth captured hers in a kiss that bordered on ravenous. She attempted to breathe through her nose but was only able to take in his spicy cologne, and as his tongue swept in between her parted lips, she got a taste of his minty toothpaste.

She kissed him back, hopefully matching his intensity, but she wasn't sure that was possible. He made her feel wanted, desired. The way his fingers curled over her body, she could tell that he needed her, craved her. And to be wanted by a powerful, sensual man like Reid...

She shuddered against his chest and her arms encircled his neck to draw him closer. He lifted her, and she wrapped her legs around his waist. He walked her to the edge of the bed, dropped her so she landed on the mattress flat on her back and spread her legs. Taking her by the ankles, he brought her legs to his shoulders. He placed a hot kiss on her ankle and unbuckled his pants with one hand.

Thankfully the box of condoms was still on the nightstand from the night before, and he reached over and grabbed one as he pushed his pants down his thighs, rolling the latex over himself. "Sorry if this is a little quick," he grumbled, as he lined himself up with her center. "I've got to get to work."

She moaned when he rubbed his length against her. "Fine by me," she told him, her eyes flutter closed at the luxurious contact. "I've got stuff to do today, too."

"Not yet, you don't," he told her, sliding inside her in one long, hard stroke.

She arched off the bed and met him thrust for thrust. The angle of his movements made his cock glide against her clit, hitting her in just the right spot, bringing her closer to orgasm with every stroke. He leaned over her as his hips thrust, capturing one nipple between his lips. With his teeth and tongue, he plucked at the strings of desire within her, playing her body like an instrument until she came with a crescendo, crying out Reid's name as he buried his face in her chest, his breath hot on her skin, and he played out his own release.

He hovered over her for a moment. Then pushed himself off her body, and tossed the condom in a nearby trash can, while she straightened her robe.

"Nice trick, Reid," she said.

"What's that?" he asked, using his fingers to comb back the black hair that had fallen over his forehead.

She shrugged. "Leaving your cell phone, just so you'd have to come back to get it?"

He picked the phone up from the table, and immediately his thumbs moved over the screen. "Is that what you think happened?"

"Isn't it?"

He didn't look up from the screen. "Did you access anything on this?" he asked, studying the screen.

That caught her off guard. "No, I just saw it on

the nightstand before you showed up. Are you accusing me of something?" she asked, instinctively tightening the robe around her waist.

He looked at her, his eyes roaming up and down her body, as if appraising her, gauging her reaction to his accusation. "No."

"What, did you think I'd hacked your phone and stolen all of your secrets?"

"No, I'm sorry," he told her, crossing the room to stand in front of her. He cupped her jaw in his long, strong fingers, and she couldn't help but lean into his touch. "I guess I'm a little paranoid. I have reasons to be cautious." She looked up at him and saw a certain vulnerability in his eyes.

"Why?"

He didn't respond, but she saw him look down at his watch.

"Time to go?" she teased.

"Yeah, I have to get to work. And if I recall, you have things to do, too."

"That's right. This is it, I guess?"

"Yeah, I guess so." He looked away. "It's probably for the best, don't you think, parting like this?" It looked like he didn't think that. Her pride stopped her from disagreeing. But she remembered that he was one of the owners of the Rexford Rum Distillery. Where she was headed later that afternoon. Maybe she would see him there. "Well, it was fun, Reid."

He turned around to smile. "Yeah, it was, Lila. I guess this is goodbye."

"I like to think of it as an 'until next time.'"

He laughed. "Next time." With that he was gone. And despite wishing he'd stayed, Lila smiled. Reid might not know it, but *next time* would come sooner than he could have imagined.

When Lila saw her agent's number on the screen of her ringing cell phone, she answered more quickly than she normally would. "James, do you have good news?" she asked by way of greeting him, hoping he would have a GO! Channel contract to offer her.

"Not yet. I was chatting with the execs and they have concerns."

"What kind of concerns?"

"They're afraid that people won't know who you are. You aren't a mainstream celebrity, and you've never carried a national campaign. They don't know if your face—as gorgeous as it is," he added, "will be able to carry a television show."

Lila closed her eyes and took in the news. "They should just look at my follower numbers, the ana-lytical information I provided to show that I know what I'm doing. People know me, and my word on a product or place means a lot."

"I know that, and so do many others. But you need to prove it to these guys. Let's come up with some-thing big," he suggested. "Get into business with a brand. Why don't we get together and brainstorm a way to convince these suits that you've got the juice?"

Lila frowned. "Fine. Listen, I've got work to do. Can we talk another time?"

"Yeah, sure thing. And we will find something for you. It might just take a little while."

"Thanks," she said without much enthusiasm. "I'll talk to you later. Bye." She leaned back on the bed. She needed the GO! Channel offer. It would be her way to settle down, find an apartment in LA—establish a home base, a place to call her own. She made a good life on the road. But she was starting to tire of it. A reduced travel schedule would be a good thing for her before she suffered burnout.

Again, Lila thought of Reid. Her body tingled in anticipation of seeing him again. They'd shared a definite connection and with her plans to visit the distillery later, while she didn't think he would bend her over his desk, she wished he would. But she wondered if maybe she could propose some sort of arrangement. Hopefully he'd be interested in a business relationship, as well as their sexual one.

CHAPTER FIVE

HAVING MET WITH Gemma and Quin to go over next week's work plans, Reid was now alone in his office. His laptop was open to his full calendar and a quarterly earnings spreadsheet, but he'd be damned if he could find an ounce of focus to actually do anything with either of them. It was thoughts of Lila that still sat at the forefront of his mind. She consumed him, even more than she had before he saw her earlier that morning.

There was a knock on his closed door. He knew it was impossible, but wouldn't it be something if it was Lila knocking? His heartbeat sped up—just a little—at the improbable idea and he shook his head. "Foolish," he scolded himself right before he called out, "Come in."

The door opened and Gemma poked her head inside. Reid felt like an idiot for even thinking it could have been Lila, even for a second. "Hey Reid, you busy?"

He looked at his open laptop. "No, what's up?"

"I have the ingredients and cost lists for the honey batch for you." She handed over a scrap of paper where she'd jotted down the ingredients.

"Thanks." At least it would give him something to train his brain on. He clearly wasn't getting anything else done. "And I only had to ask you half a dozen times."

"Yeah, I wanted you in a good mood for the favor I'm about to ask you," she said, sitting on the corner of his desk.

He narrowed his eyes at her. "What is it?"

"Remember the guy I went out with last night?"

"Okay, but no connection?" he repeated her earlier words.

"You forgot cute. Yeah, well, he called and wants to get together for happy hour. I've decided to give him another chance."

"And what's that have to do with me?"

"Welllll," she said sweetly. "Remember when we were talking about travel bloggers and influencers earlier? I set up a tour with one today. But if I'm at a bar, I can't be here."

"Still doesn't sound like my problem," he told her.

"Reid. Please. It's just an hour of your time."

"Gemma—" With the lack of sleep from the night before, he'd planned for once on having a relaxing evening, finishing up his work, crashing on the couch with a drink and watching TV. But who was he kidding? More likely, he would end up staying at the distillery until after dark, and then using his home office to finish up whatever tasks seemed necessary on a Friday night—if only to distract him from going back to Lila's hotel room. "I don't give tours."

"But you know your way around the distillery. It's nothing in-depth. You know enough to give her a basic tour and let her try a few things."

"You should know I'm too busy to show around someone who thinks she's too good for a group tour. Especially one of those Instagram influencers. Those people are all style, no substance."

"Listen to yourself. Those *influencers* have more reach than many large marketing firms. They know how to spread the word. If she likes us, Reid, she could make us huge. She's doing us a favor here. I arranged it with her weeks ago. It'll take an hour out of your oh-so-busy afternoon, and then you can get back to working on the financials for this batch."

"How did you know—"

"Because you're my brother and I know you. I could see the gears turning in your head the minute I put that bottle down in front of you last night."

"I can't do the tour."

"Can't or won't?"

"Both. Get one of your workers to do it."

"They're all gone for the day."

"I'm—"

"I know, you're *busy*," she finished for him.

"No, I'm uninterested," he told her flatly.

"No, you're impossible. And I'm out of here," she said with finality, heading to the door.

"I don't give tours," he said again.

Gemma huffed out a breath. "You're such an ass-hole. You know, maybe you need to get laid, Reid. It might put you in a better mood."

"Drop it." To the contrary, it had been just a few hours since he'd left Lila's hotel. He could still feel her on him, the need for her clawing its way up his back. Lack of great sex wasn't his problem, but he wasn't about to share that with Gemma. It would give her too much ammunition, and he would never hear the end of it if his sister knew he'd gone back to the woman's room that morning.

"I've got work to do," he tried again feebly, know-ing full well that there was no doubt he'd stick around the distillery while his sister went on her date. "But fine, I'll do your tour. She gets an hour of my time, and that's it."

Gemma smiled, knowing that, as always, she'd gotten her way with her older brother. "You're the best. And I'll forgive you being such a grumpy bitch, if you promise to do something fun today," Gemma called out to him.

Alone again, he snorted. He'd had plenty of fun already. But there was still work to be done. He had to make sure the distillery was poised for massive success, and if that meant entertaining some blogger for an hour to ensure a positive review, then so be it. Inexplicably, Lila kept making her way to front and center of his brain. And it surprised him how much he'd rather spend another hour with her than with anything having to do with rum.

When the cab stopped outside of the Rexford Rum Distillery, Lila was surprised the small, two-story building—gray concrete, unassuming—was her destination. The only thing marking it as the right place was the old wooden sign—the one she recognized from the picture of Reid and his siblings—bearing the Rexford name along with Established 1809.

She paid the driver and got out of the car. She walked up to the wooden door and pulled on the large iron handle. The door didn't budge. Locked. Her driver pulled away from the curb, and she was left standing in the empty parking lot.

"Just great."

Looking in through the small windows, she saw the equipment of the distillery, but the room appeared dark and empty. Gemma had told her that they would be closed to the public by the time she got there, but that she would be out front to meet her. Lila looked around for any sign of life, but the place was completely vacant.

She'd confirmed with Gemma the day before and double-checked the time in the email. She was on time, at the right place. She didn't have a phone number for her, besides that of the distillery, and she dialed. Several rings went in before the voice mail started, so she hung up. She knocked on the door before feebly trying the iron handle again. Still no movement. From a look around at her surroundings, she knew she wasn't in the safest area of Miami, and the sooner she could gain access to the building, the better.

Alone in the empty parking lot, she figured she'd walk around the side to see if she could find somebody, or another way in. She came to a side door. She pulled the handle, surprised when it opened. She walked inside, and was greeted by a stony silence, a sterile concrete staircase that led upstairs to the second floor. Lila took to the stairs, hoping she would find someone there. *Or I'll be kidnapped in this creepy-ass building and never seen again...*

So, doing what was almost instinctive to her, she turned on her cell phone camera and started a livestream of herself, lost and trying to find another person in the Rexford distillery.

"Hey, guys, it's Lila," she said into the lens as she climbed the stairs, "and as you know, I'm in Miami right now. I should be touring the Rexford Rum Distillery, and sampling some amazing rum, but instead I'm lost in a horribly boring hallway. There's no one around, and I have no idea where I'm going. Hopefully I find someone to help me, and not be doomed to walk these lonely hallways forever." She opened the door on the second floor, turned a corner and breathed out a sigh of relief, grateful to be in a carpeted reception area, with some furniture and uninteresting art prints. She turned back to the video recorder on her phone. "Still no signs of life, but at least I'm not in some concrete dungeon. If I don't make it out alive, avenge me." She saw that there were already hundreds of people watching her video, asking questions, leaving comments. There was a hallway past the reception desk that seemed to lead to some offices, and she walked further. Maybe she'd find someone down there.

Reid, alone in the office, cocked an eyebrow at the click of high heels and a female voice that reverberated throughout the empty hallway outside. "Oh shit," he muttered, looking at his watch. He'd missed his appointment with the travel blogger. He'd meant to go downstairs earlier to let her in, but he'd lost track of time going over the costs for Gemma's new batch of rum.

He got up from his desk and walked out into the hallway and didn't see anyone. But he could hear her down in the reception area, around the corner out of his sight. He tilted his head and listened to the far-off voice. The laughter in it was familiar. He knew that voice. He started down the hallway in the direction of the sound, turned the corner to where his receptionist's desk was located, and smacked into a small, warm body, sending the woman crashing to the floor.

The first thing he noticed was the flash of red hair. He was frozen in place. A buzz of electricity shot throughout his body as she looked up at him from the floor. "What are you doing here?" he asked.

He shook his head and, remembering his manners, reached down, extending his hand to help her to her feet.

"Well, it was either find a way in, or stand outside."

Reid frowned. "That's not what I meant. How did you find me here?"

"How self-obsessed are you?" she asked him, brushing off her skirt. "Reid, not everything is about you, you know? I'm here for a tour."

"You're the travel blogger Gemma invited?" he asked, incredulous, unable to believe that this was just a huge coincidence.

One of her perfectly shaped eyebrows arched upward. "You know, I'm sensing a lot of attitude from the person who didn't keep an appointment, leaving me stranded in the parking lot."

He relented. "I'm sorry. I was supposed to meet you outside, but I lost track of time." For several beats, he stood in dumbfounded shock. He couldn't believe that she was there. In his office.

"Why don't we start over." She extended her hand, officially introducing herself. "Lila Campbell."

Even though he knew touching her would prove to be a mistake, Reid shook her hand. "Reid Rexford." He couldn't take his eyes off her. "You know, I didn't expect to see you again, but I'm not upset about it."

She picked up her phone and looked into the camera, ignoring him. "And, ladies and gentlemen, I successfully found another human being. Everyone say hi to Reid." She turned the camera on him, and he saw himself in the screen.

Reid gave a humorless wave, and she put away her phone. "You were recording?" He couldn't stop the rigid tension that straightened his spine at the thought of her recording on premises, in an area where she shouldn't have been.

"I just went live for my audience. They like those little slices of life."

He was still tense from being on her camera, and he worried that she'd explored other parts of the distillery without supervision. Neither of them spoke until she looked around. "So, is Gemma here? She's supposed to show me the place."

He shook his head. "No, she got called away and had to leave unexpectedly, so I'll be showing you around if that's all right."

A quiet moment passed between them, and Reid knew they were both thinking about the night—and morning—they'd spent together. There was an inkling of doubt in his mind, though. He flashed back to how they'd met. Had she known who he was the entire time? Was hooking up with him part of her plan? Seducing him to get inside information? He'd been burned in the past, and he wondered if, like his ex-wife, Lila had set him up. And she had had access to his phone. He'd been hacked, manipulated before. But as he looked at Lila, he didn't think so. He hoped that it was his intuition, not his libido, telling him to trust her.

She raised one eyebrow. "You and me alone in the building, you think that's a good idea?"

It was as if she'd read his mind. He led her down the stairs to the distillery. "I think I can behave myself if you do."

Reid couldn't help but watch the sway of her short, flowy dress as she walked. He was entranced by it, filled with the familiar pulses of desire. He could still feel her. *Taste* her.

"So, where do we start?" Lila asked him, glancing at him over her shoulder, catching him in the act of checking her out.

"Start?" he asked, his eyes snapping up to meet hers.

"The tour?" she reminded him. "That's why I'm here, remember."

Right. "Yeah." He tried to recover. "We start right here. If you'll follow me, I'll show you all the ins and outs of Rexford." He hadn't intended any innuendo in his words, but as soon as they were out of his mouth, he realized exactly what he'd said. He hoped she hadn't caught it, but when Lila spoke next, he realized that he'd met his match.

"You promise?"

Lila attempted to keep her eyes off Reid's ass as she followed him around the distillery, trying her best to listen as he told her about the business and the process of making rum. She looked up at the man beside her as he walked her past copper vats, dodging hoses and other equipment as he talked. Despite its popularity, Rexford Rum was still a small family operation. "So how did you guys come to start up a distillery?"

"Rum is in our blood," he explained. He stopped in front of an old hand-drawn portrait of a man. Reid pointed at it. "Joseph Rexford was our ancestor, and also a thief and a vagrant," he said with a smile. "Generations ago, he fled Scotland evading arrest, and he somehow made his way across the Atlantic Ocean and landed in the Bahamas. He began his new life as a rumrunner, illicitly bringing Bahamian rum to the Florida coast. He was one of the first notorious distillers and bootleggers—a profession he passed on to his sons, who passed it on to their children, and so on. The Rexford clan was also responsible for sneaking rum into the US during prohibition in the 1920s. Since the 1700s, the Rexford name has been synonymous with rum.

"Rexford Rum operated on a small scale through the generations. After prohibition, our great-grandfather legitimized the business for the first time. By the time it was my father's turn to take the helm here, through bad luck and worse investments, there wasn't much left, but Mom and Dad turned it around. They made the distillery successful, but when Gemma, Quin and I took over, we made our rum the best."

Lila was certain he had just given her the speech given to most tour groups. But she wanted to know more about Reid and the Rexfords. "Was rum always your calling? Did you want to follow in the family business?"

"I was always intrigued by the lore of Joseph Rexford. I liked the idea of a family history filled with pirates and bootleggers, but when my mother passed away, my dad gave up the business and moved out west. Between myself, Gemma and Quin, we didn't want it to die on our watch." He looked around thoughtfully, as if he was recalling the memories and experiences he'd had in the room. "We all grew up in this building. It's been in the family for more than one hundred years. Our grandfather and father taught us everything we needed to know. Gemma was distilling long before she could legally drink— but that's strictly off the record," he said with a sly wink. "And now she's the master distiller. It's been about ten years now since we officially took it over, and we've acquired the neighboring buildings and expanded operations significantly."

Lila looked around the distillery. While the equipment was gleaming and kept in pristine shape, the signs of age and wear of the building itself were apparent. But she could tell Reid truly loved the place. "And even though you could work out of a new facility, you still run it out of the same small building."

"Yeah." He reached out and patted the stone wall. "This place is the heart of the business. There's a lot of history inside these walls. I couldn't imagine going anywhere else every day."

"You're a traditional guy," Lila noted.

He nodded. "I wasn't always, but yeah, I guess I am now. My brother and sister think I'm old-fashioned, but the Rexford name, my family, the rum, that's all there is, right?"

For several seconds, Lila considered her own family. Her parents who didn't support her; the ex-husband who didn't believe her capable of anything. She blinked their images from her mind, and saw that Reid was watching her. Their eyes met for a moment, before the intensity in his stare made her avert her eyes.

"Yeah, I guess." Desperate to change the topic, she brought her attention back to their surroundings. She had to get to the job at hand. Learning about the distillery, and the man himself. "Tell me more about all this—where the magic happens," she said with a sweep of her hand.

He looked relieved to again be talking about rum. "This is normally Gemma's domain, and she rarely lets us in here without supervision."

"Well, I guess we'll have to try our best to be good."

Lila noticed the way Reid's body momentarily stiffened before he went back into tour mode, leading her over to two large boilers. "Forgive me. Gemma and her guys are a lot better at this tour than I am. I rarely get the chance to come down here anymore."

"It's fine." She subtly gave Reid a once-over. "I know she's left me in good hands."

She wasn't sure he'd caught her intentionally

innuendo-laced comment, but when his eyes traveled down over her body, leaving a trail of fire in their wake, she knew he did. His hands clenched into fists at his sides, and as he pushed them into the pockets of his sensible pants, she remembered just how talented those hands were.

They regarded one another for several tension-filled beats before she forced herself to look away. She cleared her throat. "So, Gemma's the master distiller? That's impressive."

"Yeah, like I said, she's been working here since she was a teenager, but since then, she's studied all over the world, practicing with some of the greatest rum makers there are, including our grandfather. Quin and I might keep the place running, but she's the lifeblood of the business."

"And what is your job?"

"As my brother and sister like to keep reminding me, I'm the boring numbers guy. Quin is head of marketing and PR. He's the fun, charismatic one, but I handle the business side of things. It's just the three of us running it with a few small teams. We might sell internationally, but it's still the same family-run place it always has been."

She smiled. Once again, she could see how devoted he was to his family. It was commendable. He was responsible, sensible, but passionate. Sure, she'd seen that passion the night before, but responsible and sensible wasn't the impression she'd had of the man who'd seduced her in a restaurant and took her quickly, fiercely in her hotel that morning. He wasn't at all what she went for when it came to men—she liked them more adventurous and carefree—but she might be tempted to make an exception for another go-around with Reid Rexford…

Lila mentally slapped herself. *Down, girl. You're here for work!* She had to think about her future and see if Reid would be open to some sort of partnership. That was one thing that could secure her the GO! Channel deal. But she wouldn't be able to do that if she couldn't keep her hormones in check. Straightening, she tried to tamp down her attraction to him. She tried to separate herself as the woman who'd slept with him from the blogger who was there for information. "That doesn't sound boring. You keep the lights on, and keep the place running. You can be as charismatic, or make as much fabulous rum as you please, but without the boring numbers guy, there isn't a business."

Another beat of silence passed between them. And Lila was sure at that point they would never get to finish the tour. Not that that would be the worst thing… "So, why don't you tell me about making rum? What's the step-by-step process?"

"All right," Reid said, rubbing his hands together, and pointed to the drums. "It all starts with sugar cane…"

Even though the distillery was Gemma's domain, and he'd argued the opposite, Reid still knew the place inside out. Thankfully, back in control of the situation, he started the tour. He went over the process with Lila, giving her a spiel that he remembered from his days of running the tours. But he'd never had an audience like Lila.

She was a stunning woman, all generous curves and red hair. But it wasn't just her looks that drew him to her. She was vibrant, vivacious, and her energy filled the distillery as she hung on his every word. He could feel her attention so acutely that he had to concentrate to keep the words coming from his mouth. Reid gave her the chance the check out one of the giant stills, and as she walked around it, taking notes and asking questions, even the intricacies of her movements intrigued him. The way her pen went between her lips as her sharp eyes took in the process, the way she restlessly drummed her fingers against her thigh, not out of boredom, he knew, but to expel the excess energy that coursed through her.

They moved over to the charred oak barrels where they aged the rum. He saw the cognac barrels from Gemma's new batch in one corner. Her notebook— which contained her recipes—lay open on top. Rolling his eyes at Gemma's carelessness, he snatched it up before Lila could sneak a peek at the words scribbled on the pages. But all it earned him was a curious look from her. Smooth. "And that's the end of the tour," Reid said, sliding the small coil notebook into his pocket. "Now's the fun part—the tasting."

"The rest of the tour was pretty interesting. That does sounds like it's more fun, though." She smiled, laying her fingertips on his forearm. "But I know a more fun thing we could do together."

"I thought we promised to behave ourselves?"

She walked past him, and her smile was daring—and sexy. "That was you. I never promised any such thing."

Reid clenched his fists and counted to ten in his head. It was barely enough to bring down his libido. He was barely hanging on. He had to remind himself that there was something strange going on with Lila's reappearance into his life. She had called it a coincidence. But he didn't believe in coincidence. While his dick might be happy to have Lila in his presence, he had to consider the other possibilities.

On one hand, she might be a spy, sent by a rival distillery. On the other hand, she could be out to get the inside scoop into his personal life, to air his dirty laundry. Wouldn't be the first time those things happened when he wasn't careful about who he trusted.

He ground his teeth, but still couldn't stop himself from putting his hand on the small of her back to guide her into the tasting room. Immediately, he regretted the lapse in judgment. He should have kept his hands to himself; he would never have touched another distillery guest in such an intimate manner.

He was so attuned to her that he could feel Lila stiffen underneath his fingers. Her head turned in his direction, not surprised by his touch, and she gave him that same devastatingly slick grin. He knew he was done. She didn't move away from his touch, and instead settled back against his hand and continued walking with him.

He turned on the overhead lights to the tasting area—the large room was designed and lit for intimacy despite its size. Edison bulbs on strings and in sconces lit the stone walls of the room, which held several long old wooden tables, big enough to accommodate larger tour groups. He gestured to a spot on the center of the bench that ran along one of the tables. "Take a seat. I'll be right back," he told her.

He let his gaze linger on Lila for a second before he went into the next room to prepare the tasting. As he pulled out a couple of flat boards and the small glasses that went with them, he thought about the woman waiting for him. It had been a long time since he'd let any sort of need or desire rise to the surface. But since she'd come into his life the night before, she'd completely turned him upside down. He shook his head. If he wasn't careful, he would find himself in a vulnerable situation with the woman. He poured himself a shot of rum and downed it in a fortifying gulp.

But first. He had to think about the distillery. He had to put the business, his family ahead of his own goddamn sex life. Gemma and Quin were counting on him to make sure Lila left with a good impression of the Rexford distillery. He had to forget the effect that Lila had on him. He had to be on his best behavior. He had to think about the business.

"Pull it together, Reid," he muttered, giving himself a mental shake. As per the standard they'd set for the tours, Reid finished preparing the tasting boards with the selection of rum, giving visitors a range of what the distillery had to offer. And even though he would rather be laying Lila out on top of the old oak table in the next room, and burying himself deep inside her, he had to be professional.

Professionalism had never been a problem for him before. As Gemma and Quin were quick to remind him, he was the serious, boring one—the one who never let anything get in the way of work. Why Lila was such a temptation him, he didn't know, but he normally didn't have any trouble separating the business from his dick.

But that didn't mean he could stop thinking about the woman waiting for him in the main room. He'd had an incredible night—and following morning—with Lila. When they'd been completely anonymous. But now she knew who he was, and that made him feel more vulnerable than he liked.

He frowned and poured himself another shot of rum. It had been a while since he'd done the tasting spiel, but he knew the qualities of each type of rum and could explain it in detail. He wanted to give Lila the authentic, typical experience, but his desire for the woman was anything but typical.

With Reid in the other room, Lila was able to finally take a deep breath, but it did little to settle her. Reid

Rexford was as formidable as a brick wall, and seemingly unflappable despite her giving him her sexiest looks. She, however, was completely shaken. His inquisitive, even skeptical, eyes had bored through her. She'd enjoyed the tour of the distillery, but she was glad she'd recorded it because after seeing Reid, she found it difficult to remember anything he'd said to her.

Given the passion he'd exhibited the night before, she'd been surprised by how stiff and serious he looked in the distillery. It was difficult to reconcile the businessman him with the passionate lover he'd been. They could have been two different men, but when he put his hand on her, low on her back, she'd nearly sighed with pent-up pleasure.

Using the reversed camera on her phone as a mirror, she checked out her reflection, and smoothed her hair. *Still cute.* When she looked up, he came back into the room and laid down two wooden board platters that contained four small glasses each. The whole time, he kept a noticeable distance from her.

"What do we have here?" she asked, eyeing each of the glasses.

"Here's a sample of our regular rums—" he pointed to each glass "—white, amber, spiced, and we finish it off with a cream rum."

He went into a speech about each of the products, about the differences in production, laced with humorous tales of Joseph Rexford. Reid knew the family lore, but she was more interested in learning about him. "And we start with the white rum." He picked up the small glass that held the clear liquid.

They both held up their glasses of white rum, clinked them together in salute, and took a sip. The clear rum was smooth, some of the best she'd ever had. Normally her rum came mixed with fruit juice and topped with little umbrellas. But without the decoration and overpowering fruit, she was able to taste the clarity of the rum. She drank again, and their eyes connected over their glasses. When his glass was empty, he put it back on the table. His posture was rigid, his serious face set with hard features.

"Can I ask you a question?" he said after a beat of silence.

"Shoot."

"Why are you here?" he asked, surprising her.

Her mouth dropped open in shock at the almost accusatory tone he used. "What does it look like I'm doing here? I'm taking a tour of your business."

"Why though? I've got to know. Did you know who I was when we met at Arlo's? And then you show up here. It's all a little too coincidental for my liking."

"If you remember, last night, you approached me. The only thing I knew about you until today was that your name was Reid, and that you're good in bed. I've been in touch with Gemma, and she's the one who invited me for a tour. You know, I really don't like having to explain myself to you." She narrowed her eyes at him and saw that he was still suspicious.

"Whether you like it or not, it's just a coincidence. Are you accusing me of something, Reid? What's with the inquisition?"

"I don't believe in coincidence, fate or happenstance. I don't understand how we meet in a restaurant, sleep together and then you randomly show up at my business. Is this a way to get extra information, an inside scoop for your blog?"

"What, *In Bed with the Rum Baron*? You think that's a traffic booster? Please." When he didn't say anything in response, and just looked at her critically, anger quickly replaced any other feelings she might have had for Reid. "Are you fucking kidding me?" she asked, indignant, standing from the table. "I don't need a salacious story to sell people on my brand. I wanted to take a tour of the distillery because I like your sister, and maybe I wanted to see you again. Jeeze, you're so freaking hot and cold. I don't understand you."

He shook his head. "You're right. I shouldn't have said that. It seemed… Never mind."

"You can't just accuse me of what—trying to gain your information, and then say forget it. I'm just going to leave." Like that, she saw her dreams of them working together burst into flames. Without a brand partnership, she could kiss her television career goodbye. But her integrity was worth more than that. "Thanks for the tour."

"Lila." Reid's voice remained even. "Please don't go. Believe me, I'm very sorry for what I've implied. It didn't come out the way I meant." He exhaled. "I've… I've been burned before. And I don't normally see women more than once. So, my reaction to seeing you this morning, and then seeing you here—it's all too incredible for me."

Even though she knew she should be halfway out the door, she briefly forgot how insulted she'd been by him. She could see the mix of emotions on his face. He looked uncomfortable, troubled, confused, frustrated, vulnerable, and Lila was intrigued. She sat back down and watched him. "What happened? Who burned you?"

He shook his head. "It's nothing I'm eager to talk about, especially to a stranger."

A stranger. That stung.

"It's a story best left for another time," he continued. "Or never. But I'm a little more careful now than I used to be. And seeing you here today confused me." He picked up the next rum, the amber. "Shall we carry on? Forget that I even said anything?"

There was a story there, a reason for his sudden shift in attitude, and despite feeling a little hurt, instead of telling him to go fuck himself and walking away, Lila was eager to dig a little deeper to hear it. The man in front of her was intriguing. But he was also kind of a jerk. Good thing he was sexy as hell on top of it. "Sure." She picked up the next small glass, still mad at Reid, but willing to drink his rum.

He cleared his throat. "This is the amber," he told her, back in business mode. He held the small glass aloft, and Lila did the same, the light shining through a liquid gold. "It's medium-bodied, aged three years, and caramel and spicy in flavor."

He brought it to his lips, and she drank hers, as well. It was just as good as the first. It didn't have the same burn that most straight liquor had, a testament to its quality. The only burn she felt came from the infuriatingly complicated man who sat across the table.

"What do you think?" he asked.

"About the rum?" she countered, shrugging. "It's good." She looked at the two shots still in front of her. "I'm glad I had lunch, though."

"We can skip the rest if you want to leave."

"And let it go down the drain?" She laughed. "Never. I'll just carb-load later to soak it up." She picked up the next. "What's this one?"

"Our signature spiced rum. Flavored with a combination of spices. The recipe is one of Gemma's most tightly held secrets. I'll be honest, Quin and I don't even know how she makes this one."

They both drank. The spiced rum was amazing, and she hummed in approval as she savored the flavor. It was heavy, spicy but also sweet—*just like Reid*—and it felt warm in her stomach. A pleasant feeling spread to each of her extremities. "Delicious." She smiled at him.

He exhaled as he put down the glass with a heavy clunk, and she wondered if he was feeling the effects of the alcohol as well. "Lila, I really am sorry

I got so angry earlier, and I'm sorry I accused you of being unscrupulous. I acted poorly. You did nothing wrong, and you didn't deserve it."

His apology seemed heartfelt. The beast wasn't all gruff. He might have a heart, after all. "Thank you. This is a weird situation we've found ourselves in. Fate works in mysterious ways."

"I don't believe in fate. It all seems a little too coincidental." He gestured to the last glass. "Shall we drink?"

"Yes, please."

He picked up the last shot, the creamy one. "Last one. This is the cream liqueur. This one is a combination distilled rum and cream. Then Gemma added a little vanilla, cinnamon and a few other delicious spices from around the world. Once again, only Gemma and her guys know the exact recipe."

She held the glass to her nose and sniffed. It smelled sweet. "Down the hatch," she said. When he laughed, she explained. "I know it's not the fanciest toast, but whatever." She savored the flavor. "That was delicious."

When she lowered the glass, she saw that Reid was looking at her, and he was smiling.

"What?" she asked.

"You've got a little…" He reached across the table and swiped his thumb across her top lip. He pulled it away with some of the creamy rum on it, and before bringing his hand back to his side of the table, he paused, and touched it to her mouth. She parted her lips and closed them around his thumb. When she released him, she dragged her tongue along the outer edge of his thumb, tasting the rum on his skin, combined with his own flavor. She wanted more.

He groaned and without saying anything, Reid came around to her side of the table. She was still seated, and he stood behind Lila, towering over her. Resting his palms on the table, one on each side of her own hands, he hovered over her, caging her in. Lila leaned back against him and looked up. The all-too-familiar heat had returned to his eyes. Despite his accusations, he wanted her again. *So goddamn hot and cold.*

He drew the fingers of one hand along her cheek, down her throat, to the crevice of cleavage revealed by the low cut of her dress. Lila again leaned into his touch, unable to do anything else but urge him to keep touching her. His hand slid underneath the neckline of her dress and bra and cupped her breast. He pinched her nipple between two fingers, and she gasped, and it turned into a moan when he smoothed his hand over her.

"Still want to leave?"

Lila drew her bottom lip between her teeth, and closed her eyes, leaning against his chest. She in-haled his cologne, his rum-scented breath, and she moaned. Her laugh was a throaty sound. "I couldn't if I tried. I thought you said we were a one night only thing."

"I was a fool. And we already broke that rule this morning, didn't we?"

His hand left her breast and smoothed down the front of her dress to her thighs, where the material of her skirt had already ridden up. He slid his hand between her thighs, and she responded by spreading them further for him. He hummed in approval. "That's good." His fingers traveled upward to the apex of her thighs, where he found her already wet panties. He stroked her through the soaked satin and her moan filled the small room.

"I don't know what you do to me, Lila," he whispered in her ear, as he slipped his hand underneath her panties and touched her without a barrier. "I know this is a bad idea, but the minute I'm near you, it's all I can do to keep from fucking you."

"Why is this such a bad idea?" She spread her thighs wider, allowing him better access, and she was rewarded when he slid two fingers easily inside her.

"Because nothing that is this fucking sweet can be a good thing."

"Hey, Reid, I figured I'd find you in here—oops!" A male voice behind them interrupted them.

"Fuck," Reid muttered, removing his hand, straightening immediately.

Lila turned her head, and even with Reid blocking her with his body, she could see the other man standing in the doorway.

"Get the fuck out of here, Quin."

"I'm already gone. I'll call you later."

The door closed and they were alone again. But the mood had shifted. For a while, the only sounds were their matched heavy breaths, the pounding of her heart, and her hormones *screaming* to be sated.

"Who was that?"

"My brother. I'm really sorry," he told her, taking a step back from her. Apparently, the moment had passed.

"You're sorry about us being interrupted, or that anything happened in the first place?"

"Both. Damn, Lila—"

"You know, if you're just going to repeat that it was wrong, or a bad idea, or whatever, I'm not interested in hearing it. I'd better leave." Humiliated, she gathered her things as quickly as she could. "Thanks for the tour and the rum." She could still feel the ghost of his touch on her skin. "And whatever that was," she said, gesturing to the table.

"I'll call you a car," Reid said.

"That's not necessary," she said, taking her phone out of her purse and opening a rideshare app. "I get my own rides." She straightened her dress and smoothed down her hair. "See you later, Reid."

Reid was so hot one minute, threatening to rip her clothes off, and then so stern and serious the next. She couldn't read him, and goddamn if that didn't intrigue her.

CHAPTER SIX

LILA TOSSED HER hair over her shoulder as she stepped out of her hired car and onto the sidewalk in the front of the five-star hotel where the Rexford Rum party was located. She looked up, and at the very top, on the roof of the hotel, she could see bright skylights streaking the sky—X marking the spot of the most elite party in Miami. The hotel itself gave off a very you-can't-sit-with-us vibe. And it was one she normally couldn't stand. But this was the job, and she had an invitation to the hottest party in the city in her small, ultra-fashionable purse.

Not to mention that she would undoubtedly see Reid. Almost a week had passed since she'd seen him. He hadn't called like she'd expected him to, nor had she contacted him. If distance was what he'd wanted, then fine. But she was going to be at his party, whether he wanted her there or not. She grinned, thinking about what his reaction might be.

She entered the hotel and at the elevators was met by an attendant who checked her invitation and ID and escorted her to an elevator that would take her to the rooftop bar. She checked her reflection in the mirrored wall of the elevator, touched up her lipstick and fluffed her hair. Despite the Miami humidity, her blowout had held, and when she'd dressed, she'd been inspired by her encounters with Reid, so she picked the sexiest outfit in her suitcase—a black, tight spaghetti-strap cropped camisole, paired with a matching skin-tight, high-waisted skirt. Her favorite red stilettos completed the look. She knew she looked sexy.

The elevator came to a stop with a soft *ding*, and the doors parted in front of her. She was met by another attendant who again checked her ID and invitation and gave her a discreet scan with a metal-detecting wand. The Rexfords had really spared no expense, and took no risks with their security, it seemed. When she'd received the invite from Quin Rexford, she'd known it would be a high-end affair, but she hadn't been prepared for the extent.

The music, courtesy of one of the country's hottest DJs, pumped into the warm night air, but she still managed to hear the dull roar of the Atlantic Ocean against the sandy beach below them. The spotlight beams she'd seen from the street crossed each other high in the sky, and cool blue-and-purple uplighting focused on potted palms and VIP seating.

Looking around, she saw nothing, but the beautiful and glamorous people Miami was known for, with many celebrities and athletes, and their entourages scattered throughout. Lila thought about her blog and even though she had social media followers in the millions across all her platforms, and she'd rubbed shoulders with many rich and famous folks in the past, she wondered how she'd even managed to score an invite to this shindig. Rexford was still run out of their humble distillery, but they apparently knew how to throw a hot party. A passing server held a tray of drinks, and she caught his eyes.

"Cuba Libre, ma'am?" he asked.

Lila blinked in surprise. That one of the featured cocktails was the same that she'd drunk with Reid last week wasn't lost on her. "Yes, please," she told him, taking a glass from the tray. When she sipped, she was hit with notes of lime and a light rum over the cola, and she hummed in appreciation. Just drinking the cocktail brought her back to her time with Reid.

It was Friday, exactly a week since she'd seen him last, and with her time drawing short in Miami, she was starting to kiss goodbye the prospect of partnering with the rum brand. Every time she picked up the phone to call him, to suggest the business partnership between their brands, she chickened out. But was she afraid of his dismissal? His ridicule? His sexual power over her? Lila had no idea.

She drank from her glass again. The rum warmed her pleasantly. A little liquid courage would help her navigate the crowd. Her first stop would be to find her gracious hosts, the Rexfords, and thank them for inviting her.

She decided the best way to start would be to walk the perimeter—do a lap around to see if she could find someone she knew. But she knew nobody in Miami—well, except for mysterious Reid. Many interested men tried to catch her eye. But she ignored them. As she looked around at the faces of the beautiful people, part of her hoped to see Reid among them.

Distracted by the crowd around her, Lila wasn't looking when she collided with another woman, almost spilling her drink on herself. "I'm so sorry about that," she said.

"Don't worry about it," the woman told her. "As long as you didn't spill your drink."

"Thank God, I didn't," Lila said, taking a sip for emphasis. "Spilling something this good would be a sin."

She looked up and saw Gemma Rexford standing in front of her. While Lila had never met Reid's sister in person. They'd been in contact via email, and she recognized her picture from the lock screen of Reid's phone "You like the drink?" she asked.

"Yeah. It's delicious. Apparently, Rexford Rum is quickly becoming one of my favorites."

She laughed. "I'm glad to hear it." She stuck out her hand. "You must be Lila Campbell. I'm Gemma Rexford."

"It's great to finally meet you," Lila said, shaking her hand. "Thanks for the invite to the party."

"We're glad to have you here. I hope you're having a great night."

"I haven't been here long, but it looks like everyone is having a great time."

"I'm really sorry I couldn't make the tour. I trust that Reid took care of you."

He certainly had. Lila felt a flush start on her chest, and she tried to control it before it reached her cheeks.

"He never did tell me how the tour went. Did you enjoy it?"

"I did. I was going to include the distillery in a top ten in Miami list with a small section, but I wrote a full blog featuring the distillery. It's scheduled to go live on my website at midnight, to correspond with pictures and videos from here."

"Thank you so much. We really appreciate it."

This was Lila's chance to lay the groundwork for a partnership. Start small, and they could build a business relationship from there. "I'd love to follow up and do an interview with you. I'm sure my audience would be interested in hearing from the badass master distiller of Rexford Rum."

Gemma laughed. "Oh, I don't know if I'm that badass. I just make rum that I hope people love."

Lila looked around the party. "I think it's safe to say that people do. How about we schedule a time to get together?" She held out hope that the other woman would be free before she left town.

Gemma nodded. "Yeah. Are you free for late lunch tomorrow?"

"I'm in Miami until tomorrow evening. I'd love to get together for lunch."

"Fabulous," Gemma said, clinking her glass against Lila's. "It's a date."

Lila looked around the party "Is Reid here?" she asked, not sure if Gemma knew about the extent of their relationship. "I didn't really get a chance to thank him for the tour."

Gemma's face gave nothing away. "Yeah, he's right behind you."

Lila turned around and froze in place. Reid had been on her mind for the entire week. So much so she thought she'd seen him on the beach, on a scooter tour, in restaurants, behind bushes…. He was already ingrained in her memory, tattooed on her skin. As if she could still smell him, hear his laughter in the distance. Lila shook her head. She really had to get a grip on herself.

Her skin prickled and an anticipatory shiver crawled over her, as she was rooted in place. Slowly, Lila turned and once again came face-to-face with Reid Rexford.

Reid stood, dumbfounded, in front of Lila—the saucy redheaded siren who'd consumed his every waking moment since the previous weekend. He hadn't expected her to be among the personalities invited to the party, but he probably should have. Pretending that her presence had no effect on him, Reid stuck out his hand, and put a cordial smile on his face. "Hello, Ms. Campbell. Nice to see you again."

Lila shook his hand. Her hand was warm and soft, and the same current of heat that occurred each time he saw her traveled between them. "Likewise."

"Lila was telling me how much she loves our rum," Gemma said.

He watched as Lila raised her glass to those full, pouty lips. "Yeah, I really do enjoy the taste of Rexford," she told him with a wink. They looked at each other for several beats, and, as the rest of the world fell away, he focused on only Lila. If Gemma noticed the haze of sexual tension between them, she didn't let on.

Realizing it had been some time before either of them spoke, Reid cleared his throat and looked at her drink. "What do you have there?" he asked. Not giving her time to answer, he carried on. "Let me guess, Cuba Libre. One of my favorites."

She nodded. "It's delicious."

Reid was reminded of his sister's presence when she put her hand on his forearm. One look at her, and he knew that she knew something was going on. "Reid, Lila, please excuse me. There are some people over there I need to talk to. Lila, it was wonderful to meet you. I'll see you tomorrow." She pointed a finger at her brother. "Reid, be nice."

"Aren't I always nice?" he asked her, as she walked away, disappearing in the crowd.

And with that, Reid was left alone with the woman who'd completely rocked him the week before. They stood awkwardly in place for several beats. He wondered who would speak first. What would she say? How unbelievable would it be that fate had put them together like this, yet again, in a way neither could have expected? He frowned as she smiled and sipped her drink, giving him a few more seconds before he would have to say anything.

"This is certainly a strange turn of events. Another coincidence?" he asked.

Reid tried to ignore her smile, her luscious curves and the way his body reacted to her.

"Too bad I don't believe in coincidence, right?"

"So, what are you doing here?"

"I was invited."

"You didn't think to mention you'd be coming?"

"If you were really on top of things here, you would think you would have checked the RSVP list."

"Touché."

"But after everything we've been through, you still don't believe that fate can have an influence over our lives? To shape us? To change us?"

"No, the only thing that influences my life is me. I don't put my future in anyone else's hands."

"Oh really?" she asked, leaning in closer. Looking down, he was treated to a view of her ample cleavage. He could still taste the smooth skin of her chest on his tongue. It was the same taste he'd craved all week. Saliva flooded the back of his mouth as he wanted nothing more than to capture the flavor again. "That's a couple of times you've said something like that. You don't trust easily."

He kept his posture rigid, but his fist clenched to stop himself from reaching out to touch her. "I believe that trust has to be earned. And it isn't easy."

"There's something you aren't telling me, isn't there?"

Was there ever. But if the past weekend had taught him anything, it was that Lila tempted him. Around her, he'd already broken most of his rules—he'd found himself revealing far too much to her. No matter how much he wanted to get out of there and spend the rest of the night buried deep inside her, he might be tempted to spill his secrets. And given what she did for a living, peddling in information, he couldn't do that. He was strong, but somehow, she wore him down. That's what she was to him—a temptress, a siren, one that would bring about his downfall if he wasn't careful. He had to end this dalliance and put the necessary distance between them before he did something he regretted. The sooner the better.

The DJ started up again. The familiar notes of a song she knew filled the night air. "Ooh, I love this song," she told him. "Dance with me?"

He shook his head. "No, I don't dance."

"Come on, everybody dances."

"Not me."

"Fine. Suit yourself," she said, turning and heading for the dance floor without him.

She stayed within his sight, and he couldn't take his eyes off her. He watched riveted as Lila swiveled her hips to the music, rolling her body seductively to the beat. She looked over her shoulder and their eyes met, and her lips pursed into a saucy smile. He knew that was her game—he didn't want to dance so she'd at least make him regret it.

Reid's eyes were pinned to Lila as she danced with the crowd. But he knew what she was doing, she was teasing him. Trying to prod him into joining her. He barely noticed when Quin sidled up next to him.

"You're not going to dance with your girl?"

"What makes you think she's my girl?"

"It certainly looked like you two were getting pretty cozy over here. Not to mention what I walked in on at the tasting room last week."

"It was just a conversation," he insisted. "And you walked in on nothing."

"Is that right?"

"That's right." He wouldn't share with his brother that she was a woman he'd already slept with—twice. But he forgot about Quin entirely when his vision focused on the guy who was approaching Lila.

Quin had noticed him, too. "So, you're going to let some other man dance with her then."

Reid's eyebrows narrowed. No, he wasn't. He handed his glass to Quin. "I'll see you later."

Striding across the rooftop to the sunken dance floor, he came upon Lila and the guy who'd tried to insinuate himself into Reid's private show. "May I cut in here?" he asked her.

"Hey, buddy," the guy stepped forward, looked at Reid and backed up quickly. "Sorry, Mr. Rexford, I didn't realize it was you."

"Leave," Reid told him.

"That was rude," Lila told him. "What if I was enjoying his company?"

"Well, I'll apologize for scaring away a kid who ground his pelvis against you without any sort of rhythm. He was making you look bad."

"Is that right? Will you make me look good?"

His eyes swept up and down her body "You already look good. I'll make you feel good."

She drew the tip of her tongue along her upper lip. "I believe that."

It had been years since he'd danced, but it felt so right when he took her hips in his hands and moved in closer. They were chest-to-chest, with no space between them, both of them moving to the music. The song changed and the notes of a Cuban hip-hop song started playing. He shifted his hips against her, swaying with her on the dance floor. Reid turned her in his hands, so that her ass pressed against his crotch. There was no way she missed his already-stiffening cock. Turning her head over her shoulder, she raised an eyebrow at him. He smirked, unembarrassed.

"We move pretty well together, don't we?"

She wasn't just talking about their dance moves, and he knew it. "We certainly do."

The songs changed again, and then again. They danced, pressed together, their bodies moving as one to the beats of the music.

After several songs, Lila stopped, and put her hands on his shoulders, stopping him and leaned in close. "I'm done. My feet hurt," she said in his ear.

"Want to grab a table?" she asked, gesturing to the high-top tables next to the wall closest to the ocean.

"Yeah, sure." So much for staying away. Reid cursed his lack of restraint when it came to the woman.

"I'll get a table and let you buy me a drink."

"It's an open bar," he reminded her.

"Well, you could be a dear and fetch me one then," she told him.

"Cuba Libre?" he asked her.

"I'd love one." She strutted to a nearby table. Her skirt was skin-tight, and showed off her smooth, ample curves. He wanted nothing more than to run his palms over her hips, her breasts, the high curve of her ass. Instead he clenched his fists and shoved them into his pockets as he headed for the bar. He was doomed.

While the bartender mixed their cocktails, Reid watched as Lila secured them a seat at the table. She turned her back to the party, took out her phone, and snapped a picture of herself in front of the crowd, the lights, the glamour that he and his siblings had created. They'd overspent for the party, invited celebrities and personalities that he hadn't dreamed would show up, but all he could see was Lila.

He knew that spending any more time with her would be a mistake, but he just couldn't help himself. After being alone for such a long time, he'd buried himself in his work. He'd stayed guarded. But there was something about the woman that filled his well, gave him a new energy. Who she was, though, and how she made him feel was dangerous, to him and to the business.

"Here you are, Mr. Rexford." The bartender handed him two glasses.

"Thank you."

When he returned, she was staring out into the darkness, toward the sound of the ocean. Her eyes unfocused, and her lips turned down, she looked so pensive and lost in thought that he didn't want to disturb her. In the halo of the lights from the party, she looked so beautiful it made his stomach twist.

Sliding one of the glasses over, he took a seat across from her at the small table. "You okay?"

"Huh? Oh, yeah. I'm fine."

"You looked pretty deep in thought there."

She shook her head, but he wondered if she was hiding something. "I'm just thinking."

"So, what do you think of our little party?"

"Little? Are you kidding? This party is amazing. Look around. This is pretty much the best party I've ever attended. A real who's who of pop culture right now." Her eyes widened. "Which makes me wonder why you're over here talking to little ol' me."

"Maybe I like your company."

"Doesn't seem like it all the time," she pointed out.

"I apologized for that, didn't I?"

"Doesn't mean it isn't well within my rights to give you a hard time about it."

"You got me there. Honestly, the party is a bit much for me. Normally, we do this on a smaller scale. Gemma and Quin handled most of the planning. I just tried to keep them on budget."

"And did they stay on budget?"

He looked around, and her eyes followed his as she took in the spectacle around them. Celebrities, athletes and A-listers laughed and danced, and took photos with Rexford Rum in hand. It was a glamorous party on a beautiful night. Reid laughed. "Does it look like they stayed on budget?" He paused. "But I have to say, they did an awesome job."

"You have a great thing going on here. Rexford is so exclusive, such a premium spirit, though, I don't know if many of my followers even know who you are. But it's going to make a great blog post. People are going to love you guys."

"I just want people to love the rum."

She took a sip and watched him. "They will." She averted her gaze briefly. "Reid, I think we should talk about what happened. I would feel a lot more comfortable if we just addressed what we did." He nodded and waved a hand for her to start talking. "We had a lot of fun that night," she started. "And the next morning. And at the distillery." She laughed. "But I think it's probably best if we leave it at that."

Reid's eyes widened. That wasn't what he'd expected her to say. Part of him had hoped for another night, to finish what they'd started in the distillery. But it was smart for them to part ways amicably. They'd both had a good time, and Lila would give them excellent exposure on her blog. "Yeah, that's a good idea."

"You're a great guy, Reid," she kept going. "It's just that I can't let anything affect my online image. One misstep, and I could just be seen as a party girl. I want to be taken seriously, and that's hard enough for a woman in my field."

Relief came over him, knowing that she was on the same page as him. It would be easier to behave himself. "I completely agree."

"Great. Now that that's settled, you can relax."

"Why are you worried about me relaxing?"

"Because just looking at you, I can see how uptight you are. Look at how rigid you are. If you keep that up, work and stress are going to put you into an early grave."

It bothered him that she had been able to peg him so easily. "You think you know that much about me?"

She nodded. "I do."

"How?"

"Because the night you came on to me at Arlo's,

the night we spent in my hotel room, you were a completely different person. You were loose, fun, charming. But now, even at an incredible party, you're as taut as a violin string. Maybe you're due for another plucking," she surmised with a grin.

"You're terrible."

"I know. It's all part of the personality."

"I think that's enough about me," he said. They'd had the discussion they'd needed to have, but he didn't want to walk away yet. "Tell me about what you do. I never did understand the *influencer culture*," he said, using his fingers to make air quotes around the phrase. He liked Lila, but the whole thing seemed shallow to him. He was a firm believer of living in the moment and didn't think everything needed to be documented and shared online for "likes."

"What do you want to know?"

"How did you get into the business? What is it you do exactly? You're very well-known and apparently have a lot of fans."

She frowned. "I can't tell if you're making fun of me, or not."

He put up his hands. "I'm not making fun, I promise. I'm just a traditional guy. I don't follow social media or celebrities or any of that. I'm more of a private person. I like the quiet life."

She raised an eyebrow and looked around the party. "Really? This doesn't exactly scream the quiet life."

"This is all my brother and sister. I'm not that guy anymore."

"*Anymore?* Was all of this once you?"

He shook his head. He didn't want to get into it, and how he once lived his life.

"There's another story there," she said.

"There are many stories, Lila, but you aren't going to hear them. But we're off track because you distracted me. Tell me what you're all about."

"Where do I start? I've always had a lot of energy, you know? I grew up in a very small town. And I had no intention of staying there. When I turned eighteen, I had big dreams of getting out. But instead, I met the wrong guy, thought I was in love and got married."

"Really?"

"Yeah, it's really embarrassing now. It feels like it was another life from where I am now."

"What happened then?"

"Little did I know that my husband expected me to stay home and cook and clean, until it was time to have babies, and then I could raise children, along with cooking and cleaning. I'd just finished high school, and he told me I'd never have a career, so I'd be dependent on him. He isolated me from my friends and family. I didn't see it at the time, but it was such an unhealthy situation. He was a little older. He was a salesman, and he was good at it. Worked all the time and made a great living. The guy could sell water to a fish. I guess that's how he manipulated me. We looked like the perfect little family. But it was hell." She exhaled, nervously. "I don't know why I'm telling you all of this," she said, shaking her head. "It's been a while since I've talked about it."

"Keep going," he told her. He hated that Lila had been so unhappy. He wanted nothing more than to track down her ex and punch him repeatedly.

"Fine. He was content to keep me at home, but I didn't want that. I wanted to travel, to *finally* leave that town. So, one day, when he was at work, I got the hell out of there. I'd managed to squirrel-away five thousand dollars and I left and never looked back. Then I trained to be a flight attendant."

Reid admired that. "That's great. Then what?"

"I started working, and I got to see and do all the things I'd dreamed about. It was amazing. Along the way I started a blog, began tweeting about my adventures and misadventures, and posting to Instagram. And it just kind of went from there. My videos and posts got a lot of views. I know it sounds easy, but it's a lot of hard work. I started to get sponsors, and ad revenue. It's hell trying to build a dedicated following when you start with nothing."

Reid realized that they had more in common than he would have ever thought. "Tell me about it. My parents worked at the distillery when we were children. They had a small local following, but never intended to have the reach we do now. Some days it feels like marketing and building a brand comes ahead of the actual product."

"So, you know what I'm saying."

"I think I do."

"And that's why your brother invited me here," she said, pulling out her phone. "I take pictures, I write blogs, I show people what a good time they're missing." As if to prove her point, she snapped a photo of the crowd. "I give people extreme FOMO." She stopped when his head tilted at the word she'd used. *"Fear of missing out,"* she explained. "People want to live my life—travel, eat, drink, hang out with celebrities. I get people to do what I do—which in this case is drink your rum."

Before he could ask her about it, she quickly snapped a picture of her glass. Looked at it, frowned, then lifted the glass and held the camera above her to take a picture of herself drinking the rum. She looked at it and smiled. "Perfect," she muttered, and began typing furiously. "Having a wild time at the Rexford Rum party in Miami," she read aloud as she typed. "Hashtag drinks, hashtag Rexford Rum, hashtag Miami, hashtag party-time, hashtag wish you were here." She smiled at him, and then rounded the table and held her camera above them, but tilted downward, and took another picture. She started typing. "Our handsome host, Reid Rexford says hi," she said as she typed. "And post."

"So that's your job?" he asked skeptically. "You take a picture, post it, and sit back to wait for the likes."

"And the shares and comments," she retorted.

"Seems a little shallow," he told her. He hadn't meant for his words to sound as harsh as they did.

"It's all about reach. I'm no different than those fancy traditional marketing firms you hire. In fact, I might be a little more flexible and adaptable to new platforms and technology than those guys. It's all about search engine optimization and cost per click. I get more bang for your buck.

"People see and want my life—that's the product I'm pushing. Brands and events reach out because I have literally millions of followers who want just a small piece of what's perceived to be my amazing life."

Perceived stuck out to him. As much as Lila extolled the wonderful parts of her life, he wondered if it wasn't always as wonderful as it seemed. Maybe the life of a beautiful vagabond wasn't all the glitz and glamor people thought.

"What's the difference between your actual life and what you put out there?"

Her eyes shifted skyward, and then she blew out a shaky breath. "I know I'm lucky, I do have an incredible life," she told him. "I love to travel, meet new people, have new experiences. But sometimes I get tired. I get bored with the same hotel rooms, not making any of those real connections with people. I went to Bonnaroo last year, and all I wanted to do was stay in my hotel room, eat Doritos and watch *The Office* on Netflix. I don't always want to be the social one." Her laugh sounded forced. "Listen to me—poor little girl who has fun for a living."

Hearing her revelation that her life wasn't all fun and glamour, that she trusted him enough to tell him, Reid felt like they were sharing a real moment. "I get that. I'm the most reserved of my siblings. I like the quiet."

"Me too sometimes, but I'm not always allowed to have it."

"Well, why don't you do something else?"

"Why would I? I have everything I want. A fun life, and I get paid to do it. I'm my own boss. I could never be tied to a nine-to-five, Monday-to-Friday gig."

"Except you're on the clock 24/7."

"It sounds to me like you might be, too."

He thought about it, and realized she was right. That was his life. "Not everyone is cut out for it, I guess." He frowned, too, and their eyes connected. For a moment, they shared a knowing solidarity.

"Where do you live?" he asked.

She blinked. "What do you mean?"

He paused. "I'm not sure how else I could ask that question. Where do you go when you aren't globe-trotting? Where's your family?"

Lila pictured the town, and the people she'd come from, and forced the frown from her lips, replacing it with a big, easy smile. "Still in that very small town, and that's also where I escaped from. I don't stop. When I'm tired, I plan some more quiet trips, if I can get a hotel or resort comped, or maybe I'll visit some friends. I've got some stuff in storage in LA, but mostly I live out of my suitcase."

She leaned over the table, coming closer to him. "Can you keep a secret?" she whispered conspiratorially.

He leaned in as well. "My lips are sealed."

"I'm not sure why I'm telling you this. Maybe it was the rum, maybe you make me feel at ease. But here it is. I'm in negotiations with the GO! Channel for my own travel show."

"That's incredible."

"It hasn't been finalized yet, so I'd really appreciate it if you don't tell anyone."

"I know about wanting to keep secrets. Yours dies with me."

"What secrets do you have, Reid?"

He looked down into his drink and didn't say anything for a while. He didn't know what to say, so he deflected. "And what about your family?" he asked, ignoring her question entirely.

She shook her head. "They visit me on the road. Not like I'll ever go back there. My hometown represents oppression, and now I'm free."

"No plans on settling down? Putting down roots?"

"I think eventually I might get a place. Something small. But I don't have to worry about that yet. If I make the deal for my own show, I'll find something in LA. I'll still get to travel but it won't be so much." Not taking his eyes from her, Reid lifted his glass and finished his drink. There was more to Lila, with whom he'd had a one-night stand, and then a rare-for-him second round. He liked her, more than he'd liked a woman in a long time. He noticed that she'd also finished her drink. "Another?"

"So, because I missed my train, I was four hours late getting to Prague, I missed the check-in time for the room I'd arranged. I get there, and the innkeeper freaks out at me, saying that he'd given away my room, that it would teach me to plan ahead, and all that. I went to about a dozen other places and found no room anywhere. Here I am, completely alone, with no room in a strange city."

Reid laughed. "What did you do?"

"What any young woman in my predicament would do—I found a pub and got a beer. I fell in with a group of Irish girls, and they offered me a spot on the floor in their small room."

She didn't miss his frown. "Sounds risky."

Lila dismissed him with a wave. "I don't make it a habit to go off with strangers." She caught the way his eyebrows rose. That was exactly what she'd done with him. "But I always open myself up for adventure."

Lila watched as Reid laughed and sipped his drink. She was feeling light-headed, but not from the alcohol—she hadn't had that much—but it was Reid's company. He was funny, smart, but also very serious. "So, what about you?"

"What about me?"

"You have any funny travel stories?"

He shook his head. "Unfortunately, I don't get to travel much."

"Why not?" He clearly had the funds to go on any holiday he wanted.

"I'm so busy with work and everything. I don't feel comfortable leaving the distillery for long periods of time."

"Won't your brother and sister take care of things?"

Reid's eyes shifted over to the bar, where his brother, Quin, downed shots with some players she recognized as starters for the Miami Heat basketball team.

"Yeah," he said slowly. "They're my family and I love them, but they aren't the surest hands I've seen. That's Quin in a nutshell, and Gemma rarely surfaces from the distillery." He shook his head. "I'm not even sure she's ever *seen* a financial statement."

"You're the responsible older brother just trying to hold it all together."

"That's a little dramatic, but some days it feels like that."

"Are you kidding me? You're young, hot, successful. Everyone needs a break every now and then. Don't you ever want to just get away?"

"Sometimes, I might take a weekend away and go to the Everglades or Key West." He sighed. "I'll bet my life sounds boring to you."

She hesitated. The quiet, the solitude, it was what Lila typically avoided at all costs, not wanting to be alone with herself or her own thoughts. She needed the excitement, the buzz around her. But she thought about it. A visit to the Everglades, or a quiet Key West beach, especially one that came with Reid Rexford, sounded nice. She smiled, and shrugging, drained her glass. "I see the appeal. Not sure if it's what I'm looking for, but different strokes, right?"

"Definitely."

A comfortable silence surrounded them, and Lila realized the amount of time that had passed since they'd started talking. "You know, I should be making my rounds," she said. "Earn that invitation your brother sent me."

"Yeah, me too. I should go shake some hands."

"It was nice to see you again. Thanks for the drinks, and the dance. I'm glad I got to see you again tonight. And we got to clear the air a little."

"Me too. It's been fun. It's been a while since I've danced."

She looked up at him and narrowed her eyes. He looked straight ahead; his posture was rigid. "But it's over, right?" she guessed.

"Yeah. Just let the doorman know whenever you're ready to leave. He'll get you a car."

"No, it's fine. I'll just call a cab or walk. My hotel isn't far."

"Yeah, I know exactly where your hotel is," he

reminded her. Of course, he knew. He'd been there. Twice. "But I'm not letting you walk out of here alone," he told her.

"Thanks." They stood. While Lila was disappointed she hadn't set the groundwork for a partnership, she was glad to have had an actual conversation with him and get to know him a little bit better.

"How much longer do you have in Miami?" he asked.

"I fly out tomorrow night," she told him.

He nodded, but he was frowning. "Well, it's been fun."

"It sure was," she agreed. It was too bad that she was leaving soon. She knew she would miss Reid, and for the first time, she wondered if she would be leaving something behind.

Without thinking, she reached out and wrapped her arms around him, and it surprised her when he hugged her back.

His strong arms wrapped around her and the heat from his body made her melt her against him. He was standing so close she could smell the rum on his breath.

She heard a low groan from his chest. "You leave tomorrow night?" he asked, his voice low.

"Yeah," she whispered back. Turning her head put her lips within a fraction of an inch of his jaw. There was only a hairbreadth of space between their bodies, and from the way he looked down at her, there was that spark of desire in his eyes that she couldn't miss and knew he hadn't either.

"You're still staying at the same hotel?"

"I am."

"Why don't I meet you there in an hour?"

CHAPTER SEVEN

TRUE TO HIS WORD, one hour later, Reid was standing outside of Lila's hotel room. He'd been so close to a clean break with her. But instead, when he'd hugged her, the desire he felt had been too much. He'd done one final lap around the party, making sure everything was going smoothly, and avoiding the curious glances of his brother and sister, he quietly left. He knew Quin and Gemma would have questions tomorrow. But as he jogged down the street to Lila's hotel, he didn't give a damn. All he could think about was Lila.

He raised his fist and knocked three times. The force behind the knock told of his urgency.

Lila opened the door. She was still wearing the outfit she'd worn at the party. She smiled and stepped to the side, opening the door wider to let him in.

Once inside, he slammed the door shut and then pounced. He cupped her face in his hands and kissed her. She was so sweet, so hot. Perfect. When he kissed Lila, there was nothing else—no family, no business, no commitments—nothing but her full, delicious lips.

She pulled away first. "Reid," she started, putting her hand on his chest. "I'm so glad you came here. I know we agreed it was best if we didn't do this. What I said earlier—that was the smart, rational Lila speaking, but this is the Lila who wants you so badly she can barely breathe." She smoothed her palms over his chest, and he cursed the material of his shirt for separating them. "There's no reason why we can't have one more night together, is there?"

"I can't think of a goddamn one."

"You sure you aren't missing the party?"

Reid thought briefly of what he might be missing—schmoozing with celebrities, hearing from customers. He knew that the night was an important one for the distillery. If it was a success, it could put them on the map and give them mainstream success. If it failed, it could ruin them. But when he looked down at Lila, it didn't matter. "I'm not missing anything," he told her, roughly pulling her to him. He kissed her.

As he kissed her, her arms wrapped around his neck, her fingers fisting his hair, as she lowered them, running her hands over her shoulders, down his chest. Her fingers were at his buttons, loosening them, undressing him. Reid was harder than he'd ever been in his life, and his need for her was greater than anything he'd ever wanted.

He broke away only long enough to pull her shirt over her head. Her skirt was next. She stood in front of him in only her matching black bra and panties and black stilettos. "Christ," he muttered against her throat. "You're the sexiest goddamn thing I've ever seen."

Lila pushed Reid's shirt from his shoulders. "You're not so bad yourself," she told him, moving against his hardened cock, the delicious contact making him flinch. Adrenaline, the need to have her surged through his system, and his entire body clenched. His hands were on her ass. He lifted her and she wrapped her legs around his waist. She fit perfectly against him. He removed one hand from her ass and brought it to her red hair, pushing his fingers through the silky strands, until reaching the back of her head, where he wrapped her hair around his hand and pulled gently, forcing her eyes to his.

Her lips parted with a startled gasp, and his entire body hardened with the image of his dick sliding between them. Her eyes were fiery, and her thighs tightened around his waist, and he could feel her heat against his abdomen. There was no time for any preliminaries—that would come later—right now, he needed to be inside of her.

He closed his eyes and took a deep, calming breath. Lila made him feel like a wild man. He'd never been so out-of-control with a woman. His body was calling the shots, not his mind.

He brought her to the bed and lowered her. He reached for a condom on the nightstand and he made quick work of lowering his pants and covering himself with the latex. He pulled down her panties and stood between her parted thighs.

She reached for him, and when her fingers touched his dick, he thought he might explode. With a growl, he leaned over her and with one hand, he held both of her wrists over her head—pinning her to the bed.

"You okay?" he asked her, his desire-addled brain barely able to form the words.

She nodded. "Yes."

"Good." He used his free hand to guide his dick to her opening and in one hard thrust, he was inside of her.

The cry that tore from Lila's lips filled the hotel room.

Still holding both of her wrists, he pushed in and out of her. Her heat surrounded him, and it was more incredible than he remembered. Long forgotten were all his responsibilities, all his cares and worries. All that existed was Lila and his desire.

His heart was pounding, and his muscles began to tighten. He increased his pace, shifting the bed underneath them. He wouldn't last much longer. But he needed to make sure Lila found her pleasure before he took his own.

With his free hand, he found her clit, and circled the sensitive nubs with the pads of his fingers. Her eyes snapped open, and she gasped. It only took a few seconds before she tightened and spasmed around him, crying out her release.

Reid then let go and let himself succumb to the

pleasure. From the bottom of his curling toes, to the flashes of light he saw behind his closed eyes, he took every amount of bliss from the moment before he collapsed on top of her still-quivering body.

When he awoke the next morning, with the sun in his eyes and his arm slung tightly around Lila's waist, it was after noon, and Reid felt like he'd had the best sleep of his life. Lila's deep, even breaths, accompanied by the rise and fall of her chest told him that she was still sleeping, and he pulled her closer, her red wild curls tickling his nose and cheek. He inhaled deeply. He wasn't sure what had caused him to come to her the night before. He should have stayed at the party. It was his responsibility. But when it came to Lila, for whatever reason, he didn't care about anything else but being with her He'd shirked his responsibilities. Even during his marriage, he hadn't done anything like that. The distillery had always come first.

Lila gave a small whimper and burrowed herself deeper underneath the blanket. Meeting Lila had changed that. It wasn't love, of course, he barely knew her, but Reid was completely in lust with the woman. She was pure temptation. She would be leaving town later that day. And that was how he justified his attraction to her. Theirs was a red-hot affair—but it was temporary.

He heard his cell phone ring, the sound coming from his jacket, which had been left in a pile near the door. He should answer it. But that was when Lila, still asleep, rolled over in his arms to face him. There was no way he could tear himself away from her warm body. The phone quieted, and Reid closed his eyes. But when the phone rang again, he cursed.

"Is that your phone?" Lila murmured, her eyes still closed.

"Yeah," he said. "I'd better getter it."

"Could be an emergency."

Those words hit Reid like a punch to the chest. She was right. It *could* have been an emergency—that something has happened to Gemma, Quin or his father. Maybe something had happened at the distillery. There could have been a fire or mechanical breakdown, there could be batches ruined. Those were the things that plagued his mind on the short walk across the room. How many times had his phone rang and he'd slept through it? How long had he been content to ignore the calls, just as long as he was wrapped up in a woman he barely knew. Reid should know better.

After a walk that took no more than eight steps, but felt like a mile, Reid reached his coat. He pulled out his phone and saw that Quin was calling. He answered. "What's wrong?"

"About time you answered your goddamn phone," his brother admonished him.

"What's up? Is everything okay?"

"We've been fielding phone calls from distributors all morning."

A ball of worry formed in Reid's gut. "About what? What's going on?" he asked, while picturing crisis situations involving ruined shipments, the inability to pay their bills and foreclosure. What had happened while he'd been in bed with Lila.

"We're sold out," Quin told him.

The words didn't make sense at first. "Where?"

"Dude, everywhere. Florida, Georgia and Alabama are dry, and the shelves are emptying as we speak everywhere else. We've got calls from stores LA, New York, Austin, Vegas and a bunch of other cities who want to carry our rum. Gemma's got everyone working this morning, and emergency shipments going out."

"How did this happen? Was it the party?"

"The party helped. But really, I think it was Lila Campbell," he told him.

"Lila?" Just hearing her name was enough for his body to clench in response. He looked over at her, and her eyes were open, watching him. He forced his brain to focus on the business and what Quin was telling him. But that was almost impossible when he could barely hear his brother's words.

"Her blog about the distillery went live last night, and within hours it was picked up by outlets all over the country. Along with her posts and those of the celebrities who attended our party... Reid, we're trending on almost every social media platform—Twitter, Instagram, Snapchat, Facebook. Pictures and videos are being shared everywhere." He could hear the excitement in Quin's voice. "This is insane. We're on the edge, man. This is it. Rexford is going to pop off!"

"Where are you?"

"Gemma and I are here at the distillery, and we've been here since six. We've got her crew in trying to see how quickly we can restock and roll more out."

"Since six?"

"Yeah, as soon as our social media accounts started seeing the action. Then the distributors and stores started calling."

Reid's heart pounded with excitement. Rexford Rum was about to take off, and he'd missed the biggest morning they'd ever had. His siblings were dealing with supply issues, when that was supposed to be his job.

"You left pretty early last night." Quin paused. "Are you with Lila now?"

He didn't want to lie to his brother, so he said nothing. "I'm on my way over there now."

"Bring Lila with you," Quin told him.

"Why?"

"Just do it. There's something I want to discuss with her."

"You can tell me what it is." Reid did not like being left out of the loop when it came to the distillery.

"I will when you get here."

Reid wanted to know what was on his brother's mind, but he knew that the quicker he could get off the phone, the faster he could get to work. "Okay, I'll be right there." Without saying goodbye to his brother, Reid disconnected the call, and turned to Lila.

"What's going on? Is everything okay?"

"Do you have any plans today?"

Lila shook her head. "Just a late lunch with your sister."

"That's probably cancelled now. Why don't you get dressed and come with me?"

"Where?"

"The distillery."

"Why?"

He watched as Lila got out of bed. His body reacted, wanting to push her down and have her again, but instead he turned away and began gathering his clothes. He had to get to work and put all his energy to solving his current supply problem. "Wouldn't I love to know."

CHAPTER EIGHT

LILA WASN'T SURE why Reid had asked her to join him at the Rexford distillery, but she was intrigued. He'd told her that demand for the rum was high thanks to whatever had happened last night. Checking her web site analytics and social media impressions, she knew that internet stars have aligned, and the social media gods had spoken, and Rexford Rum have been struck by lightning. But when it came to social media, posts and reach were not enough. Her blog post on the distillery had been picked up, and it coincided with the posts and pictures from all the celebrities at the party. This was some once-in-a-lifetime exposure for the distillery. And herself. Those kinds of results made her happy—not just for the reach of her own blog, and the increase in ad revenue, but it also gave her something to bring to the GO! Channel. Those stuffy executives couldn't argue with raw data behind her creation of a media sensation.

From her seat in the hard, wooden chair in the distillery, she watched as Gemma's distillers worked feverishly to get product out, while Reid, Quin and Gemma were locked inside Gemma's small office. She was able to see inside, thanks to the large window over her desk. The siblings were engaged in what looked like a serious conversation. Despite their overnight success, they looked stressed. She couldn't count the number of times she watched Reid run his fingers through his hair. His features were tight, serious. She still didn't know why she was there. If only one of them would talk to her.

Lila couldn't sit any longer. She had to do something. So she stood from the uncomfortable chair, stretched her legs, and turned to check out the wall of photos behind her The inscriptions showed the evolution of the Rexford distillery starting with hand-drawn maps from the records of Joseph Rexford, the disgraced bootlegger and alleged pirate, who ran rum from Cuba and the Bahamas to what was now known as Miami Beach. Each photo showed growth, succession through the generations, until she came to the last one—a picture of Reid, Quin and Gemma, the same one she'd seen before on Reid's phone. Smiling, proud in front of their humble distillery. The picture had to have been at least ten-years-old. She could see that Reid had aged gracefully in the past decade. In the photo, he lacked some of the lines at the corners of his eyes and lips. His smile was more carefree, less forced than the ones she'd seen from him in person, and she wondered what had changed.

* * *

"How are we going to meet this demand?" Reid scrubbed his hands over his face. He looked over the production schedules Gemma had shown him, and then the demand projections over the next six months.

"We aren't," Gemma said matter-of-factly, looking as frustrated as he felt. "We can start production ASAP on new batches, so we will have an abundance in a year at the earliest. Unless I can come up with something new, there's no way to speed up the aging process on what we already have while maintaining quality. And I'm not compromising on quality."

"Nor should we. We need a way to keep this momentum, so that by the time the rum we're producing right now is ready, people will still want it." He turned to his brother. "You're the marketing expert. How do we do that?"

"I have something," she offered, opening her locked drawer. "I was going through some old records and journals a little while ago, and I found something." She took out a yellowed sheet of paper and laid it carefully on the desk in front of them.

"What is that?" Reid asked.

"It's a recipe," she told them. "It belonged to our great-grandfather. For an easy-to-make, unaged prohibition-era rum. You know how white and light batches don't need to be aged. That's how they did it back in the day. They made it and then immediately sold it. And it's simple. Simpler than mine, and if I'm right about it, it can most likely be ready, bottled and out the door in just a couple of weeks. If it turns out good, it can keep us going long enough to start production on dark and spiced batches. I just wish there was a way to quick-distill and age those."

Quin nodded. "I like that. We can call it a throw-back recipe. Boost the prohibition and rumrunner angle. Give it a good story, tie in the family history. It could work." Reid looked over the orders that had come in that morning so far, and on top of their regular orders, this was the only thing that could help them fill some of the demand for their product. "That's a good plan of attack," Reid agreed, and even though he was glad they had a way out of their current predicament, he was still irritated that he hadn't come up with it. He hadn't even been there while the rest of the employees had worked that morning. He would never let himself get so distracted again. He didn't care what happened, he would never put the family or the business on the back burner again. That was the priority—not rolling around with a gorgeous, charismatic temptress. He looked out through the window and saw Lila. He still didn't know why Quin wanted to see her.

Reid watched her shake her loose hair—those gorgeous red curls—over her shoulder. His fingers itched, wanting to twirl them around his fingers.

"All right we'll get the crews working today." Reid

hadn't even noticed when Gemma had started talking. "Meanwhile, I'm going to try to figure out a way to get the dark and spiced rums out. But I don't know if I can. I'm not making any promises."

"We just need to keep demand high. We need to sustain this spike, and not just fall off again. The new rum could help. But we need to maintain our online popularity. We've got to stay in the public eye. We're in an interesting position right now. Rexford is a hot commodity. But you're right. We can't stay on top forever if we can't get the product into people's hands. So that's why I asked you to bring Lila." Quin stood from the table.

"What does Lila—"

But before he could finish his sentence, Quin had opened the door. "Lila, can you come in here, please?"

"Sure."

She walked into his office, and Quin gestured for her to sit in the chair he'd vacated. Reid still didn't know what his younger brother had in mind, but he could tell from his smirk that he wouldn't like it.

"Lila, thanks for coming in," Quin started. "I wanted to talk to all of you about this. I've got an idea."

"What is it?" Reid and Lila asked at the same time, and their eyes met.

"Here's what I'm thinking," Quin started. "Lila, we want you to be our brand ambassador."

"What?" Again, Reid and Lila spoke at the same

time. He'd had no idea that was where the impromptu meeting Quin had called was leading.

"We'd like to offer you a corporate partnership to represent our brand."

Lila's eyes found his, and she seemed just as surprised as he was. She turned to Quin. "I'm interested. What exactly do you have in mind?"

Lila ignored Reid's stare as Quin detailed what they wanted from her. It was everything she'd wanted from them but had not yet proposed.

"Because of your posts, and the overnight jump in popularity, we have a supply problem," Quin told her.

"Quin," Reid said. "Maybe it's best if we don't talk business with outsiders."

Outsiders. Even though he was right, she was an outsider, hearing him say it hurt. She had no stake in the business. She'd just hooked-up with one of the owners a couple of times. That was it.

But Quin ignored him. "Basically, we want you to do what you've already done. We want you to promote Rexford Rum on all of your platforms, in your blog. Keep the Rexford Rum brand out there so we have time to increase production and distribution. We'll pay you, but also feature you and your brand in our own promotions."

"A corporate partnership would definitely be beneficial for me as well," she told them, leaving out that she was in talks for a television show, and that a corporate partnership with the country's most-wanted liquor brand would make her a hot commodity, as well. "What sort of things do you need me to do?"

"We can discuss specifics later, and we'll do up the paperwork. I'm just wondering if you're open to working together."

"Yeah, I am. Send me the contract and the terms when it's ready. But I just have to wonder, wouldn't featuring your rum—when you don't have enough to meet the demand—just piss people off?"

"Without getting into too many details, we're hoping to have a new product out soon," Gemma told her. "We will have rum for sale, just not everything that we have available in the small batches."

"We want you to focus on that," Quin explained. "Think prohibition, bootleggers, a real vintage feel."

"I think you're both doing a lot of talking about the confidential details of our business," Reid admonished his siblings. "Lila doesn't need to know all of our plans."

"You're right," Lila agreed. "But I'm a very trustworthy person, I figured you might agree," she said with a raised eyebrow. They'd slept together several times. He clearly didn't trust her. She turned back to Quin. "Let's work on a contract. But if we can agree to terms, I'm in." Reid interrupted. "No," he said, his voice firm.

Lila joined Gemma and Quin in turning to look at Reid with surprise.

"What?" Quin asked him. "Why not?"

"Lila, I know you're good at what you do. The

numbers prove it. We pay a lot of money to marketing firms. I don't want to pin our distillery's success, and potential failure on a slick, relatively new,
fickle marketing plan like social-media exposure. We
don't need a social media *influencer* representing our
brand." His tone and words were cruel, and they hurt.

What is his problem? As long as she lived, she
would never understand Reid Rexford. She wanted
to work with the brand, but they needed her as much
as she needed them. She knew what happened when
people and companies failed to capitalize on their
success. They were doomed to fail. But Lila knew
she was good at what she did, and she wouldn't put
her self-respect on the line to work for a man who
didn't respect her or her job.

The room was still. No one spoke until Lila took
her phone out of her purse. "That's where your
wrong," she said, moving her thumbs quickly over
the screen. "Facebook followers," she started, "five
million. Twitter: 1.3 million, Snapchat: 870,000, Instagram: 10.9 million. That's organic reach, Reid.
Your brother is right. People pay attention to what I
have to say. Look at this." She passed her phone over
and showed Reid the pictures she'd posted from the
party. She'd looked up Rexford Rum's social media
accounts. The likes, comments, shares were all more
than they'd ever received. "And I'm going to need
you to apologize for the tone you just used describ-
ing my career before we go any further with this
discussion."

Both Quin and Gemma looked to Reid, but he said nothing.

"Goddammit, Reid," Quin said.

"You've seen what I can do," she said, her lips curving upward in an innuendo-laced grin. "But if you don't want to be in business with me, Reid, fine." She looked at Quin and Gemma. "Thanks for the meeting. It was great meeting you." She stood, gathered her phone and purse and headed for the door.

When Lila walked out and slammed the door behind her, Quin turned to Reid and punched him in the arm. "What the fuck was that, man?"

Reid wasn't sure. He knew he would have to give them more of an explanation than that. But what could he say? That he didn't trust himself around her, that when she was around, he could barely focus on anything *but* her? That by leaving the party to be with her last night, it showed that he wanted her beyond everything else. And that terrified him.

He couldn't have her connected to the distillery, he couldn't keep her in his life, even if it meant missing out on the opportunity of what he knew would be a successful campaign. But if he couldn't do his actual work, what was the point?

So, he lied to his siblings. "I didn't think it was a good idea."

"Bullshit," Quin said.

"How do you think that?" Gemma asked. "You saw what she's capable of. Look at this demand. And you just sent away the woman who can keep the buzz going and sell our new batch."

"Stop being so dramatic. We're already successful. Sure, the boost is nice, but it'll still lead to long-term success whether we use Lila, or not."

"Stop being so pigheaded. Is this because you slept with her?"

"How did you know?"

"I saw you guys at the party last night. There was definitely a connection between the two of you. Why were you such a jerk to her?"

He wasn't sure why he'd been so cold to Lila. But he knew that he couldn't have her in his vicinity. Whether it was good for the business or not, he knew it wasn't good for him. And it certainly wouldn't be good for her in the long run.

"You said it yourself," Quin said simply. "We have a great marketing firm, but in the business world, especially some of the older guys have been slow to catch up to recent developments in social media marketing. She's got her finger on the pulse and can reach millions of people, who would consider us to be the rum brand their grandfathers choose. We need to get younger, sexier. We started with the party. This is how we position ourselves, and you basically chased away our shot. I don't care what happened between you guys, go get her," Quin urged him.

"And make sure you apologize," Gemma told him.

Reid knew he wouldn't win, and even though he

was caught between chasing her and letting her walk out the door, he stood. "Fine," he said. "I'll get her." Whether or not she'd want to talk to him, well, that was another story.

Fucking Reid. Lila walked down the hallway. Where did he get off, treating her like that? Well, she knew exactly right where he'd gotten off, she remembered with an eye roll. In her bed. Stopping at the main door, she flipped through her phone to a ride share app to summon a car, but she paused when she heard the even, sure footsteps approach her from behind.

"Lila, wait."

What now? Why had he followed her out the door when she'd made her indignant exit? "What do you want? A second opportunity to disrespect me and the work I do?"

"No." He paused. "I'm sorry about what I said."

"Why did you say it, then? After I explained to you everything I do. How much I told you about it. I thought you understood how much work goes into it."

He sighed and looked away. "I don't know. I panicked, maybe."

"You panicked," she repeated, not understanding him.

"Lila, we were supposed to be a one-night thing. An anonymous thing."

"We blew that out of the water, didn't we?" He said nothing. "We agreed on one night, and you want me gone."

"Yes." Her eyebrows rose. "No, not like that," he stammered. "I like you. But that's where the trouble lies. All I want to do is be near you. And when I see you, all I can think about is taking you to bed. And when Quin suggested you work with us, all I could think about was how dangerous that was."

"Dangerous? Reid, you aren't making any sense."

"I know. It doesn't make any sense to me either. But I know that having you promote us does make sense."

She sighed. If he couldn't be clearer than that, there wasn't a point in her sticking around. "Well, that's too bad. I thought I liked you, Reid. But you're just like the rest. What I do has a real value, and I can be good for your company."

"I know, and that's why I chased you out here."

"Not just because your brother and sister made you?"

He paused for too long, and Lila noticed her car pull up in front of the distillery. "Goodbye, Reid." She patted his chest and dragged her fingers over his nipple, and he flinched at the contact. His reaction made her laugh. She winked. "This time is for good. Congratulations on all your success. I had a lot of fun, and I did want to work with your family." She shrugged. "But you blew it."

Reid didn't move until Lila's car was completely out of sight. Blowing out a heavy, frustrated breath, he pushed his fingers through his hair. That hadn't played out exactly how he'd imagined it would. And he had no one to blame but himself. He'd been cruel to her. And he wasn't even sure why. He'd enjoyed her company and had shown an interest in what she did. But the prospect of having her work with the distillery had caused him to panic, and he'd lashed out.

He walked back to the distillery. He'd hoped his siblings had taken the opportunity to leave and move on to other tasks, but he had no such luck. Gemma and Quin watched him as he wordlessly walked in and took his seat next to Gemma's desk. Their faces showed contempt, anger, disappointment and—he wished he had better news for them—hope that Lila had decided to forgive him.

A heavy silence filled the room until Quin cut through it with a clearing of his throat. "Is she going to do it?" he asked.

"She's gone."

"Goddammit, Reid," Gemma scolded him. "What is wrong with you?"

Not interested in being on the receiving end of an inquisition, Reid wanted to be left alone. He stood. "I'm done. We should get out there and help the crew. We've got bottles to get out."

"Not quite yet," Quin said, stopping him. "*We're* not done. And we're not having this disagreement out there on the floor in front of the workers."

"Yeah, I'm confused about what happened here today," Gemma said. "It looked like you guys were getting along last night. I mean, it's obvious you did."

"We did." He offered nothing else in response.

Quin snorted. Despite how angry he was at Reid, his younger brother loved needling him even more. "If I walked in on what I think I did, the tour probably went better than any other we've had."

Reid flipped him off without saying a word.

Quin put up his hands. "Don't get mad at me."

No one said anything until Gemma spoke again. "So why were you such a jerk to her? This is a good thing for us, and you know it. The fact that you sabotaged it doesn't make any sense. You've always done what's best for the distillery. What's going on?"

He didn't want to respond. But he knew his siblings wouldn't let it go unless he did. He didn't want to get into the real reason he'd dismissed her and let her leave. That she was a temptation. He tried to tell himself that the attraction was physical, but he could feel something more building there. If she was connected to the business, there was no way he could keep his feelings in check. "I told you. I don't think we should be pouring our money into some slick social media campaign. That's not us."

"It's the 21st century, Reid," Quin scolded him. Reid wasn't used to being berated by Quin, and he didn't like it. He'd always been the more practical sibling. "Magazine and television ads don't cut it anymore. It's all about social media, word of mouth, an online presence, *getting clicks*. You need to make this right with her."

"I can't," he conceded. "She's gone." And rightfully so. Reid realized that he didn't deserve Lila's time or presence. He couldn't blame her for walking away after he'd treated her so shabbily. But it was best that parting happened like it did—with her walking away. He couldn't stand to be around her and not have her. The temptation would have been too much to bear.

Gemma's mouth dropped, and he saw the understanding come over her face. "I get it now," she said softly. "This is actually about Carolina, and what she did, isn't it?"

Reid frowned. He wanted to pound his fist on his desk and tell his brother and sister that his ex-wife was the furthest thing from his mind. It'd be a lie, of course. Every business decision he'd made since their divorce was at least partially colored by her betrayal. "This has nothing to do with her," he said, in a feeble attempt to convince them.

Quin shook his head. "I don't know, Reid, I would think that your lack of trust has a lot to do with a woman who betrayed you a couple of years ago."

"Can we just get to work?" Reid asked, wanting to put the issue behind them.

"You're sure that's what you want?"

"That's all I want. The business is my priority. You know that."

"What if the business wasn't your only priority?"

Reid shook his head. The one time he'd dropped the ball and let a woman in, it had almost cost them everything. "It's too late for that. Let's get to work and sell some rum." Reid was ready to roll up his sleeves, do some work to forget about the woman who'd somehow managed to turn him completely inside-out.

CHAPTER NINE

FROM HER VIEW at the table of the beachfront restaurant, Lila watched the ocean crash against the sand. She closed her eyes, sipped her mojito and listened to the roar of the waves hitting the shore.

It was late in the evening, and she watched families pack up their belongings, sun-kissed and smiling from a day at the beach. There were just a few hours before she needed to be at the airport. But Gemma had contacted her after she'd stormed out of the distillery, begging her to meet her for a drink before leaving town. Lila almost said no, still angry at Reid. But she relented. She liked Gemma and it wasn't her fault her brother was an asshole.

Again, she sipped her drink. Before arriving in Miami, she would never have called herself a rum fan, but she was starting to develop a taste for the stuff. It was like an elixir. With every taste, with every smell, she felt Reid. His essence had stayed with her, in her system, and all she could think about was getting her next taste. She was never one to fall quickly for a man, but the physical attraction between them was stronger than she'd ever experienced. It had been a while since she'd been with a man. Maybe she'd just been hornier than she knew.

Ugh. Reid. She didn't have the time or patience to figure out what was going on in his brain. He was hot and cold, night and day, a mystery wrapped in an enigma, and so on.

"Sorry I'm late," Gemma said, coming up behind her. "Traffic was insane. Typical Miami, right?" Lila hadn't spent much time in the city, but she'd been there long enough to know that traffic was a mess. "Have you been waiting long?"

Lila smiled as Gemma Rexford took the seat across from her. She was still wearing the same jeans and tank top that she'd had on at the distillery that afternoon. She looked like she'd been working all day. "Just long enough to get a drink."

"You're probably wondering why I asked you to still meet me. I really appreciate it because I know you have a flight in a few hours."

"I figured I'm just here so you can grovel."

"Yeah, pretty much," Gemma admitted.

"We, Quin and I, really want you to be our representative."

"But not Reid."

Gemma exhaled and smiled. "Reid is stubborn. I don't know what's going on with him, but the way he reacted is so out-of-character. He always does what's best for the business. And that's you, whether he wants to or not. Maybe he's just old-fashioned. I don't know."

Lila flashed back to images of Reid in her mind. In bed, Reid was fiery, impassioned, and nothing like the cold businessman he'd shown her earlier. Old-fashioned, however, wasn't how she'd describe him.

"I really want to apologize for how he acted."

"Reid's a grown man. It's not your place to apologize for him."

"Still, I'd really hate for his attitude to screw up one of the best things that's happened to us. You were a huge part of the boost we've received in the past twenty-four hours."

"So, we're here for you to tell me how great I am?"

"That and we need you. Forget about Reid for a second. We need our customers to embrace this new recipe, until our regular and premium batches are ready for distribution. We want you to work with us. And we'll pay you. Very well." Gemma named a price that made Lila's eyes widen. She received perks from her job, and revenue from ads and endorsements, but nothing close to what Gemma Rexford had just put on the table.

Lila smiled. She wanted to work with Rexford as well. She still needed them for her own reasons. Raising the profile of Rexford would boost her own brand as well. "You know what? I'm probably going to hate myself for this—the way Reid spoke to me, I should already be online canceling your whole brand." She heard Gemma inhale a gasp. "But I'm not. I like the rum, and I like you. And believe it or not, I do want to be associated with you guys." Lila paused. "But I want to make sure Reid suffers at least a little bit," she finished with a smile.

Gemma snorted out a laugh. "You and me, both, girl. I love my brother, but he's just so gruff and serious sometimes. It's been so long since he's taken any sort of break from the distillery. I think he needs a vacation before he snaps."

Reid hadn't revealed too much of himself to her, but she knew what his sister was saying was the truth. Even though he'd been a dick, she couldn't help herself. She had always been a sucker for pain, for men who would break her heart. But she'd turn the tables on him. He'd have to beg for her forgiveness.

She recalled the differences between Reid the lover and Reid the businessman. She knew that she could release his fun, passionate side. If he was forced to, that is. She took out her phone. "I have an idea." She turned on the speakerphone, asked Gemma to dial Reid's number and put the phone down in the center of the table.

A half of a ring went through before Reid's gruff voice came through the speaker. "Hello,"

"Hi Reid."

"Lila." She could hear the tinge of regret in his voice, and she smiled, hoping he felt terrible. "I—"

"Hey Reid, let me talk now. You owe me a massive apology."

"I've already tried to apol—"

"That doesn't sound like an apology to me. But we'll get there. I've been thinking about it. I'm really on the fence here."

"What do you mean?"

"I mean, I might come around," she smiled at Gemma. "For the right price, if you make it up to me, I might consider working with the distillery."

She heard the whoosh of breath come from his end. "That's great, Lila. I'll talk to marketing and get this rolling ASAP."

"Not so fast," she stopped him again. "I haven't agreed yet. You need to hear my terms." She looked up and winked at Gemma, who was hanging on every word, and clearly enjoying her brother's torture.

"What do you want?"

"I've got something I want you to do." She took a sip of her rum. "I need you packed and ready to meet me at the airport in two hours."

CHAPTER TEN

REID GRUMBLED AS he pulled his carry-on through Miami International Airport, thinking about Lila's request. The woman really had him over a barrel on this one. He should be at the distillery, making sure everything was going smoothly with Gemma's newest batch of the prohibition-era experimental rum. But Gemma and Quin had all but packed his bag for him and pushed him out the door to meet her, whether he liked it or not.

His phone pinged. He checked the screen, and saw it was a text from Lila telling him to meet him at a bar near the security line. He picked up his speed, thinking about the woman waiting for him. At least there would be alcohol. For the day he'd had, he could fucking use a drink.

He made it to the bar and easily found her at a table, sipping champagne from a flute while she picked at the high pile of nachos in front of her. He stopped and watched her as she raised the glass to her lips. Her profile was classic—her nose straight, her lips full, her chin rounded. Suddenly he wasn't quite as angry about being summoned to the airport on a Sunday evening, forcing him to take time away from the distillery when they needed him the most.

She must have felt his eyes on her because she turned to look at him. She smirked and waved with a dainty flick of her fingers. Her eyes held no humor, only irritation.

Directed at him.

Steeling himself, Reid prepared to grovel. For good reason. He'd been terrible to Lila—treated her poorly, embarrassed her—and he might not be a gentleman, but he had to make it right.

"Champagne? Celebrating?"

She shrugged and drained the glass, and before answering waved to the nearby server. "Two more. Yeah, I think we should be celebrating."

He took a seat across from her. She was right. He'd been so caught up trying to figure out the logistics getting enough rum out, that he hadn't had a chance to sit back and enjoy the success.

"We've both had a pretty incredible day," she told him. And you're here. I think that means I've won."

"You think you've won?"

She shrugged. "You're here, aren't you?"

"I don't think this hostage situation counts as winning."

"Ooh, a hostage situation? That sounds kind of hot, doesn't it?"

"I didn't realize that was your kink."

She shrugged. "You never asked." The server placed two more champagne flutes on the table.

"What am I doing here?" Reid asked, taking a nacho chip off the pile. "Why am I going to New Orleans?"

"You're here because you showed me such disrespect this afternoon. After I explained to you how much work I do, and how seriously I take it, you still took the opportunity to dismiss me. You really embarrassed me and belittled what I do. So, you're coming on the road with me."

"What?"

"Yeah, I have to be in New Orleans for a few days. You'll live how I do. You'll be my assistant—"

"Oh, come on, now."

Lila held up a finger. "But you'll cut loose, have fun. And learn that hard work doesn't just happen behind a desk. Then we'll come back here, and we'll sign the necessary paperwork to for our partnership, and I'll show you the ideas I already have for getting out the word about your new rum."

Reid's laugh was a short, incredulous guffaw. "You're insane. I can't just walk away from the distillery for three days."

"Why not? Gemma's already been talking to your assistant. Your work's been rerouted. You don't take vacations. Now, you're going to start."

Gemma. He should have figured she was behind this. Lila had him by the short hairs. "Fine. What do I have to do?"

She finished her champagne in one long swallow. "Drink up, take off your shoes and make sure all your liquids are in a sealed bag. It's almost time to board."

Several hours later, Lila was pressed against Reid in the back seat of an economy rideshare car as it pulled to a stop at the curb in front of a budget hotel. It looked fine to her. She probably could have picked a nicer place, but knowing that Reid would be in tow, she thought she'd show him how to slum it a little.

"All right, this is it," she told him, clutching her purse and getting out of the cab.

Reid looked out through the window. "I don't think so."

"Why not? I didn't take you for a snob."

"I'm not a snob. I'm just not interested in bringing bed bugs and roaches back to my own house." He leaned forward and gave the cab driver the name of a higher-end hotel chain.

When they were on the road again, Lila settled back in her seat and crossed her arms.

"Don't pout, Lila. It's a nice hotel."

She knew it was. She'd brought him on her trip to teach him a lesson. To show him how busy and chaotic her life was, and how much work was involved in her job. She wasn't pouting because he'd changed the hotel, she was just mad that already he'd started taking over her trip. And it didn't help that the warmth of his arm against hers radiated throughout her body, as his cologne tingled her nostrils. Everything about the man, even when she was angry at him, turned her on.

"I know it's a nice hotel. But I'd specifically chosen that one to be close to the action of the French Quarter. That's what I'm here for, you know. None of my readers care about the best hotels in the business sector."

"Don't be so dramatic. We can get a ride where we need to go."

"That's not the point." Soon they pulled up in front of the hotel. An upscale chain. If there was one thing she hated, it was chains—a city was best felt through its local establishments, not through corporate ones. "Let me guess," she started. "You get points for staying here?"

Reid's smile was rich. "Of course I do. I'm a diamond member," he said, before exiting the car.

Rolling her eyes and sighing, Lila gathered her purse. The cab driver caught her eye as she handed over her credit card.

"Lady, if you and your man stay this mad at each other, you're going to have a pretty miserable time."

Lila nodded and signed the printout, not bothering to correct his assumption that Reid was *her man*. "You've got that right."

By the time Lila met up with Reid in the hotel lobby, he was already checked in and waiting for her near a bank of elevators. He handed her a room key. "I got us a two-bedroom suite."

"Fine," she said, taking the key card he'd offered. Even though she was angry at Reid—and she'd invited him along out of pettiness—that didn't mean she wasn't looking forward to them sharing a room. A two-bedroom suite would really cut down the intimacy of that, though. She'd had big plans to walk around in her flimsiest pajamas, to tease him, provoke him... Desire tightened her core just thinking about it. But he'd already made the decision for them, relegating them each to their own bedrooms. "Sounds good to me. We should go up there and get settled. I need a shower, and we should get to bed. We have a busy day tomorrow."

In the suite, when the door to Lila's room closed behind her, Reid let out a heavy breath. In the hall of the suite, outside her closed door, he could hear her rustle about, opening drawers, unpacking. Then he heard the faint noise of shower spray. His body tightened and his brain conjured up images of her soft, supple body as streams of water rolled over her soft skin, imagining it was his hands. He clenched his fists to stop himself from knocking on the door. And he looked to his own room and took one step before he stopped and released the handle on his rolling bag. "Aw, fuck it," he muttered to himself, and went to her door.

Hating his lack of control, Reid couldn't help but knock on her door.

"Hold on," she called from deep within the room.

When she opened the door, her wavy red hair was loose but still dry, and she was wearing the fluffy white hotel robe. She looked impatient, still annoyed at him for changing hotels, or for what he'd said to her. Hell, he didn't know. The list of reasons why Lila might be pissed at him wasn't a short one. "What do you want?" she asked.

He didn't say a word, just went to her, cupping her face in his hands as he brought her to him. Her lips parted instantly for him, and he rewarded her with a hard, deep kiss. A surprised sound came from her throat, and her fingers clenched in the material of his shirt, urged him on. She pulled back and they walked further into her room, not separating their mouths.

With nimble fingers, Lila tackled the buttons down the front of his shirt, while he ripped the tie of the robe from her front and pushed the plush material from her shoulders. He barely noticed when it fell to the floor, soon followed by his shirt.

He lifted her and she was feather-light in his arms, and her legs wrapped around his waist. He followed the sound of the running shower and walked her into the bathroom, still not removing his mouth from hers.

She pulled away first. Her breath was heavy, and she gulped in air. "There are condoms in my makeup bag."

He chuckled, setting her on the counter next to the leather tote. "You came prepared."

"Something wrong with that?" she asked, reaching into the box and withdrawing a condom, while he unzipped his pants and pushed them and his boxers down.

"I'm just relieved that now you aren't going to give me a hard time for the box I packed in my own bag." He took the condom from her fingers and under her watchful eye, he took himself in his free hand and rolled the latex over his length.

The shower still ran, and steam began to fill the room. He took a step closer, bringing his rigid cock in contact with her hot, rich center. "Not right here," he told her, wrapping an arm around her waist and pulling her so close she was flush against him, his cock pressed upward between them. She squirmed, creating a delicious feeling up and down his dick. "Keep that up and I won't last to get inside of you. Then where will you be?"

"I'm confident you won't leave me hanging."

"You got that right." Again, he picked her up and walked into the open-stall shower. Scorching hot water poured from the rainfall and the angled shower heads and he gasped, but he soon forgot about the stinging heat when he pinned Lila to the tile wall and pushed deep inside her in one thrust, as his mouth took hers again. No rum he'd ever had could match the rich flavor of Lila's tongue.

He thrust into her, again and again, driving both of them to the heights of pleasure, as her water-slicked body slid against him, awakening new sensations in every nerve ending. She scratched and clawed at his back, and he grimaced at the way her nails dug into his skin, but every small crescent-shaped scar he was left with would be worth it. He felt Lila begin to tense in his grasp, so he tilted her hips, positioning her so that he entered her at the right angle, hitting that sweetest of spots that would take her higher.

Lila's cries tore through the steam and filled the bathroom as she came. Reid pumped a couple more times before his own climax hit him. He groaned into her shoulder, and shuddered, emptying into the condom.

Lila threw her head back lightly against the tiled wall, exposing the smooth skin of her throat. Reid trailed his lips up the sleek line and took her earlobe between his teeth. He wasn't sure how long they stayed like that, but soon Lila began to squirm against him, and he released her.

"Well," she said under the running water. "That was unexpected."

With the postcoital glow wearing off, Reid couldn't believe what he'd done. He faced the hot water, letting it wash over his face "Yeah, I know. Sorry about that."

"You're sorry? Are you married, Reid?"

"You know I'm not."

"You have a girlfriend?"

"Of course not."

"Well, what are you sorry for?"

"It's not that," he insisted, and sighed. "I feel like I've lost control of this conversation."

"It's cute that you thought you ever had it."

"Honestly, hell if I know why I'm apologizing. I can't tell if this trip is off to a great start, or a terrible one."

"You think that was terrible?"

"No, not at all. But I can't lose focus on what I'm doing here."

"And what's that?"

"I'm here to get you to represent my brand."

She turned off the water and faced him. "And that's the only reason?"

Slowly, he ran his eyes up and down her still wet and naked body. She hadn't bothered to cover up. But part of him wished she would. Lila was a woman who could make him forget everything. Every second he was with her, he felt his resolve crumble. This would be a dangerous trip for him. He had to keep the distillery at the forefront of his mind, but he knew it would be the hardest thing he'd ever done in his life.

"Yeah, that's why I'm here."

She smiled. "And that's why you also brought condoms, right? Because this is about business?"

"I brought them in case of a momentary slip-up. Like this," he explained, grabbing a towel from the nearby rack. "And look at us. I was right, wasn't I?"

"Yeah, you were."

She was standing in front of him. Water still beading and rolling down her skin. Again, he was a ball of sexual tension. No matter how hard he tried, his desire grew for her every second he was with her. "You said we had an early morning tomorrow?"

"We do."

Even though he wanted to pick her up in his arms, and bring her to the bed in his room, he didn't. It took all his fortitude to take a step back and put distance between them.

"I guess we'd better get to bed."

The steam in the bathroom had cleared, as had the fog of desire that surrounded them. Lila turned away from him and picked up her towel and wrapped it around her chest. Without saying anything, she left the bathroom. Reid wasn't sure how he would survive the next couple of days, but he knew it wouldn't be easy.

CHAPTER ELEVEN

WHEN LILA EXITED her room the next morning, Reid had taken over the large table and had turned it into a makeshift office. "I thought you weren't going to be working on this trip."

"I don't remember making that deal. You may have kidnapped me, but that doesn't mean I still don't have a company to run. I need to stay up-to-date on what's going on in production and distribution." He looked up at her. "I should be there, not here messing around with any of this."

Lila bent over and buckled her espadrille sandals, intentionally giving Reid a more than generous look at her ass. When she righted, she caught him staring. "Feel free to leave anytime, Reid. It's not like the door's locked and you're tied to a chair." *Although...* The idea of that held a certain appeal for her. She shook herself free of the image when Reid stood, and she noticed he'd changed into a pair of pants and button-down shirt, like something he would wear to work. He looked like a man who was heading to the office, and not a man who was about to hit the town in New Orleans.

"I'm here to get you to sign on as our brand ambassador."

"And that's all you're here for?"

He didn't answer but closed his laptop and placed it in the hotel safe on top of her own, and she noticed they used the same brand. "You'd better watch out. I might grab yours by mistake."

"You need a fingerprint and three different passwords to access anything on mine," he explained. "So, there's no chance of that happening."

"What? No retinal scan?"

"That comes on the next model."

"What industry secrets do you have on that thing?" she asked with a laugh.

She caught the way he stiffened at her question. "It's confidential."

"Fine," she said, putting her hands up in surrender, moving on, and she wondered what nerve she'd accidentally touched. "Let's get going."

"What's first on the agenda?" he asked, as they left their room and headed for the elevator. "Espresso and beignets at Café du Monde?"

"How'd you know?"

"We're in New Orleans. It's what people do, isn't it?"

Lila snorted, and rolled her eyes. "It's what *everyone* does. A city is best observed through the eyes of a local, not through the touristy areas."

"Why are we going there, then?"

"Because I'm a travel blogger. Of course, I'm going to do the touristy things. I have to get those out of the way. Then I do the things I want to do."

"We all have to do things we don't want to do for work, don't we?"

"That's the nature of work,"

They arrived in the lobby. "Okay what now?" he asked.

"We've got a tour of the French Quarter. Plus, there are some museums, a haunted hike. And whatever other stops strike our fancy. Anything you want to see?"

It surprised Lila when he nodded. "Actually, yeah. There are some spots I wouldn't mind checking out. There are records of Joseph Rexford bootlegging in New Orleans. I'd love to see some of the landmarks he wrote about. There are some prohibition-era speakeasys that are still operating today. If you'd like to go."

"Yeah, and that would be an excellent tie-in to your new rum." She started mentally writing the blog in her head. "Look at us, collaborating already. I'm proud of you, getting into the vacation spirit—even if it is directly related to work."

Reid laughed. "I think we've collaborated before," he said, his eyebrows waggling suggestively. Slowly but surely, Reid was loosening up, turning into the funny, charming man she'd met at Arlo's in Miami.

"Yeah, we have, but that's nothing I can blog about."

* * *

Several hours later, they were strolling side by side in an already crowded French Quarter. They'd stopped at a couple of museums, and the spots that Reid wanted to see, and had enjoyed more food than she would care to admit. But what stood out during the day was how loose Reid had become. Get him away from the distillery, and he was quite a fun guy, and with every touch, smile and glance, she could feel herself falling for him more and more.

With every step, the back of Lila's hand grazed against his, and she felt the sizzle of electricity zap from his skin to hers. It frustrated her that he pretended not to notice, because if he did, he didn't show it.

"What now?" he asked.

"I was thinking about hitting a few food trucks but with how much we've already eaten today, I think that can wait."

They'd already stopped at several food spots, and he rubbed his flat stomach. "So, we eat all day, and your fans eat it up?"

"I'm not posting everything today. I'll spread it out. Swap spots with other bloggers. It's all about creating content. And you never stop creating it."

"That's what your life is? Content?"

"Digital lifespans are short. I've got to plug as much as I can, for as long as I can. The same goes for your rum. If you don't capitalize on the number of people talking about you now—" she shrugged "—you'll lose all interest in your product."

"Well, I guess that means corporate sponsorship is important to you, right? Seeing as how you're hot right now, who's to say how long that'll last? You might as well say yes to us, while you're a hot commodity. If you wait, you might not be any good to us."

She arched an eyebrow, but still it stung. She knew he was right, but she wouldn't give him the satisfaction. "You trying to neg me into submission?"

"Is it working?"

"Not a chance. Would you be satisfied if it did?"

He shook his head. "No. But I think we can negotiate mutually beneficial terms."

"I think we've already been mutually beneficial," she said, poking into his ribs with her elbow.

He was quiet for a moment. "You know, though, that if we agree to this, and we work together, our relationship has to be strictly business. We have to stop whatever it is we have going on, and we'll be just two people who work together."

"I know. I meant what I said to you at the party. It is best if we do that—stay away from each other, but staying away is harder than it should be, isn't it?"

"Yeah," she admitted.

"And seeing as how sex is all we have in common, why do you think I'd agree to anything you guys propose?"

"I'm hoping you'll see reason, and what we can do for each other."

"You're only working so hard on this because your brother and sister are mad at you, right?"

"Well, I agreed to come with you because they were mad at me, but I'm still here because I like a challenge. I want you. And I always get what I want."

"You want me?"

"I want you to rep my rum."

"Is that all you want?"

He stopped walking and they turned to face each other. "That's all we can have. That's all I'm offering." Reid wasn't a good liar, and Lila wasn't convinced. His eyes bored into hers, and she felt the same passion from him that she'd seen when he'd come to her the night before. Even though his body was rigid, and his body language kept him off limits, his eyes, they showed fire, passion. And they were trained solely on her.

He looked down the street at the passing crowds, and when he looked back, it was as if the spell had been broken. He was all business again. "Okay, where to next?" "I think we're done for the day. We can go back to the hotel if you want. I have to write about today and catch up on my interactions."

"Sounds good to me," he said as he started walking.

Lila narrowed her eyes on his back as he remained several steps ahead of her. Maybe this trip would also be a chance for Reid to loosen up. She'd never been one to chase a guy who didn't want her, but she knew Reid wanted her. She'd show him. A little hard work didn't scare her.

CHAPTER TWELVE

IT WAS LATER that evening, and Reid sat at the makeshift desk he'd made at the table, and poured some of the dark Rexford Rum from the bottle he'd bought earlier into a short glass. Already tense and tight from his day with Lila, he'd gone to the hotel minibar for some refreshment, but found only Cain rum—their biggest competitor—and Reid would rather drink used mouthwash than imagine Carolina and her *new family* seeing one cent of profit from him. So he'd left the room again and hit the nearest liquor store to get himself a bottle of Rexford's finest rum.

He grimaced at the bar fridge. He had no idea that Cain had secured a deal with the hotel chain. Quin and Gemma were right, they needed Lila's help to branch out. And he turned back to the laptop in front of him as he scanned the projections the distribution team had sent him. Rexford Rum had gone viral, and they hadn't counted on that. They'd aimed for slow growth and had become a well-known name in high-end circles. Rexford may have been the drink of choice of the elite, but overnight mainstream success was not something they'd planned for. Now they were now scrambling to keep up with demand. Things had never been better for the company but now he was struggling to keep afloat.

If the projections were to be trusted, expanded operations, and a larger facility would be the only way they would be able to keep up in the long-term. But he thought about his office back home, the one where he'd spent his summers working with his grandfather, who'd sneaked teenage Reid cigars and glasses of fine rum. But he was sitting in a hotel suite in New Orleans, and he felt a pang of sadness. He missed the office, the comfort the four walls of the distillery provided him. But there was no time for sentimentality. He had to get some work done, before Lila pulled him off on some other adventure.

He turned back to his open spreadsheets, but his attention kept being drawn to her closed bedroom door, behind which she'd sequestered herself in her room to do her own work.

His eyes blurred under the blue light of his laptop, as his gaze again drifted to Lila's closed door. She'd managed to turn his life completely upside down, as he missed his first day of work in years.

He heard her laugh again, and he pictured her on that king bed that matched the one in his own room. Her underneath him, bringing them both to the heights they'd reached in the shower that morning.

He let go a deep sigh and took another large mouthful of rum, in an attempt to get his body under control, and numb the desire that ate at his gut, before he did something else stupid.

He stared at his laptop, but the numbers on the screen blurred, and his eyes landed on the closed door once more. When it opened, he quickly averted his gaze, so as to not look like he was staring. Lila emerged from the room. She was wearing a flesh-colored tank top—no bra, he noted—and shorts that he had no doubt would ride up over the curve of her ass if she bent over even at the slightest angle. She'd scrubbed off the makeup she didn't need, and her red hair was piled high in a messy knot at the top of her head. She looked incredible, like a bare-bones version of the woman who'd posted vibrant pictures and videos of herself online all day.

He stood up from his desk, the notes, diagrams, charts, reports all but forgotten. "Lila."

Lila smiled at Reid's dumbfounded expression, and she laughed lightly. "Did you forget I was here, or something?"

How could he have forgotten about temptation incarnate in the other room?

"No."

"You're just embarrassed that I caught you staring at my bedroom door?" She took a step closer.

"Absolutely not." He busied himself with straightening the papers.

She looked over her shoulder at the room she'd

just vacated, and when she turned back, a wicked smile and mischievous gleam masked the innocent facade he'd just seen. "Were you wondering what I was doing in there?" she asked.

"I wasn't thinking about you at all," he responded, trying to maintain his stiff, serious composure. "I'm busy working out here."

"Is that right? Why don't I believe you? I think you were out here, trying to work, but instead, you were thinking about what I was doing. Were you wondering if I was naked, wrapped up in my sheets…" She stepped closer and dropped her voice to a whisper. "Were you imagining me *touching myself*?"

He didn't want to admit how accurate she'd been. "No, I was working. And I thought you were doing the same. I was live-chatting with fans. What were you doing?"

But for fantasizing about what was going on behind her closed door. "If you'll excuse me, I have to get back to work."

He felt her eyes travel down his body until her gaze settled on his middle, his stiffening cock, emboldened by her stare, growing, tenting out his pants. *Fucking traitor.*

She laughed. "You sure?" She took a step closer, and it brought her to the table. She sat on it and crossed her legs. And he pictured himself licking a trail up those smooth, delicious thighs.

He frowned at her. "We've discussed this."

"You discussed it." She shrugged. "But I don't follow directions that well. There's no reason we can't have some fun in the meantime."

"If you're going to represent our company—"

"I haven't signed anything yet, Reid," she reminded him.

"I have work to do, if I could just get some peace to do it."

"Nothing that can wait?"

"It shouldn't."

"Sounds important."

"It is."

"Take a break," she said, shoving his chest so he fell into his chair.

"I'm not going to win here, am I?" He found himself lost in the depths of her cleavage as she bent over him, her hands going to his middle.

Lila unbuckled his belt. "Oh, I think you're going to win pretty soon."

With Reid in his chair, Lila put a hand on each of his firm thighs and dropped to the floor. He didn't try to stop her as she loosened the button and zipper of his pants. He was already hard for her. Perfect.

She lowered the elastic of his boxer briefs, and he lifted his hips so she could pull them lower. His cock sprang forth, standing tall and proud. Keeping her eyes on his, she took him in her hand, swirling her palm over the head of his dick, spreading moisture around. His eyes stayed on her, unblinking, but his nostrils flared and a muscle in his jaw ticked. Her touch had the desired effect. She did that to him.

Leaning in, she swept her tongue from the base of his dick to the head and took him into her mouth. She sucked lightly on the head and heard a low growl and a rumble roll through him and into her. She grasped his base in a fist, and dipped her head, taking more of him, not stopping until her lips met her hand.

His breath was heavy, and his hands were on her head. He loosened the bun she'd used to restrain her hair and gripped the loose tendrils in his fist. She increased her speed and pressure as she raised and lowered her head, as his own hold on her hair tightened.

Lila could feel the moisture between her own legs, and she needed to alleviate the pressure, so she squeezed her thighs together and continued her work.

"Lila," he said. "Stop." His voice was low. With a groan, and a firm grip on her hair, he pulled her head back. "I said stop," he told her. He stood and pulled her so she was as well. She thought he would push her away, but instead he turned her around, and with a dramatic movement, he swept the table clear of everything, including his laptop, which crashed to the floor. He didn't even seem to notice, as he bent her over the table.

Now breathless at this turn of events, him completely taking over, she watched out of the corner of her eye when he reached for his wallet and took out a condom. He pulled down her shorts and smacked a hand across her bare ass. She cried out, mostly from the shock, and not the pleasant sting that lingered.

He ran his hand over her ass. His skilled fingers went lower and skirted along the outer lips of her core. Then he delved deeper—pressing the pad of one finger on her clit, and she urged him to go close, to give her the relief she sought. His touch was magical. If he didn't take her soon, she might explode.

Finally, he obliged, and circled her clit with his fingers. She panted under his touch, and he stroked her until she came. When she settled, catching her breath with her cheek against the cool marble of the tabletop, he grabbed her hips and pushed inside her. He was fast, intense, as he pounded his hips against her ass, taking her, fucking her hard.

Reid's fingers dug into her hip and her shoulder. Holding her in place as he took what he wanted from her. She'd come on to him, looking to play with him a little, but he'd quickly turned the tables—and she couldn't have been happier about it.

Feeling another orgasm rise in her, she allowed herself to be completely taken over by him and how he was making her feel. Lila cried out, and as if he'd been waiting for her, he stiffened and hollered out his own release.

They stayed together for a moment, catching their breaths, but then he pushed away. Without speaking, they both straightened their clothes. He picked up his laptop, and she saw that the lid was bent at an unnatural angle and the screen was shattered.

"Might have to get this replaced," he muttered.

"Hopefully you backed up your work."

"I always do," he assured her, bending to pick up the papers, and she did the same.

She picked up one and saw a roughly hand-drawn outline of a distillery. She looked over the rest of the papers that covered the floor. They were scribbles, notes, and hand-drawn charts and diagrams. "What are you working on?" she asked. "Are you expanding? Getting a new distillery?"

Before answering, he took the papers from her. "No. How do you know that?" She raised her eyebrows at his brusque tone, and he noticed. "I didn't. I just guessed from your sketches. What's with the tone?"

"Sorry," he said.

"It's okay. Not really my business." She wouldn't want him snooping in her private matters either. But Reid was so mysterious that she wondered what was behind it. She watched him as he straightened the papers and put them into his bag. "You have some real trust issues, Reid. What happened to you?"

"What are you talking about?"

"What happened to you that you're so secretive, so unable to trust?"

"Nothing."

"Come on," Lila prodded. "I shared all of my painful history with you—my small-town life, my marriage. I know we don't know each other well. But I can see there's something dark brewing within you."

"I don't want to talk about it."

"That's your choice, I guess. You don't trust easily, and I know you don't trust me. I'd just like to know why."

He sighed and sat heavily in his chair. "It's not just you," he told her. "Except for my family, I don't trust anyone." His words were blunt, and she could see the pain on his face.

"Why not?"

He took a deep breath. "Fine. I'm like you, I guess. I too married the wrong person." Lila sat on the edge of the desk, as Reid continued. "We met when we were young. We were in love. We shared everything. She even worked for the distillery. Life was good."

"And then?"

"I didn't know she came with a price. We were at convention, where she met John Cain, the founder of Cain Rum in New York, one of our biggest competitors. I didn't know it at the time, but that was when their affair had commenced."

"She cheated on you?" Lila was shocked. Lila abhorred cheaters. And a woman who would cheat on a man like Reid? The woman must be vile.

Reid laughed. "If that was all she did, it wouldn't have been such a big deal." Bitterness contorted his handsome features. "She took a lot of our recipes and gave them to Cain Rum Distillery."

"What? How did she get away with it?"

"We didn't pursue legal action. I didn't want the

press scrutiny or the spotlight. I screwed up. It was my fault—"

"You were the victim. She stole from you. What she did was corporate espionage."

"It was an embarrassment. Despite what Quin, Gemma and my dad said, and how much they had my back. It was me who was weak. I let it happen. I trusted the wrong person. We rebuilt and moved on. I'm a lot more careful now."

"What happened to Carolina?"

He let out a humorless laugh. "She ended up marrying John Cain."

"Shut up."

"It's true."

"Bitch."

"I try not to think about it. It's best to focus on work and building the best future we can."

"You're right. Getting married was my biggest mistake. But I know I wouldn't have the life I have now without that asshole." She shook her head. "You know, I'm glad you told me about Carolina, but let's not talk about our exes anymore." She stood and reached out for his hand. "Let's just focus on us."

The anger that had transformed his face smoothed, and he smiled up at her. "I like that idea."

Reid held Lila's hand as he led her to his bedroom.

After telling Lila about what had happened during his marriage to Carolina, Reid felt lighter than he had in years. It had been a secret, one known only by the members of his immediate family. He'd expected to be embarrassed, but he wasn't. Telling her his deepest, darkest secret had been easier than he'd expected. She hadn't laughed, she hadn't blamed him for being an idiot. And what surprised him the most was that he trusted Lila.

When they reached the foot of the bed, he stopped, and turned to face her. Cupping her cheeks in his hands, he drew her to him and kissed her. Her lips were full, soft and waiting for him. Her mouth parted, and he took the kiss deeper. He stroked her tongue with his own, entwining, dancing, dueling for who could get the most taste from the other. He needed her again, didn't think he'd ever get enough of her.

He lowered them both to the bed, each pulling at the clothing they'd just straightened only minutes ago.

He reached for a condom from the box he'd left on the nightstand and rolled the latex over his painfully rock-hard dick.

Lining up with her, he pushed inside her, and he was home. Each time with Lila was better than the last. It shocked him how quickly she'd managed to get under his skin. A serious voice in his brain told him that he should be keeping his feelings for her separate from the business. He shouldn't want her. Especially since they would soon be collaborating in business. It was reckless. It was stupid. Somehow, when it came to Lila, he didn't give a damn about anything but being with her. And he had no idea how he would give her up when she signed the papers agreeing to work with them.

Soon, she was pushing back on him, matching his pounding rhythm, her breaths were short, her movements frantic. He knew she was as far-gone as he was. His stomach tightened, and his heartbeat stuttered in his chest.

He looked down at the curve of Lila's body, and he realized that he would do anything for her. She'd managed to awaken long-dormant feelings within him, and he wasn't sure how she'd sneaked in past his barriers and gotten to him. Somewhere along the way, he'd developed feelings for her, and he knew there would be no going back. But he couldn't help that now. He gripped her hips, stilling her as he buried himself deeply within her heat, taking what he wanted, bringing them both to a hard, powerful finish, as their satisfied cries mingled in the quiet of the hotel room.

The waiter removed their dinner plates and replaced them with dishes of chocolate mousse. It was their final night in New Orleans and Reid had insisted they go to dinner. Lila knew she would miss this time alone with Reid. In just a few short days, between exploring the city in the day and making love at night, they'd managed to get so close. But she knew that their time together like this would be short. He'd already made it clear that once she signed on to work with the distillery, they wouldn't have any sort romantic relationship.

"How did you like dinner?" He looked across the table at Lila. They were seated on a balcony and the full moonlight cast a soft white glow over them, while the warm, night air surrounded them.

"Delicious," she said, spooning up some of the mousse. As the creamy, chocolate hit her tongue, she closed her eyes in surrender, and hummed her appreciation. When she opened her eyes, she saw that Reid was watching her, stock still. His fork frozen halfway way to his mouth.

"What?"

"Nothing," he said, and took his own taste of mousse. "Oh, that is good." Watching pleasure cross over his face—whether in bed, or while eating dinner—was something to behold. But his expression grew serious when he put down his spoon and straightened. "I know you made me come on this trip to make me forget about the business, but can we talk about it now?"

"God, you're so boring and predictable, Reid. But I guess it had to come up eventually."

"It did. I need to know if you'll agree to work on our social media campaigns."

Of course, Lila had already agreed to do it, a contract had appeared in her inbox that morning. She looked forward to working with the brand. She wanted to laugh, but Reid face was so serious. And then she remembered that he was only there to get her to sign on. It might feel like they were a couple, but that wasn't reality. She'd extorted him to come on the trip.

"You've seen the offer. It's very fair for the work you'll have to do. Have you looked it over?"

"I have."

"So, you know I've already put—literally—everything on the table, dinner included. Can we just put this to bed already?"

"Well, that sounds like a good idea."

"Lila, what's your answer?"

"I'm going to do it," she told him.

His smile was broad. "That's fantastic."

"I'm going to LA tomorrow," she told him. "I've got a few meetings and I'm going to talk to my agent about your offer."

"You know, that's a huge relief," he told her. "There's a real weight off my shoulders."

He held his glass aloft. "To the beginning of a profitable, professional partnership."

She clinked her glass against his and turned her attention back to her dessert. The Rexford deal would be amazing for her. The exposure, the money, the clout it gave her during her negotiations with the GO! Channel would greatly benefit her. Reid had been quick to remind her of their forthcoming *professional* relationship. That was what he wanted from her. It should be what she wanted, too.

She looked at Reid. He seemed happier than she had ever seen him. It served as a reminder that getting her on board with the distillery was his goal for the trip and nothing else. *Mission accomplished.*

"Lila, I know I was hesitant at first, but I have to say, I've had a great time here with you. Thanks for kidnapping me."

"Anytime. I had a great time, too. It's nice to have some company every now and again. But let's not pretend you didn't spend a lot of the time working remotely."

"It's baby steps," he insisted. "But maybe you're right, I don't always get to enjoy what life has to offer."

"You could have everything you could ever want, but you never leave the office."

"If I don't work, then I can't afford all of the things I have no time to enjoy."

"Why not? You should be able to enjoy the fruits of your success."

"The fruits of my success are continued success. Unlike Quin and Gemma, I can't take my eyes off the prize. Gemma creates an incredible product, and Quin ensures that people see it. But I've got to work behind the scenes to make sure it all comes together."

"So, you work 24/7?"

"Gotta keep my eye on the prize, right?"

"Oh please. I know you guys have been successful for a while. You're doing fine and were doing well before this recent boost."

"You've done your homework."

"I'm a businessperson, too, Reid. I wasn't going

to sign anything until I knew you guys would be good for my own brand. I'm not going to jump into bed blind."

"Like you did with me?" he goaded with a smile.

She rolled her eyes. "I think we were both wearing blinders that first night." She took his hand in hers. "Reid, you can have anything you want. There are so few people in the world who get an experience like this. You're one of the lucky ones."

"I know I am," he said. "But I slipped up once. I took my attention from the distillery and it almost cost us everything."

"You can't hold on to that forever," she told him. "you did nothing wrong."

"It doesn't matter. Still feels like it."

"It's in the past," she told him. "Let's focus on the future and everything we can do for each other."

"I'll drink to that."

CHAPTER THIRTEEN

FINALLY, BACK IN Miami at the distillery, Reid was a ball of tension as he sat at the conference table with Quin and Gemma as they discussed what Reid had missed during his New Orleans trip. During his three days away, he'd stayed up to date on the happenings at the distillery, but Quin had moved forward independently, scouting new locations to set up and expand, which would give them the space they needed, and keep everything under one roof. But Reid disagreed, and he was starting his first day back with an argument with his brother.

"We're not moving operations," he told Quin. "This is where Rexford started. This is where we continue."

"Reid, listen to reason. There's no way we can continue and produce rum to meet the demand in our current distillery. Gemma, tell him."

"I'm with Reid," she said. "I can't imagine not working in this building. It makes us who we are. But I do need more room."

"Well, how about an expansion?" Reid suggested. "We build on and connect with the neighboring buildings that we already own. It keeps everything under one roof, but we stay here."

Gemma nodded. "I like that. Does that work for you, Quin?"

"That could work. But I can't help but feel it'd be a lot easier—and probably cheaper—to find a new place."

Reid knew Quin was probably right, but Reid couldn't imagine leaving the building that was as much a part of the business as he was. "Why don't we get some quotes on what it would cost and we can come back to it later?"

"Fine," Quin relented. "If you're willing to consider an opinion you don't necessarily agree with, you must have had a good time in Louisiana?"

Reid's body tensed. He hadn't seen Lila since they'd parted ways in New Orleans. He'd boarded a flight to Miami as she boarded one to Los Angeles. She'd texted him a couple of times but that was it. He missed her. "It was fine."

"Just fine?" Quin asked, with a smirk that Reid wanted to punch.

"Yes."

"Did you make things right with her?" Gemma asked."

"I believe we came to an understanding," he said vaguely. "She has the paperwork. She's going through it and will get it back to us soon." Gemma smiled. "And you guys had a good time together?"

"I think we did."

"Well," Gemma said. "I'm looking forward to seeing her tomorrow. I really like her."

"What do you mean? Tomorrow?"

"She'll be back in Miami."

"How do you know that?"

"She told me on the phone last night."

"You talk to her on the phone?"

"Yeah, we've been in touch."

"Then why are you asking me if she's signing the contracts? Why am I on the hook for being the one unable to convince her to work for us?"

"Because you're the one with the obvious attraction to her. And we don't generally discuss work when there are far more interesting things to talk about," she told him with a wink. "What's that supposed to mean?" "Oh, nothing," Gemma said, standing from the table. "If you'll excuse me, I've got to head down to the distillery. Just do me a favor, Reid."

"What's that?"

"Make sure you call Lila tomorrow."

"And why should I do that?"

"Because when I look at you—I can tell you're relaxed, refreshed, you're smiling. I think she's good for you."

CHAPTER FOURTEEN

BACK IN MIAMI, Lila sat on the bed in her hotel room and looked over the offer from Go! Channel production team. They'd been thoroughly impressed by her social media reach and by her screen test, so they gave the green light to develop her show. She still couldn't believe their offer. The papers in front of her represented everything she wanted, but there was something about the deal that didn't sit right with her. In her career, she'd always done what she wanted. And as she reviewed the proposed itinerary that the travel channel had given her, the things she could and couldn't do, she started to feel the control slip away from her. She craved the security that came from the network deal, but at what price to the life she wanted to live? She'd already lived one lifetime under the thumbs of her parents, and then her husband. Did she really want to do it again?

She had planned to stay in LA for a couple more days, but after seeing what the television execs wanted her to do, she panicked. She needed to get away. And she booked the next flight across the country to Miami. She hadn't had a *home* in about five years—she'd spent her time traveling. But there was something that drew her to Miami, and she knew that *something* was Reid.

While she'd been in contact with Gemma, she hadn't called Reid. Why would he want to see her? He'd gotten what he wanted and had made it clear they would only have a professional relationship from here out.

Her phone rang. When she picked it up, she tried to quell the rush of excitement that went through her when she saw Reid's name on her screen. *Well, speak of the devil.*

"Reid Rexford," she purred in greeting. "I didn't think I'd be hearing from you so soon. Did you really miss me that much?"

"I heard you were back in town."

"Yeah, just a short stopover."

"How short?"

"It's up in the air."

He chuckled and the sound warmed her. "How do you live like that?"

"Easily. There's no pressure to do things I don't want to do," she told him, thinking of the things the GO! Channel asked of her. "So, what's up? Why are you calling me?"

A beat of silence was followed by a chuckle. "Okay, Lila," he said, and she tried not to shiver at the way he said her name. Clearly, he had more control than either of them thought. "I was wondering if you had any plans for dinner."

"I don't. But I'd like to."

"All right. Why don't I send a car for you at seven? We can have dinner here."

"Sounds good to me." She smiled. The prospect of seeing Reid again thrilled her. "I'll be ready. I just have one question, though."

"What is it?"

"Is this a professional dinner, where we discuss our collaboration, or something else?"

"It can be whatever you want it to be."

"Good answer. See you then."

So much for a professional dinner, Lila thought as Reid wrapped his arms around her waist.

She had barely stepped into his foyer when he was on her, his lips pressing against hers. He was frantic, but no more than she was. Their discarded clothing littered the floor as they made their way into the house. They got as far as the kitchen, wearing only their underwear, and Lila knew they wouldn't make it any further than that.

She didn't have a chance to look around, take in the view of the backyard, or even check out what he'd cooked, food which was simmering on the stovetop. But that was fine. She could get the tour later.

Reid lifted her onto the countertop, and ran his hands down her body, while she busied herself with his. She reached down and squeezed his length through the material of his boxers, and he groaned in response, letting her touch him for only a moment before he pushed her hand away and dropped his own between her thighs.

Touching her, he found her wet, needy. The minute his fingers met her clit, a bolt of electricity shot through her. Reid was different than any other man that she'd been with. Just his touch was enough to set her ablaze.

He stroked her and her heart rate increased, as he slipped past the satin barrier of her panties and slid a finger inside of her. She could feel herself tighten around his finger and she gripped him even harder when he inserted another. He moved his hand back and forth, plunging his fingers in and out of her, circling her clit with the master's touch of his thumb. He was driving her crazy, as she was splayed on the countertop, trapped between the wall behind her and the hard muscles of his chest. Her breathing increased, and she clenched her hands into tight, little fists, finding it difficult to hold on.

It had only been a couple of days since she'd been with him in New Orleans, but even that had been far too long. She needed him again. Now!

"Reid," she gasped. "Condoms. In my purse," she told him, apparently unable to form complete sentences.

"Aren't you eager?" he teased, slowly the speed of his touches, lazily drawing out her pleasure.

"Reid, now. Please," she pleaded.

"You don't have to ask me again," he told her, pulling his hand away from her and bringing his fingers to his mouth, licking his digits free of her juices. She was so far gone, that just the sight of the pleasure he took from it, almost pushed her over the edge. She squeezed her eyes shut, to get her hormones under control, but it was useless.

When she opened her eyes again, she watched, riveted, as Reid rolled the latex over himself, and took position again between her spread thighs. He roughly grabbed her hips in his large, strong hands and entered her. Her eyes fluttered shut in relief, but she opened them again, not wanting to miss the look on Reid's face as he pushed into her over and over.

The look that came over him was rough, serious, as he possessed her, rearing back, almost pulling his entire length from her, before slamming back into her again. He squeezed her hips in a tight grip as he filled her, possessing her so fully, as he held her in place, thrusting his hips against her with a force that made her head crash against the wall cupboard door. Immediately, he put a hand at the back of her head, cushioning the blows, but not slowing his pace.

Lila felt her orgasm grow again. His movements grew more strained and she knew that he was close, as well. He pulled her close, and hit her just right, and soon, her orgasm erupted with force, and bliss overcame her, as he continued pumping his hips. "Reid," she yelled out, barely recognizing her own voice, as she exploded. But her cries were muted by his lips, as he entered her one more time, before he stiffened and came with his own thick groan.

Waking up in Reid's bed the next morning, Lila felt warm, firm chest at her back. A strong arm was draped over her middle and it took her several seconds to remember where she was. But when she inhaled Reid's spicy cologne and the unmistakable scent of their lovemaking, it all came rushing back to her.

She turned in his arms, and he kept his eyes closed, still sleeping. His face was soft, but day-old stubble peppered his chin. Her fingers itching to touch it, she reached out and felt the rough bristles under her fingertips. His eyes opened slowly and when they focused on her, he smiled.

"Morning."

"Sorry to wake you."

His eyes shifted downward, at their naked bodies pressed together, and his smile turned devilish. "I'm glad you did." Between them, his cock hardened, and she felt him grow against her belly.

"Well, hello down there," she said, and he flexed his hips against her.

He laughed and cupped her cheek, coming close to kiss her, but she drew back, and covered her mouth with the back of her hand. "Watch out," she warned him. "Morning breath."

He moved her hand and leaned in, kissing her

anyway, before he pulled back and grimaced. "Yeah, you're right."

Lila laughed. "Jerk."

Reid laughed and kissed her again, taking his time, his tongue brushing against hers. "I'm kidding. You're good," he assured her, before kissing her again to prove his point.

She moaned into his mouth, and he rolled her over onto her back, holding himself over her with his strong forearms. She ran her fingernails up the soft dark hair and wrapped her arms around his neck. She pulled Reid closer, and they kissed more before he pulled away. "Aw, damn," he muttered against her skin, his lips skimming down her throat.

"What's wrong?"

"We used all of my condoms last night."

The bubble of desire popped. "Are you serious? For such a responsible guy, you don't keep your place stocked with the necessities?"

"Sorry for my poor planning. But that doesn't mean we can't improvise."

Lila spread her legs, and flexed her hips upward, allowing his midsection to rest more fully on top of hers. "What do you have in mind?"

He quirked an eyebrow upward. "This," he said, before disappearing below the thin blanket that covered them.

Reid kissed, licked, nibbled his way across her chest, stopping to circle one tight nipple with his lips. He sucked and swished his tongue across the bud.

He cupped the other breast with his large hands and pinched the nipple between his fingers, making her cry out. Her back arched off the bed as he worked, played over her breasts, plucking at strings of desire that settled in her center. "Reid," she gasped, not understanding how it was possible that he could have such an effect on her, as he played with her breasts. "I can't wait anymore."

He released one rosy bud from his rounded lips with a light pop, and he grinned. "You got it, sweetheart." He ventured lower, dipping his tongue into her belly button, before he found his destination. He threw off the blanket, left her exposed to the chilly air of his room and maneuvered her legs so that they draped over his back, thighs on his shoulders.

From his position, he looked up at her, a playful smile perched on wicked lips, amusement putting a glisten in his eyes. This was a different Reid—not the hard, serious, callous jerk, with a tongue that could cut. No, he was having fun—he was playful, funny, cute, even. *With an even more wicked tongue.* His mouth descended upon her flesh again, his tongue snaking between her folds, and hit the spot she needed him to. He closed his lips around the bud and applied pressure, giving her the same attention he'd given her nipples. Stroking, pinching, licking, feasting.

While one hand fisted the cotton bedsheet, her other gripped the back of his head. Wanting him to get closer and relieve the delicious pressure. The feeling was almost too much for her, and she whined, pushing her hips closer to his mouth. He pulled back momentarily and flipped over so that he was on his back, and he pulled her to him, so that she straddled his head between her thighs, he held her so closely, that she wasn't sure how he was able to breathe down there. He nipped her clit with his lips just right and she let out a wild yell. She began to move her hips, riding his face, surely cutting off his air supply. And yet he still didn't stop. She swayed and shook her hair behind her shoulders as she chased her own pleasure. *If he dies, he dies,* she reasoned, not caring about anything how he made her feel. Every muscle in her body tensed, as he ate from her, and she barely noticed the hand he snaked across her ass, and the finger he pressed into the crevice.

Her breath went short and her orgasm powered through her and she continued to ride him, as he held on to her, guiding her climax. When her body quieted from the rapturous pleasure, she rolled over in a heap on the bed. Her heart was pounding, and she tried to regain her breath. Reid lay by her side, his chest rising and falling rapidly.

"You okay?" she asked him, putting a hand on his sweat-glistened chest.

"Yeah," he said in between breaths. "I thought I might black out there for a moment," he added with a laugh.

"Sorry I almost killed you."

"It was worth it. It would have been a good way to go."

She smiled, and then rolled over onto him so that she straddled his hips. "Well, don't go anywhere yet," she told him, grabbing his length. "It's your turn now."

CHAPTER FIFTEEN

ON MONDAY MORNING, Reid walked into the distillery with a smile on his face, whistling as made the way to his office. He'd had a spectacular weekend with Lila. She'd gotten under his skin, and no matter how much he scratched that itch there was no relief like being inside her. He may have resisted her at first, but he'd found himself wanting to be with her. It was a need at this point. And he'd almost skipped work to stay with her in his bed.

"Well, aren't you in a good mood this morning," he heard Quin say, coming up behind him. "What's put the jump in your step?"

"I'm in a good mood," he told him. "Is that allowed?"

"It's allowed. It's just not very common, coming from you." His little brother narrowed his eyes at him. "What were you up to this weekend?"

"If you have to know, I was with Lila."

"Oh really? Just discussing business, right?" he asked with a wink.

"We did a little, but really, I barely thought about work at all."

"The woman deserves an award for keeping your mind off the office."

Reid rolled his eyes. Quin could use his imagination if he wanted. Reid wouldn't provide any more details about Lila. "Can I help you with something? Or do you not have enough of your own work to do?"

"I stopped by to tell you that Gemma wants to see both of us in the distillery."

Reid checked his phone and didn't see a message from her.

"She texted me this morning," Quin explained. "And you weren't anywhere to be found so I told her I'd let you know."

"Thanks."

Side by side they made their way down to the distillery where Gemma was waiting for them.

"So, Lila, huh?" Quin asked.

"Yeah, I guess so. You have anything to say about it?"

"Not at all. Good for you, man," he said. "I really like her. And you guys are so different, it seems like a great fit. Do you see a future there?"

"You're getting way ahead of this," Reid told him. "It's nothing serious. We're just hanging out. She's got her work, I've got mine. Especially if she's partnering with us. We're having fun for the time being because it won't last forever." There was no way that two people as different as he and Lila would ever be able to work romantically in the real world.

"Why not?" Quin asked.

Reid was about to give him reasons he'd given himself—their differences, work, propriety, blah, blah, blah—but he didn't. The more he thought about the reasons, the less sense they made.

Reid walked into the distillery alongside Quin. Gemma was standing next to the large copper fermenters with several of her employees, directing them. Reid was proud of the way she ran her distillery. She was a fierce, talented leader with a firm but gentle hand, all wrapped up in a small package.

"About time you guys got here," she told Reid and Quin.

"What did you want?"

"I've got some news," she told them. "Let's talk in my office."

They followed her to the small, cluttered office in the distillery, and Reid and Quin took seats on the battered couch next to her desk. "What have you got?" Reid asked.

Gemma handed over a notebook, and when he flipped through the pages, he found diagrams, notes, recipes, random scribbles. "What am I looking at, Gem?"

"It's very preliminary at the moment. But I may have come up with a way to quick-distill and quickly age our rum."

"Are you serious?"

"I'm not sure. But here's what might work," she said before going into an in-depth discussion of the science behind distilling. Reid was impressed. She had come up with a way to speed up the aging process, taking what would typically be at least a five-year process for their dark and spiced rums and turning it into a six-month one. But he had reservations.

"Will the quality suffer?" Quin asked.

"That's the beauty of it," she told them. "I won't know for sure until we get some test batches done. But I don't think it will. I've played with something before, but nothing on a grand scale like this."

"So along with the prohibition recipe, you'll be quick-aging all other batches. What about space or equipment?" Reid asked.

"I already ordered the special equipment we'll need. If this works, we'll need to expand, so the sooner we get to converting our current properties, or buying new ones, the better."

"That really puts some pressure on us. We haven't planned on expanding this quickly. I guess you'd better get started and we'll handle the facilities," Quin told her. "This is a lot," Reid said. "It's risky. I hope it's worth it."

"It will be."

"I'm not one to take a risk."

"We all have to be on board here," Quin reminded them. "It's how we do this. Either we waste the opportunity we've been given with this newfound popularity, or we let it ride on expansion and a procedure that's completely new to us."

"All in favor of *new to us*?" Gemma asked, raising her hand. Quin did also.

"Guys, we have to be careful here," Reid maintained.

"Raise your hand, Reid," Quin warned him. "We're doing this."

"Fine," Reid relented. "We'll do this your way." He raised his hand and he hoped to God the decision wouldn't ruin them.

No matter how hard she tried, Lila couldn't will herself to get out of bed, not as long as she could smell Reid on the bedsheets, still see the indent of his head on the pillow next to her. She'd slept so soundly in his bed, against his chest with his arms wrapped tightly around her that it had felt like only minutes had passed when his alarm sounded that morning and he'd gone to work. They'd spent the night wrapped up in each other. They ran so hot and cold—between goading each other and tearing each other's clothes off. Teasing him provided her with just as much a rush as sex with him. Maybe it was all part of the same emotion.

She pushed herself up from Reid's bed and looked around his room—so masculine, neat, and ordered. Just like the man himself.

She picked up the shirt he'd discarded the night

before and held it to her nose, taking in his scent before throwing it into his clothes hamper.

She hadn't gotten a good look at the place last night. When she'd showed up, they'd immediately taken things to the bedroom. Not that she had any complaints, of course. Her stroll to the kitchen took her past a couple more immaculate bedrooms, a living room, a dining room, and his office.

Knowing that Reid didn't trust easily, it meant a lot to her that he let her stay there without him. In such a short time, they'd come a long way.

Her phone rang and she saw it was a call from her agent in LA.

"Lila, where are you?" he asked, skipping the traditional greetings.

"I'm in Miami," she told him. "Why?"

"You were supposed to stay in LA for the contract negotiations."

Lila sighed, and despite the great opportunity that a television network provided her, she increasingly felt doubt about signing the contract. "I had to take care of something in Miami first," she told him.

"That rum thing?" he asked, indifferent. Lila knew he didn't care about it because she'd lined it up without him, excluding him from ten percent of her paycheck. "That's not your future. This internet fame you have—you're a flash in the pan, girl. You have to strike while the iron is hot," he said, mixing metaphors in a way that bugged her every time.

He was right. She had to take advantage of every

lucrative opportunity that came her way. Even if it meant doing something she didn't really want to do—like sign her name, image, brand over to a corporation. "Can I do a video chat with them?" She still had things to take care of with the distillery. And whether she admitted it to herself not, that was the deal she wanted to sign.

"No, we'll need you back in LA as soon as possible."

"Okay," Lila agreed with a frown. Sure, it was just a matter of hopping a flight, but part of her felt like she would be cutting off an important piece of her life. Her independence, her freedom.

And Reid.

With another trip across the country on the horizon, Lila wanted to soak up as much of Miami as she could. But Reid's home was the only place she wanted to be. She lay next to his pool and sprayed more sunblock over her skin.

Reaching behind her back, she smoothed in the spray as best she could.

"Want me to get that for you?" The deep baritone that set her panties ablaze came from somewhere behind her. She turned her head and saw Reid walk out onto the pool deck with an easy gait. He was smiling and looked relaxed with the first couple of buttons of his shirt unbuttoned and his sleeves rolled halfway up his corded, tanned forearms.

He sat next to her, took the bottle from her hands

and sprayed the sunscreen on her back and shoulders before spreading it over her skin. Looking over her shoulder, she saw that he looked like he was surprisingly in a good mood. "Look, he *does* smile," she teased. He swatted her ass and she giggled and rolled over. "What's gotten into you?"

"God, a guy can't smile once in a while without getting the third degree? I had a good day. It might be too soon to say, but we think we might have solved our supply problem for good. Gemma's working on it now with her crew."

"Oh, that's great. What is it?" Reid paused. "Trade secrets?" she asked.

Again, he hesitated. "Gemma may have come up with a way to quick-distill and age the rum."

"Oh really?"

"Yeah, it's highly experimental. But, besides the prohibition-era recipe it's pretty much our only option to get all our product on the shelves and to the people who want it. Hopefully it'll work out. Otherwise, it could be a bust."

"I think that if Gemma believes she can do it, she will."

"Me too. Any word from your agent?"

"Yeah, I have to head back to Los Angeles tomorrow. Negotiations for the GO! Channel," she said with a sigh.

"You don't sound very happy."

"I know. He isn't happy I left LA so quickly."

"You couldn't stay away, though, huh?" His smile was cocky as he lay back in the chair.

"That's right."

"Why exactly aren't you happy about the TV deal?"

"I don't know. I should be happier. This is everything I wanted."

"But?" he prompted.

"I don't know. Something just doesn't feel right about it. My agent and everyone else on the team tells me it's the right thing to do, that it's a good deal. But it feels like they're just going to strip me of my independence and put restrictions on what I want to do."

"Don't sign anything if it doesn't feel right. If you're going to do it, do it right. Go into negotiations and kick their asses. Get what you want."

"What if they say no?"

He shrugged. "Then you tried. But you've got to take that risk, right? But if this is what you want, fight for it," he told her. He sounded serious. Lila watched him for a moment from behind her sunglasses. He stared off into the distance, as if he was deep in thought about something.

"Are you talking about my contract, or us?"

"I'm talking about everything. A very smart woman taught me that life should be fun. Not all serious work stuff," he said, pouncing on her and rolling back over so she sprawled on his chest.

"Sounds like a smart woman," she said, kissing the underside of his jaw. "In the meantime, I have something more fun we can do."

CHAPTER SIXTEEN

REID SAT IN HIS OFFICE, working on the next step of their expansion. The team had worked quickly and based on the price quotes and time estimations they received from several contractors, they'd decided to go ahead with expanding the current distillery into the adjacent properties, which they also owned. He was glad that they would be staying in the building. It was part of what tied them to their past. Reid couldn't imagine going to work every day in another building—nor would he. He would take the old, worn, hurricane-and-sun-battered exterior over any flashy new designs. The old distillery was just as much a part of the business as he and his siblings were.

He signed off on an invoice for their contractor and scanned over the orders for the new equipment Gemma would need to quick-distill her recipes. He still wasn't completely on board with the idea. If it failed, it would cost them a lot of resources—*a lot* of money. And there was the risk that the quality would suffer. That was what didn't sit well with him. Rexford Rum had a reputation to uphold. It was a huge risk, but if there was anything that Lila had taught him, it was that he should take more risks, live a little. Have some fun.

Lila. A smile formed on his lips as he thought of her. In such a short time, she had transformed his entire life. He never thought he would get close to another woman, but she had managed to break through each of the walls he'd erected around himself.

The door to his office opened and he looked up. His smile turned down, as in walked the woman who'd caused him to build them those walls.

His jaw became tight and clenched. "What are you doing here?" he asked Carolina without standing.

"Is that how you greet your ex-wife?"

"It's the politest way I could muster," he told her.

She ignored him. "I'm in Miami with some girlfriends. I thought I'd pay you a visit, and I knew I'd find you here." She looked around his simple office with disdain. "The place looks exactly the same."

"I'll ask again, why are you here?"

"I wanted to see you."

"Why, old man Cain can't keep you satisfied?" Reid smiled at the anger in her eyes.

"He keeps me plenty satisfied. Thank you for your concern. But I've seen pictures of you around the internet with that little blogger of yours."

"Lila is none of your concern. I've had enough of this tête-à-tête. You should leave."

"I just wanted to stop by and congratulate you,

Quin and Gemma. I've been hearing a lot of buzz about Rexford Rum."

"Get out," he told her, not wanting to discuss rum, or anything else with the woman who'd almost ruined him.

"Word on the street has it that Gemma is up to something here. She's placed orders for some very specialized equipment. Just makes everyone wonder what she's up to. Seeing as how you're the hot commodity right now, and I know how long Gemma ages her stuff. I don't have any idea how you're going to fill the demand your popularity has created. You haven't got enough stock, have you?"

He wasn't about to confirm or deny anything she thought. "You're lucky I don't pick you up and bodily remove you from my building," he warned her.

"You would never do such a thing, Reid. I know you. I also know you guys aren't as slick as you pretend to be. Whatever you're planning down here, and I think I know exactly what it is, just give up, because you're going to lose."

"What do you think we're doing?"

"Those five-to-ten-year batches that Gemma is so proud of, there's no way they're ready to hit shelves. My theory is that Gemma's found a way to quick-distill rum." Reid kept his face impassive, not letting on the anger or surprise he felt at finding out their little secret wasn't so secret. "I know Gemma is smart, but that's pretty good."

"Is that what you think? Where did you hear that?"

She shrugged. "A little bird told me. Don't think that the master distiller at Cain Rum isn't currently working on a way to do the same."

"Carolina, I could stay here and chat all day, but I've really got to go. I have actual work to do. Like you would know anything about that."

"So, it sounds like nothing's changed for you, then. Work, work, work. That's too bad."

"Did I say that *I* had to go? I clearly meant you. Leave before I call the police."

"Fine, you're no fun. Good luck, Reid."

Carolina turned and with a swivel in her hips that he'd once found appealing, she sashayed out of his office, and hopefully out of his life for the last time.

In the silence of his office, Reid stewed over his ex-wife's visit. How had word gotten out what they were doing? They'd kept it in house. The only people who knew were him, his brother and sister, Gemma's workers in the distillery...

And Lila.

"Fuck," Reid muttered. Had Lila sold him out? She was the only person on the outside he'd told about the expansion and their new production plans. And she was alone in his house. Following a hunch, he turned to his laptop and typed the names *Lila Campbell* and *Carolina Cain.* The results were what he'd suspected and yet hoped to never see.

There were pictures of Lila and Carolina attending the same Cain party. The women were all smiles as photographers captured them deep in conversation, smiling for the cameras, their arms around each other. Reid slammed his laptop shut. He'd trusted Lila, let her in, told her things. Is this why she was here? Why she'd stayed close and gotten under his skin?

He pushed back from his desk. Lila was at his house right now. He had to go there and get to the bottom of this.

When Reid came into the house, Lila could tell something was wrong. He said nothing, and she followed him to the study, where he stalked to the wet bar and poured himself a glass of the ten-year-aged dark rum that she knew he preferred.

"You okay?" she asked.

He didn't say anything for a moment, as he watched her over the rim of his glass. His eyes were full of fire, but it wasn't from passion, how she'd grown accustomed to having him watch her. There was anger there. He lowered the glass. "No," he said finally.

"What's up?"

"What do you know about Carolina Cain?"

She thought for a moment. "Carolina? Carolina Cain?" She flashed back to several Cain rum parties and events she'd attended, and the tall, slim, glamorous woman she'd met. "I can't believe I never connected it before. Carolina is your ex-wife?"

"As if you didn't know."

"What's that supposed to mean?"

"You didn't think to mention you were at any of their parties?"

"I go to a lot of parties, Reid. I greet the hosts. I know Carolina by name, and that's it."

He didn't seem to hear her. "I told you. I told you everything. About me, Carolina, about the distillery, and the whole time, you're playing me for a fucking idiot."

"Whoa," she said, putting up a hand, cutting him off. "What are you accusing me of?"

"You sold me out."

"To who?"

"Carolina."

"I met the woman two or three times in my life, and I haven't seen her since I went to their Labor Day party in the Hamptons last year."

"Then how did she know all about our plans at the distillery? Why was Gemma ordering new equipment even on her radar?"

"I don't know. Are you accusing me of leaking your secrets? You barely tell *me* anything about the distillery. Do you think I have such little integrity?"

"I know that Carolina and Cain Rum will pay any price to take us out."

Lila figured it out, and the realization hit her like a ton of bricks. "You never trusted me."

"I trusted you enough to tell you about our plans,

to leave you alone in my house. And this happens. Christ!"

"No, you didn't trust me. You gave me a basic run-down of what you were doing. Then you changed the topic to sex—like you always do when we're having a deep or intense conversation. And then you think I did what, exactly? Went right to Carolina and told her everything while she cut me a check?"

"It wouldn't be the first time something like that happened."

"I know she screwed you over. But I'm not her. And the fact that you don't trust me, after everything we've been through? That you think I can do that?"

"No. I don't know. I barely know you. But I do know what Carolina is. And she's capable of charming the devil. This is why I didn't want you working for us. I wanted to keep you separate from the business. But I couldn't. That's why I knew this was a bad idea."

"You want to keep me in a separate box? That's not good enough for me, Reid. I don't want to be involved in one part of your life. I want all of you."

"Clearly, I can't give you that."

"You know, you're a lot more fun when you're away from work."

"Is that right? Because not all of us have the luxury of traveling and eating and taking in festivals for income. I have responsibilities. I'm not like you. You don't even have a home."

She shook her head in disbelief. "You're just getting all your shots in now? You think I don't have any responsibilities?"

"That's not what I meant."

"Yes, it is. You still don't take me seriously, do you? You think I'm breezing through life. I tried to show you how hard I work, how my life isn't all a party."

"You can agree that our lives are very different."

"Yeah, because you close yourself off to joy, and love, and everything else but your fucking office and bottles of rum. You're going to work yourself to death." Lila took a deep breath. "I should leave."

"Where are you going?"

"I don't know. The airport, I guess, seeing as how I don't have a home or anything."

"Lila, don't, wait."

"What?"

"Don't go. Let's talk."

"You've already said enough. But what I need to know is this—did you say all those things, try to hurt my feelings in order to push me away?

"Are you going to take the chance, and welcome me into your life, or are you going to keep me separate? Because I don't do half measures, Reid. I don't settle down, especially not with someone who won't make me a priority. Hell, you won't make anything but your work a priority. You're *too* settled down, if you ask me."

He turned away from her, not bothering to answer all of her questions. "I don't have anything to give you, Lila. I'm needed at the distillery and keeping it running smoothly is what I do. It's my family, my name."

Reid wouldn't look at her, and she didn't believe he meant the hurtful words he'd said. She hadn't known him long, but she knew him well enough to read his face, his actions. But she wouldn't chase a man who didn't want her. Her head bobbed. "Okay. You've made your decision, I guess. I should go."

"Should we get together to nullify the contract we signed?"

"If you want to get out of it, we can arrange it. But I don't think we need to cut professional ties. Just whatever this—" she motioned between the two of them "—was."

"Okay."

"I'll just contact Quin for anything I might need," she told him.

"I'll let him know."

They were both quiet, and Lila knew the conversation was over. This was it. "I'll go get my things."

CHAPTER SEVENTEEN

LILA STOOD IN front of the camera, and with a shake of her head, tossed her hair over her shoulders. The microphone buried between her breasts was invisible to anyone who looked at her, but it felt as foreign as she did in front of the green screen in the studio. She should be outside, using her phone's camera, speaking to her audience, not to the besuited men in the room who looked as bored as she was.

"Okay, from the top, Lila," the cameraman said in an indifferent tone.

"Hey, it's Lila Campbell and I'm coming to you live from—" she looked over her shoulder at the screen that would project an image later "—where am I again?"

"Spring break in Cozumel," one of the suits told her without looking up from his phone.

"Spring break? It's summer."

"This commercial will launch in March, during spring break. We're going to send you there."

"You know I'm in my thirties, right? Spring break isn't exactly my thing."

"Well, you look twenty-one in TV years. Should we remind you that this is what you're being paid for."

"From the top again," the director said.

She looked over at herself in the monitor and saw that they'd projected a video of raucous spring breakers behind her. But she stared at herself. Her hair and makeup done within an inch of her life, the wardrobe that she would have never picked for herself, and she frowned.

Lila took a deep breath and turned on her brightest smile, reminding herself that she was living every online influencer's dream—a deal with a television network, worldwide exposure. She tamped down her frustration and looked back into the camera lens.

"Hey guys, it's Lila Campbell…"

Later, she was seated at a table in the conference room above the studio. Across from her sat her three studio executives from the GO! Channel.

"Ms. Campbell," the woman started. "We loved your reel from this morning. We're so excited about this partnership."

"Thank you. It was definitely a different experience for me. But I'm used to being a little more hands-on when it comes to my content."

The male exec in the middle waved off her concern. "We'll get you out in the field soon. But you'll find we record a lot of segments here in the studio.

It's cheaper, easier and safer than some of the exotic locales you may be used to."

"That sounds pretty inauthentic. Why would a travel channel operate like that—"

"Ms. Campbell, here is your updated contract." The third executive slid the papers across the table. "I'm sure you'll see the contract is in order and contains the provisions we discussed previously."

Lila nodded. She and James had negotiated an excellent contract for her. GO! Channel was going to pay her handsomely. But it was the heavily detailed itinerary that bothered her the most. Even with the segments that would be produced in-house, it was loaded with stops, and some left her in a town for only a day at a time—some places for a few hours. Also included was something new she hadn't seen before—a list of brands she could use and advertise on her personal blog.

"Excuse me," she spoke over the executives who had barely let her say two words since she sat down with them. "This list of products and brands—"

"Yes, they're affiliated with the network and our advertisers."

"Rexford Rum isn't here."

"No," one of the suits said, checking his own notes. "Our network has a deal with Cain rum."

"I needed a provision to still work with Rexford, since I have a promotion deal with them." She and Reid may have fought, but she still had a professional responsibility to them. She wouldn't renege on that.

The executives exchanged looks. "You'll have to terminate that. It doesn't align with our advertisers."

She looked at her agent. "Why wasn't I consulted on this before the contract was drafted? That was on my list of provisions. Did you think I wouldn't notice?"

"We were hoping it wouldn't matter. Do we have to remind you that this is a television deal?"

She'd heard enough. With the pressure that came along with the channel, she felt herself snap. She could do it. She didn't want it. If she wanted success, she would do it on her own. Not everything was about money and stability. "You know that cable TV is basically obsolete, right?"

"Lila—" James warned.

"No, I'm not going to sell out, sell my soul, and turn on people who have been good to me." Reid might have been a dick, but she was still a professional, and wouldn't renege on their contract. She put down the contact and slid it back to the executives. "I'm not signing this."

"You're a blogger, and you should be counting yourself lucky that we're even talking to you," the woman executive said.

"You know what? I'm done. Thank you for your time and consideration, but I think I'm better off remaining independent."

"Lila, wait—" her agent called to her.

She stopped and turned, felt herself become light, and free. "James, you're fired."

CHAPTER EIGHTEEN

IT WAS THE first day Reid had called in sick since he'd taken over the distillery. He'd even gone to work with walking pneumonia, fractured ribs, that bout of flu that kept him quarantined in his office. But as he sat on his couch, he tried to summon the strength to sit up. He failed. He wasn't physically sick, he reasoned, but tell that to the painful hollow beneath his breastbone. He missed Lila. There was no way around it. He sipped the rum from the crystal glass beside him. He'd done it to himself.

Knowing he would regret it, he pulled up her Instagram account—her pictures were fun, colorful, and he could see the passion in them. His thumb slipped and he accidentally double-tapped, liking one of her old photos. "Shit." But his eyes were glued to the picture, one from Belize, where she wore an emerald-colored bikini on a beautiful beach. His heart throbbed. He regretted what had happened between them, but there was nothing he could do about it now. It was best to keep her separate from his personal life. She was a good brand ambassador. There was no room for a romantic relationship. It was what they'd both wanted from the start. He should have listened to reason and stayed away from her. If he had, he wouldn't be in this situation.

"I thought we'd find you here," he heard Gemma say. He raised his head and saw her and Quin walking toward him. They each took a seat on a lounger flanking him, boxing him in. "I heard you called in sick. Feeling okay?"

"No, I'm sick," he told her, pointedly taking a drink from his glass.

"You're hardly ever sick," she reminded him. "And even if you were, it's never kept you from work."

"That's how we know I'm *really* sick," he told her.

Quin ripped his phone from his hand. "Looks like *lovesick* to me, big brother."

"Give that back," Reid demanded, reaching to grab it from his brother's hand, but he was too slow as Quin tossed the phone over him to Gemma.

"You're stalking her social media now?" Gemma asked. "What happened? I thought you guys had a good thing going."

"We did. Until I fucked it up."

"What did you do?"

"I said some things to her. Cruel."

"Why?"

He shrugged. "I don't know. I think I did it to drive her away."

"Reid Rexford caught in deep introspection?" Quin teased.

"Shut up."

"What did driving her away accomplish?" Gemma asked. "Besides make you miserable."

He shook his head. "Check out the pictures. *I'm* miserable and she's having a ball."

"No, she isn't," Gemma said. "I might not know her as intimately as you do, but I know she really cares for you."

"I thought Carolina did, too."

"Holy shit," Quin whispered. "That's what this is about? What Carolina did to you?"

"You know she isn't like Carolina. You can tell that right away," Gemma said.

"I fell too deep, too fast for Lila. She was too close. I had to end it, to protect the distillery."

"That's bullshit and you know it," Gemma said. "You drove her away because you're afraid. You're afraid of being burned again."

Reid didn't answer. He couldn't because Gemma had nailed it. "Can I have my phone back?"

She handed it back to him without a fight. "Figure out your life, Reid, or you'll end up miserable and alone." She took a deep breath. "But that's not why we're here."

The grave look on her face got Reid's attention. "What's going on?"

"After Carolina's visit, I asked my crew if anyone had leaked anything to our competitors. I found out one of them has been feeding information to Cain Rum."

"What?" There was a sinking feeling in Reid's stomach.

"He came to me this morning. He's remorseful. They paid him to tell them what we're doing. I fired him. It sucks."

Reid put his head in his hands. He'd blamed Lila. He had pushed her away because he jumped to conclusions, and automatically believed the worst when he thought she'd betrayed him.

"Are you okay, Reid?" Quin asked him.

"No. I blamed Lila for the leak."

"How could you?" Gemma whispered. "I didn't know that was why she left. You've got to call her and apologize."

"I can't. She won't talk to me. Nor should she."

In her hotel room in San Francisco, Lila checked her planner. Her day was completely filled. But at least it was her own schedule, not some television network telling her where to go and what to do there. Even though she'd wanted a little downtime, she'd packed her day with activities. She forced herself to stay busy. If she didn't, it might lead to too much thinking. And she knew the subject of those thoughts would be Reid.

She picked up the package that had been delivered to the hotel. It proudly bore the Rexford logo. She opened it and saw the promotional materials that she would start wearing and giving away. She picked up a cropped tank top. She wasn't sure why, but she brought it to her nose. It didn't smell like Reid. It just smelled like cotton and cardboard. She sighed and went to lie on her bed. She had it bad.

She rolled over and looked at her phone. It was time to check her notifications. She spent time every day moderating her feeds, responding to comments and messages. Instagram had hundreds of likes, but one stuck out to her. @RRexford. Reid. He'd liked one of her photos from a year ago. Someone was internet-stalking.

She smiled. So, he'd been creeping her feed. She brought up his contact information and debated whether or not she should dial. Before she could stop herself, she did. One ring went through. Two rings. She toyed with the idea of hanging up, but she couldn't. There was no going back now. Even if he didn't answer, he would still see her name on his caller ID.

"Hello?" he answered.

"Hi, Reid."

"How are you?"

"I'm good. And yourself?"

"I can't complain. I'm in San Francisco. So that's always good."

"Nice city."

Their conversation was so strained, so formal that it made her heart ache.

"What can I do for you, Lila?"

I miss you. What could she say? "I received that promotional package from you guys. Everything looks fine."

"Great. And the payment went through fine?"

"Yeah it did."

"That's good."

She could hear him take a deep breath.

"Lila, I need to say something."

She almost gasped with anticipation of what Reid might have to say.

"I owe you an apology. We found out who was behind the leak. I know it wasn't you. And I shouldn't have blamed you."

That's it? She appreciated the apology, but she'd wanted to hear more. That he wanted her to come back. He wanted to try again. But those words never came.

"And if you have any other concerns, don't be afraid to contact Quin. You have his number, right?"

Her eyes squeezed shut. "Yeah," she said, feeling her eyes water and her throat tighten. "Listen, I'm really busy at the moment. Why don't we talk later?" She managed to squeak out the words.

She heard his sigh on the other end. "Okay. Take care, Lila."

"You too, Reid."

CHAPTER NINETEEN

THE MAIN STAGE held little interest for Lila, as she made her way through the throngs of festival-goers. She was tired, wanted to go home. *Home.* That was a thought she'd never had before. But where was home, exactly? The only place she could think of was Miami.

"You ready?" one of the organizers asked her.

She had set up a booth at the music festival event to distribute the Rexford gear she'd been sent. "All set," she muttered. She should be interacting, creating posts, going live from the festival. But she was tired and not feeling it. She gave herself a shake to relax. Her phone buzzed in her pocket. She considered ignoring it, but she pulled it out. It was a text from Reid—the first she'd heard from him in more than a month.

All it said was French toast truck.

She looked up from the screen and took in her surroundings. The food truck area was nearby. Not caring that the organizer was calling after her, or that he was ready to start, Lila took off in the direction of the smell of the food, not sure what she was looking for, but hoping against hope that she would see Reid when she got there.

Lila wasn't disappointed.

When she stopped in front of the food truck, the scent of maple syrup and butter tickling her nostrils, all she could focus on was Reid. He looked casual, in khaki-colored linen pants and a button-down shirt. He'd grown a short, dark beard since she'd last seen him, and his hair was mussed, as if he'd pushed his fingers through it more than once in the ninety-degree heat.

"What are you doing here?" she asked.

"I came hoping to find you, not that I was certain you'd want to see me."

She looked around at the crowd. "You thought you'd find me among thousands of people?"

"It was a bit of long shot, I know, but I thought I'd try my luck drawing you to the food."

She laughed. "I guess you know me after all."

"Can I get you some French toast?"

She nodded. "Share an order?"

"Sure. Why don't you find somewhere for us to sit?"

The few tables were all full, so she walked a short distance and found a mostly flat section of grass where they could sit. When he joined her, they picked at their food.

"Drop the crap, Reid. Why are you here?"

"I really wanted to see you. In fact, that's all I've wanted to do since you left my house that day when I was a huge asshole to you. I missed you."

"I missed you, too."

"And I wasn't fair to you. You were right, I didn't trust you. But it wasn't because you gave me a reason not to. It was my own inability to let someone get close. I got scared and found a reason to push you away."

Lila nodded. Reid had been terrible, but she couldn't put the blame fully on Reid. She'd run, too. The move to Los Angeles had been the easy option, not staying to work it out. "I'm pretty sure I was the one who ran. Like, literally. I moved across the country."

He shook his head. "I wouldn't even listen to you. I should have known you weren't responsible for the leak."

"We can discuss this in circles all day, and I'll miss Childish Gambino's set. So why don't we say what we want. What do you want?"

"I want you," he said simply. He took a swallow of his beer, and Lila marveled at the scene. Reid Rexford, the buttoned-down businessman, always in control of his life, his appearance always impeccable, sitting cross-legged with her in a field, in rumpled clothes, drinking from a beer can, eating a piece of French toast on a paper plate. "And I'm so used to getting what I want. I don't know if you noticed this, but I might be just a little bit spoiled."

She faked a gasp. "You?" she asked, clutching her chest.

He laughed, but the sound was hollow. "When I realized you weren't coming back, I was miserable. I tried to bury myself in the business, but that didn't work. Nothing let me forget about you. Especially since I've been following your social media accounts. I wouldn't let myself forget about you. Especially since it you looked like you'd moved on. You're out here having a blast. It just reminds me that I'm not as fun and carefree as you. I like the quiet. What I held onto the most was that we couldn't be together if we were working together. I know I was just making excuse."

"Reid, you're plenty fun. Think of all the fun we had together."

He looked around. "We did have fun. But it's not like this. Your life is so much bigger than mine." He shook his head, laughing. "Can you make me stop talking?"

"No, I'm liking this. Talk some more."

"I know you have a life in LA now, and God, I don't even know what I'm asking you, or how we can make this work, but I don't care. I want you in my life."

She leaned forward and kissed him. She tasted the maple syrup and butter on his lips. "I want you in my life, too." She looked around. "I know my life is more chaotic than yours. You're more settled, I'm a little wild. I'm carefree, you're serious. The balance is what makes us good together."

"I know you're living out here now, but we can make the distance work. If you want, I can take leave from the distillery and travel with you."

"You'd take leave from the distillery?"

He nodded. "I know Quin and Gemma have everything under control. I can stay away for short periods of time. You taught me that." He blew out a breath. "And you showed me that I can love again. I love you, Lila, and I'll do anything to keep you in my life."

She couldn't believe the words he was saying. "I don't want you to think that you can just come here and say some nice things, and all is forgiven."

"I don't expect that," he told her. "I'm just grateful you're willing to listen to me."

"I love you, too, Reid."

Reid dropped his food and drew Lila into an embrace. His mouth found hers and they kissed, and she poured every bit of love and emotion she could muster into him. She couldn't believe they'd been given a second chance.

"I don't want you to walk away from the distillery," she told him when she broke away. "That place is everything to you."

"It isn't anymore," he assured her. "You are. Why don't we get out of here?"

"I would, but I have a whole box of Rexford swag to give away."

"Just leave the boxes open on the ground, and let people take what they want."

"Are you suggesting I bail on work?" she teased.

"Lila," he said against her lips, kissing her lightly. "When are you going to learn that there is more to life than just work?"

* * * * *

UNTAMED
BILLIONAIRE'S
INNOCENT BRIDE

CAITLIN CREWS

I can't believe that this is my 50th book for Mills & Boon! What a delightful ride it's been so far!

I want to thank Jane Porter, whose novels inspired me to try to write my first Modern Romance and whose friendship, mentorship and stalwart sisterhood have changed my life in a million glorious ways.

I want to thank my two marvelous editors, Megan Haslam and Flo Nicoll, who I simply couldn't do without. What would these stories be without your guidance, encouragement, excitement, fantastic editing and endless help? I shudder to think! And I want to thank the wonderful Jo Grant as well, for always being such a shining light for category romance and those of us who write it.

But most of all I want to thank you, my readers, for letting me tell you my stories.

Here's to fifty more!

xoxox

CHAPTER ONE

LAUREN ISADORA CLARKE was a Londoner, born and bred.

She did not care for the bucolic British countryside, all that monotonous green with hedges this way and that, making it impossible to *get* anywhere. She preferred the city, with all its transportation options endlessly available—and if all else failed, the ability to walk briskly from one point to the next. Lauren prized punctuality. And she could do without stiff, uncomfortable footwear with soles outfitted to look like tire tread.

She was not a hiker or a rambler or whatever those alarmingly red-cheeked, jolly hockey-sticks sorts called themselves as they brayed about in fleece and clunky, sensible shoes. She found nothing at all entertaining in huffing up inclines only to slide right back down them, usually covered in the mud that accompanied all the rain that made England's greenest hills that color in the first place. Miles and miles of tramping about for the dubious pleasure of "taking in air" did not appeal to her and never had.

Lauren liked concrete, bricks, the glorious Tube and abundant takeaways on every corner, thank you. The very notion of *the deep, dark woods* made her break out in hives.

Yet, here she was, marching along what the local innkeeper had optimistically called a road—it was little better than a footpath, if that—in the middle of the resolutely thick forests of Hungary.

Hive-free thus far, should she wish to count her blessings.

But Lauren was rather more focused on her grievances today.

First and foremost, her shoes were not now and never had been sensible. Lauren did not believe in the cult of *sensible shoes*. Her life was eminently sensible. She kept her finances in order, paid her bills on time, if not early, and dedicated herself to performing her duties as personal assistant to the very wealthy and powerful president and CEO of Combe Industries at a level of consistent excellence she liked to think made her indispensable.

Her shoes were impractical, fanciful creations that reminded her that she was a woman—which came in handy on the days her boss treated her as rather more of an uppity appliance. One that he liked to have function all on its own, apparently, and without any oversight or aid.

"My mother gave away a child before she married my father," Matteo Combe, her boss, had told her one fine day several weeks back in his usual grave tone.

Lauren, like everyone else who had been in the vicinity of a tabloid in a checkout line over the past forty years, knew all about her boss's parents. And she knew more than most, having spent the bulk of her career working for Matteo. Beautiful, beloved Alexandrina

San Giacomo, aristocratic and indulged, had defied reason and her snooty Venetian heritage when she'd married rich but decidedly unpolished Eddie Combe, whose ancestors had carved their way out of the mills of Northern England—often with their fists. Their love story had caused scandals, their turbulent marriage had been the subject of endless speculation and their deaths within weeks of each other had caused even more commotion.

But there had never been the faintest whisper of an illegitimate son.

Lauren had not needed to be told that once this came out—and it would, because things like this always came out eventually—it wouldn't be whispers they'd have to be worried about. It would be the all-out baying of the tabloid wolves.

"I want you to find him," Matteo had told her, as if he was asking her to fetch him a coffee. "I cannot begin to imagine what his situation is, but I need him media-ready and, if at all possible, compliant."

"Your long-lost brother. Whom you have never met. Who may, for all you know, loathe you and your mother and all other things San Giacomo on principle alone. This is who you think might decide to comply with your wishes."

"I have faith in you," Matteo had replied.

And Lauren had excused that insanity almost in that same instant, because the man had so much on his plate. His parents had died, one after the next. His fluffy-headed younger sister had gone and gotten herself pregnant, a state of affairs that had caused Matteo to take a swing at the father of her baby. A perfectly reasonable reaction, to Lauren's mind—but unfortunately, Matteo had taken said swing at his father's funeral.

The punch he'd landed on Prince Ares of Atilia had been endlessly photographed and videoed by the assorted paparazzi and not a few of the guests, and the company's board of directors had taken it as an opportunity to move against him. Matteo had been forced to subject himself to an anger management specialist who was no ally, and it was entirely possible the board would succeed in removing him should the specialist's report be unflattering.

Of course, Lauren excused him.

"Do you ever *not* excuse him?" her flatmate Mary had asked idly without looking up from her mobile while Lauren had dashed about on her way out the morning she'd left London.

"He's an important and very busy man, Mary."

"As you are always on hand to remind us."

The only reason Lauren hadn't leaped into *that* fray, she told herself now as she stormed along the dirt path toward God knew where, was because good flatmates were hard to find, and Mary's obsession with keeping in touch with her thirty thousand best friends in all corners of the globe on all forms of social media at all times meant she spent most of her time locked in her room obsessing over photo filters and silly voices. Which left the flat to Lauren on the odd occasions she was actually there to enjoy it.

Besides, a small voice inside her that she would have listed as a grievance if she allowed herself to acknowledge it, *she wasn't wrong, was she?*

But Lauren was here to carry out Matteo's wishes, not question her allegiance to him.

Today her pair of typically frothy heels—with studs and spikes and a dash of whimsy because she didn't own a pair of sensible shoes appropriate for mud and woods and never would—were making this unplanned trek through the Hungarian woods even more unpleasant than she'd imagined it would be, and Lauren's imagination was quite vivid. She glared down at her feet, pulled her red wrap tighter around her, thought a few unkind thoughts about her boss she would never utter out loud and kept to the path.

The correct Dominik James had not been easy to find.

There had been almost no information to go on aside from what few details Matteo's mother had provided in her will. Lauren had started with the solicitor who had put Alexandrina's last will and testament together, a canny old man better used to handling the affairs of aristocrats than entertaining the questions of staff. He had peered at her over glasses she wasn't entirely convinced he needed, straight down his nose as he'd assured her that had there been any more pertinent information, he would have included it.

Lauren somehow doubted it.

While Matteo was off tending to his anger management sessions with the future of Combe Industries hanging in the balance, Lauren had launched herself into a research frenzy. The facts were distressingly simple. Alexandrina, heiress to the great San Giacomo fortune, known throughout the world as yet another poor little rich girl, had become pregnant when she was barely fifteen, thanks to a decidedly unsuitable older boy she shouldn't have met in the first place. The family had discovered her pregnancy when she'd been unable to keep hiding it and had transferred her from the convent school she had been attending to one significantly more draconian.

The baby had been born in the summer when Alexandrina was sixteen, spirited away by the church, and Alexandrina had returned to her society life come fall as if nothing had happened. As far as Lauren could tell, she had never mentioned her first son again until she'd made provisions for him in her will.

To my firstborn son, Dominik James, taken from me when I was little more than a child myself, I leave one third of my fortune and worldly goods.

The name itself was a clue. James, it turned out, was an Anglicized version of Giacomo. Lauren tracked all the Dominik Jameses of a certain age she could find, eventually settling on two possibilities. The first she'd dismissed after she found his notably non–San Giacomo DNA profile on one of those ancestry websites. Which left only the other.

The remaining Dominik James had been raised in a series of Catholic orphanages in Italy before running off to Spain. There he'd spent his adolescence, moving from village to village in a manner Lauren could only describe as itinerant. He had joined the Italian Army in his twenties, then disappeared after his discharge. He'd emerged recently to do a stint at university, but had thereafter receded from public view once more.

It had taken some doing, but Lauren had laboriously tracked him down into this gnarled, remote stretch of Hungarian forest—which Matteo had informed her, after all her work, was the single notation made in the paper version of Alexandrina's will found among Matteo's father's possessions.

"That was what my father wrote on his copy of my mother's will," Matteo had said cheerfully. *Cheerfully*, as if it didn't occur to him that knowing the correct Dominik James was in Hungary might have been information Lauren could have used earlier.

She didn't say that, of course. She'd thanked him.

Matteo's father might have made notes on Alexandrina's will, but he'd clearly had no intention of finding the illegitimate child his wife had given away long before he'd met her. Which meant it was left to Lauren to not only make this trek to locate Dominik James in the first place, but also potentially to break the news of his parentage to him. Here.

In these woods that loomed all about her, foreign and imposing, and more properly belonged in a fairy tale.

Good thing Lauren didn't believe in fairy tales.

She adjusted her red wrap again, pulling it tighter around her to ward off the chill.

It was spring, though there was no way of telling down here on the forest floor. The trees were thick and tall and blocked out the daylight. The shadows were intense, creeping this way and that and making her feel...restless.

Or possibly it wasn't shadows cast by tree branches that were making her feel one way or another, she told herself tartly as she willed her ankles not to roll or her sharp heels to snap off. Perhaps it was the fact that she was here in the first place. Or the fact that when she'd told the innkeeper in this remote mountain town that she was looking for Dominik James, he'd laughed.

"Good luck with that," he had told her, which she

had found remarkably unhelpful. "Some men do not want to be found, miss, and nothing good comes of ignoring their issues."

Out here in these woods, where there were nothing but trees all around and the uneasy sensation that she was both entirely alone and not alone at all, that unhelpful statement felt significantly more ominous.

On and on she walked. She had left the village behind a solid thirty minutes ago, and that was the last she'd seen of anything resembling civilization. She tried to tell herself it was lucky this path didn't go directly up the side of the brooding mountains, but it was hard to think in terms of luck when there was nothing around but dirt. Thick trees. Birds causing commotions in the branches over her head. And the kind of crackling sounds that assured her that just because she couldn't see any wildlife, it didn't mean it wasn't there.

Watching. Waiting.

Lauren shuddered. Then told herself she was being ridiculous as she rounded another curve in her path, and that was when she saw it.

At first, she wasn't sure if this was the wooded, leafy version of a desert mirage—not that she'd experienced such a thing, as there were no deserts in London. But the closer she got, the more she could see that her eyes were not deceiving her, after all. There was a rustic sort of structure peeking through the trees, tucked away in a clearing.

Lauren drew closer, slowing her steps as the path led her directly toward the edge of the clearing. All she'd wanted this whole walk was a break from the encroaching forest, but now that there was a clearing, she found it made her nervous.

But Lauren didn't believe in nerves, so she ignored the sensation and frowned at the structure before her. It was a cottage. Hewn from wood, logs interlocking and tidy. There was smoke curling up from its chimney, and there was absolutely no reason that a dedicated city dweller like Lauren should feel something clutch inside her at the sight. As if she'd spent her entire life wandering around without knowing it, half-lost in forests of wood and concrete alike, looking for a cozy little home exactly like this one.

That was ridiculous, of course. Lauren rubbed at her chest without entirely meaning to, as if she could do something about the ache there. She didn't believe in fairy tales, but she'd read them. And if any good had ever come from seemingly perfect cottages slapped down in the middle of dangerous forests, well. She couldn't remember that story. Usually, an enchanted cottage led straight to witches and curses and wolves baring their teeth—

But that was when she noticed that the porch in front of the cottage wasn't empty as she'd thought at first glance. That one of the shadows there was a man.

And he was staring straight at her.

Her heart did something acrobatic and astonishing inside her chest, and she had the strangest notion that if she surrendered to it, it could topple her straight to the ground. Right there on that edge where the forest fought to take back the clearing.

But Lauren had no intention of crumpling.

No matter who was lurking about, staring at her.

"Mr. Dominik James?" she asked briskly, making her voice as crisp and clear as possible and projecting it across the clearing as if she wasn't the slightest bit unnerved, because she shouldn't have been.

Though she was standing stock-still, she couldn't help but notice. As if her legs were not necessarily as convinced as she was that she could continue to remain upright. Especially while her heart kept up its racket and ache.

The man moved, stepping out from the shadow of the porch into the sunlight that filled the clearing but somehow did nothing to push back the inky darkness of the forest.

It only made her heart carry on even worse.

He was tall. Much too tall, with the kind of broad shoulders that made her palms itch to…do things she refused to let herself imagine. His hair was dark and thick, worn carelessly and much too long for her tastes, but it seemed to make his strong, bold jaw more prominent somehow. His mouth was flat and unsmiling, yet was lush enough to make her stomach flip around inside her. He was dressed simply, in a long-sleeved shirt that clung to the hard planes of his chest, dark trousers that made her far too aware of his powerful thighs, and boots that looked as if they'd been chosen for their utility rather than their aesthetics.

But it was his eyes that made everything inside Lauren ring with alarm. Or maybe it was awareness.

Because they were gray. Gray like storms, just like Matteo's.

San Giacomo gray, Lauren thought, just like Alexandrina's had been. Famously.

She didn't need him to identify himself. She had no doubt whatsoever that she was looking at the lost San Giacomo heir. And she couldn't have said why all the tiny hairs on the back of her neck stood up straight as if in foreboding.

She willed herself to forge on.

"My name is Lauren Clarke," she informed him, trying to remember that she was meant to be efficient. Not…whatever she was right now, with all these strange sensations swishing around inside her. "I work for Matteo Combe, president and CEO of Combe Industries. If you are somehow unfamiliar with Mr. Combe, he is, among other things, the eldest son of the late Alexandrina San Giacomo Combe. I have reason to believe that Alexandrina was also your mother."

She had practiced that. She had turned the words over and over in her head, then gone so far as to practice them in the mirror this morning in her little room at the inn. Because there was no point hemming and hawing and beating around the bush. Best to rip the plaster off and dive straight in, so they could get to the point as quickly as possible.

She'd expected any number of responses to her little speech. Maybe he would deny the claim. Maybe he would launch into bluster, or order her away. She'd worked out contingency plans for all possible scenarios—

But the man in front of her didn't say a word.

He roamed toward her, forcing her to notice the way he moved. It was more liquid than it ought to have been. A kind of lethal grace, given how big he was, and she found herself holding her breath.

The closer he came, the more she could see the expression on his face, in his eyes, that struck her as a kind of sardonic amusement.

She hadn't made any contingency plan for that.

"When Mrs. Combe passed recently, she made provisions for you in her will," Lauren forced herself to continue. "My employer intends to honor his mother's wishes, Mr. James. He has sent me here to start that process."

The man still didn't speak. He slowed when he was face-to-face with Lauren, but all he did was study her. His gaze moved all over her in a way that struck her as almost unbearably intimate, and she could feel the flush that overtook her in reaction.

As if he had his hands all over her body. As if he was testing the smoothness of the hair she'd swept back into a low ponytail. Or the thickness of the bright red wool wrap she wore to ward off the chill of flights and Hungarian forests alike. Down her legs to her pretty, impractical shoes, then back up again.

"Mr. Combe is a man of wealth and consequence." Lauren found it was difficult to maintain her preferred crisp, authoritative tone when this man was so...close. And when he was looking at her as if she were a meal, not a messenger. "I mention this not to suggest that he doesn't wish to honor his commitments to you, because he does. But his stature requires that we proceed with a certain sensitivity. You understand."

She was aware of too many things, all at once. The man—Dominik, she snapped at herself, because it had to be him—had recently showered. She could see the suggestion of dampness in his hair as it went this way and that, indicating it had a mind of its own. Worse still, she could smell him. The combination of soap and warm, clean, decidedly healthy male.

It made her feel the slightest bit dizzy, and she was

sure that was why her heart was careening about inside her chest like a manic drum.

All around them, the forest waited. Not precisely silent, but there was no comforting noise of city life—conversations and traffic and the inevitable sounds of so many humans going about their lives, pretending they were alone—to distract her from this man's curious, penetrating, unequivocally gray glare.

If she believed in nerves, she'd have said hers were going haywire.

"I beg your pardon," Lauren said when it was that or leap away from him and run for it, so unsettled and unsteady did she feel. "Do you speak English? I didn't think to ask."

His stern mouth curled the faintest bit in one corner. As Lauren watched, stricken and frozen for reasons she couldn't begin to explain to herself, he reached across the scant few inches between them.

She thought he was going to put his hand on her—touch her face, or smooth it over her hair, or run one of those bluntly elegant fingers along the length of her neck the way she'd seen in a fanciful romantic movie she refused to admit she'd watched—but he didn't. And she felt the sharpest sense of disappointment in that same instant he found one edge of her wrap, and held it between his fingers.

As if he was testing the wool.

"What are you doing?" Lauren asked, and any hope she'd had of maintaining her businesslike demeanor fled. Her knees were traitorously weak. And her voice didn't sound like her at all. It was much too breathy. Embarrassingly insubstantial.

He was closer than he ought to have been, because

she was sure there was no possible way *she* had moved. And there was something about the way he angled his head that made everything inside her shift.

Then go dangerously still.

"A beautiful blonde girl walks into the woods, dressed in little more than a bright, red cloak." His voice was an insinuation. A spell. It made her think of fairy tales again, giving no quarter to her disbelief. It was too smoky, too deep and much too rich, and faintly accented in ways that kicked up terrible wildfires in her blood. And everywhere else. "What did you think would happen?"

Then he dropped his shockingly masculine head to hers, and kissed her.

CHAPTER TWO

HE WAS KISSING HER.

Kissing her, for the love of all that was holy.

Lauren understood it on an intellectual level, but it didn't make sense.

Mostly because what he did with his mouth bore no resemblance to any kiss she had ever heard of or let herself imagine.

He licked his way along her lips, a temptation and a seduction in one, encouraging her to open. To him.

Which of course she wasn't going to do.

Until she did, with a small sound in the back of her throat that made her shudder everywhere else.

And then that wicked temptation of a tongue was inside her mouth—*inside* her—and everything went a little mad.

It was the angle, maybe. His taste, rich and wild. It was the impossible, lazy mastery of the way he kissed her, deepening it, changing it.

When he pulled away, his mouth was still curved.

And Lauren was the one who was shaking.

She assured herself it was temper. Outrage. "You can't just...go about *kissing* people!"

That curve in his mouth deepened. "I will keep that

in mind, should any more storybook creatures emerge from my woods."

Lauren was flustered. Her cheeks were too hot and that same heat seemed to slide and melt its way all over her body, making her nipples pinch while between her legs, a kind of slippery need bloomed.

And shamed her. Deeply.

"I am not a storybook creature." The moment she said it, she regretted it. Why was she participating in whatever bizarre delusion this was? But she couldn't seem to stop herself. "Fairy tales aren't real, and even if they were, I would want nothing to do with them."

"That is a terrible shame. What are fairy tales if not a shorthand for all of mankind's temptations? Fantasies. Dark imaginings."

There was no reason that her throat should feel so tight. She didn't need to swallow like that, and she certainly didn't need to be so *aware* of it.

"I'm sure that some people's jobs—or lack thereof—allow them to spend time considering the merit of children's stories," she said in a tone she was well aware was a touch too prissy. But that was the least of her concerns just then, with the brand of his mouth on hers. "But I'm afraid my job is rather more adult."

"Because nothing is more grown-up than doing the bidding of another, of course."

Lauren felt off-kilter, when she never did. Her lips felt swollen, but she refused to lift her fingers to test them. She was afraid it would give him far too much advantage. It would show him her vulnerability, and that was unconscionable.

The fact she had any vulnerability to show in the first place was an outrage.

"Not everyone can live by their wits in a forest hut," she said. Perhaps a bit acerbically.

But if she expected him to glower at that, she was disappointed. Because all he did was stare back at her, that curve in the corner of his mouth, and his eyes gleaming a shade of silver that she felt in all those melting places inside her.

"Your innkeeper told me you were coming." He shifted back only slightly, and she was hyperaware of him in ways that humiliated her further. There was something about the way his body moved. There was something about him. He made her want to lean in closer. He made her want to reach out her hands and—

But of course she didn't do that. She folded her arms across her chest, to hold him off and hold herself together at the same time, and trained her fiercest glare upon him as if that could make all the uncomfortable feelings go away.

"You could have saved yourself the trouble and the walk," he was saying. "I don't want your rich boss and yes, I know who he is. You can rest easy. I'm not interested in him. Or his mother. Or whatever 'provisions' appeared in the wills of overly wealthy people I would likely hate if I'd known them personally."

That felt like a betrayal when it shouldn't have felt like anything. It wasn't personal. She had nothing to do with the Combe and San Giacomo families. She had never been anything but staff, for which she often felt grateful, as there was nothing like exposure to the very wealthy and known to make a person grateful for the things she had—all of which came without the scrutiny and weight of all those legacies.

But the fact this man didn't want his own birthright…rankled. Lauren's lips tingled. They felt burned, almost, and she could remember the way his mouth had moved on hers so vividly that she could taste him all over again. Bold and unapologetic. Ruthlessly male.

And somehow that all wrapped around itself, became a knot and pulled tight inside her.

"My rich boss is your brother," she pointed out, her voice sharper than it should have been. "This isn't about money. It's about family."

"A very rich family," Dominik agreed. And his gaze was more steel than silver then. "Who didn't want me in the first place. I will pass, I think, on a tender re-union brought about by the caprice of a dead woman."

Her heart lurched when he reached out and took her chin in his hand. She should have slapped him away. She meant to, surely.

But everything was syrupy, thick and slow. And all she could feel was the way he gripped her. The way he held her chin with a kind of certainty that made everything inside her quiver in direct contrast to that firm hold. She'd gone soft straight through. Melting hot. Impossibly…changed.

"I appreciate the taste," he rumbled at her, sardonic and lethal and more than she could bear—but she still didn't pull away from him. "I had no idea such a sharp blonde could taste so sweet."

And he had already turned and started back toward his cabin by the time those words fully penetrated all that odd, internal shaking.

Lauren thought she would hate herself forever for the moisture she could feel in her own eyes, when she hadn't permitted herself furious tears in as long as she could remember.

"Let me make certain I'm getting this straight," she threw at his back, and she certainly *did not* notice how muscled he was, everywhere, or how easy it was to imagine her own hands running down the length of his spine, purely to marvel in the way he was put together. *Certainly not.* "The innkeeper called ahead, which means you knew I was coming. Did he tell you what I was wearing, too? So you could prepare this Red Riding Hood story to tell yourself?"

"If the cloak fits," he said over his shoulder.

"That would make you the Big Bad Wolf, would it not?"

She found herself following him, which couldn't possibly be wise. Marching across that clearing as if he hadn't made her feel so adrift. So shaky.

As if he hadn't kissed her within an inch of her life, but she wasn't thinking about that.

Because she couldn't think about that, or she would think of nothing else.

"There are all kinds of wolves in the forests of Europe." And his voice seemed darker then. Especially when he turned, training that gray gaze of his on her all over again. It had the same effect as before. Looking at him was like staring into a storm. "Big and bad is as good a description as any."

She noticed he didn't answer the question.

"Why?"

Lauren stopped a foot or so in front of him. She found her hands on her hips, the wrap falling open. And she hated the part of her that thrilled at the way his gaze tracked over the delicate gold chain at her throat. The silk blouse beneath.

Her breasts that felt heavy and achy, and the nipples

that were surely responding to the sudden exposure to colder air. Not him.

She had spent years wearing gloriously girly shoes to remind herself she was a woman, desperately hoping that each day was the day that Matteo would see her as one for a change. He never had. He never would.

And this man made her feel outrageously feminine without even trying.

She told herself what she felt about that was sheer, undiluted outrage, but it was a little too giddy, skidding around and around inside her, for her to believe it.

"Why did I kiss you?" She saw the flash of his teeth, like a smile he thought better of at the last moment, and that didn't make anything happening inside her better. "Because I wanted to, little red. What other reason could there be?"

"Perhaps you kissed me because you're a pig," she replied coolly. "A common affliction in men who feel out of control, I think you'll find."

A kind of dark delight moved over his face.

"I believe you have your fairy tales confused. And in any case, where there are pigs, there is usually also huffing and puffing and, if I am not mistaken, blowing." He tilted that head of his to one side, reminding her in an instant how untamed he was. How outside her experience. "Are you propositioning me?"

She felt a kind of red bonfire ignite inside her, all over her, but she didn't give in to it. She didn't distract herself with images of exactly what he might mean by *blowing*. And how best she could accommodate him like the fairy tale of his choice, right here in this clearing, sinking down on her knees and—

"Very droll," she said instead, before she shamed

herself even further. "I'm not at all surprised that a man who lives in a shack in the woods has ample time to sit around, perverting fairy tales to his own ends. But I'm not here for you, Mr. James."

"Call me Dominik." He smiled at her then, but she didn't make the mistake of believing him the least bit affable. Not when that smile made her think of a knife, sharp and deadly. "I would say that Mr. James was my father, but I've never met the man."

"I appreciate this power play of yours," Lauren said, trying a new tactic before she could get off track again, thinking of *knives* and *blowing* and *that kiss*. "I feel very much put in my place, thank you. I would love nothing more than to turn tail and run back to my employer, with tales of the uncivilized hermit in the woods that he'd be better off never recognizing as his long-lost brother. But I'm afraid I can't do that."

"Why not?"

"Because it doesn't matter why you're here in the woods. Whether you're a hermit, a barbarian, an uncivilized lout unfit for human company." She waved one hand, airily, as if she couldn't possibly choose among those things. "If I could track you down, that means others will, as well, and they won't be nearly as pleasant as I am. They will be reporters. Paparazzi. And once they start coming, they will always come. They will surround this cabin and make your life a living hell. That's what they do." She smiled. Sunnily. "It's only a matter of time."

"I spent my entire childhood waiting for people to come," he said softly, after a moment that stretched out between them and made her...edgy. "They never did. You will forgive me if I somehow find it difficult to believe that now, suddenly, I will become of interest to anyone."

"When you were a child you were an illegitimate mistake," Lauren said, making her voice cold to hide that odd yearning inside her that made her wish she could go back in time and save the little boy he'd been from his fate. "That's what Alexandrina San Giacomo's father wrote about you. That's not my description." She hurried to say that last part, something in the still way he watched her making her stomach clench. "Now you are the San Giacomo heir you always should have been. You are a very wealthy man, Mr. James. More than that, you are part of a long and illustrious family line, stretching back generations."

"You could not be more mistaken," he said in the same soft way that Lauren didn't dare mistake for any kind of weakness. Not when she could see that expression on his face, ruthless and lethal in turn. "I am an orphan. An ex-soldier. And a man who prefers his own company. If I were you, I would hurry back to the man who keeps you on his leash and tell him so." There was a dangerous gleam in his eyes then. "Now, like a good pet. Before I forget how you taste and indulge my temper instead."

Lauren wanted nothing more. If being a pet on Matteo's leash could keep her safe from this man, she wanted it. But that wasn't the task that had been set before her. "I'm afraid I can't do that."

"There is no alternative, little red. I have given you my answer."

Lauren could see he meant that. He had every intention of walking back into this ridiculous cottage in the middle of nowhere, washing his hands of his birthright and pretending no one had found him. She felt a surge of a different kind of emotion at that, and it wasn't one that spoke well of her.

Because *she* wouldn't turn up her nose at the San Giacomo fortune and everything that went along with it. She wouldn't scoff at the notion that maybe she'd been a long-lost heiress all this time. Far better that than the boring reality, which was that both her mother and father had remarried and had sparkly new families they'd always seemed to like a whole lot more than her, the emblem of the bad decisions they'd made together.

They'd tossed her back and forth between them with bad grace and precious little affection, until she'd finally come of age and announced it could stop. The sad truth was that Lauren had expected one of them to argue. Or at least pretend to argue. But neither one of them had bothered.

And she doubted she would mind that *quite* so much if she had aristocratic blood and a sudden fortune to ease the blow.

"Most people would be overjoyed to this news," she managed to say without tripping over her own emotions. "It's a bit like winning the lottery, isn't it? You go along living your life only to discover that all of a sudden, you're a completely different person than the one you thought you were."

"I am exactly who I think I am." And there was something infinitely dangerous beneath his light tone. She could see it in his gaze. "I worked hard to become him. I have no intention of casting him aside because of some dead woman's guilt."

"But I don't—"

"I know who the San Giacomos are," Dominik said

shortly. "How could I not? I grew up in Italy in their shadow and I want no part of it. Or them. You can tell your boss that."

"He will only send me back here. Eventually, if you keep refusing me, he will come himself. Is that what you want? The opportunity to tell him to his face how little you want the gift he is giving you?"

Dominik studied her. "Is it a gift? Or is it what I was owed from my birth, yet prevented from claiming?"

"Either way, it's nothing if you lock yourself up in your wood cabin and pretend it isn't happening."

He laughed at that. He didn't fling back his head and let out a belly laugh. He only smiled. A quick sort of smile on an exhale, which only seemed to whet Lauren's appetite for real laughter.

What on earth was happening to her?

"What I don't understand is your zeal," he said, his voice like a dark lick down the length of her spine. And it did her no favors to imagine him doing exactly that, that tongue of his against her flesh, following the flare of her hips with his hands while he… She had to shake herself slightly, hopefully imperceptibly, and frown to focus on him. "I know you have been searching for me. It has taken you weeks, but you have been dogged in your pursuit. If it occurred to you at any point that I did not wish to be found, you did not let that give you the slightest bit of pause. And now you have come here. Uninvited."

"If you knew I was searching for you—" and she would have to think about what that meant, because that suggested a level of sophistication the wood cabin far out in these trees did not "—why didn't you reach out yourself?"

"Nobody sets himself apart from the world in a tiny cottage in a forest in Hungary if they wish to have visitors. Much less unannounced visitors." His smile was that knife again, a sharp, dangerous blade. "But here you are."

"I'm very good at my job." Lauren lifted her chin. "Remarkably good, in fact. When I'm given a task to complete, I complete it."

"He says jump and you aim for the moon," Dominik said softly. And she could hear the insult in it. It sent another flush of something like shame, splashing all over her, and she didn't understand it. She didn't understand any of this.

"I'm a personal assistant, Mr. James. That means I assist my employer in whatever it is he needs. It is the nature of the position. Not a character flaw."

"Let me tell you what I know of your employer," Dominik said, and his voice went lazy as if he was playing. But she couldn't quite believe he was. Or that he ever did, come to that. "He is a disgrace, is he not? A man so enamored of this family you have come all this way to make me a part of that he punched his sister's lover in the face at their father's funeral. What a paragon! I cannot imagine why I have no interest involving myself with such people."

Lauren really was good at her job. She had to remind herself of that at the moment, but it didn't make it any less true. She pulled in a breath, then let it out slowly, trying to understand what was actually happening here.

That this man had a grudge against the people who had given him to an orphanage was clear. Understandable, even. She supposed it was possible that he wasn't turning his nose up at what Matteo was offering so much as the very idea that an offer was being made at all, all these years too late to matter. She could understand that, too, having spent far more hours than she cared to admit imagining scenarios in which her parents begged for her time—so she could refuse them and sweep off somewhere.

And if she had been a man sent to find him, she supposed Dominik would have found a different way to get under her skin the same way he would any emissary sent from those who had abandoned him. All his talk of kissing and fairy tales was just more misdirection. Game-playing. Like all the scenarios she'd played out in her head about her parents.

She had to assume that his refusal to involve himself with the San Giacomos was motivated by hurt feelings. But if she knew one thing about men—no matter how powerful, wealthy or seemingly impervious—it was that all of them responded to hurt feelings as if the feelings themselves were an attack. And anyone in the vicinity was a collaborator.

"I appreciate your position, Dominik," she said, trying to sound conciliatory. Sweet, even, since he was the first person alive who'd ever called her that. "I really do. But I still want to restore you to your family. What do I have to do to make that happen?"

"First, you go wandering around the forbidding woods in a red cloak." Dominik shook his head, making a faint *tsk*-ing sound. "Then you let the Big Bad Wolf find out how you taste. Now an open-ended offer? My, my. What big eyes you have, little red."

There was no reason she should shiver at that, as if he was making predictions instead of taking part in this same extended game that she had already given too much of her time and attention.

But the woods were all around them. The breeze whispered through the trees, and the village with all its people was far, far away from here.

And he'd already kissed her.

What, exactly, are you offering him? she asked herself.

But she had no answer.

Looking at Dominik James made Lauren feel as if she didn't know herself at all. It made her feel like her body belonged to someone else, shivery and nervous. It made her tongue feel as if it no longer worked the way it should. She didn't like it at all. She didn't like *him*, she told herself.

But she didn't turn on her heel and leave, either.

"There must be something that could convince you to come back to London and take your rightful place as a member of the San Giacomo family," she said, trying to sound reasonable. Calmly rational. "It's clearly not money, or you would have jumped at the chance to access your own fortune."

He shrugged. "You cannot tempt me with that kind of power."

"Because, of course, you prefer to play power games like this. Where you pretend you have no interest in power, all the while using what power you do have to do the exact opposite of anything asked of you."

It was possible she shouldn't have said that, she reflected in some panic as his gaze narrowed on her in a way that made her...shake, deep inside.

But if she expected him to shout or issue threats, he

didn't. He only studied her in that way for another moment, then grinned. Slowly.

A sharp blade of a grin that made her stop breathing, even as it boded ill.

For her. For the heart careening around and battering her ribs.

For all the things she wanted to pretend she didn't feel, like a thick, consuming heat inside her.

"By all means, little red," he said, his voice low. "Come inside. Sit by my fire. Convince me, if you can."

CHAPTER THREE

DOMINIK JAMES HAD spent his entire life looking for his place in the world.

They had told him his parents were dead. That he was an orphan in truth, and he had believed that. At first. It certainly explained his circumstances in life, and as a child, he'd liked explanations that made sense of the orphanage he called home.

But when he was ten, the meanest of the nuns had dropped a different truth on him when she'd caught him in some or other mischief.

Your mother didn't want you, she had told him. *And who could blame her with you such a dirty, nasty sneak of a boy. Who could want you?*

Who indeed? Dominik had spent the next ten years proving to everyone's satisfaction that his mother, whoever she was, had been perfectly justified in ridding herself of him. He had lived down to any and all expectations. He'd run away from the orphanage and found himself in Spain, roaming where he pleased and stealing what he needed to live. He'd considered that happiness compared to the nuns' version of corporal punishment mixed in with vicious piety.

He had eventually gone back to Italy and joined the

army, more to punish himself than as any display of latent patriotism. He'd hoped that he would be sent off to some terrible war where he could die in service to Italy rather than from his own nihilistic urges. He certainly hadn't expected to find discipline instead. Respect. A place in the world, and the tools to make himself the kind of man who deserved that place.

He had given Italy his twenties. After he left the service, he'd spent years doing what the army had taught him on a private civilian level until he'd gotten restless. He'd then sold the security company he'd built for a tidy fortune.

Left to his own devices as a grown man with means, he had bettered himself significantly. He had gotten a degree to expand his thinking. His mind. And, not inconsiderably, to make sure he could manage his newfound fortune the way he wanted to do.

He didn't need his long-lost family's money. He had his own. The computer security company he had built up almost by accident had made him a very wealthy man. Selling it had made him a billionaire. And he'd enjoyed building on that foundation ever since, expanding his financial reach as he pleased.

He just happened to enjoy pretending he was a hermit in the Hungarian woods, because he could. And because, in truth, he liked to keep a wall or a forest between him and whatever else was out there. He liked to stay arm's length, at the very least, from the world that had always treated him with such indifference. The world that had made him nothing but bright with rage and sharp with fury, even when he was making it his.

Dominik preferred cool shadows and quiet trees these days. The comfort of his own company. Nothing brighter than the sun as it filtered down through the trees, and no fury at all.

Sharp-edged blondes with eyes like caramel who tasted like magic made him…greedy and hot. It made him feel like a long-lost version of himself that he had never meant to see resurrected.

He should have sent her away at once.

Instead, he'd invited her in.

She walked in front of him, those absurd and absurdly loud shoes of hers making it clear that she was not the sort of woman who ever expected to sneak up on a person, especially when they hit the wood of his porch. And he regretted letting her precede him almost at once, because while the cloak she wore—so bright and red it was almost as if she was having a joke at his expense—hid most of that lush and lean body from his view, it couldn't conceal the way her hips swung back and forth like a metronome.

Dominik had never been so interested in keeping the beat before in his life. He couldn't look away. Then again, he didn't try that hard.

When she got to his front door, a heavy wood that he'd fashioned himself with iron accents because perhaps he really had always thought of himself as the Big Bad Wolf, he reached past her. He pushed the door open with the flat of one hand, inviting her in.

But that was a mistake, too.

Because he had already tasted her, and leaning in close made him…needy. He wanted his mouth right there on the nape of her neck. He wanted his hands on the full breasts he'd glimpsed beneath that sheer blouse she wore. He wanted to bury his face between her legs, then lose himself completely in all her sweet heat.

Instead, all he did was hold the door for her. Meekly, as if he was some other man. Someone tamed. Civilized.

A hermit in a hut, just as he pretended to be.

He watched her walk inside, noting how stiff and straight she held herself as if she was terrified that something might leap out at her. But this cabin had been made to Dominik's precise specifications. It existed to be cozy. Homey.

It was the retreat he had never had as a boy, and he had absolutely no idea why he had allowed this particular woman to come inside. When no one else ever had.

He wasn't sure he wanted to think about that too closely.

"This is a bit of a shock," she said into the silence that stretched taut between them, her gaze moving from the thick rugs on the floor to the deep leather chairs before the fire. "I expected something more like a hovel, if I'm honest."

"A hovel."

"I mean no disrespect," she said, which he thought was a lie. She did that thing with her hand again, waving at him in a manner he could only call dismissive. It was…new, at least. "No one really expects a long-haired hermit to live in any kind of splendor, do they?"

"I am already regretting my hospitality," Dominik murmured.

He looked around at the cabin, trying to see it through the eyes of someone like Lauren, all urban chic and London snootiness. He knew the type, of course, though he'd gone to some lengths to distance himself from such people. The shoes were a dead giveaway. Expensive and pointless, because they were a statement. She wanted everyone who saw them to wonder how she walked in them, or wonder how much they cost, or drift away in a sea of their own jealousy.

Dominik merely wondered what it said about her that her primary form of expression was her shoes.

He also wondered what she was gleaning about him from this cabin that was his only real home. He didn't know what she saw, only what he'd intended. The soaring high ceilings, because he had long since grown tired of stooping and making himself fit into spaces not meant for him. The warm rugs, because he was tired of being cold and uncomfortable. The sense of airiness that made the cottage feel as if it was twice its actual size, because he had done his time in huts and hovels and he wasn't going back. The main room boasted a stone fireplace on one end and his efficient kitchen on the other, and he'd fashioned a bedchamber that matched it in size, outfitted with a bed that could fit two of him—because he never forgot those tiny cots he'd had to pretend to be grateful for in the orphanage.

"It's actually quite lovely," she said after a moment, a note of reluctant surprise in her voice. "Very…comfortable, yet male."

Dominik jerked his chin toward one of the heavy chairs that sat before his fire. Why there were two, he would never know, since he never had guests. But when he'd imagined the perfect cabin and the fireplace that would dominate it, he had always envisioned two cozy leather chairs, just like these. So here they were.

And he had the strangest sensation, as Lauren went and settled herself into one of them, that he had anticipated this moment. It was almost as if the chair had been waiting for her all this time.

He shook that off, not sure where such a fanciful notion had come from. But very sure that he didn't like it. At all.

He dropped into the chair opposite hers, and lounged there, doing absolutely nothing at all to accommodate her when he let his long legs take over the space between them. He watched her swallow, as if her throat was dry, and he could have offered her a drink.

But he didn't.

"I thought you intended to convince me to do your bidding," he said after a moment, when the air between them seemed to get thick. Fraught. Filled with premonition and meaning, when he wanted neither. "Perhaps things are different where you're from, but I would not begin an attempt at persuasion by insulting the very person I most wanted to come around to my way of thinking. Your mileage may vary, of course."

She blinked at him, and it was almost as if she'd forgotten why they were there. She shrugged out of that wrap at last, then folded her hands in her lap, and Dominik let his gaze fall all over her. Greedily. As if he'd never seen a woman before in all his days.

She was sweet and stacked, curvy in all the right places. Her hair gleamed like gold in the firelight, the sleek ponytail at her nape pulled forward over one shoulder. There was a hint of real gold at her throat, precisely where he wanted to use his teeth—gently, so gently, until she shuddered. Her breasts begged for a man's hands and his face between them, and it would take so little. He could shift forward, onto his knees, and take her in hand that easily.

He entertained a few delicious images of himself doing just that.

And she didn't exactly help matters when she pulled

that plump lower lip of hers between her teeth, the way he'd like to do.

But Dominik merely sank deeper into his chair, propped his head up with his fist, and ignored the demands of the hardest, greediest part of him as he gazed at her.

"I would be delighted to persuade you," she said, and did he imagine a certain huskiness in her voice? He didn't think he did. "I expected to walk in here and find you living on a pallet on the floor. But you clearly like your creature comforts. That tells me that while you might like your solitude, you aren't exactly hiding from the world. Or not completely. So what would it take to convince you to step back into it?"

"You have yet to explain to me why that is something I should want, much less consider doing."

"You could buy a hundred cabins and litter them about all the forests of Europe, for a start."

He lifted one shoulder, then let it fall. "I already have a cabin."

And properties across the globe, but he didn't mention that.

"You could outfit this cabin in style," she suggested brightly. "Make it modern and accessible. Imagine the opportunities!"

"I never claimed to live off the grid, did I? I believe you are the one who seems to think this cabin belongs in the Stone Age. I assure you, I have as much access to the modern world as I require."

Not to mention his other little shack that wasn't a shack at all, set farther up the mountainside and outfitted with the very latest in satellite technology. But that was yet another thing that could remain his little secret.

"You could buy yourself anything you wanted."

"All you have to offer me is money," he said after a moment. "I already told you, I have my own. But the fact that you continue to focus on it tells me a great deal about you, I think. Does this brother of mine not pay you well?"

She stiffened at that, and a crease appeared between her brows. "Mr. Combe has always been remarkably generous to me."

He found the color on her cheeks…interesting. "I cannot tell if that means he does or does not pay you what you deserve. What's the going rate for the kind of loyalty that would lead a woman clearly uncomfortable with the outdoors to march off into the forest primeval, deep into the very lair of a dangerous stranger?"

Her chin tipped up at that, which he should not have found as fascinating as he did. "I fail to see how my salary is your business."

"You have made anything and everything my business by delivering yourself to my door." And if he was overly intrigued by her, to the point his fingers itched with the need to touch her all over that curvy body until she sounded significantly less cool, that was his burden to carry. "Why don't you tell me why you're really here?"

The color on her cheeks darkened. The crease between her brows deepened. And it shouldn't have been possible to sit any straighter in that chair, but she managed it.

"I have already told you why I'm here, Mr. James."

"I'm sure they told you in the village that I come in at least once a week for supplies. You could have waited for me there, surrounded by creature comforts and room service. There was no need at all to walk through the woods to find me, particularly not in those shoes."

She looked almost smug then. As if he'd failed some kind of test.

"You don't need to concern yourself with my shoes," she said, and crossed her legs, which had the immediate effect of drawing his attention to the shoes in question. Just as she'd intended, he assumed. "I find them remarkably comfortable, actually."

"That you find them comfortable, or want me to think you do, doesn't mean they are. And it certainly doesn't make them practical for a brisk hike on a dirt path."

That gaze of hers was the color of a sweet, sticky dessert, and he wanted to indulge. Oh, how he wanted to indulge. Especially when her eyes flashed at him, once again letting him know that she felt superior to him.

Little did she know, he found that entertaining.

Even as it made him harder.

"In my experience, anyone who is concerned with the practicality of my footwear is casting about in desperation for some way to discount what I have to say," she told him. "Focus on my shoes and we can make sweeping generalizations about what sort of person I am, correct? Here's a little secret. I like pretty shoes. They don't say anything about me except that."

Dominik grinned, taking his time with it and enjoying it when she swallowed. Hard.

"Let me hasten to assure you that I'm in no way desperate. And I would love nothing more than to discount what you say, but you have said very little." He held her gaze. "Make your case, if you can. Explain to me why I should leave the comfort of my home to embrace this family who have ignored me for a lifetime already. I'm assuming it would be convenient for them in some way. But you'll understand that's not a compelling argument for me."

"I already told you. The paparazzi—"

He shook his head. "I think we both know that it is not I who would dislike it if your reporters found me here. I am perfectly content to deal with trespassers in my own way." He could see by the way her lips pressed together that she was imagining exactly how he might handle trespassers, and grinned wider. "But this rich boss of yours would not care for the exposure, I imagine. Is that not why you have made your way here, after searching for me so diligently? To convince me that his sudden, surpassing concern for my privacy is a genuine display of heretofore unknown brotherly love rather than his own self-interest?"

"Mr. Combe was unaware that he had a brother until recently," she replied, but her voice had gone cool. Careful, perhaps. "If anything should convince you about his intentions, it should be the fact that he reached out to find you as soon as he knew you existed."

"I must remember to applaud."

She didn't sigh or roll her eyes at that, though the tightness of her smile suggested both nonetheless. "Mr. Combe—"

"Little red. Please. What did you imagine I meant when I asked you to convince me? I've already had my mouth on you. Do you really think I invited you in here for a lecture?"

He didn't know what he expected. Outrage, perhaps. Righteous indignation, then a huffy flounce out of the cabin and out of his life. That was what he wanted, he assured himself.

Because her being here was an intrusion. He'd invited her in to make certain she'd never come back.

Of course you did, a sardonic voice inside him chimed in.

But Lauren wasn't flouncing away in high dudgeon. Instead, she stared back at him with a dumbfounded expression on her face. Not as if she was offended by his suggestion. But more as if…such a thing had never occurred to her.

"I beg your pardon. Is this some kind of cultural divide I'm unfamiliar with? Or do you simply inject sex into conversations whenever you get bored?"

"Whenever possible."

She laughed, and what surprised him was that it sounded real. Not part of this game at all.

"You're wasting your time with me." Her smile was bland. But there was a challenge in her gaze, he thought. "I regret to tell you, as I have told every man before you who imagined they could get to my boss through me, that I have no sexual impulses."

If she had pulled a grenade out of her pocket and lobbed it onto the floor between them, Dominik could not have been more surprised.

He could not possibly have heard her correctly. "What did you just say?"

There before him, his very own Little Red Riding Hood…relaxed back against the leather of her armchair. Something he also would have thought impossible moments before. And when she smiled, she looked like nothing so much as an oversatisfied cat.

"I'm not a sexual person," she told him, and Dominik

was sure he wasn't mistaking the relish in her voice. It was at odds with the sheen of something a whole lot like vulnerability in her gaze, reminding him of how she'd melted into his kiss. "It's a spectrum, isn't it? Some people's whole lives are completely taken over by the endless drive for sex, but not me. I've never understood all the fuss, to be honest."

He was half convinced he'd gone slack-jawed in astonishment, but he couldn't seem to snap out of it long enough to check. Not when she was sitting there talking such absolute nonsense with an expression that suggested to him that she, at least, believed every word she was saying.

Or, if he looked closer, *wanted* to believe it, anyway.

"You are aware that a kiss is a sexual act, are you not?"

"I've kissed before," Lauren said, and even shook her head at him, wrinkling up her nose as if he was... silly. Him. *Silly.* "I experimented with kissing when I was at university. As you do. That's how I know that it isn't for me."

"You experimented," he repeated as if that would make sense of what she was saying with such astonishing confidence—though, again, when he looked closer he was almost sure it was an act. Did he merely want it to be? "With kissing."

"As I said, there are all sorts. Not everyone is consumed with the urge to flail about naked. Not that there's anything wrong with that, but some of us have other things to think about." Her expression turned virtuous and Dominik was sure, then, that while she might believe what she was saying, he'd...rocked her foundations. She was overselling it. "More important things."

"And what, dare I ask, is it that consumes your thoughts if not…flailing?"

"You've made quite a few references to my being at Mr. Combe's bidding, but I take my job very seriously. It requires dedication. Focus and energy. I couldn't possibly siphon all of that off into all that trawling about from pub to pub every night, all to…"

"Flail. Naked."

"Exactly."

Dominik knew two things then as surely as he knew himself, his own capabilities and the fact she was lying about her own sexuality. One, if he wasn't misunderstanding what she was telling him, his sharp, majestically shoed and caramel-eyed blonde was a virgin. And two, that possibility made him hard.

Very nearly desperately so.

Because he already knew how she tasted. He'd heard the noises she'd made when he kissed her, and no matter what she told herself and was trying to tell him now, he did not believe that she had been unaffected.

He knew otherwise, in fact, as surely as he knew his own name.

"I can see how you're looking at me," Lauren said. She was still entirely too relaxed, to his way of thinking, leaning back in the leather chair as if she owned it. Clearly certain that she was in total control of this conversation. And him. "I don't understand why men take this as such a challenge."

Dominik's mouth curved. "Do you not?"

It was her turn to shrug. "I'm perfectly comfortable with who I am."

"Obviously." He settled back against his chair until he mirrored her. And for a long moment, every second of which he could feel in the place where he was hardest, he simply…studied her. Until her smile faded and she looked a whole lot less *certain*. "For reference, little red, people who are perfectly comfortable with themselves rarely mentioned their sexuality at all, much less bludgeon others over the head with it."

"Oh, I see." Her smile was bland again, and this time, distinctly pitying besides, though he could see the uncertainty she tried to hide. "You're upset because you think I'm saying this because I didn't like your kiss. Don't worry, Mr. James. I don't like any kissing. Not just yours."

"Of the two of us sitting here, Lauren," he said, enjoying the taste of her name in his mouth and the faint tremor in her sweet lower lip that told him the truths she couldn't, "I am the one who is actually comfortable with himself. Not to mention fully aware. I know exactly how much you liked my kiss without you needing to tell me all these stories."

"I'm glad to hear it." Her chin tipped up again, her eyes flashing as if that could hide the glint of doubt there. "I've seen this a thousand times before, you know. First, you will proposition me. Then you'll throw a temper tantrum when I decline your kind offer to see what I'm missing, with you as selfless guide. It's always the same old story."

"Is it? Why don't you tell it to me?"

She waved that hand of hers again. "You will want to kiss me, certain that a mere touch of your lips will awaken me to the joys of the flesh. It won't work, it's already failed to awaken me to anything, but you won't believe me. I can see you already don't believe me." She had the gall to try to look bored. "And if it's all the same to you, I'd rather fast-forward straight through that same old song and dance. It's tedious."

"If you insist." He found himself stroking his jaw with his fingers, because he knew that if he reached over to put them on her, she would take it as evidence of this theory of hers. This *song and dance.* No matter how much she liked it. "And what is on the other side? Once we're finished with all this fast-forwarding?"

"Why, business, of course. What else?"

"But in this case, little red, your business and mine are the same. Aren't you here to tempt me out of my humble cabin and into the great, wide world?"

"I am. All you need to do is name your price."

And Dominik was not an impulsive man. Not anymore. He had learned his lesson, time and again, in his misspent youth.

But there was something about this woman that got to him. She was still smiling at him in that pitying way when he'd already tasted her. When he knew better. He couldn't tell if she was lying to herself as well as him, but try as he might, he couldn't think of a single good reason to deny himself.

Not when Lauren Clarke was the most entertainment he'd had in ages.

And Dominik was no longer in the army. He no longer ran his security company. If he wanted to live his life in pursuit of his own amusement, he could now.

Even if it meant involving himself with the blood relations he had located when he was still in the army, but had never seen any reason to contact.

Because like hell would he go begging for scraps.

"You must let me kiss you whenever I wish," he said, keeping his voice mild so she wouldn't see that driving need for her inside him, greedy and focused. "That's it. That is my price. Agree and I will go wherever you wish for me to go and do whatever you wish me to do."

"Don't be ridiculous."

He could tell she thought he was kidding, because she didn't bother to sit up straight. Her cheeks didn't flush, and she was still smiling at him as if he was a fool. He felt like one. But that didn't make him want to take back what he'd said.

Especially when he could see the truth all over her, where she couldn't smile it away.

"This fairy tale obsession of yours has gone too far, I think. Let's return to the real world, which I understand is hard out here in an enchanted cottage in the deep, dark woods."

"The first thing you will learn about me is that I'm never ridiculous," Dominik told her, his voice low. "And when I make a promise, I keep it. Will you? You must let me kiss you whenever I like. However I like. This is a simple request, surely. Particularly for a person such as you who doesn't care one way or the other about kissing."

"I already told you, I know how this goes." She'd lost that smile, and was frowning at him then. "You say *kissing*, but that's not what you mean. It always goes further. There's always a hand."

"I do have a hand, yes. Two, in fact. You've caught me."

"One way or another it always leads back to the same discussion. When we can just have it now." She shook her head. "I'm just not sexual. That's the beginning and the end of it."

"Marvelous. Neither am I, by your definition."

Dominik gazed at her, and hoped he didn't look as wolf-ish as he felt. "Let's be nonsexual together."

She blinked at him, then frowned all the more. "I don't think…"

"We can make rules, if you like." It was his turn to smile, and so he did, all the better to beguile her with. "Rule number one, as discussed, you must allow me to kiss you at my whim. Rule number two, when you no longer wish me to kiss you, you will tell me to stop. That's it. That's all I want."

"But…" Her voice was faint. He counted that as a victory.

"And in return for this, little red, I will trot back to England on your boss's leash and perform the role of long-lost brother to his satisfaction. What will that entail, do you think? Will it be acts of fealty in public view? Or will it simply be an appropriate haircut, the better to blend with the stodgy aristocracy?"

She looked bewildered for a moment, and if Dominik had ever had the slightest inkling to imagine himself a good man—which he hadn't—he knew better then. Because he liked it. He liked her off balance, those soft lips parting and her eyes dazed as if she hardly knew what to do with herself.

Oh, yes, he liked it a great deal.

"I don't understand why, when you could have any-thing in the world, you would ask for…a kiss."

He could feel the edge in his own smile then. "You cannot buy me, Lauren. But you can kiss me."

She looked dubious, but then, after a moment or two, she appeared to be considering it.

Which Dominik felt like her hands all over his body, skin to skin.

"How long do you imagine this arrangement will go on?" she asked.

He shrugged. "As long as your Mr. Combe requires I remain in his spotlight, I suppose."

"And you give me your word that you will stop when I tell you to."

"I would not be much of a man if I did not," he said, evenly. "There are words to describe those who disregard such clear instructions, but *man* is not among them."

"All you want from the news that you're one of the richest men alive is a kiss," she said after another moment, as if she was selecting each word with care. "And I suppose you can't get much kissing out here in the middle of nowhere, so fair enough, if that's what you like. But why would you choose me?"

Dominik restrained himself—barely—from allowing his very healthy male ego to tell her that he had no trouble finding women, thank you very much. That this cabin was a voluntary retreat, not an involuntary sentence handed down from on high. But he didn't say that.

"What can I say? I've always had a weakness for Little Red Riding Hood."

She sighed, and at the end, it turned into a little laugh. "Very well. If that's what you want, I'll kiss you. But we leave for England as soon as possible."

"As you wish," Dominik murmured, everything in him hot and ready, laced through with triumph and something far darker and more intense he didn't want to name. Not when he could indulge it instead. "But first, that kiss. As promised."

CHAPTER FOUR

LAUREN WAS BAFFLED.

Why would anyone want a kiss—or, she supposed, a number of kisses—when there were so many other things he could have asked for? When the world was at his feet with the combined Combe and San Giacomo fortunes at his service?

She had met a great many men in her time, most of them through work, so she considered herself something of an expert in the behavior of males who considered themselves powerful. But she'd never met anyone like Dominik James. He had no power at all that she could see, but acted like he was the king of the world. It didn't make sense.

But it didn't matter. She wasn't here to understand the man. All she had to do was bring him back to London, and no matter that she felt a good deal less steady than she was pretending.

"Now?" she asked. She looked around the cabin as if sense was another rug tossed over the wood floor that could rise up and assert itself if she could only locate it. "You want me to kiss you *now*?"

Dominik lounged there before her, something glittering in the depths of his gray eyes, though the rest of his face was perfectly serious. He patted his knee with his free hand while what she thought was a smile *almost* changed the stern line of his mouth.

She pushed herself to her feet, still feeling that odd, liquid sensation all throughout her body. It was the way she felt when she slipped on a new pair of the shoes she loved. It made her feel…dangerous, almost. She'd always loved the feeling, because surely that was what a woman was meant to feel.

She'd long thought that if Matteo ever looked at her the way she looked at her shoes, she'd feel it. But he never had.

Lauren didn't understand why she felt it now, in a cabin in the middle of the woods. Or why Dominik was so determined to ruin it with more kissing.

Because the way he'd kissed her out there in the clearing had been different from her halfhearted youthful experiments, true. But Lauren knew it wouldn't last, because it never did. She knew that sooner or later he would grow ever more keen while she became less and less interested.

That was how it had always gone. She had discovered, time and again, that *thinking* about kissing was far preferable to the unfortunate reality of kissing.

She preferred this moment, right now. The moment when a man looked at her and imagined she was a desirable woman. Feminine straight through and capable of feeling all those things that real women did.

Capable of wanting and being wanted in return, when the truth was, *want* wasn't something that Lauren was capable of.

But he had already kissed her, and she told herself that was a good thing. She already knew what she'd agreed to. And it wasn't as if kissing Dominik had been as unpleasant as it always had been in the past.

Quite the opposite, a sly voice deep inside her very nearly purred.

She brushed that aside. It was the unexpected hike, no doubt, that had made her feel so flushed. So undone. She was unaccustomed to feeling those sorts of sensations in her body—all over her body—that was all.

"Perhaps you do not realize this, since you dislike kissing so much, but it is generally not done while standing across the room," Dominik said with that thread of dark amusement woven into his voice that she couldn't quite track. She could feel it, though. Deep inside all those places where the hike through the woods had made her sensitive.

She didn't understand that, either.

"Do you expect me to perch on your knee?" she asked without trying all that hard to keep the bafflement out of her voice.

"When and where I want," he said softly, gray eyes alight. "How I want."

And Lauren was nothing if not efficient. She had never been wanted, it was true, and was lacking whatever that thing was that could make her want someone else the way others did so readily. So she had learned how to be needed instead.

She had chosen to pursue a career as a personal assistant because there was no better way to be needed—constantly—than to take over the running of someone's life. She liked the high stakes of the corporate world, but what she loved was that Matteo truly *needed* her. If she didn't do her job he couldn't do his.

He needed her to do this, too, she assured herself. He wanted his brother in the fold, media-ready and compliant, and she could make it happen.

And if there was something inside her, some prickle of foreboding or something much sweeter and more dangerous, she ignored it.

The fire crackling beside them seemed hotter all of a sudden. It seemed to lick all over the side of her body, and wash across her face. She had never sat on a man's lap before, or had the slightest desire to do such a thing, and Dominik did nothing to help her along. He only watched her, no longer even the hint of a smile anywhere on his face, save the suggestion of one like silver in the endless gray of his gaze.

She stepped between his legs, thrust out before him in a way that encouraged her to marvel at both their length and strength, and then she eased herself down, putting out a hand to awkwardly prop herself against him as she sat.

"Do you plan to kiss me from this position?" She could swear he was laughing at her, though his face remained stern. "You are aware that kissing requires that lips meet, are you not?"

He had kissed her so smoothly out there at the edge of the woods. So easily. And now that Lauren thought about it, she had never been the one to initiate a kiss. She had always been a recipient. But there was something deep inside her that refused to tell him that.

It was the same something that bloomed with shame—because it had to be shame, surely—there between her legs.

She shouldn't have thought about that just then. Because she was sitting there on his hard, muscled thighs, so disastrously and intriguingly hot beneath her, and she couldn't seem to help herself from squirming against him.

And as she did she could feel something tense and electric hum to life in the space between them.

The fire was so hot. The air seemed to thicken with it as if there were flames dancing up and down the length of her arms, and the strangest part was that it didn't hurt. Burning should hurt, surely, but in this case it only seemed to make her breathless.

She eased closer to the wall of his chest, twisting herself so she was level with his face, and close enough to kiss him. Or she thought it was the correct distance, having never experimented with this position before.

He moved, but only a little, sliding his hands to grip her lightly at her waist.

Lauren couldn't think of a single reason why that should make her shudder.

Everywhere.

She gulped in a breath, aware of too many things at once. Those broad, blunt fingers of his like brands through the thin shell of her blouse. The iron forge of him beneath her, making her pulse and melt in places she'd never felt much of anything before.

This close, and knowing that a kiss was about to happen, she noticed things she hadn't before. The astonishing lines of his face, from his high cheekbones to the blade of his nose. The supremely male jut of his chin. And that thick, careless hair of his, that for some reason, she longed to sink her fingers into.

Her heartbeat slowed, but got louder. And harder, somehow, as if it was trying to escape from her chest.

She searched that implacable gray gaze of his, though

she couldn't have said what she was looking for. She burned still, inside and out, and the fire seemed to come at her from all sides, not just from the fireplace.

Slowly, carefully, she lowered her mouth.

Then she pressed her lips against his.

For one long beat, there was only that. The trembling inside her, the feel of his firm lips beneath hers.

There, she thought, with a burst of satisfaction. *This is even easier than I expected—*

But that was when he angled his head.

And he didn't kiss the way she had, halting and unsure.

He smiled against her mouth, then licked his way inside, and Lauren…ignited.

It was as if the cabin caught fire and she was lost in the blaze.

She couldn't seem to get close enough. Dominik's big hands moved from her waist, snaking around her back to hold her even more fiercely. And she moved closer to him, letting her own hands go where they liked. His wide, hard shoulders. His deliciously scratchy jaw. And all that gloriously dark hair of his, thick and wild, like rough silk against her palms.

And still he kissed her, lazy and thorough at once, until she found herself meeting each thrust of his wicked tongue. Until she was the one angling her head, seeking that deliriously sweet fit.

As if they were interlocking parts, made of flame, intoxicating and dangerous at once.

Lauren was the one meant to be kissing him, and this was nothing but a bargain—but she forgot that. She forgot everything but the taste of him. His strength and all that fire, burning in her and around her until she thought she might have become her own blaze.

And she felt a different kind of need swell in her then, poignant and pointed all at once. It swept her from head to toe, then pooled in the place between her legs where she felt that fire most keenly and pulsed with a need too sharp to be shame—

She wrenched her lips from his, startled and shamed and something else that keened inside her, like grief.

For a moment there was nothing but that near-unbearable fire hanging in the air between them. His eyes were silver and bright, and locked to hers. That mouth of his was a temptation and a terror, and she didn't understand how any of this was happening.

She didn't understand much of anything, least of all herself.

"You promised," Lauren managed to say.

And would likely spend the rest of her life reliving how lost and small she sounded, and how little she thought she had it in her to fix it. Or fight her way back to her efficient and capable self.

"I did," he agreed.

His voice was a dark rasp that made her quiver all over again, deep inside.

"You promised and you've already broken that promise. It didn't even take you—"

Her voice cut off abruptly when he ran his palm down the length of her ponytail and tugged it. Gently enough, so there was no reason she felt…scalded straight through.

"What promise did I break?" he asked mildly. So mildly she found herself frowning at him, because she didn't believe it.

"One kiss," she said severely.

And the way his mouth curved then, there below the knowing silver of his gaze, made her shiver.

"You're the one who has to say stop, little red. I don't remember you saying anything of the kind. Do you?"

And for another beat she was…stupefied.

Unable to breathe, much less react. Unable to do anything but gape at him.

Because he was quite right. She hadn't said anything at all.

In the next second she launched herself off him, leaping back in a way that she might have found comical, had she not been so desperate to put space between her and this man she'd made a devil's bargain with.

"This was our agreement, was it not?" Dominik asked, in that same mild voice. He only watched her—looking amused, she couldn't help but notice—as she scrambled around to the back of the chair facing him. "I hope you do not plan to tell me that you are already regretting the deal we made."

And Lauren did not believe in fairy tales. But it occurred to her, as she stared back at this man who had taken her over, made her a stranger to herself, and made her imagine that she could control something she very much feared was far more likely to burn her alive—she realized that she'd been thinking about the wrong kind of fairy tale.

Because there were the pretty ones, sweeping gowns and singing mice. Everything was princesses and musical numbers, neat and sweet and happy-ever-afters all around.

But those weren't the original fairy tales. There were darker ones. Older versions of the same stories, rich with the undercurrent of blood and sacrifice and grim consequences.

There were woods that swallowed you whole. Thorn bushes that stole a hundred years from your life. There were steep prices paid to devious witches, locked rooms that should have stayed closed, and children sent off to pay their fathers' debts in a variety of upsetting ways.

And there were men like Dominik, whose eyes gleamed with knowledge and certainty, and made her remember that there were some residents of hidden cottages who a wise girl never tried to find in the first place.

But Lauren hadn't heeded all the warnings. The man so difficult to find. The innkeeper's surprise that anyone would seek him out. That damned uninviting path through the woods.

She'd been so determined to prove her loyalty and capabilities to Matteo during this tough period in his life. If he wanted his long-lost older brother, she, by God, would deliver said older brother—once again making it clear that she alone could always, always give her boss what he needed.

Because she did so like to be needed.

She understood that then, with a lurch deep inside her, that once Matteo had mentioned Dominik this had always been where she would end up. This had always been her destination, which she had raced headlong toward with no sense of self-preservation at all.

This deal she'd made. And what it would do to her.

And she knew, with that same lurch and a kind of spinning sensation that threatened to take her knees out from under her, that it was already much too late to save herself from this thing she'd set in motion.

"I don't regret anything," she lied through lips that no longer felt like hers. And though it was hard to meet that too-bright, too-knowing gray gaze of his, she forced herself to do it. And to hold it. "But we need to head back to England now. As agreed."

His lips didn't move, but she could see that smile of his, anyway. All wolf. All fangs.

As if he'd already taken his first bite.

"But of course," he said quietly. "I keep my promises, Lauren. Always. You would do well to remember that."

CHAPTER FIVE

BY THE TIME they made it down out of the mountains in the hardy SUV Dominik kept back behind the cabin, then onto the private plane Lauren had waiting for them at the nearest airfield, she'd convinced herself that she'd simply…gotten carried away.

Once out of the woods, the idea that she'd let *trees* get into her head and so deep beneath her skin struck her as the very height of foolishness.

She was a practical person, after all. She wasn't excitable. It was simply the combination of hiking around in heels and a man who considered kissing currency.

It was the oddness that had gotten to her, she told herself stoutly. And repeatedly.

By the time they boarded the plane, she had regained her composure. She was comfortable on the Combe Industries jet. In her element. She bustled into her usual seat, responded to her email and informed Matteo that she had not only found his brother, but would also shortly be delivering him to England. As requested.

It was amazing how completing a few basic tasks made her feel like herself again.

As if that strange creature who had lost herself on a strange man's lap had never existed at all.

She threw herself into the work that waited for her, delighted that it gave her the opportunity to continue pretending she had no idea who that girl could have been, wild with abandon on Dominik's knee. The farther they got from those woods, the farther she felt from all those bizarre sensations that had been stirred up in her.

Fairy tales, for God's sake. What had she been thinking?

Lauren resolved that she would do whatever she could to make sure she never succumbed to that kind of nonsense again, no matter what bargains she might have made to get Dominik on this plane.

But all through the short flight, no matter how ferociously she tried to concentrate on her computer screen and all the piled-up emails that required her immediate attention, she was aware of Dominik. Of that considering gray gaze of his, following her every move.

And worse, the heat it kicked up in its wake, winding around and around inside her until she was terribly afraid it would make her burst wide open.

Fairy tale nonsense, she told herself sharply. People didn't *burst*, no matter what they felt.

That was what came of tramping about in the wilderness. Too much clean air obviously made her take leave of her senses.

Back in London she felt even more like herself. Calm. Competent. In control and happily surrounded by tarmac. Concrete. Brick buildings. All the solid reminders of the world she knew. And preferred to inhabit, thank you very much.

"England's greenest hills appeared to be rather more gray puddles and a procession of dingy, squat holdings,"

Dominik said from beside her in the backseat of the car that picked them up from the private airfield outside the city. "What a disappointment."

Lauren congratulated herself on her total lack of reaction to him. He was nothing more than a business associate, sharing a ride.

"Surely, you must know that it rains in England," she said, and even laughed. "A great deal, in fact."

She would have said nothing could possibly divert her attention from her mobile, but every cell in her body went on high alert when Dominik turned. And then faced her, making it impossible for her to pretend she didn't notice the way his big body took up more than his fair share of room in the car. His legs were too long, and those boots of his fascinated her. They seemed so utilitarian. So ruthlessly masculine.

And she couldn't even bring herself to think about the rest of him. All those long, smoothly muscled limbs. All that strength that simmered in him, that she was dimly surprised he managed to contain.

He didn't sit like a San Giacomo. He might look like one of them, or a feral version, anyway, but he was far more...elemental. Matteo and his sister, Pia, shared those same gray eyes, and they had both looked stormy at one time or another.

But Lauren couldn't help thinking that Dominik *was* a storm.

And her body reacted appropriately, prickling with unease—or maybe it was electricity.

Lightning, something in her whispered.

"What happens now?" Dominik asked, but his voice was lazy. Too lazy. She didn't believe he cared what happened now. Or ever. This was all a game to him.

Just as she was.

That thought flustered her, and she didn't make it any better by instantly berating herself for feeling anything at all. She tried to settle her nerves—the ones she didn't believe in—as she stared at him sternly.

"What would you like to happen?" she asked, and told herself she didn't know why she felt as if she were made of glass.

"I assume you are even now in the process of delivering me safely into the bosom of my warm, welcoming family." His smile was as sharp as she felt inside. Jagged. "Will there be a fatted calf?"

"I'm currently delivering you to the London headquarters of Combe Industries," Lauren replied as crisply as she could manage. Especially when all she could seem to concentrate on was his sardonic mouth. "Once there, you and I will wait for further instructions from Mr. Combe."

"Instructions." Dominik looked amused, if darkly. "I can hardly wait."

Lauren gripped her mobile in her hand and made herself stop when she realized she was making her palm ache.

"Mr. Combe is actually not in England at present," she said, and she didn't know why she was telling him this now. It could have waited until they were out of this car. Until they were safely in the office, the place where she felt most at home. Most capable. "He is currently in Perth, Australia. He's personally visiting each and every Combe Industries office."

If Lauren had expected Matteo to greet the news that she'd found his brother by leaping onto a plane and heading straight home to meet him, she kept that to herself. Because Matteo showed no sign of doing anything of the kind.

And it felt disloyal to find that frustrating, but she did.

"The great saint is not in England?" Dominik asked in mock outrage. "But however will we know how best to serve him if he isn't here to lay out his wishes?"

"He is perfectly able to communicate his wishes at all times," she assured him. "It's actually my job to make certain he can, no matter where he is. Don't worry. You'll know exactly what he expects of you."

That was the wrong thing to say, but she only realized that once the words were out there between them. And Dominik's eyes gleamed like silver as he gazed at her.

"Between you and me, little red, I have never done well with expectations." His voice was much too low for her peace of mind. It was too intimate. Too…insinuating. "I prefer to blaze my own trail."

"There is no blazing of trails in the San Giacomo family," she retorted with far more fervor than she'd intended. But she tried to keep her expression impassive when his dark brows rose. "The San Giacomos have existed in some form or another for centuries. They were once a major economic force in the Venetian Empire. While their economic force might have faded over time, their social capital has not."

"They sound marvelous," Dominik murmured. "And wholly without the blood of innocents on their hands, I am sure."

"I couldn't say what the San Giacomo family did in the eighth century, of course. But I think you'll find that Matteo Combe is a good and decent man."

"And you his greatest defender," Dominik said, and there was something less lazy about his voice then. "He must pay you very well indeed."

Her breath caught, but Lauren pushed on. "Whether you like expectations or do not, I'm afraid that the blood in your veins means you must meet them, anyway."

That dark amusement in Dominik's eyes made them bright against the rain outside. "Must I?"

"There are more eyes on the San Giacomos now than usual," Lauren said, and wasn't nervous. Why would she be nervous?

"It would seem to me that those eyes are more focused on the Combe side of the family," Dominik said after a moment. "Less Venetian economic might and more Yorkshire brawler, if I remember correctly."

Lauren didn't instantly bristle at that, which struck her as evidence of more disloyalty on her part.

"I'm not sure that there's any particular model of behavior for how a man is expected to act at his father's funeral," she said quietly. "Especially when his mother died only weeks before."

"I wouldn't know," Dominik replied, and that voice of his wasn't the least bit lazy any longer. "Having never met anyone who would claim me as a son in the first place."

Lauren felt as if he'd slapped her. Worse, she felt a flush of shame as if she deserved the slap he hadn't actually given her.

"Why don't we wait to have this argument—"

Dominik laughed. "Is this an argument? You have a thin skin indeed, little red. I would have called this a discussion. And a friendly one, at that."

"—until we are in the office, and can bring Mr.

Combe in on a call. Then he can answer all these questions instead of me, which seems more appropriate all around."

"Wonderful," Dominik said, and then his mouth curved in a manner she could only call challenging. "Kiss me."

And she had truly convinced herself that the bargain they'd struck had been some kind of hiking-inspired dream. A Hungarian-woods-inspired nightmare, made of altitude and too much wildlife. She had been sure it had all been some kind of hallucination. She'd been *sure*.

You're such a liar, a voice deep inside her told her.

"You can't mean now. Here."

"Will you make me say it every time?" Dominik's voice was soft, but the look on his face was intense. Intent. "When, where and how I want. Come now, Lauren. Are you a woman of your word or not?"

And it was worse, here. In the back of a town car like so many other town cars she'd ridden in, on this very same stretch of motorway. Here in England, on the outskirts of London, where she had always prided herself on her professionalism. Her competence and efficiency. Where she had built a life made entirely of needs she could meet, and did.

She still hadn't figured out who the Lauren Isadora Clarke was who had kissed this man with such abandon and hunger. But the intrusion of the fairy tale story she refused to accept was real into her life—her real life—was a shock. A jolt.

Her stomach went into free fall.

And Dominik shook his head sadly, making that *tsk*-ing sound as if he could read her every thought right there on her face. "You agreed to this bargain, Lauren. There's no use pretending you suddenly find the notion disgusting." His eyes were much too bright. "It is almost as if kissing makes you feel things, after all."

That shook her out of the grip of her horror—because that was what she told herself it had to be, that wild, spinning sensation that made her feel drunk from the inside out. It spurred her into action, and she didn't stop to question why it was she was so determined that this man never know that his kiss was the only one that had ever gotten to her at all.

It was information he never, ever needed to know.

She hardly wanted to admit it to herself.

And she threw herself across the backseat, determined that whatever else happened, she would do what she'd promised she would. That way, he would never know that she didn't want to do it *because* she wasn't bored by him the way she wanted to be.

Dominik caught her as she catapulted herself against his chest, then shifted her around so that she was sitting draped over his lap, which didn't help anything at all.

He was much too hard. There was the thick, enticing steel of his thighs, and that hard ridge that rose between them. And Lauren felt…soft and silly, and molten straight through.

And she was sitting on him again, caught in the way he gazed at her, silver in his eyes and his hands at her waist again.

"I know you know how to do this, little red," he said, his voice a soft taunt. "Or are you trying to play games with me?"

"I don't play games," she said stiffly.

As if, should she maintain proper posture and a chilly

tone, she might turn this impossible situation to her advantage. Or at least not drown in it.

"So many things you don't do," Dominik murmured, dark and sardonic. "Until you do."

She wanted him to stop talking. And she wanted to get this over with, as quickly as possible, and somehow those two things fused together and made it seem a terrific idea to lift her hands and use them to frame his face.

He stopped talking.

But the trouble with that was, her brain also stopped working.

She was entranced, suddenly and completely, with that strong jaw of his. She marveled at the feel of him, the rasp of his unshaven jaw beneath her palms.

A giant, hot fist she hadn't known lurked there inside her opened then. Slowly, surely, each finger of pure sensation unfurled, sending ribbons of heat to every last part of her.

She studied the sweep of his cheekbones, the lush shape of his mouth, and felt the shiver of it, so deep inside her it made parts she hadn't known she had bloom into life.

And she had the craziest urge to just…rub herself against him.

But instead, she kissed him.

She had some half-baked notion that she would deliver a peck, then retreat, but the moment she tasted him again she forgot about that. His mouth was a temptation and sin at once, and she was giddy with it. With his taste and heat.

With him, full stop.

So she angled her head and took the kiss deeper.

Just the way he'd taught her.

And for a little while, there was nothing at all but the slide of her tongue against his. The tangle of their breath, there in the close confines of the back of the car as it moved through the London streets.

Nothing but that humming thing that kicked up between them, encircling them both, then shuddering through Lauren until she worried, in some distant part of her head, that she would never be the same.

That she was already forever changed.

She kissed him and kissed him, and when she pulled her mouth away from his she fully expected him to follow her.

But he didn't.

She couldn't begin to describe the expression on his face then, or the steady sort of gleam in his gaze as he reached over and traced the shape of her mouth.

"Good girl," he said, and she knew without having to ask that he was deliberately trying to be provocative. "It's nice to know that you can keep your promise even after you get what you want."

"I am a woman of my word, Mr. James," she said crisply, remembering herself as she did.

And suddenly the fact that she was sitting on him, aware of all those parts of him pressed so intimately against her, was unbearable.

She scrambled off him and had the sinking suspicion that he let her go. And then watched her as if he could see straight through her.

And that was the thing. She believed he could.

It was unacceptable.

"The only thing you need to concern yourself about is the fact that you will soon be meeting your family for the first time," she said, frowning at him. "It wouldn't be surprising if you had some feelings around that."

"I have no feelings at all about that."

"I understand you may wish—"

"You do not understand." His voice was not harsh, but that somehow made the steel in it more apparent. "I was raised in an orphanage, Lauren. As an orphan. That means I was told my parents were dead. When I was older, I learned that they might very well be alive, but they didn't want me, which I believed, given no one ever came to find me. I don't know what tearful, emotional reunion you anticipate I'm about to have with these people."

Lauren was horrified by the part of her that wanted to reach over to him again. This time, just to touch him. It was one more thing that didn't make sense.

"You're right, I can't understand. But I do know that Mr. Combe will do everything in his power to make sure this transition is easy for you."

"You are remarkably sure of your Mr. Combe. And his every thought."

"I've worked for him for a long time."

"With such devotion. And what exactly has he done to deserve your undying support?"

She flexed her toes in her shoes, and she couldn't have said why that made her feel so obvious, suddenly. Silly straight through, because he was looking at her. As if he could see every last thing about her, laid out on a plate before him.

Lauren didn't want to be known like that. The very notion was something like terrifying.

"I see," Dominik said, and there was a different sort of darkness in his voice then. "You are not sexual, you tell me with great confidence, but you are in love with your boss. How does that work, exactly?"

"I'm not in…" She couldn't finish the sentence, so horrified was she. "And I would never…" She wanted to roll down the window, let the cool air in and find her breath again, but she couldn't seem to move. Her limbs weren't obeying her commands. "Matteo Combe is one of the finest men I have ever known. I enjoy working for him, that's all."

She would never have said that she was in love with him. And she would certainly never have thought about him in any kind of sexual way. That seemed like a violation of all the years they'd worked together.

All she wanted—all she'd ever wanted—was for him to appreciate her. As a woman. To see her as something more than his walking, talking calendar.

"And this paragon of a man cannot stir himself to return home to meet the brother you claim he is so dedicated to? Perhaps, Lauren, you do not know the man you love so much as well as you think."

"I know him as well as I need to."

"And I know he's never tasted you," Dominik said with all his dark ruthlessness. It made her want to cry. It made her want to…*do something* with all that restlessness inside her. "Has he?"

Lauren could barely breathe. Her cheeks were so red she was sure they could light up the whole of the city on their own.

"Not answering the question is an answer all its own, little red," Dominik murmured, his face alight with what she very much feared was satisfaction.

And she was delighted—relieved beyond measure— that the car pulled up in front of the Combe Industries building before she was forced to come up with some kind of reply.

But she didn't pretend it was anything but a reprieve, and likely a temporary one, when she pushed open the door and threw herself out into the blessedly cool British evening.

Where she tried—and failed, again and again—to catch her breath and recover from the storm that was Dominik James.

CHAPTER SIX

THERE WAS NO doubt at all that the man on the video screen was Dominik's brother. It was obvious from the shape of his jaw to the gray of his eyes. His hair was shorter, and every detail about him proclaimed his wealth and high opinion of himself. The watch he wore that he wasn't even bothering to try to flash. The cut of his suit. The way he sat as if the mere presence of his posterior made wherever he rested it a throne.

This was the first blood relative Dominik had ever met, assuming a screen counted as a meeting. This… aristocrat.

He couldn't think of a creature more diametrically opposed to him. He, who had suffered and fought for every scrap he'd ever had, and a man who looked as if he'd never blinked without the full support of a trained staff.

They stared at each other for what seemed like another lifetime or two.

Dominik stood in Lauren's office, which was sprawling and modern and furnished in such a way to make certain everyone who entered it knew that she was very important in her own right—and even more so, presumably, as the gatekeeper to the even more massive and dramatically appointed office beyond.

Matteo Combe's office, Dominik did not have to be told.

His only brother, so far as he knew. The man who had received all the benefit of the blood they shared, while Dominik had been accorded all the shame.

Matteo Combe, the man whose bidding Lauren did without question.

Dominik decided he disliked the man on the screen before him. Intensely.

"I would have known you anywhere," Matteo said after they'd eyed each other a good long while.

It would have pained Dominik to admit that he would have known Matteo, too—it was the eyes they shared, first and foremost, and a certain similarity in the way they held themselves—so he chose not to admit it.

"Brother," Dominik replied instead, practically drawling out the word. Making it something closer to an insult. "What a pleasure to almost meet you."

And when Lauren showed him out of the office shortly after that tender reunion, Dominik took a seat in the waiting area that was done up like the nicest and most expensive doctor's office he'd ever seen, and reflected on how little he'd thought about this part. The actually having family, suddenly, part.

Because all he'd thought about since she'd walked into his clearing was Lauren.

When he'd searched for his parents, he'd quickly discovered that the young man who'd had the temerity to impregnate an heiress so far above his own station had died in an offshore oil rig accident when he was barely twenty. An oil rig he'd gone to work on because he couldn't remain in Europe, pursuing his studies, after his relationship with Alexandrina had been discovered.

And when Dominik had found all the Combes and San Giacomos with precious little effort—which, of course, meant they could have done the same—he'd had wanted nothing to do with them. Because he wanted nothing from them—look what they'd done to the boy who'd fathered him. They had gotten rid of both of them, in one way or another, and Dominik had risen from the trash heap where they'd discarded him despite that abandonment. His mother's new boy and girl, who had been pampered and coddled and cooed over all this time in his stead, were nothing to him. What was the point of meeting with them to discuss Alexandrina's sins?

He'd been perfectly content to excel on his own terms, without any connection to the great families who could have helped him out of the gutter, but hadn't. Likely because they'd been the ones to put him there.

But it hadn't occurred to him to prepare himself to look into another man's face and see...his own.

It was disconcerting, to put it mildly.

That they had different fathers was evident, but there was no getting around the fact that he and Matteo Combe shared blood. Dominik scowled at the notion, because it sat heavily. Too heavily.

And then he transferred that scowl back to the screen inside Lauren's office, where Matteo was still larger than life and Lauren stood before him, arguing.

He didn't have to be able to hear a word she said to know she was arguing. He knew some of her secrets now. He knew the different shapes she made with that mouth of hers and the crease between her brows that broadcast her irritation. He certainly knew what she looked like when she was agitated.

And he found he didn't much care for the notion that whatever she called it or didn't call it, she had a thing for her boss.

Her boss. His brother.

"Is he one of the ones you've experimented with?" he asked her when she came out of the office, the screen finally blank behind her.

She was frowning even more fiercely than before, which he really shouldn't have found entertaining, especially when he hadn't had the pleasure of causing it. He lounged back in his seat as if it had been crafted specifically for him and regarded her steadily until she blinked. In what looked like incomprehension.

"I already declined to dignify that question with a response."

"Because dignity is the foremost concern here. With your boss." He refused to call the man *Mr. Combe* the way she did. And calling him by his Christian name seemed to suggest that they had more of a personal relationship—or any personal relationship, for that matter—than Dominik was comfortable having with anyone who shared his blood. "I want to know if he was one of your kissing experiments."

Lauren maintained her blank expression for a moment.

But then, to his eternal delight, she went pink and he couldn't seem to keep from wondering about all the other, more exciting ways he could make her flush like that.

"Certainly not." Her voice was frigid, but he'd tasted her. He knew the ice she tried to hide behind was a lie. "I told you, I admire him. I enjoy the work we do together. I have never *kissed*—"

She cut herself off, then pulled herself up straight. It only made Dominik wonder what she might have said if she hadn't stopped herself. "You and I have far more serious things to talk about than kissing experiments, Mr. James."

"I have always found kissing very serious business indeed. Would you like me to demonstrate?"

That pink flush deepened and he wanted to know where it went. If it changed as it lowered to her breasts, and what color her nipples were. If it made it to her hips, her thighs. And all that sweetness in between. He wanted to peel off that soft silk blouse she wore and conduct his own experiments, at length.

And the fact that thinking about Lauren Clarke's naked body was far preferable to him than considering the fact he'd met his brother, more or less, did not escape him. Dominik rarely hid from himself.

But he had no need, and less desire, to tear himself open and seek out the lonely orphan inside.

"Mr. Combe thinks it best that we head to Combe Manor. It is the estate in Yorkshire where his father's family rose to prominence. He understands you are not a Combe. But he thinks it would cause more comment to bring you directly to any of the San Giacomo holdings in Italy at this point."

Dominik understood that *at this point* was the most important part of Lauren's little speech. That and the way she delivered it, still standing in her own doorway too stiffly, her voice a little too close to nervous. He studied her and watched her grow even more agitated—and then try to hide it.

It was the fact that she wanted to hide her reactions from him that made him happiest of all, he thought.

"I don't know who you think is paying such close attention to me," Dominik said after a moment. "No one has noticed that I bear more than a passing resemblance to a member of the San Giacomo family in my entire lifetime so far. I cannot imagine that will change all of a sudden."

"It will change in an instant should you be found in a San Giacomo residence, looking as you do, as the very ghost of San Giacomos past."

He inclined his head. Slightly. "I am very good at living my life away from prying eyes, little red. You may have noticed."

"Those days are over now." She stood even straighter, and he had the distinct impression she was working herself up to say something else. "You may not feel any sense of urgency, but I can tell you that the clock is ticking. It's only a matter of time before Alexandrina's will is leaked, because these things are always leaked. Once it is, the paparazzi will tear apart the earth to find you. We need to be prepared for when that happens."

"I feel more than prepared already. In the sense of not caring."

"There are a number of things it would make more sense for us to do now, before the world gets its teeth into you."

"How kinky," he murmured, just to please himself.

And better still, to make her caramel eyes flash with that temper he suspected was the most honest thing about her.

"First, we must make your exterior match the San Giacomo blood that runs in your veins."

He found his mouth curving. "Are you suggesting a makeover? Have I strayed into a fairy tale, after all?"

"I certainly wouldn't call it that. A bit of tailoring and a new wardrobe, that's all. Perhaps a lesson or two in minor comportment issues that might arise. And a haircut, definitely."

Dominik's grin was sharp and hot. "Why, Lauren. Be still my heart. Am I the Cinderella in this scenario? I believe that makes you my Princess Charming."

"There's no such thing as a Princess Charming." She sniffed. "And anyway, I believe my role here is really as more of a Fairy Godmother."

"I do not recall Cinderella and her Fairy Godmother ever being attached at the lips," he said silkily. "But perhaps your fairy tales are more exciting than mine ever were."

"I hate fairy tales," she threw at him. "They're strange little stories designed to make children meek and biddable and responsible for the things that happen to them when they're not. And also, we need to get married."

That sat there between them, loud and not a little mad.

Dominik's gaze was fused to hers and, sure enough, that flush was deepening. Darkening.

"I beg your pardon." He lingered over each word, almost as if he really was begging. Not that he had any experience with such things. And there was so much to focus on, but he had to choose. "All this urban commotion must be getting to me." He made a show of looking all around the empty office, then, because he had never been without a flair for the dramatic when it suited him—and this woman brought it out in him in spades. "Did you just ask me to marry you?"

"I'm not *asking* you, personally. I'm telling you that

Mr. Combe thinks it's the best course of action. First, it will stop the inevitable flood of fortune hunters who will come out of the woodwork once they know you exist before they think to start. Second, it will instantly make you seem more approachable and civilized, because the world thinks married men are less dangerous, somehow, than unattached ones. Third, and most important, it needn't be real in any sense but the boring legalities. And we will divorce as soon as the furor settles."

Dominik only gazed back at her, still and watchful.

"Come now, Lauren. A man likes a little romance, not a bullet-pointed list. The very least you could do is bend a knee and mouth a sweet nothing or two."

"I'm not *proposing* to you!" Her veneer slipped at that, and her face reddened. "Mr. Combe thinks—"

"Will I be marrying my own brother?" He lay his hand over his heart in mock astonishment. "What sort of family *is* this?"

He thought her head might explode. He watched her hands curl into fists at her sides as if that alone could keep her together.

"You agreed to do whatever was asked of you," she reminded him, fiercely. "Don't tell me that you're the one who's going to break our deal. Now. After—"

After kissing him repeatedly, he knew she meant to say, but she stopped herself.

The more he stared back at her without saying a word, the more agitated she became. And the more he enjoyed himself, though perhaps that made him a worse man than even he'd imagined. And he'd spent a great quantity of time facing his less savory attributes head-on, thanks in part to the ministrations of the nuns who had taught him shame and how best to hate himself for existing. The army had taken care of the rest.

These days Dominik was merrily conversant on all his weaknesses, but Lauren made him…something else again.

But that was one more thing he didn't want to focus on.

"What would be the point of a marriage that wasn't real?" he asked idly. "The public will need to have reason to believe it's real for it to be worth bothering, no?"

The truth was that Dominik had never thought much about marriage one way or the other. Traditional family relationships weren't something he had ever seen modeled in the orphanage or on the streets in Spain. He had no particular feelings about the state of marriage in any personal sense, except that he found it a mystifying custom, this strange notion that two people should share their lives. Worse, themselves.

And odder still, call it love—of all things—while they did it.

What Dominik knew of love was what the nuns had doled out in such a miserly way, always shot through with disappointment, too many novenas and demands for better behavior. Love was indistinguishable from its unpleasant consequences and character assassinations, and Dominik had been much happier when he'd left all that mess and failure behind him.

He had grown used to thinking of himself as a solitary being, alone by choice rather than circumstance. He liked his own company. He was content to avoid others. And he enjoyed the peace and quiet that conducting his affairs to his own specifications, with no outside opinion and according to his own wishes and whims, afforded him. He was answerable to no one and chained to nothing.

The very notion of marrying anyone, for any reason, should have appalled him.

But it didn't.

Not while he gazed at this woman before him—

That pricked at him, certainly. But not enough to stop. Or leave, the way he should have already.

He told himself it was because this was a game, that was all. An amusement. What did he care about the San Giacomo reputation or public opinion? He didn't.

But he did like the way Lauren Clarke tasted when she melted against him. And it appeared he liked toying with her in between those meltings, too.

"What we're talking about is a publicity stunt, nothing more," she told him, frowning all the while. "You understand what that means, don't you? There's nothing real about it. It's entirely temporary. And when it ends, we will go our separate ways and pretend it never happened."

"You look distressed, little red," he murmured, because all she seemed to do as she stood there before him was grow redder and stiffer, and far more nervous, if the way she wrung her hands together was any indication.

He didn't think she had the slightest idea what she was doing. Which was fair enough, as neither did he. Evidently. Since he was still sitting here, lounging about in the sort of stuffy corporate office he'd sworn off when he'd sold his company, as if he was obedient. When he was not. Actually subjecting himself to this charade.

Participating in it wholeheartedly, in point of fact, or he never would have invited her into his cabin. Much less left it in her company—then flown off to rainy, miserable England.

"I wouldn't call myself distressed." But her voice told him otherwise. "I don't generally find business concerns *distressing*. Occasionally challenging, certainly."

"And yet I am somehow unconvinced." He studied the way she stood. The way she bit at her lower lip. Those hands that telegraphed the feelings she claimed not to have. "Could it be that your Mr. Combe, that paragon of virtue and all that is wise and true in an employer by your reckoning, has finally pushed you too far?"

"Of course not." She seemed to notice what she was doing with her hands then, because she dropped them back to her sides. Then she drew herself up in that way she did, lifted her chin and met his gaze. With squared shoulders and full-on challenge in her caramel-colored eyes—which, really, he shouldn't have found quite as entertaining as he did. What was it about this woman? Why did he find her so difficult to resist? He, who had made a life out of resisting everything? "Perhaps you've already forgotten, but you promised that you would do whatever was asked of you."

He stopped trying to control his grin. "I recall my promises perfectly, thank you. I am shocked and appalled that you think so little of the institution of marriage that you would suggest wedding me in some kind of cold-blooded attempt to fool the general populace, all of whom you appear to imagine will be hanging on our every move."

He shook his head at her as if disappointed unto his very soul at what she had revealed here, and had the distinct pleasure of watching her grit her teeth.

"I find it difficult to believe that you care one way

or the other," she said after a moment. "About fooling anyone for any reason. And, for that matter, about marriage."

"I don't." He tilted his head to one side. "But I suspect you do."

He thought he'd scored a hit. She stiffened further, then relaxed again in the next instant as if determined not to let him see it. And then her cheeks flamed with that telltale color, which assured him that yes, she cared.

But a better question was, why did he?

"I don't have any feelings about marriage at all," she declared in ringing tones he couldn't quite bring himself to believe. "It was never something I aspired to, personally, but I'm not opposed to it. I rarely think about it at all, to be honest. Are you telling me that you lie awake at night, consumed with fantasies about your own wedding, Mr. James?"

"Naturally," he replied. And would have to examine, at some point, why he enjoyed pretending to be someone completely other than who he was where this woman was concerned. Purely for the pleasure of getting under her skin. He smiled blandly. "Who among us has not dreamed of swanning down an expensive aisle, festooned in tulle and lace, for the entertainment of vague acquaintances?"

"Me," she retorted at once. And with something like triumph in her voice.

"Of course not, because you are devoid of feelings entirely, as you have taken such pains to remind me."

"I'm not sentimental." Except she looked so deeply pleased with herself just then it looked a whole lot like an emotion, whether she wanted to admit such things or not. "I apologize if you find that difficult to accept."

"You have no feelings about marriage. Sex. Even kissing, no matter how you react while doing it. You're an empty void, capable only of doing the bidding of your chosen master. I understand completely, Lauren."

That she didn't like that description was obvious by the way she narrowed her eyes, and the way she flattened her lips. Dominik smiled wider. Blander.

"How lucky your Mr. Combe is to have found such devotion, divorced of any inconvenient sentiment on your part. You might as well be a robot, cobbled together from spare parts for the singular purpose of serving his needs."

If her glare could have actually reached across the space between them and struck him then, Dominik was sure he would have sustained mortal blows. What he was less certain of was why everything in him objected to thinking of her as another man's. In any capacity.

"What I remember of my parents' marriage is best not discussed in polite company," she said, her voice tight. He wondered if she knew how the sound betrayed her. How it broadcast the very feelings she pretended not to possess. "They divorced when I was seven. And they were both remarried within the year, which I didn't understand until later meant that they had already moved on long before the ink was dry on their divorce decree. The truth is that they only stayed as long as they did because neither one wanted to take responsibility for me." She shook her head, but more as if she was shaking something off than negating it. "Believe me, I know better than anyone that most marriages are nothing but a sham. No matter how much tulle and expense there might be. That doesn't make me a robot. It makes me realistic."

Something in the way she said that clawed at him, though he couldn't have said why. Or didn't want to know why, more accurately, and accordingly shoved it aside.

"Wonderful," he said instead. "Then you will enjoy our sham of a marriage all the more, in all its shabby realism."

"Does that mean you'll do it, then?"

And he didn't understand why he wanted so badly to erase that brittleness in her tone. Why he wanted to reach out and touch her in ways that had nothing to do with the fire in him, but everything to do with that hint of vulnerability he doubted she knew was so visible. In the stark softness of her mouth. In the shadows in her eyes.

"I will do it," he heard himself say. "For you."

And every alarm he'd ever wired there inside him screeched an alert then, at full volume.

Because Dominik did not do things for other people. No one was close enough to him to ask for or expect that kind of favor. No one got close to him. And in return for what he'd always considered peace, he kept himself at a distance from everyone else. No obligations. No expectations.

But there was something about Lauren, and how hard she was clearly fighting to look unfazed in the face of her boss's latest outrageous suggestion. As if an order to marry the man's unknown half brother was at all reasonable.

You just agreed to it, a voice in him pointed out. *So does it matter if it's reasonable?*

One moment dragged on into another, and then it was too late to take the words back. To qualify his acceptance. To make it clear that no matter what he might have said, he hadn't meant it to stand as any form of obligation to this woman he barely knew.

Much less that boss of hers who shared his blood.

"For me?" she asked, and it was as if she, too, had suddenly tumbled into this strange, hushed space Dominik couldn't seem to snap out of.

He didn't want to call it sacred. But he wasn't sure what other word there was for it, when her caramel eyes gleamed like gold and his chest felt tight.

"For you," he said, and he had the sense that he was digging his own grave, shovelful by shovelful, whether he wanted it or not. But even that didn't stop him. He settled farther back against his chair, thrust his legs out another lazy inch and let one corner of his mouth crook. "But if you want me to marry you, little red, I'm afraid I will require a full, romantic proposal."

She blinked. Then swallowed.

"You can't be serious."

"I don't intend to make a habit of marrying. This will have to be perfect, the better to live on all my days." He nodded toward the polished wood at his feet. "Go on, then. On your knees, please."

And he was only a man. Not a very good one, as he'd acknowledged earlier. There was no possibility of issuing such an order without imagining all the other things she could do once she was there.

So he did. And had to shift slightly where he sat to accommodate the hungriest part of him.

"You agreed that any marriage between us will be a sham," she was saying, her voice a touch too husky for someone so dedicated to appearing unmoved. "You used that very word. It will be a publicity stunt, and only a publicity stunt, as I said."

"Whatever the marriage is or isn't, it begins right here." He ignored the demands that clamored inside him, greedy and still drunk on his last taste of her. "Where there is no public. No paparazzi. No overbearing employer who cannot stir himself to greet his long-lost brother in person."

She started to argue that but subsided when he shook his head.

"There are only two people who ever need to know how this marriage began, Lauren. And we are both right here, all alone, tucked away on an abandoned office floor where no one need ever be the wiser."

She rolled her eyes. "We can tell them there was kneeling all around, if that's really what you need."

"We can tell them anything you like, but I want to see a little effort. A little care, here between the two of us. A pretty, heartfelt proposal. Come now, Lauren." And he smiled at her then, daring her. "A man likes to be seduced."

Her cheeks had gone pale while he spoke, and as he watched, they flooded with bright new color.

"You don't want to be seduced. You want to humiliate me."

"Six of one, half dozen of another." He jutted his chin toward the floor again. "You need to demonstrate your commitment. Or how else will I know that my heart is safe in your hands?"

The color on her cheeks darkened, and her eyes flashed with temper. And he liked that a hell of a lot more than her robot impression.

"No one is talking about hearts, Mr. James," she snapped at him. "We're talking about damage control. Optics. PR."

"You and your Mr. Combe may be talking about all of those things," he said and shrugged. "But I am merely a hermit from a Hungarian hovel, too long-haired to make sense of your complicated corporate world. What do I know of such things? I'm a simple man, with simple needs." He reached up and dramatically clasped his chest, never shifting his gaze from hers. "If you want me, you must convince me. On your knees, little red."

She made a noise of sheer, undiluted frustration that nearly made him laugh. Especially when it seemed to make her face that much brighter.

He watched as she forced her knees to unlock. She took a breath in, then let it out. Slowly, as if it hurt, she took a step toward him. Then another.

And by the time she moved past his feet, then insinuated herself right where he wanted her, there between his outstretched legs, he didn't have the slightest urge to laugh any longer. Much less when she sank down on her knees before him, just as he'd imagined in all that glorious detail.

She knelt as prettily as she did everything else, and she filled his head as surely as his favorite Hungarian *palinka*. He couldn't seem to look away from her, gold and pink and that wide caramel gaze, peering up at him from between his own legs.

The sight of her very nearly unmanned him.

And he would never know, later, how he managed to keep his hands to himself.

"Dominik James," she said softly, looking up at

him with eyes wide, filled with all those emotions she claimed she didn't feel—but he did, as if she was tossing them straight into the deepest part of him, "will you do me the honor of becoming my husband? For a while?"

He didn't understand why something in him kicked against that qualification. But he ignored it.

He indulged himself by reaching forward and fitting his palm to the curve of her cheek. He waited until her lips parted because he knew she felt it, too, that same heat that roared in him. That wildfire that was eating him alive.

"But of course," he said, and he had meant to sound sardonic. Darkly amused. But that wasn't how it came out, and he couldn't think of a way to stop it. "I can think of nothing I would like to do more than marry a woman I hardly know to serve the needs of a brother I have never met in the flesh, to save the reputation of a family that tossed me aside like so much trash."

There was a sheen in her gaze that he wanted to believe was connected to that strangely serious thing in him, not laughing at all. And the way her lips trembled, just slightly.

Just enough to make the taste of her haunt him all over again.

"I… I can't tell if that's a yes or no."

"It's a yes, little red," he said, though there was no earthly reason that he should agree to any of this.

There was no reason that he should even be here, so far away from the life he'd carved out to his specifications. The life he had fought so hard to win for himself.

But Lauren had walked into his cabin, fit too neatly into the chair that shouldn't have been sitting there, waiting for her, and now he couldn't seem to keep himself from finding out if she fit everywhere else, too.

A thought that was so antithetical to everything he was and everything he believed to be true about himself that Dominik wasn't sure why he didn't trust her away from him and leave. Right now.

But he didn't.

Worse, he didn't want to.

"It's a yes," he said, his voice grave as he betrayed himself, and for no reason, "but I'm afraid, as in most things, there will be a price. And you will be the one to pay it."

CHAPTER SEVEN

LAUREN DIDN'T UNDERSTAND anything that was happening.

She had been astounded when Matteo had suggested marriage, so offhandedly as if it was perfectly normal to run around marrying strangers on a whim because he thought that would look better in some theoretical tabloid.

"Marry him," he'd said, so casually, from the far side of the world. "You are a decent, hardworking sort and you've been connected to the family without incident for years."

"I think you mean employed by the family and therefore professional."

"You can take him in hand. Make sure he's up to the task. And by the time the shock fades over my mother's scandalous past, you'll have made him everything he needs to be to take his place as a San Giacomo."

"Will this new role come with combat pay?" she'd asked, with more heat than she normally used with her boss, no matter what was going on. But then, she wasn't normally dispatched into the hinterland, made to *hike*, and then kissed thoroughly and repeatedly. She was... not herself. "Or do you expect me to give up my actual life for the foreseeable future for my existing salary, no questions asked?"

She never spoke to Matteo that way. But he didn't normally react the way he had then, either, with nothing but silence and what looked very much like sadness on his face. It made Lauren wish she hadn't said anything.

Not for the first time, she wondered exactly what had gone on between Matteo and the anger management consultant the Combe Industries board of directors had hired in a transparent attempt to take Matteo down. He'd gone off with her to Yorkshire, been unusually unreachable and then had set off on a round-the-world tour of all the Combe Industries holdings.

A less charitable person might wonder if he was attempting to take the geographic tour.

"You can name your price, Lauren," he said after what felt like a very long while, fraught with all the evidence she'd ever needed that though they might work very closely together, they had no personal relationship. Not like that. "All I ask is that you tame this brother of mine before we unleash him on the world. The board will not be pleased to have more scandal attached to the Combe name. And the least we can do is placate them a little."

And she'd agreed to ask Dominik, because what else could she do? For all Dominik's snide commentary, the truth was that she admired Matteo. He was not his father, who had always been willing to take the low road—and usually had. Matteo had integrity, something she knew because no matter how she might have longed for him to *see* her, he never had. He treated her as his personal assistant, not as a woman. It was why she felt safe while she wore her outrageously feminine heels. It was why she felt perfectly happy dedicating herself to him.

If he had looked at her the way Dominik did, even once, she would never have been able to work for him at all. She would never have been able to sort out what was an appropriate request and what wasn't, and would have lost herself somewhere in the process.

She'd been reeling from that revelation when she'd walked out to pitch the marriage idea, fully expecting that Dominik would laugh at the very notion.

But he hadn't.

And she'd meant to present the whole thing as a very dry and dusty sort of business proposition, anyway. Just a different manner of merger, that was all. But instead of a board meeting of sorts, she was knelt down between his legs, gazing up at him from a position that made her whole body quiver.

And unless she was very much mistaken, he had actually agreed to marry her.

For a price.

Because with this man, there was always a price.

How lucky you want so badly to pay it, an insinuating, treacherous voice from deep inside her whispered. *Whatever it is.*

"What kind of price?" Lauren frowned at him as if that could make them both forget that she was kneeling before him like a supplicant. Or a lover. And that he was touching her as if at least one of those things was a foregone conclusion. "I have already promised to kiss you whenever you like. What more could you want?"

His palm was so hard and hot against the side of her face. She felt it everywhere, and she knew that seemingly easy touch was responsible for the flames she could feel licking at her. All over her skin, then deeper still, sweet and hot in her core.

Until she *throbbed* with it. With him.

"Do you think there are limits to what a man might want?" he asked quietly, and his voice was so low it set her to shattering, like a seismic event. Deep inside, where she was already molten and more than a little afraid that she might shake herself apart.

"You're talking about sex again," she said, and thought she sounded something like solemn. Or despairing. And neither helped with all that unbearable *heat*. "I don't know how many ways I can tell you—"

"That you are not sexual, yes, I am aware." He moved his thumb, dragging it gently across her lower lip, and his mouth crooked when she hissed in a breath. His eyes blazed when goose bumps rose along her neck and ran down her arms, and his voice was little more than a growl when he spoke again. "Not sexual at all."

Something in the way he said that made her frown harder, though she already knew it was futile. And it only seemed to make that terrible, knowing blaze in his gray eyes more pronounced.

And much, much hotter. Inside her, where she still couldn't tell if she hated it—or loved it.

"What do you want from me?" she asked, her voice barely above a whisper.

And she thought that whatever happened, she would always remember the way he smiled at her then, half wolf and all man. That it was tattooed inside her, branded into her flesh, forever a part of her. Whether she liked it or not.

"What I want from you, little red, is a wedding night."

That was another brand, another scar. And far more dangerous than before.

Lauren's throat was almost too dry to work. She wasn't sure it would. "You mean…?"

"I mean in the traditional sense, yes. With all that entails."

He shifted, and she had never felt smaller. In the sense of being delicate. *Precious*, something in her whispered, though she knew that was fanciful. And worse, foolish.

Dominik smoothed his free hand over her hair, and let it rest at the nape of her neck. And the way he held her face made something in her do more than melt.

She thought maybe it sobbed.

Or she did.

"Find a threshold, and I will carry you over it," he told her, his voice low and intent. And the look in his gray eyes so male, very nearly *possessive*, it made her ache. "I will lay you down on a bed and I will kiss you awhile, to see where it goes. And all I need from you is a promise that you will not tell me what you do and do not like until you try it. That's all, Lauren. What do you have to lose?"

And she couldn't have named the things she had to lose, because they were all the one thing—they were all *her*—and she was sure he would take them, anyway.

He would take everything.

Maybe she'd known that from the moment she'd seen the shadows become a man, there in that clearing so far from the rest of the world. There in those woods that had taunted her from the first, whispering of darkness and mystery in a thousand ways she hadn't wanted to hear.

Maybe it had always been leading straight here.

But between the heat of his hands and that shivering deep inside her, she couldn't seem to mind it as much as she should have.

As much as she suspected she would, once she survived this. *If* she survived this.

She should get up right this minute. She should move herself out of danger—out of arm's reach. She should tell Dominik she didn't care what he did with his new-found name and fortune, just as she should ring Matteo back and tell him she had no intention of marrying a stranger on command.

She knew she should do all those things. She *wanted* to do all those things.

But instead, she shivered. And in that moment, there at his feet with all his focus and intent settled on her, she surrendered.

If surrender was a cliff, Lauren leaped straight off it, out into nothing. She hadn't done anything so profoundly foolish since she was nine years old and had thought she could convince her parents to pay more attention to her by acting out. She'd earned herself instead an unpleasant summer in boarding school.

But surrendering here, to Dominik, didn't feel like that. It didn't feel like plummeting down into sharp rocks.

It felt far more like flying.

"I will give you a wedding night," she heard herself agree, her voice very stern and matter-of-fact, as if that could mask the fact that she was capitulating. As if she could divert his attention from the great cliff she'd just flung herself over. "But that's all."

"Perhaps we will leave these intimate negotiations until after the night in question," Dominik said, that undercurrent of laughter in his voice. "You may find you very much want a honeymoon, little red. Who knows? Perhaps even an extended one. This may come as a surprise to you, but there are some women who would clamor for the opportunity to while away some time in my bed."

Wedding nights. Honeymoons. *Time in bed.* This was all a farce. It had to be.

But Lauren was on her knees in the offices of Combe Industries, and she had just proposed marriage to a man she'd only met this morning.

So perhaps *farce* wasn't quite the right word to describe what was happening.

Something traitorous inside her wanted to lean in closer, and that terrified her, so she took it as an opportunity to pull away. Cliff or no cliff.

Except he didn't let her.

That hand at her nape held her fast, and something about that…lit her up. It was as if she didn't know what she was doing any longer. Or at all. But maybe he did.

And suddenly she was kneeling up higher, her hands flat on his thighs, her face tilted toward his in a manner she could have called all kinds of names.

All of them not the least bit her. Not the person she was or had ever been.

But maybe she was tired of Lauren Isadora Clarke. And everything she'd made herself become while she was so busy not feeling things.

Like this. Like him.

"It's not a real proposal until there's a kiss, Lauren," Dominik told her. Gruffly, she thought. "Even you must know this."

"Isn't it enough that I promised you a wedding

night?" she asked, and she might have been horrified at the way her voice cracked at that, but there were so many horrors to sift through. Too many.

And all of them seemed to catch fire and burn brighter as she knelt there between his legs, not sure if she felt helpless or far more alarming, *alive*.

Alive straight through, which only made it clear that she never had been before. Not really.

"Kiss me, little red," he ordered her, almost idly. But there was no mistaking the command in his voice all the same. "Keep your promise."

His voice might have been soft, but it was ruthless. And his gray eyes were pitiless.

And he didn't seem to mind in the least when she scowled at him, because it was the only thing she knew how to do.

"Now, please," he murmured in that same demanding way. "Before you hurt my feelings."

She doubted very much that his feelings had anything to do with this, but she didn't say that. She didn't want to give him more opportunity to comment on hers. Or call her a robot again.

"I don't understand why you would want to kiss someone who doesn't wish to kiss you," she threw at him in desperation.

"I wouldn't." Those gray eyes laughed at her. "But that description doesn't apply to either one of us, does it?"

"One of us is under duress."

"One of us, Lauren, is a liar."

She could feel the heat that told her that her cheeks were red, and she had the terrible notion that meant he was right. And worse, that he could see it all over her face.

She had no idea.

In a panic, she mimicked him, hooking one hand around the hard column of his neck and pulling his mouth to hers.

This man who had agreed to marry her. To pretend, anyway, and there was no reason that should work in her the way it did, like a powder keg on the verge of exploding. Like need and loss and yearning, tangled all together in an angry knot inside her.

And she was almost used to this now. The delirious slide, the glorious fire, of their mouths together.

He let her kiss him, let her control the angle and the depth, and she made herself shiver as she licked her way into his mouth. All the while telling herself that she didn't like this. That she didn't want this.

And knowing with every drugging slide of his tongue against hers that he'd been right all along.

She was a liar.

Maybe that was why, when his hands moved to trace their way down her back, she moaned at the sensation instead of fighting it. And when he pulled her blouse from the waistband of her formal trousers, she only made a deeper noise, consumed with the glory of his mouth.

And the way he kissed her and kissed her, endless and intoxicating.

But then his bare hand was on her skin, moving around to the front of her and then finally—finally, as if she'd never wanted anything more when she'd never wanted it in the first place, when it had never occurred to her to imagine such a thing—closing over the swell of one breast.

And everything went white around the edges.

Her breast seemed to swell, filling his palm, with her nipple high and hard.

And every time he moved his palm, she felt it like another deep lick—

But this time in the hottest, wildest, most molten place of all between her legs.

She could feel his other hand in her hair, cradling the back of her head and holding her mouth where he wanted it, making absolutely no bones about the fact that he was in charge.

And it was thrilling.

Lauren arched her back, giving him more of her, and it still wasn't enough.

The kiss was wild and maddening at the same time, and she strained to get closer to him, desperate for something she couldn't name. Something just out of reach—

And when he set her away from him, with a dark little laugh, she thought she might die.

Then thought that death would be an excellent escape when reality hit her.

Because she was a disheveled mess on the floor of her office, staring up at the man who'd made her this way.

Perilously close to begging for things she couldn't even put into words.

She expected him to taunt her. To tell her she was a liar again, and remind her of all the ways he just proved it.

But Dominik stayed where he was, those gray eyes of his shuttered as he gazed back at her.

And she knew it was as good as admitting a weakness out loud, but she lifted her fingers and pressed them to her lips, not sure how she'd spent so many years on this earth without recognizing the way her own flesh could be used against her. And then tingle in the aftermath, like it wasn't enough.

As if she was sexual, after all.

"The company maintains a small number of corporate flats in this building," she managed to tell him when she'd composed herself a little, and she didn't sound like herself. She sounded like a prerecorded version of the woman she'd been when she'd left these offices to fly to Hungary. She wasn't sure she had access to that woman anymore. She wasn't sure she knew what had become of her.

But she was very sure that the creature she was now, right there at his feet, would be the undoing of her.

Assuming it wasn't already too late.

She climbed off the floor with as much dignity as she could muster. For the first time in her life, she cursed the fact that she wore such ridiculous shoes, with such high heels, that it was impossible to feel steady even when she was standing.

Right, a little voice inside her murmured archly. *Blame the shoes. It's definitely the* shoes.

"Corporate flats," he repeated after another long moment, that dark gaze all over her. "How...antiseptic."

But when she called down to the security desk to have one of the guards come and escort him there, he didn't argue.

Lauren told herself that she liked the space he left behind him. That it wasn't any kind of emptiness, but room for her to breathe.

And once she was alone, there was no one to see her when she sank down into her chair behind her desk, where she had always felt the most competent. There was no one to watch as she buried her face in her hands—still too hot, and no doubt too revealing—and let all those emotions she refused to look at and couldn't name spill down her cheeks at last.

CHAPTER EIGHT

By MORNING SHE'D pulled herself together. The tears of the night before seemed to have happened to someone else. Someone far more fragile than Lauren had ever been, particularly in the crisp light of day. She showered in the bathroom off the executive suite, rinsing away any leftover emotion as well as the very long previous day, and changed into one of the complete outfits she kept at the office precisely for mornings like this.

Well. Perhaps not *precisely* like this. She didn't often plan and execute her own wedding. She'd worn her highest, most impractical pair of heels as a kind of tribute. And she was absolutely not thinking—much less overthinking—about the many questionable bargains she'd made with the strange man she'd found in the forest.

She knocked briskly on the door to the corporate flat at half nine on the dot, aware as she did that she didn't expect him to answer. A man as feral as Dominik was as likely to have disappeared in the night as a stray cat, surely—

But the door swung open. And Dominik stood there, dressed in nothing but a pair of casual trousers slung low on his hips, showing off acres and acres of...*him*.

For a moment—or possibly an hour—Lauren couldn't seem to do anything but gape at him.

"Did you imagine I would run off in the night?" he asked, reading her mind yet again. And not the most embarrassing part, for a change. She tried to swallow past the dryness in her throat. She tried to stop staring at all those ridges and planes and astonishing displays of honed male flesh. "I might have, of course, but there were restrictions in place."

She followed him inside the flat, down the small hall to the efficient kitchen, bright in the morning's summer sunlight. "You mean the security guards?"

He rounded the small counter and then regarded her over his coffee, strong enough that she could smell the rich aroma and blacker than sin. "I mean, Lauren, the fact I gave you my word."

Lauren had allowed sensation and emotion and all that nonsense to get the best of her last night, but that was over now. It had to be, no matter how steady that gray gaze of his was. Or the brushfires it kicked up inside her, from the knot in her belly to the heat in her cheeks. So she cleared her throat and waved the tablet she carried in his direction, completely ignoring the tiny little hint of something bright like shame that wiggled around in all the knots she seemed to be made of today.

"I've sorted everything out," she told him, aware that she sounded as pinched and knotted as she felt. "We will marry in an hour."

Dominik didn't change expression and still, she felt as if he was laughing at her.

"And me without my pretty dress," he drawled.

"The vicar is a friend of the Combe family," she said as if she hadn't heard him. And she had to order herself not to fuss with her own dress, a simple little shift that was perfect for the office. And would do for a fake wedding, as well. "I took the liberty of claiming that ours is a deep and abiding love that requires a special license and speed, so it would be best all round if you do not dispute that."

"I had no intention of disputing it," Dominik said in that dark, sardonic voice of his that made her feel singed. "After all, I am nothing but a simple, lonely hermit, good for nothing but following the orders of wealthy aristocrats who cannot be bothered to attend the fake weddings they insisted occur in the first place. I am beside myself with joy and anticipation that I, too, can serve your master from afar in whatever way he sees fit. Truly, this is the family I dreamed of when I was a child in the orphanage."

He displayed his joy and anticipation by letting that impossible mouth of his crook, very slightly, in one corner, and Lauren hated that it felt like a punch. Directly into her gut.

"It is the romance of it all that makes my heart beat faster, little red," Dominik continued, sounding very nearly merry. If she overlooked that hard gleam in his eyes. "If you listen, I am certain you can hear it."

Lauren placed her tablet down on the marble countertop in a manner that could only be described as pointed. Or perhaps aggressive. But she kept her eyes on Dominik as if he really was some kind of wolf. As if looking away—for even an instant—could be the death of her.

And it wasn't his heart that she could hear, pounding loud enough to take down the nearest wall. It was hers.

"Could you take this seriously?" she demanded. "Could you at least try?"

He studied her for another moment as he lifted his coffee to his mouth and took a deep pull. "I didn't run off in the night as I assure you I could have done if I wished, regardless of what laughable corporate security you think was in place. The vicar bears down on us even as we speak. How much more seriously do you imagine I can take this?"

"You agreed to do this, repeatedly. I'm not sure that *I* agreed to submit myself to your…commentary."

She didn't expect that smile of his, bright and fierce. "Believe me, Lauren, there are all manner of things you might find yourself submitting to over the course of this day. Do not sell yourself short."

And she hated when he did that. When he said things in that voice of his, and they swirled around inside her—heat and madness and something like hope—making it clear that he was referring to all those dark and thorny things that she didn't understand.

That she didn't *want* to understand, she told herself stoutly.

"I've already agreed," she reminded him, with more ferocity than was strictly required. But she couldn't seem to bite it back. She had always been in such control of herself that she'd never learned how to *take* control of herself. If there were steps toward becoming composed, she didn't know them, and she could blame that on Dominik, too. "There's no need for all these insinuations."

"You've agreed? I thought it was I who agreed. To everything. Like a house pet on a chain."

His voice was mild but his gaze was…not.

"You asked me for a wedding night," she reminded him, her heart still pounding like it wanted to knock her flat. "And you know that I keep my promises. Every time you've asked to kiss me, I've allowed it."

"Surrendered to it, one might even say, with notable enthusiasm. Once you get started."

"My point," she said through her teeth, not certain why she was suddenly so angry, only that she couldn't seem to keep it inside her, where she was shaky and too hot and not the least bit *composed*, "is that you don't have to continue with all the veiled references. Or even the euphemisms. You demanded sex in return for marrying me, and I agreed to give it to you. The end."

It was a simple statement of fact, she thought. There was no reason at all that he should stare at her that way as if he was stripping all the air from the flat. From the world.

"If it is so distasteful to you, Lauren, don't."

But his voice was too smooth. Too silky. And all she could hear was the undercurrent beneath it, which roared through her like an impenetrable wall of flame.

"Don't?" she managed to echo. "Is that an option?"

"While you are busy marinating in the injustice of it all, remind yourself that it is not I who tracked you down in the middle of a forest, then dragged you back to England. If I wish to go through with a sham marriage for the sheer pleasure of the wedding night you will provide me as lure, that is my business." Dominik tilted his head slightly to one side. "Perhaps you should ask yourself what you are willing to do for a paycheck. And why."

"It's a little more complicated than that."

"Is it? Maybe it is time you ask yourself what you

wouldn't do if your Mr. Combe asked it. You may find the answers illuminating."

"You obviously enjoy keeping to yourself." Lauren wasn't sure why all that breathless fury wound around and around inside her, or why she wanted nothing more than to throw it at him. She only wished she could be sure of her aim. "But some people prefer to be on a team."

"The team that is currently enjoying a holiday in scenic Australia? Or the one left here with a list of instructions and a heretofore unknown half brother to civilize through the glorious institution of marriage?" He smirked. "Go team."

Her jaw ached and she realized, belatedly, that she was clenching her teeth. *"You agreed."*

"So I did." And all he was doing was standing there across a block of marble, so there was no reason he should make her feel so...dizzy. "But then again, so did you. Is that what this is about, little red? Are you so terrified of the things you promised me?"

That took the wind out of her as surely as if she'd fallen hard and landed worse.

"What does it matter if I'm terrified or not?" She only realized after she'd said it that it was as good as an admission. "Would it change your mind?"

"It might change my approach," he said, that gleaming, dark thing in his gaze again, and she didn't understand how or why it connected to all that breathlessness inside her. Almost as if it wasn't *fury* at all. "Then again, it might not."

"In any case, congratulations are in order," she managed to say, feeling battered for no good reason at all. "In short order you will have a wife. And shortly after that, a wedding night sacrifice, like something out of the history books."

He laughed, rich and deep, and deeper when she scowled at him. "Do you think to shame me, Lauren? There are any number of men who might stand before you and thunder this way and that about how they dislike the taste of martyrdom in their beds, but not me."

"I am somehow unsurprised."

Dominik didn't move and yet, again, Lauren felt as if he surrounded her. As if those hands of his might as well have been all over her. She felt as if they were.

"You're not terrified of me," he said with a quiet certainty that made her shake. "You're terrified of yourself. And all those things you told yourself you don't know how to feel." That laughter was still all over his face, but his gray gaze made her feel pinned to the floor where she stood. "You're terrified that you'll wake up tomorrow so alive with feeling you won't know who you are."

"Either that or even more bored than I am right now," she said, though her throat felt scraped raw with all the things she didn't say. Or scream.

"Yes, so deeply bored," he said, and laughed again. Then he leaned forward until he rested his elbows on the countertop between them, making it impossible to pretend she didn't see the play of his muscles beneath the acres and acres of smooth male skin that he'd clearly shared with the sun in that Hungarian clearing. "But tell me this, Lauren. Does your boredom make you wet?"

For a moment she couldn't process the question. She couldn't understand it.

Then she did, and a tide of red washed over her, igniting her from the very top of her head to the tender spaces between her toes. No one had ever asked her a question like that. She hadn't known, until right now, that people really discussed such things in the course of an otherwise more or less regular day. She told herself she was horrified. Disgusted. She told herself she didn't even know what he meant, only that it was vile. That *he* was.

But she did know what he meant.

And she was molten straight through, red hot and flush with it, and decidedly not bored.

"You have twenty minutes," she told him when she could be sure her voice was clipped and cold again. "I trust you will be ready?"

"I will take that as a yes," he rumbled at her, entirely too male and much too sure of himself. "You are so wet you can hardly stand still. Don't worry, little red. You might not know what to do about that. But I do."

He straightened, then rounded the counter. Lauren pulled herself taut and rigid as if he was launching an attack—then told herself it was sheer relief that wound its way through her when he made no move toward her at all. He headed toward the flat's bedroom instead.

"You're welcome to join me in the shower," he said over his shoulder, and she didn't have to see his face to know he was laughing at her. "If you dare."

And she was still standing right where he'd left her when she heard the water go on. Frozen solid at the edge of the counter with her hands in fists, curled up so tight her nails were digging into her palms.

She made herself uncurl her fingers, one at a time. She made herself breathe, shoving back the temper and the fury until she could see what was beneath it.

And see that once again, he was right. It was fear.

Not of him. But of herself.

And how very much she wanted to see, at last, what it was she'd been missing all this time.

That was the thought that had kept sneaking into her head over the course of the long night.

She'd hardly slept, there on that couch in her office where she spent more time than she ever had in the flat she shared with Mary. And Lauren had always prided herself on not feeling the things that others did. She'd congratulated herself on not being dragged into the same emotional quagmires they always were. It made her better at doing her job. It made it easier to navigate the corporate world.

But Dominik had forced her to face the fact that she *could* feel all kinds of things, she just…hadn't.

Lauren had spent so long assuring herself she didn't want the things she couldn't feel. Or couldn't have. Her parents' love, the happy families they made without her, the sorts of romantic and sexual relationships all her friends and colleagues were forever falling in and out of with such abandon. She'd told anyone who asked that she wasn't built for those sorts of entanglements.

Secretly, she'd always believed she was above them. That she was better than all that mess and regret.

But one day of kissing Dominik James on demand and she was forced to wonder—if it wasn't about better or worse, but about meeting someone who made her feel things she hadn't thought she could, where did that leave her except woefully inexperienced? And frozen in amber on a shelf of her own making?

Lauren didn't like that thought at all. She ran her hands over her sensible shift dress, her usual office wear, and tried to pretend that she wasn't shaking.

But what if you melted? whispered a voice deep inside her that she'd never heard before, layered with insinuation and something she was terribly afraid might be grief. *What if you let Dominik melt you as he pleased?*

She let out a breath she hadn't known she was holding. And she swayed on her feet, yet knew full well it wasn't because of the skyscraper height of her shoes.

And she entertained a revolutionary thought. If she had to do this, anyway—if she was going to marry this man, and stay married to him for as long as it took to ride out the public's interest in yet another family scandal—shouldn't she take it as an opportunity?

She already knew that Dominik could make her feel things that she never had before. And yes, that was overwhelming. A mad, wild whirl that she hardly knew how to process. Especially when she'd been certain, all her life, that she wasn't capable of such things.

Maybe she didn't know how to want. But it had never occurred to her before now that she hadn't been born that way. That maybe, just maybe, that was because no one had ever wanted her—especially the people who should have wanted her the most.

She didn't know why Dominik wanted to play these games with her, but he did. He clearly did, or he wouldn't be here. Lauren was persuasive, but she knew full well she couldn't have forced that man to do a single thing he didn't want to do.

So why shouldn't she benefit, too?

She had spent a lot of time and energy telling herself that she didn't care that she was so clearly different from everyone else she met. That she was somehow set apart from the rest of the human race, unmoved by their passions and their baser needs. But what if she wasn't?

What if she wasn't an alien, after all?

That was what one of her kissing experiments had called her when she had declined his offer to take their experiment in a more horizontal direction. Among other, less savory names and accusations.

Just as Dominik had called her a robot.

What if she…wasn't?

What if she melted, after all?

Lauren waited until he reemerged from his bedchamber, dressed in a crisp, dark suit that confused her, it was so well-made. His hair was tamed, pushed back from his face, and he'd even shaved, showing off the cut line of his ruthlessly masculine jaw. He looked like what he was—the eldest son of the current generation of San Giacomos. But she couldn't concentrate on any of the surprisingly sophisticated male beauty he threw around him like light, because she knew that if she didn't say what she wanted right here and now, she never would.

"I will give you a wedding night," she told him.

"So we have already agreed," he said in that silky way of his that made her whole body turn to jelly. And her stomach doing flips inside her didn't exactly help. "Is this a renegotiation of terms?"

"If it takes more than one night, that's all right," she forced herself to tell him, though it made her feel queasy. And light-headed. Especially when he stopped tugging at his shirt cuffs and transferred all his considerable attention to her. "I want to learn."

"Learn what?"

And maybe his voice wasn't particularly, dangerously quiet. Maybe it just sounded like that in her head, next to all that roaring.

"Everyone has all this sex," she said, the words

crashing through her and out of her. She couldn't control them. She couldn't do anything but throw them across the room like bombs. "People walk around *consumed* by it, and I want to know why. I don't just mean I want you to take my virginity, though you will. And that's fine."

"I'm delighted to hear you're on board," he said drily, though it was the arrested sort of gleam in his eyes that she couldn't seem to look away from. Because it made her feel as if a great wind was blowing, directly at her, and there was nothing she could do to stop it. "No one likes an unenthusiastic deflowering. Gardening metaphors aside, it's really not all that much fun. Anyone who tells you otherwise has never had the pleasure. Or any pleasure, I can only assume."

"I have no idea what you're on about." He looked even more taken aback by that, and she moved toward him—then thought better of it, as putting herself in arm's reach of this man had yet to end well for her. Even if that was her current goal. "I want to understand why people *yearn.* I want to understand what all the fuss is about. Why people—you among them—look at me like something's wrong with me if I say I'm not interested in it. Can you do that, Dominik?"

Maybe it was the first time she'd called him by his name. She wasn't sure, but she felt as if it was. And he looked at her as if she'd struck him.

"I've spent my whole life never quite understanding the people around me." And Lauren knew she would be horrified—later—that her voice broke then, showing her hand. Telling him even more than she'd wanted. "Never really getting the joke. Or the small, underlying assumptions that people make about the world because of these feelings they cart about with them wherever they go. I never got those, either. Just once I want to know what the big secret is. I want to know what all the songs are about. I want to know what so many parents feel they need to protect their children from. I want to *know*."

"Lauren…"

And she didn't recognize that look on his face then. Gone was the mocking, sardonic gleam in his eyes. The theatrics, the danger. The challenge.

She was terribly afraid that what she was seeing was pity, and she thought that might kill her.

"I know this is all a game to you," she said hurriedly, before he could crush her, and had that out-of-body feeling again. As if she was watching herself from far away, and couldn't do a single thing to stop the words that kept pouring out of her mouth. "Maybe you have your own dark reasons for wanting to do what Mr. Combe wants, and I don't blame you. Family dynamics are difficult enough when you've known the players all your life. But you said that there could be certain things that were between the two of us. That are only ours. And I want this to be one of them." Her heart was in her throat and she couldn't swallow it down. She could only hope she didn't choke on it. "I want to know *why*."

He straightened then, and she couldn't read the expression he wore. Arrested, still. But there was a different light in those near-silver eyes of his. He held out his hand, that gray gaze steady on hers, as if that alone could hold her up.

She believed it.

Lauren was tempted to call the way he was looking at her *kind*. And she had absolutely no idea why that should make her want to cry. Or how she managed to keep from doing just that when her sight blurred.

"Come," Dominik said, his voice gruff and sure as if he was already reciting his vows before the vicar. And more shocking by far, as if those vows meant something to him. "Marry me, little red, and I will teach you."

CHAPTER NINE

WHEN HE LOOKED back on this episode and cataloged his mistakes—something Dominik knew he would get to as surely as night followed day—he would trace it all back to the fatal decision to step outside his cabin and wait for the Englishwoman the innkeeper had called from town to tell him was headed his way.

It had seemed so innocuous at the time. No one ever visited his cabin, with or without an invitation, and he hadn't known what would come of entertaining the whims of the one woman who had dared come find him. He'd been curious. Especially when he'd seen her, gold hair gleaming and that red cloak flowing around her like a premonition.

How could he have known?

And now Dominik found himself in exactly the sort of stuffy, sprawling, stately home he most despised, with no one to blame but himself. Combe Manor sat high on a ridge overlooking the Yorkshire village that had once housed the mills that had provided the men who'd lived in this house a one-way ticket out of their humble beginnings.

They had built Combe Manor and started Combe Industries. Dominik had also fought his way out of a rocky, unpleasant start…but he'd chosen to hoard his wealth and live off by himself in the middle of the woods.

Dominik felt like an imposter. Because he was an imposter.

He might have shared blood with the distant aristocrat he'd seen on the screen in a London office, but he didn't share…this. Ancient houses filled with the kind of art and antiques that spoke of wealth that went far beyond the bank. It was nearly two centuries of having more. Of having everything, for that matter. It was generations of men who had stood where he did now, staring out the windows in a library filled with books only exquisitely educated men read, staring down at the village where, once upon a time, other men scurried about adding to the Combe coffers.

And he knew that the Combe family was brand-spanking-new in terms of wealth when stood next to the might and historic reach of the San Giacomos.

Dominik might share that blood, but he was an orphan. A street kid who'd lived rough for years and had done what was necessary to feed himself, keep himself clothed and find shelter. A soldier who had done his duty and followed his orders, and had found himself in situations he never mentioned when civilians were near.

Blood was nothing next to the life he'd lived. And he was surprised this fancy, up-itself house didn't fall down around his ears.

But when he heard the soft click of much too high heels against the floor behind him, he turned.

Almost as if he couldn't help himself.

Because the house still stood despite the fact he was here, polluting it. And more astonishing still, the woman who walked toward him, her blond hair shining and a wary look on her pretty face, was his wife.

His wife.

The ceremony, such as it was, had gone smoothly. The vicar had arrived right on time, and they had recited their vows in a pretty sort of boardroom high on top of the London building that housed his half brother's multinational business. Lauren had produced rings, proving that she did indeed think of everything, they had exchanged them and that was that.

Dominik was not an impulsive man. Yet, he had gone ahead and married a woman for the hell of it.

And he was having trouble remembering what *the hell of it* was, because all he could seem to think about was Lauren. And more specific, helping Lauren out of those impossible heels she wore. Peeling that sweet little dress off her curves, and then finally—*finally*—doing something about this intense, unreasonable hunger for her that had been dogging him since the moment he'd laid eyes on her.

The moment he'd stepped out of the shadows of his own porch and had put all of this into motion.

There had been no reception. Lauren had taken a detour to her office that had turned into several hours of work. Afterward she had herded him into another sleek, black car, then back to the same plane, which they'd flown for a brief little hop to the north of England. Another car ride from the airfield and here they were in an echoing old mausoleum that had been erected to celebrate and flatter the kinds of men Dominik had always hated.

It had never crossed his mind that he was one of them. He'd never wanted to be one of them.

And the fact he'd found out he was the very thing he loathed didn't change a thing. He couldn't erase the life he'd led up to this point. He couldn't pretend he'd had a different life now that he was being offered his rich mother's guilt in the form of an identity that meant nothing to him.

But it was difficult to remember the hard line he planned to take when this woman—his *wife*, to add another impossibility to the pile—stood before him.

"I have just spoken to Mr. Combe," she began, because, of course, she'd been off the moment they'd set foot in this house. Dominik had welcomed the opportunity to ask himself what on earth he was doing here while she'd busied herself with more calls and emails and tasks that apparently needed doing *at once*.

And Dominik had made any number of mistakes already. There was the speaking to her in the first place that he would have to unpack at some later date, when all of this was behind him. Besides, he'd compounded that error, time and again. He should never have touched her. He should certainly never have kissed her. He should have let her fly off back to London on her own, and he certainly, without any doubt, should never have married her.

The situation would almost be funny if it wasn't so… preposterous.

But one thing Dominik knew beyond a shadow of any doubt. He did not want to hear about his damned brother again. Not tonight.

"Do me this one favor, please," he said in a voice that came out as more of a growl than he'd intended. Or maybe it was exactly the growl that was called for, he thought, when her eyes widened. "This is our wedding night. We have a great many things to accomplish, you and I. Why don't we leave your Mr. Combe where he belongs—across the planet, doing whatever it is he does that requires you to do five times as much in support."

He expected her to argue. He was sure he could see the start of it kicking up all over her lovely face and in the way she held her shoulders so tight and high.

But she surprised him.

She held his gaze, folded her hands in front of her and inclined her head.

Giving him what he wanted.

And the same demon that had spurred him on from the start—pushing him to walk out onto that porch and start all of this in the first place—sat up inside him, clearly not as intimidated by a stately library and a grand old house the way he was.

"What's this?" he asked quietly. "Is that all it took to tame you, little red? A ring on your finger and a few vows in front of the vicar? That's all that was required to make you soft? Yielding? Obedient?"

She made a sound that could as easily have been a cough as a laugh. "I am not certain I would call myself any of those things, no matter what jewelry I wear on my fingers. But I agreed to the wedding night. And…whatever else. I have every intention of going through with it."

"You make it sound so appealing." He eyed her, not sure if he was looking for her weaknesses or better yet, the places she was likely to be most sensitive. "You could do worse than a little softness. Yielding will make it sweeter for the both of us. And obedience, well…"

He grinned at that, as one image after the next chased through his head.

"I've never been much good at that, either, I'm

afraid." She said it with such confidence, tipping her chin up to go with it. And more than that, pride. "If you're looking for obedience, I'm afraid you're in for some disappointment."

"You cannot truly believe you are not obedient." He moved toward her, leaving the window—and its view of the ruins of the mills that had built this place—behind him. "You obey one man because he pays you. What will it take, I wonder, for you to obey your husband with even a portion of that dedication?"

And he had the distinct pleasure of watching her shiver, goose bumps telling him her secrets as they rippled to life on her skin.

He was so hard he thought it might hurt him.

Dominik crossed the vast expanse of the library floor until he was in front of her, and then he kept moving, wandering in a lazy circle around her as if she was on an auction block and he was the buyer.

Another image that pulsed in him like need.

"I asked you to teach me." And he could hear all the nerves crackling in her voice. As obvious as the goose bumps down the length of her arms. "Does that come with extra doses of humiliation or is that merely an add-on extra?"

"It's my lesson to teach, Lauren. Why don't you stop trying to top from the bottom?"

He'd made a full circle around her then, and faced her once more. And he reveled in the look on her face. Wariness and expectation. That sweet pink flush.

And a certain hectic awareness in her caramel-colored eyes.

She was without doubt the most beautiful woman he had ever seen. And she was his.

She had made herself his.

"What do you want me to do?" Lauren asked, her voice the softest he'd ever heard it.

He reached out to smooth his hand over all her gleaming blond hair, still pulled back in that sleek, professional ponytail. He considered that tidy ponytail part of her armor.

And he wanted none of that armor between them. Not tonight.

"It's time to play Rapunzel," he told her. When she only stared back at him, he tugged on the ponytail, just sharp enough to make her hitch in a breath. "Let down your hair, little red."

He watched the pulse in her throat kick into high gear. Her flush deepened, and he was fairly certain she'd moved into holding her breath.

But she obeyed him all the same, reaching back to tug the elastic out of her hair. When it was loose she ran her free hand through the mass of it, letting it fall where it would, thick and gold and smelling of apples.

She kept saying she didn't believe in fairy tales, but Dominik was sure he'd ended up in the midst of one all the same. And he knew the price of taking a bite out of a sweet morsel like Lauren, a golden-haired princess as innocent as she was sweet to look upon, but he didn't care. Bake him into a pie, turn him into stone— he meant to have this woman.

He made a low, rumbling sound of approval, because with her hair down she looked different. Less sharp. Less sleek. More accessible. The hair tumbled over her shoulders and made her seem…very nearly romantic.

Dominik remembered the things he'd promised her, and that ache in him grew sharper and more insistent by the second, so he simply bent and scooped her up into his arms.

She let out the breath she'd been holding in a kind of gasp, but he was already moving. He held her high against his chest, a soft, sweet weight in his arms, and after a startled moment she snuck her arms around his neck.

And that very nearly undid him.

The sort of massive, theatrical staircase that had never made sense to him dominated the front hall, and he took the left side, heading upstairs.

"Oh, the guest suites are actually—" she began, shifting in his arms and showing him that frown of hers he liked far too much.

"Is anyone else here?"

He already knew the answer. She had told him the house was empty when they'd landed in Yorkshire. She'd told him a lot of information about the house, the grounds, the village, the distant moors and mountains—as if she'd believed what he truly wanted today was a travelogue and a lecture on the Combe family.

"You know that Mr. Combe is in Australia, and his sister, Pia—" She cut herself off, her gaze locking to his. "Well. She's your sister, too, of course. And she is currently in the kingdom of Atilia."

"The island."

"Yes, it's actually several islands in the Ionian Sea—"

"I don't care." He didn't. Not about Matteo Combe or Pia Combe or anything at all but the woman in his arms. "How many beds are there in a house like this?"

"Fifteen," she replied, her gaze searching his. Then widening as he smiled.

"Never fear, Lauren. I intend to christen them all."

He took the first door he found, carrying her into a sprawling sitting room that led, eventually, into an actual bedroom. The bed itself was a massive thing, as if they'd chopped down trees that could have been the masts of ships to make all four posters, but Dominik found his normal disgust about class issues faded in the face of all the lovely possibilities.

There were just so many things an imaginative man could do with bedposts and a willing woman.

He set her down at the side of the bed and smiled wider when she had to reach out to steady herself. "Those shoes may well be the death of you. It is the shoes, is it not? And not something else entirely that leaves you so…unbalanced?"

She shot him a look, but she didn't say anything. She reached down, fiddled with the buckle around one delicate ankle, then kicked her shoe off. She repeated it on the other side, and when she was done she was nearly a foot shorter.

And then she smiled up at him, her gaze as full of challenge as it was of wariness.

"I didn't realize all the witty banter came as part of the package. I thought it would just be, you know, straight to it. No discussion."

"You could have gotten that in any pub you've ever set foot in with precious little effort on your part."

He shrugged out of the formal suit jacket he'd been wearing all day, like the trained monkey he'd allowed himself to become. And he was well aware of the convulsive way she swallowed, her gaze following his shoulders as if she couldn't bring herself to look away from him.

Dominik liked that a little too much. "Why didn't you?"

He started on his buttons then, one after the next, unable to keep his lips from quirking as she followed his fingers as they moved down his chest. And took much too long to raise her gaze back to his.

"Pardon?"

"If you were curious about experimenting with your nonsexual nature, Lauren, why not get off with a stranger after a few drinks? I think you'll find it's a tried and true method employed by people everywhere."

"As appealing as that sounds, I was never curious before. I was never curious before—"

She looked stricken the moment the words were out. And the word she'd been about to say hung between them as surely as if she'd shouted it. *You.*

I was never curious before you.

And Dominik felt...hushed. Something like humbled.

"Don't worry," he found himself saying, though his voice was gruff and he'd planned to be so much more smooth, more in control, hadn't he? "I promise you will enjoy this far more than a drunken fumble in the toilets after too much liquid courage and a pair of beer goggles."

She blinked as if she was imagining that, and Dominik didn't want a single thing in her head but him.

He tossed his shirt aside, then nodded at her. "Your dress, wife. Take it off."

Her breath shuddered out of her, and her hands trembled when she reached down to grip the hem of the shift dress she wore. She had to wiggle as she lifted it, peeling it up and off and displaying herself to him as she went.

Inch by luscious inch.

At last, he thought as she tossed the dress aside and stood there before him wearing nothing but a delicate lace bra that cupped her perfect breasts, and a pair of pale pink panties that gleamed a bit in the last of the light of the waning summer afternoon.

She made his mouth water.

And God, how she made him ache.

He reached over and put his hands on her, finally. He drew her hair over her shoulders, then followed the line of each arm. Down to find her fingers, particularly the one that wore his ring, then back up again. He found the throat where her pulse pounded out a rhythm he could feel in the hardest part of him, and each soft swell of her breast above the fabric that covered them and held them aloft.

She was like poured cream, sweet and rich, and so soft to the touch he had to bite back a groan. He traced his way over the tempting curve of her belly, her hips made for his hands, and then behind to her pert bottom.

She was warm already, but she became hot beneath his palms.

And he was delighted to find that when she flushed, she turned bright red all the way down to her navel. Better by far than he'd imagined.

He dropped to his knees, wrapped his arms around her and dropped his mouth to a spot just below her navel, smiling when she jolted against him.

Because touching her wasn't enough. He wanted to taste her.

First, he retraced his steps, putting his mouth everywhere he could reach, relishing each shocked and greedy little noise she made. The way she widened her stance, then sagged back against the high bed as if her knees could no longer hold her. She buried her hands in his hair, but either she didn't know how to guide him, or didn't want to, so he made his own path.

And when her eyes looked blind with need, he reached up and unhooked her bra, carefully removing it so he could expose her breasts to his view.

Perfect. She was perfect, and he leaned in close so he could take his fill of her. He pulled one nipple deep into his mouth, sucking until she cried out.

And Dominik thought it was the most glorious sound he had ever heard.

When he was finished with both nipples, they stood harder and more proud. And she was gripping the bed sheets behind her, her head tipped back so all of her golden hair spread around her like a halo.

He shifted forward, lifting her up and setting her back on the bed so he could peel the panties from her hips.

As he pulled them down her satiny legs, she panted. And was making the slightest high-pitched sounds in the back of her throat, if he wasn't mistaken.

She only got louder when he lifted up her legs and set them on his shoulders so they dangled down his back, and then he lost himself in the fact he had full, unfettered access to all that molten sweetness between her legs.

The scent of her arousal roared in him, making him crazy.

Making him as close to desperate as he'd ever been.

He looked up and let his lips curve when he found her gazing back at him, a look of wonder on her face.

And something like disbelief in her eyes.

"You… My legs…" She hardly sounded like herself.

"All the better to eat you with, my dear," he said, dark and greedy.

And then he set his mouth to the core of her, and showed her exactly how real the fairy tales were, after all.

CHAPTER TEN

IT HIT HER like a punch, thick and deep, setting Lauren alight from the inside out.

It made her go rigid, then shake.

But that didn't stop Dominik.

Her husband.

He was licking into her as if he planned to go on forever. He was using the edge of his teeth, his wicked tongue and the scrape of his jaw. His shoulders kept her thighs apart, and he didn't seem to care that her hands were buried in his hair. And tugging.

And after the first punch, there was a different, deeper fire. A kind of dancing flame she hardly knew how to name, and then there was more.

A shattering.

As if there were new ways to burn, and Dominik was intent on showing her each and every one of them.

The third time she exploded, he pulled his mouth away from her, pressing his lips against her inner thigh so she could feel him smile.

He stood, hauling her with him as he went, and then somehow they were both in the middle of a giant bed in one of the family's suites she had never dared enter on her previous trips to Combe Manor.

He rolled over her, and Lauren realized she must have lost time somewhere, because he was naked, too. She had no memory of him stripping off his trousers.

Not that she cared.

Because she could feel him everywhere, muscled legs between her, and the heat of his skin. All that lean weight of his. The crispness of the hair that dusted his decidedly male body. His eyes were like silver, hot and indulgent at once, and he braced himself over her as she ran her hands down all the planes and ridges of his beautiful chest, the way she'd wanted to since he'd opened the door this morning.

It was finally her turn to touch him. And she was determined to touch *all* of him, with all the fascination she hadn't know she held inside her. But there was no denying it as she followed her fingers wherever they wanted to go. There was no pretending it didn't swell and dance inside her.

"I don't understand how a man can be so beautiful," she whispered, and if that was betraying herself the way she feared it was, she couldn't bring herself to care about that.

Because he took her mouth then, a hard, mad claiming, and it thrilled her.

She surged against him, unable to get close enough. Unable to process each and every sensation that rolled over her, spiraled around inside her and made her want nothing more than to press every part of her against every part of him.

And she could feel it then. The hardest part of him, there between them. Velvet and steel, insistent against the soft skin of her belly.

It made her shudder all over again.

He slanted his mouth over hers, and then his hands were working magic between them. She heard the faint sound of foil, and then he settled himself between her legs as if all this time, her whole life, she had been made to hold him just like this.

Dominik had asked her if she was wet before. And now she knew what he meant in an entirely different way.

But he growled his approval as his fingers found the neediest part of her, playing with her until she bucked against him, her head thrashing back against the mattress.

He lifted her knees, then settled himself even more completely between them, so he was flush against her.

"Tell me if you don't feel anything," he said, his voice nearly unrecognizable, there at her ear.

"If I don't..." she began.

But then she could feel him, there at her center.

He pressed against the resistance he found; her body protested enough to make her wince, and then it was over.

Or just beginning, really.

Because he kept pressing. In and in, and there was too much. She couldn't name the things she felt; she could barely experience them as they happened—

"Remember," and his voice was a growl again. "You are nonsexual, little red. You do not feel what others do. Is that how this feels?"

But she couldn't answer him.

She couldn't do anything but dig her fingers into his shoulders as he opened her, pressed deeper and stretched her farther still.

Then finally, and yet too soon, he stopped.

And for a moment he only gazed down at her, propped up on his elbows with nothing but silver in his gaze and that very nearly stern set to his mouth.

While he was buried completely within her body.

And the knowledge of that, mixed with the exquisite sensation, so full and so deep, made her break apart all over again.

Less like a fist this time, and more like a wave. Over and over, until it wore itself out against the shore.

And when she opened her eyes again, she could see Dominik's jaw clenched tight and something harder in his gaze. Determination, perhaps.

"You're killing me," he gritted out.

She tried to catch her breath. "Am I doing it wrong?"

And he let out a kind of sigh, or maybe it was a groan, and he dropped down to gather her even more firmly beneath him.

"No, little red, you're not doing it wrong."

But she thought he sounded tortured as he said it.

Then Lauren couldn't care about that, either, because he began to move.

And it was everything she'd never known she wanted. She had never known she could want at all. It was the difference between a dark, cloudy sky, and a canopy of stars.

And she couldn't breathe. She couldn't *think*. She could only feel.

She was all sensation. All greed and passion, longing and desire, and all of it focused on the man who moved within her, teaching her with every thrust.

About need. About want.

About everything she had been missing, all these lonely years.

He taught her about hope, and he taught her about wonder, and still he kept on.

Lesson after lesson, as each thrust made it worse. Better.

As he made her undeniably human, flesh and passion made real, as surely as any kiss in a fairy tale story.

Until there was nothing between them but fire.

The glory of flames that danced and consumed them, made them one, and changed everything.

And when she exploded that time, he went with her.

He shouldn't have gone out on that porch, Dominik thought grimly a long while later as the sky outside darkened to a mysterious deep blue, and Lauren lay sprawled against his chest, her breathing even and her eyes closed.

He should have stayed in Hungary. He should have laughed off the notion that he was an heir to anything.

And he never, ever should have suggested that they make this marriage real.

He felt...wrecked.

And yet he couldn't seem to bring himself to shift her off him. It would be easy enough to do. A little roll, and he could leave her here. He could leave behind this great house and all its obnoxious history. He could pretend he truly didn't care about the woman who'd rid herself of him, then later chosen this.

But he had promised to take part in this whole charade, hadn't he? He'd promised not only to marry Lauren, but to subject himself to the rest of it, too. Hadn't she mentioned comportment? The press?

It was his own fault that he'd ended up here. He accepted that.

But he could honestly say that it had never occurred to him that sex with Lauren could possibly be this... ruinous.

Devastating, something in him whispered.

He hadn't imagined that anything could get to him. Nothing had in years. And no woman had ever come close.

Dominik had never experienced the overwhelming sensation that he wasn't only naked in the sense of having no clothes on—he was naked in every sense. Transparent with it, so anyone who happened by could see all the things in him he'd learned to pack away, out of view. First, as an orphan who had to try his best to act perfect for prospective parents. Then as a kid on the street who had to act tough enough to be left alone. Then as a soldier who had to act as if nothing he was ordered to do stayed with him.

And he couldn't say he much cared for the sensation now.

He needed to get up and leave this bed. He needed to go for a long, punishing run to clear his head. He needed to do something physical until he took the edge off all the odd things swirling around inside him, showing too much as if she'd knocked down every last boundary he had, and Dominik certainly couldn't allow that—

But she stirred then, shifting all that smooth, soft heat against him, and a new wave of intense heat washed over him.

She let out a sigh that sounded like his name, and what was he supposed to do with that?

Despite himself, he held on to her.

Especially when she lifted her head, piled her hands beneath her chin and blinked up at him.

And the things he wanted to say appalled him.

He cleared his throat. "Do you feel sufficiently indoctrinated into the sport?"

He hardly recognized his own voice. Or that note in it that he was fairly certain was...playfulness? And his hands were on her curves as if he needed to assure himself that they were real. That she was.

"Is it a sport? I thought of it more as a pastime. A habit, perhaps." She considered it, and what was wrong with him that he enjoyed watching a woman *think*? "Or for some, I suppose, an addiction."

"There are always hobbyists and amateurs, little red," he found himself saying, a certain...*warmth* in his voice that he wanted to rip out with his own fingers. But he didn't know where to start. "But I have never counted myself among them."

He meant to leave, and yet his hands were on her, smoothing their way down her back, then cupping her bottom. He knew he needed to let her go and make sure this never happened again, but she was smiling.

And he hardly knew her. Gone was all that sharpness, and in its place was a kind of soft, almost dreamy expression that made his chest hurt.

As if she was the one teaching him a lesson here.

"I beg your pardon. I didn't realize I was addressing such a renowned star of the bedroom," she said, and her lovely eyes danced with laughter.

It only served to remind him that she didn't laugh nearly enough.

"I will excuse it," he told her. "Once."

He needed to put distance between them. Now. Dominik knew that the way he knew every other fact of his existence. He knew it like every single memory he had of the nuns. The streets. The missions he'd been sent on.

He wasn't a man built for connection. He didn't want to be the kind of man who could connect with people, because people were what was wrong with the world. People had built this house. A person had given him away. He wanted nothing to do with *people*, or he never would have taken himself off into the woods in the first place.

But this pretty, impossible person was looking at him as if he was the whole world, her cheeks heating into red blazes he couldn't keep from touching. He ran his knuckles over one, then the other, silky smooth and wildly hot.

"It is still our wedding night," she pointed out.

"So it is."

Lauren lowered her lashes, then traced a small pattern against his chest with one fingertip.

"I don't know how this works. Or if you can. Physically, I mean. But I wondered… I mean, I hoped…" She blew out a breath. "Was that the whole of the lesson?"

And Dominik was only a man, after all, no matter how he'd tried to make himself into a monster, out there in his forest. And the part of him that had been greedy for her since the moment he'd seen her could never be happy with so small a taste.

Will you ever be satisfied? a voice in him asked. *Or will you always want more?*

That should have sent him racing for the door. He needed to leave, right now, but he found himself lifting her against him instead. He drew her up on her knees so she straddled him, and watched as she looked down between them, blinked and then smiled.

Wickedly, God help him.

"By all means," he encouraged her, his hands on her hips. "Allow me to teach you something else I feel certain you won't feel, as shut off and uninterested in these things as you are."

She found him then, wrapping her hands around the hardest expression of his need and guiding him to the center of her heat.

As if she'd been born for this. For him.

"No," she murmured breathlessly. And then smiled as she took him inside her as if he'd been made to fit her so perfectly, just like that. "I don't expect I'll feel anything at all."

And there was nothing for it. There was no holding back.

Dominik gave himself over to his doom.

CHAPTER ELEVEN

THE SITUATION DID not improve as the days slid by and turned inevitably into weeks.

Dominik needed to put a stop to the madness. There was no debate on that topic. The pressing need to leave the mess he'd made here, get the hell out of England, and away from the woman he never should have married, beat in him like a drum. It was the first thing he thought of when he woke. It dogged him through the long summer days. It even wormed its way into his dreams.

But one day led into the next, and he went nowhere. He didn't even try to leave as if he was the one who'd wandered into the wrong forest and found himself under some kind of spell he couldn't break.

Meanwhile, they traded lesson for lesson.

"I know how to use utensils, little red," he told her darkly one morning after he'd come back from a punishing run—yet not punishing enough, clearly, as he'd returned to Combe Manor—and had showered and changed only to find the formal dining room set with acres of silver on either side of each plate. There was a mess of glasses and extra plates everywhere he looked.

And Lauren sat there with her hair pulled back into

the smooth ponytail he took personally and that prissy look on her face.

The very same prissy look that made him hard and greedy for her, instantly.

"This won't be a lesson about basic competence with a fork, which I'll go ahead and assume you mastered some time ago," she told him tartly. Her gaze swept over him, making him feel as if he was still that grubby-faced orphan, never quite good enough. He gritted his teeth against it, because that was the last thing he needed. The present was complicated enough without dragging in the past. "This will be about formal manners for formal dinners."

"Alternatively, I could cook for myself, eat with own my fingers if I so desire and continue to have the exact same blood in my veins that I've always had with no one the least bit interested either way. None of this matters."

He expected her to come back at him, sharp and amusing, but she didn't. She studied him for a moment instead, and he still didn't know how to handle the way she looked at him these days. It was softer. Warmer.

It was too dangerous. It scraped at him until he felt raw and he could never get enough of it, all the same.

"It depends on your perspective, I suppose," she said. "It's not rocket science, of course. The fate of the world doesn't hang in the balance. History books won't be written about what fork you use at a banquet. But the funny thing about manners is that they can often stand in for the things you lack."

"And what is it I lack, exactly? Be specific, please. I dare you."

"I'm talking about me, Dominik. Not you."

And when she smiled, the world stopped.

He told himself it was one more sign he needed to get away from her. Instead, he took the seat opposite her at the table as if he really was under her spell.

Why couldn't he break it?

"When I was nine my parents had been divorced for two years, which means each of them was married again. My stepmother was pregnant. I didn't know it at the time, but my mother was, too. I still thought that they should all be spending a great deal more time with me. So one day I decided I'd run away, thereby forcing them to worry about me, and then act like parents."

She smiled as if at the memory, but it wasn't a happy smile. And later Dominik would have to reflect on how and why he knew the difference between her *smiles*, God help him. As if he'd made a study against his will, when he wasn't entirely paying attention.

"I rode the buses around and around, well into the evening," she said with that same smile. "And they came together, just as I'd hoped, but only so they could blame each other for what a disaster I was. Within an hour of my return they'd agreed to send me off to boarding school for the summer, so others could deal with me and they wouldn't have to do it themselves."

"I understand that not all parents are good ones," Dominik said, his voice low. "But I would caution you against complaining about your disengaged, yet present, parents while in the presence of a man who had none. Ever. Disengaged or otherwise."

"I'm not complaining about them," Lauren replied quietly. "They are who they are. I'm telling you how I came to be at a very posh school for summer. It was entirely filled with children nobody wanted."

"Pampered children, then. I can assure you no orphanage is *posh*."

"Yes. Someone, somewhere, paid handsomely to send us all to that school. But it would have been hard to tell a lonely nine-year-old, who knew she was at that school because her parents didn't want anything to do with her, that she was *pampered*. Mostly, I'm afraid, I was just scared."

Dominik stared back at her, telling himself he felt nothing. Because he ought to have felt nothing. He had taught her that sensation was real and that she could feel it, but he wanted none of it himself. No sensation. No emotion.

None of this scraping, aching thing that lived in him now that he worried might crack his ribs open from the inside. Any minute now.

"They taught us manners," Lauren told him in the same soft, insistent tone. "Comportment. Dancing. And it all seemed as stupid to me as I'm sure it does to you right now, but I will tell you this. I have spent many an evening since that summer feeling out of place. Unlike everyone else my age at university, for example, with all their romantic intrigue. These days I'm often trotted off to a formal affair where I am expected to both act as an emblem for Combe Industries as well as blend into the background. All at once. And do you know what allows me to do that? The knowledge that no matter what, I can handle myself in any social situation. People agonize over which fork to choose and which plate is theirs while I sit there, listening to conversations I shouldn't be hearing, ready and able to do my job."

"Heaven forbid anything prevent you from doing your job."

"I like my job."

"Do you? Or do you like imagining that your Mr. Combe cannot make it through a day without you?" He shrugged when she glared at him. "We are all of us dark creatures in our hearts, little red. Think of the story from the wolf's point of view next time. Our Red Riding Hood doesn't come off well, does she?"

He thought she had quite a few things to say to that, but she nodded toward the silverware before them instead. "We'll work from the outside in, and as we go we'll work on appropriate dinner conversation at formal occasions, which does not include obsessive references to fairy tales."

Dominik couldn't quite bring himself to tell her that he already knew how to handle a formal dinner, thank you. Not when she thought she was giving him a tool he could use to *save himself,* no less.

Just as he couldn't bring himself—allow himself—to tell her all those messy things that sloshed around inside him at the thought of her as a scared nine-year-old, abandoned by her parents and left to make *manners* her sword and shield.

He showed her instead, pulling her onto his lap before one of the interminable courses and imparting his own lesson. Until they were both breathing too heavily to care that much whether they used the correct fork—especially when his fingers were so talented.

He meant to leave the following day, but there was dancing, which meant he got to hold Lauren in his arms and then sweep her away upstairs to teach her what those bed posts were for. He meant to leave the day after that, but she'd had videos made of all the San Giacomo holdings.

There was something every day. Presentations on all manner of topics. Lessons of every description, from comportment to conversation and back again. Meetings with the unctuous, overly solicitous tailors, who he wanted to hate until they returned with beautiful clothes even he could tell made him look like the aristocrat he wasn't.

Which he should have hated—but couldn't, not when Lauren looked at him as if he was some kind of king.

He needed to get out of there, but he had spent an entire childhood making up stories about his imaginary family in his head. And he didn't have it in him to walk away from the first person he'd ever met who could tell him new stories. Real stories, this time.

Because Lauren also spent a significant part of every day teaching him the history of the San Giacomos, making sure he knew everything there was to know about their rise to power centuries ago. Their wealth and consequence across the ages.

And how it had likely come to pass that a sixteen-year-old heiress had been forced to give up her illegitimate baby, whether she wanted to or not.

He found that part the hardest to get his head around—likely because he so badly wanted to believe it.

"You must have known her," he said one day as summer rain danced against the windows where he stood.

They were back in the library, surrounded by all those gleaming, gold-spined books that had never been put on their self-important shelves for a man like him, no matter what blood ran in his veins. Lauren sat with her tablet before her, stacks of photo albums arrayed on the table, and binders filled with articles on the San Giacomo family. All of them stories that were now his, she told him time and time again. And all those stories about a family that was now his, too.

Dominik couldn't quite believe in any of it.

He'd spent his childhood thirsty for even a hint of a real story to tell about his family. About himself. Then he'd spent his adulthood resolved not to care about any of it, because he was making his own damned story.

He couldn't help thinking that this was all…too late. That the very thing that might have saved him as a child was little more than a bedtime story to him now, with about as much impact on his life.

"Alexandrina," he elaborated when Lauren frowned at him. "You must have known my mother while she was still alive."

And he didn't know how to tell her how strange those words felt in his mouth. *My mother*. Bitter and sweet. Awkward. Unreal. *My mother* was a dream he'd tortured himself with as a boy. Not a real person. Not a real woman with a life, hopes and dreams and possibly even *reasons*.

It had never occurred to him that his anger was a gift. Take that away and he had nothing but the urge to find compassion in him somewhere…and how was a man meant to build his life on that?

"I did know her," Lauren said. "A little."

"Was she…?"

But he didn't know what to ask. And he wasn't sure he wanted to know the answers.

"I couldn't possibly be a good judge." Lauren was choosing her words carefully. And Dominik didn't know when he'd become so delicate that she might imagine he needed special handling. "I worked for her son, so we were never more than distantly polite the few times we met. I don't know that any impression I gleaned of her would be the least bit worthwhile."

"It is better than no impressions, which is what I have."

Lauren nodded at that. "She was very beautiful."

"That tells me very little about her character, as I think you know."

"She could be impatient. She could be funny." Lauren thought a moment. "I think she was very conscious of her position."

"Meaning she was a terrible snob."

"No, I don't think so. Not the way you mean it. I never saw her treat anyone badly. But she had certain standards that she expected to have met." She smiled. "If she was a man, people would say she knew her own mind, that's all."

"I've read about her." And he had, though he had found it impossible to see anything of him in the impossibly glamorous creature who'd laughed and pouted for the cameras, and inspired so many articles about her *style*, which Dominik suspected was a way to talk about a high-class woman's looks without causing offense. "She seemed entirely defined by her love affairs and scandals."

"My abiding impression of her was that she had learned how to be pretty. And how to use that prettiness to live up to the promise of both the grand families she was a part of. But I don't think it ever occurred to her that she could be happy."

"Could she?" Dominik asked, sardonic straight through. "I didn't realize that was on offer."

"It should always be on offer," Lauren replied with a certain quiet conviction that Dominik refused to admit got to him. Because it shouldn't have. "Isn't that the point?"

"The point of what, exactly?"

"Everything, Dominik."

"You sound like an American advertisement," Dominik said after a moment, from between his teeth. "No one is owed happiness. And certainly, precious few find it."

He hadn't meant to move from the windows, but he had. And he was suddenly standing in front of that sofa, looking down at Lauren.

Who gazed straight back at him, that same softness on her face. It connected directly to that knot inside him he'd been carrying for weeks now. That ache. That infernal clamoring on the inside of his ribs that demanded he leave, yet wouldn't let him go.

"Maybe if we anticipated happiness we might find a little along the way." Her voice was like honey, and he knew it boded ill. He knew it was bad for him. Because he had no defenses against that kind of sweetness. Caramel eyes and honey voice—and he was a goner. "Why not try?"

"I had no idea that our shabby little marriage of convenience would turn so swiftly into an encounter group," he heard himself growl. When she didn't blanch at that the way he'd expected she would, he pushed on. "So-called happiness is the last refuge and resort of the dim-witted. And those who don't know any better, which I suppose is redundant. I think you'll find the real world is a little too complicated for platitudes and whistling as you work."

Lauren lifted one shoulder, then dropped it. "I don't believe that."

And it was the way she said it that seemed to punch holes straight through Dominik's chest. There was no defiant tilt to her chin. There was no angry flash of temper in her lovely eyes. It was a simple statement, more powerful somehow for its softness than for any attempt at a show of strength.

And there was no reason he should feel it shake in him like a storm.

"You don't believe that the world is a terrible place, as complicated as it is harsh, desperate people careening about from greed to self-interest and back again? Ignoring their children or abandoning them in orphanages as they see fit?"

"The fact that people can be awful and scared only means that when we happen upon it, we should cling to what happiness we can."

"Let me guess. You think I should be more grateful that after all this time, the woman who clearly knew where I was all along told others where to find me. But only after her death, so they could tell me sad stories about how she *might* have given me away against her will. You want me to conclude that I ended up here all the same, so why dwell on what was lost in the interim? You will have to forgive me if I do not see all this as the gift you do."

"The world won't end if you allow the faintest little gleam of optimism into your life," Lauren said with that same soft conviction that got to him in ways he couldn't explain. And didn't particularly want to analyze. "And who knows? You could even allow yourself to hope for something. Anything. It's not dim-witted and it's not because a person doesn't see the world as it is." Her gaze was locked to his. "Hope takes strength, Dominik. Happiness takes work. And I choose to believe it's worth it."

"What do you know of either?" he demanded. "You, who locked yourself away from the world and convinced yourself you disliked basic human needs. You are the poster child for happiness?"

"I know because of you."

The words were so simple.

And they might as well have been a tornado, tearing him up.

"Me." He shook his head as if he didn't understand the word. As if she'd used it to bludgeon him. "If I bring you *happiness*, little red, I fear you've gone and lost yourself in a deep, dark woods from which you will never return."

She stood up then, and he was seized with the need to stop her somehow. As if he knew what she was going to say when of course, he couldn't know. He refused to know.

He should have left before this happened.

He should have left.

His gaze moved over her, and it struck him that while he'd certainly paid close attention to her, he hadn't truly *looked* at her since they'd arrived here weeks ago. Not while she was dressed. She wasn't wearing the same sharp, pointedly professional clothing any longer—and he couldn't recall the last time she had. Today she wore a pair of trousers he knew were soft like butter, and as sweetly easy to remove. She wore a flowing sort of top that drooped down over one shoulder, which he liked primarily because it gave him access to the lushness beneath.

Both of those things were clues, but he ignored them.

It was the hair that was impossible to pretend hadn't changed.

Gone was the sleek ponytail, all that blond silk ruthlessly tamed and controlled. She wore it loose now, tumbling around her shoulders, because he liked his hands in it.

Had he not been paying attention? Or had he not wanted to see?

"Yes, you," she said, answering the question he'd asked, and all the ones he hadn't. "You make me happy, Dominik. And hopeful. I'm sorry if that's not what you want to hear."

She kept her gaze trained on his, and he didn't know what astounded him more. That she kept saying these terrible, impossible things. Or that she looked so fearless as she did it, despite the color in her cheeks.

He wanted to tell her to stop, but he couldn't seem to move.

And she kept right on going. "I thought I knew myself, but I didn't. I thought I knew what I needed, but I had no idea. I asked you to teach me and I meant very specifically about sex. And you did that, but you taught me so much more. You taught me everything." She smiled then, a smile he'd never seen before, so tremulous and full of hope—and it actually hurt him. "I think you made me whole, Dominik, and I had no idea I wasn't already."

If she had thrust a sword into the center of his chest, then slammed it home, he could not have felt more betrayed.

"I did none of those things," he managed to grit out. "Sex is not happiness. It is not hope. And it is certainly no way to go looking for yourself, Lauren."

"And yet that's who I found." And she was still aiming that smile at him, clearly unaware that she was killing him. "Follow the bread crumbs long enough, even into a terrible forest teeming with scary creatures and wolves like men, and there's no telling what you'll find at the other end."

"I know exactly what you'll find on the other end. Nothing. Because there's no witch in a gingerbread house. There's no Big Bad Wolf. You were sent to find me by a man who was executing a duty, nothing more. And I came along with you because—"

"Because why, exactly?" Again, it was the very softness and certainty in her voice that hit him like a gut punch. "You certainly didn't have to invite me into your cabin. But you did."

"Something I will be questioning for some time to come, I imagine." Dominik slashed a hand through the air, but he didn't know if it was aimed at her—or him. "But this is over, Lauren. You had your experiment and now it's done."

"Because I like it too much?" She had the audacity to laugh. "Surely, you've done this before, Dominik. Surely, you knew the risks. If you open someone up, chances are, they're going to like it. Isn't that what you wanted? Me to fall head over heels in love with you like every virgin cliché ever? Why else would you have dedicated yourself to *my experiment* the way you did?"

He actually backed away from her then. As if the word she'd used was poison. Worse than that. A toxic bomb that could block out the sun.

It felt as if she'd blinded him already.

"There is no risk whatsoever of anyone falling in love with me," he told her harshly.

"I think you know that isn't true." She studied him as if he'd disappointed her, as if he was *currently* letting her down, right there in full view of all the smug volumes of fancy books he'd never read and never would. "I assumed that was why you stayed all this time."

"I stayed all this time because that was the deal we made."

"The deal we made was for a wedding night, Dominik. Maybe a day or so after. It's been nearly two months."

"It doesn't matter how long it's been. It doesn't matter why. I'm glad that you decided you can feel all these emotions." But he wasn't glad. He was something far, far away from *glad*. "But I don't. I won't."

"But you do." And that was the worst yet. Another betrayal, another weapon. Because it was so matter-of-fact. Because she stared right back at him as if she knew things about him he didn't, and that was unbearable. Dominik had never been *known*. He wanted nothing to do with it. "I think you do."

And Dominik never knew what he might have said to that—how he might have raged or, more terrifying, how he might not have—because the doors to the library were pushed open then, and one of Combe Manor's quietly competent staff members stood there, frowning.

"I'm sorry to interrupt," she said, looking back and forth between them. "But something's happened, I'm afraid." She gestured in the direction of the long drive out front. "There are reporters. Everywhere. Cameras, microphones and shouting."

The maid's eyes moved to Dominik, and he thought she looked apologetic. When all he could feel was that emptiness inside him that had always been there and always would. Even if now, thanks to Lauren, it ached.

The maid cleared her throat. "They're calling for you, sir. By name."

CHAPTER TWELVE

IN THE END, Lauren was forced to call the Yorkshire Police to encourage the paparazzi to move off the property, down to the bottom of the long drive that led to Combe Manor from the village proper and away from the front of the house itself.

But the damage was done. The will had been leaked, as Lauren had known it would be eventually, and Dominik had been identified. That he had quietly married his half brother's longtime personal assistant had made the twenty-four-hour news cycle.

She quickly discovered that she was nothing but a shameless gold digger. There was arch speculation that Matteo had dispatched her to corral Dominik, marry him under false pretenses and then…work him to Matteo's advantage somehow.

It was both close to the truth and nothing like the truth at all, but any impulse she might have had to laugh at it dissipated in the face of Dominik's response.

Which was to disappear.

First, he disappeared without actually going anywhere. It was like looking into a void. One moment she'd been having a conversation—admittedly, not the most pleasant conversation—with him. The next, it was as if the Dominik she'd come to know was gone and a stranger had taken his place.

A dark, brooding stranger, who looked at her with icy disinterest. And as far as she could tell, viewed the paparazzi outside the same. He didn't call her *little red* again, and she would have said she didn't even like the nickname.

But she liked it even less when he stopped using it.

Her mobile rang and rang, but she ignored the calls. From unknown numbers she assumed meant more reporters. From Pia, who had likely discovered that she had another brother from the news, which made Lauren feel guilty for not insisting Matteo tell her earlier. And from the various members of the Combe Industries Board of Directors, which she was more than happy to send straight to voice mail.

"It's Mr. Combe," she said when it rang another time. "At last."

"You must take that, of course," Dominik said, standing at the windows again, glaring off into the distance. "Heaven forfend you do not leap to attention the moment your master summons you."

And Lauren couldn't say she liked the way he said that. But she didn't know what to do about it, either.

"We always knew this day would come," she told him, briskly, when she'd finished having a quick damage control conversation with Matteo. "It's actually surprising that didn't happen sooner."

"We have been gilding this lily for weeks now," Dominik replied, his voice that dark growl that made everything in her shiver—and not entirely from delight. "We have played every possible Pygmalion game there is. There is nothing more to be accomplished here."

"Where would you like to go instead?" She had opened up the cabinet and turned on the television earlier, so they could watch the breathless news reports and the endless scroll of accusation and speculation at the bottom of the screen. Now she turned the volume up again so she could hear what they were saying. About her. "I suppose we should plan some kind of function to introduce you to—"

"No."

"No? No, you don't want to be introduced to society? Or no, you don't want—"

"You fulfilled your role perfectly, Lauren." But the way he said it was no compliment. It was…dangerous. "Your Mr. Combe will be so proud, I am sure. You have acted as my jailer. My babysitter. And you have kept me out of public view for very nearly two months, which must be longer than any of you thought possible. You have my congratulations. I very nearly forgot your purpose in this."

His voice didn't change when he said that. And he didn't actually reach out and strike her.

But it felt as if he did.

"I thought this would happen sooner, as a matter of fact," Lauren managed to say, her heart beating much too wildly in her chest. Her head spinning a little from the hit that hadn't happened. "And my brief was to give you a little polish and a whole lot of history, Dominik. That's all. I found a hermit in a hut. All Mr. Combe asked me to do was make you a San Giacomo."

"And now I am as useless as any one of them. You've done your job well. You are clearly worth every penny he pays you."

It was harder to keep her cool than it should have

been. Because she knew too much now. He was acting like a stranger, but her body still wanted him the way it always did. He had woken her this morning by surging deep inside her, catapulting her from dreams tinged with the things he did to her straight into the delirious reality.

She didn't know how to handle this. The distance between them. The fury in his dark gaze. The harsh undercurrent to everything he said, and the way he looked at her as if she had been the enemy all along.

She should have known that the price of tasting happiness—of imagining she could—meant that the lack of it would hurt her.

More than hurt her. Looking at him and seeing a stranger made her feel a whole lot closer to broken.

She should have known better than to let herself *feel*.

"I know this feels like a personal attack," she said, carefully, though she rather thought she'd been the one personally attacked. "But this is about how the San Giacomo and Combe families are perceived. And more, how Matteo and his sister have been portrayed in the press in the wake of their father's death. No one wanted you to be caught up in that."

"And yet here I am."

"Dominik. Please. This is just damage control. That's the only reason Mr. Combe didn't proclaim your existence far and wide the moment he knew of you."

That gaze of his swung to her and held. Hard, like another blow. It made her want to cry—but she knew, somehow, that would only make it worse.

"You cannot control damage, Lauren. I would think you, of all people, would know this. You can only do your best to survive it."

And she had no time to recover from that.

Because that was when the self-satisfied newscaster on the television screen started talking about who Dominik James really was.

"We've just been made aware that Dominik James is not merely the long-lost heir to two of Europe's most prominent families," the man said. "Our sources tell us he is also a self-made billionaire who ran his own security company until he sold it recently for what is believed to be a small fortune in its own right. Dominik himself has been widely sought after by celebrities and kings alike, and a number of governments besides."

Then they flashed pictures of him, in case Lauren had somehow missed the implications. There were shots of Dominik in three-piece suits, his hair cropped close to his head, shaking hands with powerful, recognizable men. In and out of formal balls, charity events and boardrooms.

Nothing like a feral hermit at all.

"Oh, dear," Dominik said when the newscast cut to some inane commercial, too much darkness in his voice. "Your table settings will not save you now, Lauren. It has all been a lie. I am not at all who you thought I was. Why don't you tell me more about how happy you are?"

And Lauren remembered exactly why she'd decided emotion wasn't for her. She had been nine years old and sent off to a terrifying stone building filled with strangers. She'd stayed awake the whole of that first night, sobbing into her pillow so her roommate didn't hear her.

Since then, she'd forgotten that these terrible emotions could sit on a person like this. Crushing her with their weight. Suffocating her, yet never quite killing her.

Making her own heartbeat feel like an attack.

"You didn't need me at all," she managed to say, parts of her breaking apart on the inside like so many earthquakes, stitched together into a single catastrophe she wasn't sure she would survive. No matter what he'd said about damage.

But she didn't want to let him see it.

"No," Dominik said, and there was something terrible there in his gray eyes that made her want to reach out to him. Soothe him somehow. But his voice was so cold. Something like cruel, and she didn't dare. "I never needed you."

"This was a game, then." She didn't know how she was speaking when she couldn't feel her own face. Her outsides had gone numb, but that paralysis did not extend inside, where she was desperately trying to figure out what to do with all that raw upheaval before it broke her into actual pieces. "You were just playing a game. I can understand that you wanted to find out who your family really was. But you were playing the game with me."

And maybe later she would think about how he stood there, so straight and tall and bruised somehow, that it made her ache. With that look on his face that made her want to cry.

But all she could do at the moment was fight to stay on her feet, without showing him how much he was hurting her. It was crucial that she swallow that down, hide it away, even as it threatened to cut her down.

"Life is damage, Lauren," he said in that same dark, cold way. "Not hope. Not happiness. Those are stories fools tell to trick themselves into imagining otherwise. The true opiate of the masses. The reality is that people lie. They deceive you. They abandon you whenever possible, and may use you to serve their own ends. I never needed you to polish me. But you're welcome all the same. Someday you'll thank me for disabusing you of all these damaging notions."

Her mobile rang again, Matteo's name flashing on her screen.

And for the first time in as long as she could remember, Lauren didn't want to answer. She wanted to fling her mobile across the room and watch it shatter against the wall. Part of her wanted very much to throw it at Dominik, and see if it would shatter that wall.

But she did neither.

She looked down at the mobile, let her thoughts turn violent, and when she looked up again Dominik was gone.

And she sat where she was for a very long time, there on a Combe family sofa before a television screen that repeated lie after lie about who she was until she was tempted to believe it herself.

Her mobile rang. It rang and rang, and she let it.

Outside, the endless summer day edged into night, and still Lauren sat where she was.

She felt hollowed out. And yet swollen somehow. As if all those unwieldy, overwhelming emotions she'd successfully locked away since she was a child had swept back into her, all at once, until she thought they might break her wide open.

It was the first time in almost as long that she didn't have the slightest idea what to do. How to fix this. Or even if she wanted to.

All she knew was that even now, even though Dominik had looked at her the way he had, and said those things to her, he was still the one she wanted to go to. It was his arms she longed for. His heat, his strength.

How could she want him to comfort her when he was the one who had hurt her?

But she wasn't going to get an answer to that question.

Because when she went looking for him, determined to figure at least some part of this out, she discovered that Dominik hadn't simply disappeared while he'd stood there before her.

He'd actually gone.

He'd packed up his things, clearly, as there was nothing to suggest he'd been here at all. And then he must have let himself out while she'd been sitting there in the library where he'd left her, trying her best not to fall apart.

And she didn't have to chase after him to know he had no intention of coming back.

Because she had fallen for him, head over heels. But he had only ever been playing a game.

And Lauren would have to learn to live with that, too.

Lauren launched herself back into her life.

Her real life, which did not include mysterious men with hidden fortunes who lived off in the Hungarian woods. The life she had built all by herself, with no support from anyone.

The life that she was sure she remembered loving, or at least finding only a few months ago.

"You still love it," she snapped at herself one morning, bustling around her flat on her way to work. "You love every last part of it."

"You know when you start talking to yourself," Mary

said serenely, splashing the last of the milk into her tea, "that's when the stress has really won."

Lauren eyed her roommate and the empty jug of milk. "Is that your mobile ringing?"

And as Mary hurried out of the room, she told herself that she was fine. Good.

Happy and hopeful, as a matter of fact, because neither one of those things had anything to do with the surly, angry man who'd done exactly what she'd asked him to do and then left after staying much longer than she'd expected he would.

She had what she wanted. She knew what other people felt. She understood why they went to such great lengths to have sex whenever possible. And she was now free to go out on the pull whenever she pleased. She could do as Dominik had once suggested and take herself off to a local pub, where she could continue conducting the glorious experiment in her own sexual awakening. On her own.

He didn't need her. And she certainly didn't need him.

Lauren decided she'd get stuck into it, no pun intended, that very night.

She thought about it all day long. She made her usual assenting, supportive sounds during the video conference from wherever Matteo was in the world today, but what she was really thinking about was the debauchery that awaited her. Because Dominik had been no more than a means to an end, she told herself. Merely a stepping-stone to a glorious sensual feast.

She left work early—which was to say, on time for once—and charged into the first pub she saw.

Where she remained for the five minutes it took to

look around, see all the men who weren't Dominik and want to cry.

Because it turned out that the only kind of awakening she wanted was with him.

Only and ever with him, something in her said with a kind of finality that she felt knit itself inside her like bone.

And maybe that was why, some six weeks after the tabloids had discovered Dominik—when all that bone had grown and gotten strong—she reacted to what ought to have been a perfectly simple request from Matteo the way she did.

"I'll be landing in San Francisco shortly," he told her from his jet.

"And then headed home, presumably," she interjected. "To attend to your empire."

"Yes, yes," he said in a way that she knew meant, *or perhaps not*. "But what I need you to do is work on that marriage."

Lauren had him on the computer monitor at her desk so she could work more easily on her laptop as he fired his usual instructions at her.

But she stopped what she was doing at that and swiveled in her chair, so she could gaze at him directly.

"Which marriage would that be?" she asked. Tartly, she could admit. "Your sister's? You must know that she and her prince are playing a very specific cat and mouse game—"

Matteo was rifling through papers, frowning at something off screen, and she knew that his sister's romantic life was a sore point for him. Was that why she'd brought it up? When she knew that wasn't the marriage he meant?

"I mean your marriage, Lauren," he said in that distracted way of his. She knew what that meant, too. That her boss had other, more important things on his mind. Something she had always accepted as his assistant, because that was her job—to fade into his background and make certain he could focus on anything he wished. But he was talking about *her*. And the marriage he'd suggested, and she'd actually gone ahead and done on his command. "There's a gala in Rome next week. Do you think your husband is sufficiently tamed? Can he handle a public appearance?"

"Well, he's not actually a trained bear," she found herself replying with more snap in her voice than necessary. "And he was handling public appearances just fine before he condescended to come to Combe Manor. So no need to fear he might snap his chain and devour the guests, I think."

"You can field the inevitable questions from paparazzi," Matteo said, frowning down at the phone in his hand. The way he often did—so there was no reason for it to prick at Lauren the way it did. *Maybe it is time you ask yourself what you* wouldn't *do if your Mr. Combe asked it*, Dominik had said. *You may find the answers illuminating.* But what about what Matteo wouldn't do for her? Like pay attention to the fact she was an actual person, not a bit of machinery? "You know the drill."

"Indeed I do. I know all the drills."

She'd created the drills, for that matter. And she wasn't sure why she wanted to remind Matteo of that.

"Just make sure it looks good," Matteo said, and he looked at her then. "You know what I mean. I want a quiet, calm appearance that makes it clear to all that the

San Giacomo scandal is fully handled. I want to keep the board happy."

"And whether the brother you have yet to meet is happy with all these revelations about the family he never knew is of secondary interest, of course. Or perhaps of no interest at all."

She was sure she'd meant to say that. But there it was, out there between them as surely as if she'd hauled off and slapped her boss in the face.

Matteo blinked, and it seemed to Lauren as if it took a thousand years for him to focus on her.

"Is my brother unhappy?" he asked. Eventually.

"You will have to ask him yourself," she replied. And then, because she couldn't seem to stop herself, "He's your brother, not mine."

"He is your husband, Lauren."

"Do you think it is the role of a wife to report on her husband to her boss? One begins to understand why you remain unmarried."

Something flashed over his face then, and she didn't understand why she wasn't already apologizing. Why she wasn't hurrying to set things right.

"You knew the role when you took it." Matteo frowned. "Forgive me, but am I missing something?"

And just like that, something in Lauren snapped.

"I am your personal assistant, Mr. Combe," she shot at him. "That can and has included such things as sorting out your wardrobe. Making your travel arrangements. Involving myself more than I'd like in your personal life. But it should never have included you asking me to marry someone on your behalf."

"If you had objections you should have raised them

before you went ahead and married him, then. It's a bit late now, don't you think?"

"When have I ever been permitted to have objections in this job?" She shook her head, that cold look on Dominik's face flashing through her head. And the way he'd said *your master.* "When have I ever said no to you?"

Matteo's frown deepened, but not because he was having any kind of emotional response. She knew that. She could see that he was baffled.

"I value you, Lauren, if that's what this is about. You know that."

But Lauren wasn't the same person she had been. It wasn't the value Matteo assigned to her ability to do her job that mattered to her. Not anymore.

She could look back and see how all of this had happened. How she, who had never been wanted by anyone, threw herself into being needed instead. She'd known she was doing it. She'd given it her all. And she'd been hired by Matteo straight out of university, so it had felt like some kind of cure of all the things that ailed her to make sure she not only met his needs, but anticipated them, too.

She had thought they were a team. They had been, all these years. While he'd had to work around his father and now he was in charge.

But Dominik had taught her something vastly different than how to make herself indispensable to the person who paid her.

He had taught her how to value herself.

He'd taught her how to want. How to *be wanted.*

And in return, he'd taught her how to want *more.*

Because that was the trouble with allowing herself

to want anything at all when she'd done without for so long. She wasn't satisfied with half measures, or a life spent giving everything she had to a man who not only couldn't return it, but whom she didn't want anything from.

She didn't want to sacrifice herself. It turned out that despite her choice of profession, she wasn't a martyr. Or she didn't want to be one.

Not anymore.

She knew what she wanted. Because she knew what it felt like now to be wanted desperately in return—no matter that Dominik might not have admitted that. She still knew.

He had stayed so long at Combe Manor. He had showed her things that she'd never dared dream about before. And he had taken her, over and over again, like a man possessed.

Like a man who feared losing her the same way she'd feared losing him.

If he hadn't cared, he wouldn't have snuck away. She knew that, too.

Lauren looked around the office that was more her home than her flat had ever been. The couch where she'd slept so many nights—including the night before her wedding. The windows that looked out over the city she'd loved so desperately not because she required its concrete and buildings, she understood now, but because it had been her constant. The one kind of parent that wouldn't turn its back on her.

But she didn't need any of these things any longer.

Lauren already had everything she needed. Maybe she always had, but she knew it now. And it was time instead to focus on what she *wanted*.

"And I have valued these years, Mr. Combe," she said now, lifting her head and looking Matteo in the eye. "More than you know. But it's time for me to move on." She smiled when he started to protest. "Please consider this my notice. I will train my replacement. I'll find her myself and make certain she is up to your standards. Never fear."

"Lauren." His voice was kind then.

But it wasn't his kindness she wanted.

"I'm sorry," she said quietly. "But I can't do this anymore."

And that night she lay in her bed in the flat she paid for but hardly knew. She stared at her ceiling, and when that grew old, she moved to look out the window instead.

There was concrete everywhere. London rooftops, telephone wires and the sound of traffic in the distance. The home she'd made. The parent she'd needed. London had been all things to her, but in the end, it was only a city. Her favorite city, true. But if it was any more than that, she'd made it that way.

And she didn't want that any longer. She didn't need it. She craved…something else. Something different.

Something wild, a voice in her whispered.

Lauren thought about want. About need. About the crucial distinction between the two, and why it had taken her so long to see it.

And the next morning she set off for Hungary again.

By the time she made it to the mountain village nestled there at the edge of the forest it was well into the afternoon.

But she didn't let that stop her. She left the hired car near the inn she'd stayed in on the last night of her life before she'd met Dominik and everything changed, and she began to walk.

She didn't mind the growing dark, down there on the forest floor. The temperature dropped as she walked, but she had her red wrap and she pulled it closer around her.

The path was just as she remembered it, clear and easy to follow, if hard going against the high, delicate heels she wore. Because of course she wore them.

Lauren might have felt like a new woman. But that didn't mean she intended to betray herself with sensible shoes.

On she walked.

And she thought about fairy tales. About girls who found their way into forests and thought they were lost, but found their way out no matter what rose up to stop them. Especially if what tried to stop them was themselves.

It was only a deep, dark forest if she didn't know where she was going, she told herself. But she did. And all around her were pretty trees, fresh air and a path to walk upon.

No bread crumbs. No sharp teeth and wolves. No witches masquerading as friends, tucked up in enchanted cottages with monstrous roses and questionable pies.

No foreboding, no wicked spells.

There was only Lauren.

And she knew exactly what she wanted.

When she reached the clearing this time, she marched straight through it. There was no one lurking in the shadows on the front porch, but she hadn't really expected there would be. She walked up, anyway, went straight to the front door and let herself in.

The cabin was just as she remembered it. Shockingly cozy and inviting, and entirely too nice. It was a clue, had she bothered to pay attention to it, that the man she'd come to find—her husband—wasn't the mountain man she'd expected he would be.

Best of all, that same man sat before the fire now, watching her with eyes like rain.

"Turn around, Lauren," he said, his voice like gravel. "If you leave now, you'll make it back to the village before full dark. I wouldn't want to be wandering around the woods at night. Not in those shoes. You have no idea what you might encounter."

"I know exactly what I'll find in these woods," she replied. And she let her gaze go where it liked, from that too-long inky-black hair he'd never gotten around to cutting to her specifications to that stern mouth of his she'd felt on every inch of her body. "And look. There you are."

He shook his head. "You shouldn't have come here."

"And yet I did. Without your permission. Much as you ran off from Combe Manor without so much as a hastily penned note."

"I'm sure whatever mission you're on now is just as important as the last one that brought you here to storm about in my forest," he said, and something like temper flashed over his face—though it was darker. Much, much darker. "But I don't care what your Mr. Combe—"

"He didn't send me. I don't work for him anymore, as a matter of fact." She held his gaze and let the storm in it wash over her, too. "This is between you and me, Dominik."

The air between them shifted. Tightened, somehow.

"There is no you and me."

"You may have married me as a joke," she said softly, "but you did marry me. That makes me your wife."

"I need a wife about as much as I need a brother. I don't do family, Lauren. Or jokes. I want nothing to do with any of it."

"That is a shame." She crossed her arms over her chest and she stared him down as if he didn't intimidate her at all. "But I didn't ask you if you needed a wife. I reminded you that you already have one."

"You're wasting your time."

She smiled at him, and enjoyed it when he blinked at that as if it was a weapon she'd had tucked away in her arsenal all this time.

God, she hoped it was a weapon. Because she needed all of those she could find.

And she had no qualms about using each and every one she put her hands on.

"Here's the thing, Dominik," she said, and she wanted to touch him. She wanted to bury her face in the crook of his neck. She wanted to wake up with him tangled all around her. She wanted him, however she could get him. She wanted whatever a life with him looked like. "You taught me how to want. And don't you see? What I want is you."

CHAPTER THIRTEEN

"YOU CAN'T HAVE ME," Dominik growled at her, because that was what he'd decided. It was what made sense. "I never was a toy for you to pick up and put down at will, Lauren. I assumed that was finally clear."

And yet all he wanted to do was get his hands on her.

He knew he couldn't allow that. Even if he was having trouble remembering the *why* of that at the moment, now that she was here. Right here, in front of him, where he'd imagined her no less than a thousand times a night since he'd left England.

But he didn't. Because touching her—losing himself in all that pink and gold sweetness of hers—was where all of this had gone wrong from the start.

"I introduced you to sex, that's all," he said through gritted teeth, because he didn't want to think about that introduction. The way she'd yielded completely, innocent and eager and so hot he could still feel it. As if he carried her inside him. "This is the way of things. You think it means more than it does. But I don't."

"I tested that theory," she told him, and it landed on him like a punch, directly into his gut. "You told me I could walk into any pub in England and have whatever sex I wanted."

"Lauren." And he was surprised he didn't snap a few teeth off, his jaw was so tight. "I would strongly advise you not to stand here in my cabin and brag to me about your sexual exploits."

"Why would you care? If you don't want me?" She smiled at him again, self-possessed and entirely too calm. "But no need to issue warnings or threats. I walked in, took a look around and left. I don't want sexual exploits, Dominik. I told you. I want you."

"No," he growled, despite the way that ache in his chest intensified. "You don't."

"I assure you, I know my own mind."

"Perhaps, but you don't know me."

And he didn't wait for her to take that on board. He surged to his feet, prowling toward her, because she had to understand. She had to understand, and she had to leave, and he had to get on with spending the rest of his life trying to fit the pieces back together.

After she'd torn him up, crumpled him and left him in this mess in the first place.

Because you let her, the voice in him he'd tried to ignore since he'd met her—and certainly since he'd left her—chimed in.

"I thought at first it was the media attention that got to you, but you obviously don't mind that. You've had it before. Why should this be any different?"

And she didn't remind him of his lies of omission. They rose there between them like so much heat and smoke, and still, the only thing he could see was her.

"I don't care about attention." He wanted things he couldn't have. He wanted to *do* something, but when he reached out his hand, all he did was fit it to her soft, warm cheek.

Just to remind himself.

And then he dropped his hand to his side, but that didn't make it better, because she felt even better than he remembered.

"Dominik. I know that you feel—"

"You don't know what I feel." His voice was harsh, but his palm was on fire. As if touching her had branded him, and he was disfigured with it. And maybe it was the fact she couldn't seem to see it that spurred him on. "You don't have great parents, so you think you know, but you don't. There's no doubt that it's your parents who are the problem, not you. You must know this."

"They are limited people," she said, looking taken aback. But she rallied. "I can't deny that I still find it hurtful, but I'm not a little girl anymore. And to be honest, I think they're the ones who are missing out."

"That sounds very adult. Very mature. I commend you. But I'm not you. This is what I'm trying to tell you." And then he said the thing he had always known, since he was a tiny child. The thing he'd never said out loud before. The thing he had never imagined he even needed to put into words, it was so obvious. "There's something wrong with me, Lauren."

Her eyes grew bright. And he saw her hands curl into fists at her sides.

"Oh, Dominik." And he would remember the way she said his name. Long after she was gone, he would replay it again and again, something to warm him when the weather turned cold. It lodged inside him, hot and shining where his heart should have been. "There's nothing wrong with you. Nothing."

"This is not opinion. This is fact." He shook his head, harshly, when she made to reach for him. "I was six days old when I arrived in the orphanage. And brand-new babies never stay long in orphanages, because there are always those who want them. A clean slate. A new start. A child they can pretend they birthed themselves, if they want. But no one wanted me. Ever."

She was still shaking her head, so fiercely it threatened the hair she'd put in that damned ponytail as if it was her mission to poke at him.

"Maybe the nuns are the ones who wanted you, Dominik. Did you ever think of that? Maybe they couldn't bear to give you up."

He laughed at that, though it was a hollow sound, and not only because her words had dislodged old memories he hadn't looked at in years. The smiling face of the nun they'd called Sister Maria Ana, who had treated him kindly when he was little, until cancer stole her away when he was five. How had he forgotten that?

But he didn't want to think about that now. The possibility that someone had been kind to him didn't change the course of his life.

"Nobody wanted me. Ever. With one or two people in your life, even if they are your parents, this could be coincidence. Happenstance. But when I tell you that there is not one person on this earth who has ever truly wanted me, I am not exaggerating." He shoved those strange old memories aside. "There's something wrong with me inside, Lauren. And it doesn't go anywhere. If you can't see it, you will. In time. I see no point in putting us both through that."

Because he knew that if he let her stay, if he let her do this, he would never, ever let her go. He knew it.

"Dominik," she began.

"You showed me binders full of San Giacomos,"

he growled at her. "Century upon century of people obsessed with themselves and their bloodlines. They cataloged every last San Giacomo ever born. But they threw me away. *She* threw me away."

"She was sixteen," Lauren said fiercely, her red cloak all around her and emotion he didn't want to see wetting her cheeks. But he couldn't look away. "She was a scared girl who did what her overbearing father ordered her to do, by all accounts. I'm not excusing her for not doing something later, when she could have. But you know that whatever else happened, she never forgot you. She knew your name and possibly even where you lived. I can't speak for a dead woman, Dominik, but I think that proves she cared."

"You cannot care for something you throw away like trash," he threw at her.

And her face changed. It…crumpled, and he thought it broke his heart.

"You mean the way you did to me?" she asked.

"I left you before it was made perfectly obvious to you and the rest of the world that I don't belong in a place like that. I'm an orphan. I was a street kid. I joined the army because I wanted to die for a purpose, Lauren. I never meant for it to save me."

"All of that is who you were, perhaps," she said with more of that same ferocity that worked in him like a shudder. "But now you are a San Giacomo. You are a self-made man of no little power in your own right. And you are my husband."

And he didn't understand why he moved closer to her when he wanted to step away. When he wanted—needed—to put distance between them.

Instead, his hands found their way to her upper arms and held her there.

He noticed the way she fit him, in those absurd shoes she wore just as well as when she was barefoot. The way her caramel-colored eyes locked to his, seeing far too much.

"I don't have the slightest idea how to be a husband."

"Whereas my experience with being a wife is so extensive?" she shot right back.

"I don't—"

"Dominik." And she seemed to flow against him until she was there against his chest, her head tipped back so there was nothing else in the whole of the world but this. Her. "You either love me or you don't."

He knew what he should say. If he could spit out the words he could break her heart, and his, and free her from this.

He could go back to his quiet life, here in the forest where no one could disappoint him and he couldn't prove, yet again, how little he was wanted.

Dominik knew exactly what he should say.

But he didn't say it.

Because she was so warm, and he had never understood how cold he was before she'd found him here. She was like light and sunshine, even here in the darkest part of the forest.

And he hadn't gone with her to England because she was an emissary from his past. He certainly hadn't married her because she could tell him things he could have found out on his own about the family that wanted to claim him all of a sudden.

The last time Dominik had done something he didn't

want to do, simply because someone else told him to do it, he'd been in the army.

He could tell himself any lie at all, if he liked—and Lord knew he was better at that by the day—but he hadn't married this woman for any reason at all save one.

He'd wanted to.

"What if I do?" he demanded, his fingers gripping her—but whether to hold her close or keep her that crucial few inches away, he didn't know. "What do either one of us know about love, of all things?"

"You don't have to know a thing about love." And she was right there before him, wrapping her arms around his neck as if she belonged there. And fitting into place as if they'd been puzzle pieces, all this time, meant to interlock just like this. "Think about fairy tales. Happy-ever-after is guaranteed by one thing and one thing only."

"Magic?" he supplied. But his hands were moving. He tugged the elastic from her gleaming blond hair and tossed it aside. "Terrible spells, angry witches and monsters beneath the bed?"

"What big worries you have," she murmured, and she was smiling again. And he found he was, too.

"All the better to save you with, little red," he said. "If you'll let me."

"I won't." She brushed his mouth with hers. "Why don't we save each other?"

"I don't know how."

"You do." And when he frowned at her, she held him even closer, until that ache in his chest shifted over to something sweeter. Hotter. And felt a lot like forever.

"Happy-ever-after is saving each other, Dominik. All it takes is a kiss."

And this was what she'd been talking about in that sprawling house in Yorkshire.

Hope. The possibility of happiness.

Things he'd never believed in before. But it was different, with her.

Everything was different with her.

So he gathered her in his arms, and he swept her back into the grandest kiss he could give her, right there in their enchanted cottage in the deep, dark woods.

And sure enough, they lived happily ever after.

Just like a fairy tale.

Twelve years later Dominik stood on a balcony that overlooked the Grand Canal in Venice as night fell on a late summer evening. The San Giacomo villa was quiet behind him, though he knew it was a peace that wouldn't last.

His mouth curved as he imagined the chaos his ten-year-old son could unleash at any moment, wholly unconcerned about the disapproving glares of the ancient San Giacomos who lurked in every dour portrait that graced the walls of this place.

To say nothing of his five-year-old baby girls, a set of the twins that apparently ran in the family, that neither he nor Lauren had anticipated when she'd fallen pregnant the second time.

But now he couldn't imagine living without them. All of them—and well did he remember that he was the man who had planned to live out his days as a hermit, all alone in his forest.

The truth was, he had liked his own company. But he exulted in the family he and Lauren had made together.

The chaos and the glory. The mad rush of family life, mixed in with that enduring fairy tale he hadn't believed in at first—but he'd wanted to. Oh, how he'd wanted to. And so he'd jumped into, feet first, willing to do anything as long as she was with him.

Because she was the only one who had ever wanted him, and she wanted him still.

And he wanted her right back.

Every damned day.

They had built their happy-ever-after, brick by brick and stone by stone, with their own hands.

He had met his sister shortly after Lauren had come and found him in the forest. Pia had burst into that hotel suite in Athens, greeted him as if she'd imagined him into being herself—or had known of him, somehow, in her heart of hearts all this time—until he very nearly believed it himself.

And he'd finally met his brother—in the flesh— sometime after that.

After a perfectly pleasant dinner in one of the Combe family residences—this one in New York City—he and Matteo had stood out on one of the wraparound terraces that offered a sweeping view of all that Manhattan sparkle and shine.

"I don't know how to be a brother," Dominik had told him.

"My sister would tell you that I don't, either," Matteo had replied.

And they'd smiled at each other, and that was when Dominik had started to believe that it might work. This strange new family he would have said he didn't want. But that he had, anyway.

His feelings about Matteo had been complicated, but he'd realized quickly that most of that had to do with the fact Lauren had admired him so much and for so long. Something Matteo put to rest quickly, first by marrying the psychiatrist who had been tasked with his anger management counseling, who also happened to be pregnant with his twin boys. But then he'd redeemed himself entirely in Dominik's eyes by telling Lauren that Combe Industries couldn't function without her.

And then hiring her back, not as his assistant, but as a vice president.

Dominik couldn't have been prouder. And as Lauren grew into her new role in the company she'd given so much of her time and energy, he entertained himself by taking on the duties of the eldest San Giacomo. He found that his brother and sister welcomed the opportunity to allow him to be the face of their ancient family. A role he hadn't realized anyone needed to play, but one it shocked him to realize he was...actually very good at.

He heard the click of very high heels on the marble behind him, and felt his mouth curve.

Moments later his beautiful wife appeared. She'd taken some or other call in the room set aside in the villa for office purposes, and she was already tugging her hair out of the sleek ponytail she always wore when she had her professional hat on. She smiled back at him as the faint breeze from the water caught her hair, still gleaming gold and bright.

"You look very pleased with yourself," she said. "I can only hope that means you've somehow encouraged the children to sleep. For a thousand hours, give or take."

"That will be my next trick." He shifted so he could pull her into his arms, and both of them let out a small sigh. Because they still fit. Because their puzzle pieces connected even better as time passed. "I was thinking about the banquet last night. And how it was clearly my confident use of the correct spoon midway through that won the assembled patrons of the arts over to my side."

Lauren laughed at that and shook her head at him. "I think what you meant to say was thank you. And you're very welcome. No one knows how difficult it was to civilize you."

He kissed her then, because every kiss was another pretty end with the happy-ever-after that went with it. And better yet, another beginning, stretching new, sweeter stories out before them.

And he wanted nothing more than to lift her into his arms and carry her off to the bed they shared here—another four-poster affair that he deeply enjoyed indulging himself in—but he couldn't. Not yet, anyway.

Because it wasn't only the two of them anymore. And he knew his daughters liked it best when their mama read them stories before bed.

He held her hand in his as they walked through the halls of this ancient place, amazed to realize that he felt as if he belonged here. And he imagined what it might have been like to be raised like this. With two parents who loved him and cared for him and set aside whatever it was they might have been doing to do something like read him a bedtime story.

He couldn't imagine himself in that kind of family.

But he'd imagined it for his own kids, and then created it, and he had to think that was better. It was the future.

It was his belief made real, every time his children smiled.

"I love you," Lauren said softly when they reached the girls' room as if she could read every bittersweet line in his heart.

And he knew she could. She always had.

"I love you, too, little red," he told her.

More than he had back then, he thought. More all the time.

And then he stood in the doorway as she swept into the room where her daughters waited. He watched, aware by now that his heart wouldn't actually burst—it would only feel like it might—as his two perfect little girls settled themselves on either side of their gorgeous mother. One with her thumb stuck deep in her mouth. The other with her mother's beautiful smile.

And when his son came up beside him, a disdainful look on his face because he was ten years old and considered himself quite a man of the world, Dominik tossed an arm over the boy's narrow shoulders.

"I'm going to read you a fairy tale," Lauren told the girls.

"Fairy tales aren't real," their son replied. He shrugged when his sisters protested. "Well, they're not."

Lauren lifted her gaze to meet Dominik's, her caramel-colored eyes dancing.

And every time Dominik thought he'd hit his limit, that he couldn't possibly love her more—that it was a physical and emotional impossibility—she raised the bar.

He felt certain that she would keep right on doing it until the day they both died.

And he thought that was what happy-ever-after was all about, in the end.

Not a single kiss, but all the kisses. Down through the years. One after the next, linking this glorious little life of theirs together. Knitting them into one, over and over and over again.

Hope. Happiness. And the inevitable splashes of darkness in between, because life was life, that made him appreciate the light all the more.

And no light shined brighter than his beautiful wife. His own little red.

The love of his life.

"Of course fairy tales are real," he told his son. And his two wide-eyed little girls. Because he was living proof, wasn't he? "Haven't I told you the story of how your mother and I met?"

He ruffled his son's hair. And he kept his eyes on the best thing that had ever wandered into the deep, dark woods, and then straight into his heart.

"Once upon a time, in a land far, far away, a beautiful blonde in a bright red cloak walked into a forest," he said.

"And it turned out," Lauren chimed in, "that the big bad wolf she'd been expecting wasn't so bad, after all."

And that was how they told their favorite story, trading one line for the next and laughing as they went, for the rest of their lives.

* * * * *

BEST FRIENDS, SECRET LOVERS

JESSICA LEMMON

For Jules. I'm so blessed to call you a friend.

Prologue

"Twenty minutes *minimum*, or else she'll tell everyone you're horrendous in bed."

"If you're down there for longer than seven minutes, you dumb Brit, you have no idea what you're doing."

"Spoken like a guy who has no idea what he's doing."

Flynn Parker leaned back in his chair, his broken leg propped on the ottoman, and listened to his two friends argue about sex. Pleasing women in particular.

"If either of you knew what you were doing, you wouldn't be single," he informed his buddies.

Gage Fleming and Reid Singleton blinked over at Flynn as if they'd forgotten he was sitting there. Drunk as they were, they might have. Gage grabbed the nearly empty whiskey bottle resting on Flynn's footstool and splashed another inch into Reid's glass and his own.

But not Flynn's. Thanks to the pain medication he was on, the only buzz he would be enjoying was courtesy of Percocet.

"You're one to talk," Reid said, his British accent

slurred from the drink. "Your ring finger is currently un-inhabited."

"The reason for this trip." Gage clanked his glass with Reid's, then with Flynn's water bottle.

Flynn would drink to that. His recent split from Veronica was what drove them all up here, to the mountains in Colorado to go skiing. The last time they were in Flynn's father's cabin had been their sophomore year in college. The damn place must be a time machine because they'd devolved into kids just by being here.

Gage and Reid had been nonstop swapping stories, bragging about their alleged prowess, and Flynn had been foolish enough to try the challenging slope…again. His lack of practice led to his taking a snowy tumble down the hill. Just like the last time, he'd ended up in the hospital. *Unlike* the last time, he'd broken a bone.

Skiing wasn't his forte.

So. Veronica.

The ex-wife who had recently ruined his life and his outlook. His buddies had come here under the guise of pulling him out of his funk, but he knew they were mostly here because they hadn't left each other's sides since they were in college. Sure, Reid had fled back home to London for a short time, but he'd come back. They'd all known he would.

Before he boarded the plane for this vacation, Flynn had learned two things: One, that his father's diagnosis of "pneumonia" was terminal cancer and Emmons Parker would likely die soon, making fifty-three the age to beat for Flynn; and two, that when he returned home he'd be sitting in his father's office with the title of president behind his name.

Running Monarch was all Flynn had ever wanted.

Was.

Despite years of showing an interest and trying to please

his father, Emmons Parker had shooed Flynn away rather than pulled him in. Now the empire was on Flynn's shoulders, and his alone.

Reid howled with laughter at something Gage said and Flynn blinked his friends into focus. No, he wasn't alone. He had Reid, and Gage, and the best friend who'd been a part of his life longer than those two, Sabrina Douglas. His best friends worked at Monarch with him, and with them in his corner, Flynn knew he could get through this.

The senior employees were going to freak out when they found out Flynn was going to be president. He'd been accused of "coasting" before and would be in charge of all of their well-beings, which Flynn took as seriously as his next line of thought—the pact he'd been ruminating about since before his leg snapped in two on that slope.

"Remember that pact we made in college? The one where we swore never to get married."

Reid let out a hearty "Ha!" UK-born Reid Singleton was planning on staying as unattached as his last name implied. "Right here in this room, I believe."

Gage pursed his lips, his brows closing in the slightest bit over his nose. "We were hammered on Jägerbombs that night. God knows what else we said."

"I didn't adhere to it. I should have." Flynn had been swept up by love and life. He hadn't taken that pact seriously. A mistake.

Gage frowned. "It's understandable why you'd say that now. You've been through the wringer. Back then no one expected to find permanence."

"None of us *wanted* to," Reid corrected.

Flynn pointed at Gage with his water bottle. "You and this new girl have been dating, what, a month?"

"Something like that."

"Get out now." Reid offered a hearty belch. He lifted his eyebrows and downed his portion of whiskey, cheeks filling before he swallowed it down. "You and I, Gage, we stuck to the pact." He smiled, then added, "If you were Flynn, you'd have married her by now."

Reid wasn't exaggerating. Flynn and Veronica had been married on their thirty-day dating anniversary. Insanity. That they'd lasted three years was more a testament to Flynn's stubbornness than their meant-to-be-ness.

The final straw had been Veronica screwing his brother. *Whatever*, he thought, as the sting of betrayal shocked his system afresh. He'd never liked Julian much anyway.

"He's doing the thing," Reid muttered *not* quietly, given his state of inebriation. His gaze met Flynn's, but he spoke to Gage. "Where he's thinking of her."

"I can hear you, *wanker*." Flynn lost his marriage, not his hearing. Though "lost" would imply he'd misplaced it. It hadn't been misplaced, it'd been disassembled. Piece by piece until the felling blow was Veronica's head turning for none other than his older, more artsy brother. She was the free spirit, and Flynn was the numbers guy. The boring guy. The emotionally constipated guy.

Her words.

"Hey." Gage snapped his fingers. "Knock it off, Flynn. We're here to celebrate your divorce, not have you traipse down depression trail."

But Flynn wasn't budging on this. He'd given it a lot of thought since he'd tumbled down that hill. It was like life had to literally knock him on his ass to get him to wake up.

"I'm reinstating the pact," Flynn said, his tone grave. Even Reid stopped smiling. "No marriage. Not ever. It's not worth the heartache, or the broken leg, or hanging out with the two worst comrades in this solar system."

At that Reid looked wounded, Gage affronted.

"Piss off, Parker."

"Yeah," Gage agreed. "What Reid said."

With effort, Flynn sat up, carefully moving every other limb save his broken leg so he could lean forward. "I don't want either of you to go through this. Not ever."

"You're serious," Gage said after a prolonged silence.

Flynn remained silent.

Gage watched him a moment, a flash of sobriety in the depths of his brown eyes. "Okay. What'd we say?"

"We promised never to get married," Reid said. "And then we swore on our tallywackers."

Gage chuckled at Reid's choice of phrasing.

"Which means yours should have fallen off by now." Reid's face contorted as he studied Flynn. "It didn't, did it?"

"No." Flynn gave him an impatient look. "It didn't."

Reid swiped his hand over his brow in mock relief.

"Come on, Parker, you're high on drugs," Gage said with a head shake. "We made that pact because your mom was sick and your dad was miserable, and because Natalie had just dumped me. We were all heartbroken then." He considered Reid. "Except for Reid. I'm not sure why he did it."

"Never getting married anyway." Reid shrugged. "All for one."

"So? Swear again," Flynn repeated. "On your *tallywackers*." That earned a smile from Reid. "Big or small, they count."

The first time they'd made the pact none of them truly knew heartache. Breakups were hard, but the decimation of a marriage following the ultimate betrayal? Much worse. Reid and Gage didn't know how bad things could get and Flynn would like to keep it that way. He didn't want either of them to feel as eviscerated as he did right now—as he had for the last three months. All pain he could have avoided if he'd taken that pact seriously.

His buddies might never find themselves dating women who slept with their family members, but it wouldn't matter how the divorce happened, only that it did. He'd heard the statistics. That 50 percent of marriages ending in divorce was up to around 75 nowadays.

He'd heard some people say they didn't harbor regret because if they'd never married, and divorced, they wouldn't have learned life's lessons. Blah, blah, blah.

Bullshit.

Flynn regretted saying "I do" to Veronica all the way down to his churning stomach. The heartbreak over her choosing his brother would have been more bearable if she'd told him up front rather than three years into an insufferable marriage.

"I swear," Reid said, almost too serious as he crashed his glass into Flynn's water bottle, then looked at Gage expectantly.

"Fine. This is stupid, but fine." Gage lifted his glass.

"Say it," Flynn said, not cracking the slightest smile. "Or it doesn't count."

"I promise," Gage said. "I won't get married."

"Say *never*, and we all drink," Flynn said.

"Wait." Reid held up a finger. "What if one of us caves again? Like hearts-and-flowers Gage over here."

"Shut up, Reid."

"One of your monthlong girlfriends could turn into the real thing if you're not careful."

"I'm careful," Gage growled.

"You'd better be." Flynn stared down his friends. The enormity of the situation settled around them, the only sound in the room the fire crackling in the background. "The lie of forever isn't worth it in the end."

Reid eyed Flynn's broken leg, a reminder of what Flynn's stupidity had cost him, and then exchanged glances with Gage. These men were more like Flynn's brothers than his own flesh and blood. They'd do anything for him—including vowing to remain single forever.

"Never," Gage agreed, holding up his own glass.

Reid and Flynn nodded in unison, and then they drank on it.

One

Flynn Parker, his stomach in a double knot, attempted to do the same to his tie. His hands were shaking from too much coffee and not enough sleep. It wasn't helping that the tiny room in the back of the funeral home was nearing eighty degrees.

Sweat beaded on his forehead and slicked his palms. He closed his eyes, shutting out his haggard reflection, and blew out a long, slow breath.

The service for his father was over, and when Flynn had left the sweltering room, the first thing he'd done was yank at his tie. Bad move. He'd never return it to its previous state.

God help him, he didn't know if he could watch his father being lowered into the dirt. They'd had their differences—about a million of them at last count. Death was final, but burial even more so.

"There you are." Sabrina Douglas, his best friend since college, stepped into view in the tall mirror at the back of the funeral home. "Need help?"

"Why is it so hot in here?" he barked rather than answer her.

She clucked her tongue at his overreaction. Much like this moment, she'd come in and out of focus over the years, but she'd always been a constant in his life. She'd been at his side at work, diligently ushering in the new age as he acclimated as president of the management consulting firm he now owned. She'd been with him for every personal moment from his and Veronica's wedding to his thirtieth birthday—*their* thirtieth birthday, he mentally corrected. Sabrina was born four minutes ahead of him on the same damn day. She'd jokingly called them "twins" when they first met in psych class at the University of Washington, but that nickname quickly fizzled when they realized they were nothing alike.

Nothing alike, but unable to shake each other.

Her brow crinkled over a black-framed pair of glasses as she reached for the length of silk around his neck and attempted to retie it.

"I do it every morning," he muttered, Sabrina's sweet floral perfume tickling his nose. She always smelled good, but he hadn't noticed in a while.

A long while.

His frown deepened. They hadn't been as close in the years he was married to Veronica. His hanging out with Reid and Gage hadn't changed, but it was as if Veronica and Sabrina had an unspoken agreement that Sabrina wasn't welcome into the inner circle. As a result, Flynn mostly saw her at work rather than outside it. The thought bothered him.

"I don't know what's wrong with me." He was speaking of his own reverie as much as his lack of ability to tie his necktie.

"Flynn…"

He put his hands on hers to stop whatever apology-slash-life-lesson he suspected was percolating. As gently as he could muster, he said, "Don't."

Sabrina leveled him with a wide-eyed hazel stare. Her eyes were beautiful. Piercing green-gold, and behind her glasses they appeared twice as large. She'd been with him through the divorce from Veronica, through his father's illness and subsequent death. The last couple of months for Flynn had started to resemble the life of Job from the Bible. He hadn't contracted a case of boils as the Monarch offices collapsed in on themselves, *yet*. He wasn't going to tempt fate by stating he was out of the woods.

Emmons Parker knew what his sons had been through, so when he'd had his lawyer schedule the meetings to read the will, he'd made sure they happened on separate days.

Flynn on a Sunday. Julian on a Monday.

Unfortunately, Flynn knew Veronica had gone to the reading with Julian, even though he'd rather not know a thing about either of them. Goddamn Facebook.

Julian inherited their father's beloved antique car collection and the regal Colonial with the cherry tree in the front yard where they'd grown up. Flynn inherited the cabin in Colorado as well as the business and his father's penthouse apartment downtown. Julian was "starting a family," or so the lawyer had read from the will, so that was why Emmons had bequeathed their mother's beloved home with the evenly spaced shutters to his oldest, and least trust-worthy, son.

The son who was starting a family with Flynn's former wife.

Today Flynn had accepted hugs and handshakes from family and friends but had successfully avoided Julian and Veronica. His ex-wife kept a close eye on Flynn, but he refused to approach her. Her guilt was too little and way too late.

"I don't know what to do." Sabrina spoke around what

sounded like a lump clogging her throat. She was hurting for him. The way she'd hurt for him when Veronica left him. Her pink lips pressed together and her chin shook. "Sorry."

Abandoning the tie, she swiped the hollows of her eyes under her glasses, careful of the eye makeup that had been applied boldly yet carefully as per her style.

He didn't hesitate to pull her close, shushing her as she sniffed. The warmth of that embrace—of holding on to someone who cared for him so deeply and knew him so well—was enough to make a lump form in his own throat. She held on to him like she might shatter, and so he concentrated on rubbing her back and telling her the truth. "You're doing exactly what you need to do, Sabrina. Just your being here is enough."

She let go of him and snagged a tissue from a nearby box. She lifted her glasses and dabbed her eyes, leaning in and checking her reflection. "I'm not helping."

"You're helping." She was gloriously sensitive. Attuned. Empathetic. Some days he hated that for her—it made her more at risk of being hurt. He watched her reflection, wondering if she saw herself as he did. A tall, strong, beautiful woman, her sleek brown hair framing smooth skin and glasses that made her appear approachable and smart at the same time. She wore a black dress and stockings, her heeled shoes tall enough that when she'd held him a moment ago she didn't have to stretch onto her toes to wrap her arms around his neck.

"Okay. I'm okay. I'm sorry." She nodded, the tissue wadded in one hand. Evidently this okay/sorry combo marked the end of her cry and the beginning of her being his support system. "If there's anything you need—"

"Let's skip it," he blurted. The moment the words were out of his mouth, he knew it was the right thing to do.

"Skip…the rest of the funeral?" Her face pinched with indecision.

"Why not?" He'd seen everyone. He'd listened as the priest spoke of Emmons as if he was a saint. Frankly, Flynn had heard enough false praise for his old man to last a life-time.

Her mouth opened, probably to argue, but he didn't let her continue.

"I can do it. I just don't want to." He shook his head as he tried to think of another cohesive sentence to add to the protest, but none came. So he added, "At all," and hoped that it punctuated his point.

She jerked her head into a nod. "Okay. Let's skip it."

Relief was like a third person in the room.

"Chaz's?" she offered. "I'm *dying* for fish and chips." Her eyes rounded as her hand covered her mouth. "Oh. That was…really inappropriate phrasing for a funeral."

He had to smile. Recently he'd noticed how absent from his life she'd been. It'd be good to go out with her to some-where that wasn't work. "Let's get outta here."

"Are you kidding me?" His brother, Julian, appeared in the doorway, his lip curled in disgust. "You're walking out on our father's funeral?"

Like he had any room to call Flynn's ethics into question.

Veronica's blonde head peeked around Julian's shoulder. Her gaze flitted to Flynn and then Sabrina, and Flynn's limbs went corpse-cold.

"Honey," she whispered to Julian. "Let's not do this here."

Honey. God, what a mess.

Sabrina took a step closer to Flynn in support. His best friend at his side. He didn't need her to defend him, but he appreciated the gesture more than she knew.

Julian shrugged off Veronica's hand from his suit jacket and glared at his brother. It was one of Dad's suits—too wide in the shoulders. A little short in the torso.

Julian didn't own a suit. He painted for a living and his

creativity was why Veronica said he'd won her heart. Evidently, she found Flynn incapable of being "spontaneous," or "thoughtful," or "monogamous."

No, wait. That last one was *her*.

"You're not going to stand over your own father's grave?" Julian spat. Veronica murmured another "honey," but he ignored it.

"You've made it clear that it's none of my business what you do or don't do." Flynn tore his gaze from Julian to spear Veronica with a glare. "Both of you. Same goes for me."

Her blue eyes rounded. He used to think she was gorgeous—with her full, blond hair and designer clothes. The way her nails were always done and her makeup perfectly painted on. Now he'd seen what was under the mask.

Selfishness. Betrayal. Lies.

So many lies.

"Don't judge me, Flynn," she snapped.

"You used to be more attractive." The sound of his own voice startled him. He hadn't meant to say that out loud.

"Son of a bitch!" Julian lunged, came at him with a sloppy swing that Flynn easily dodged. He'd learned how to fistfight from Gage and Reid, and Julian only dragged a paint-filled brush down a canvas.

Flynn ducked to avoid a left, weaved when Julian attempted a right, cracked his fist into his older brother's nose. Julian staggered, lost his balance and fell onto his ass on the ground. Sabrina gasped, and Veronica shrieked. Julian puffed out a curse word as blood streamed from his nose.

"Honey. *Honey.* Talk to me." Veronica was on her knees over Julian's groaning form and Flynn didn't know what sickened him more. That his ex-wife cared about his brother's well-being more than the man she'd vowed to love forever, or that Flynn had lost his temper with Julian and hit him.

Both made his stomach toss.

"Are you okay?" Sabrina came into focus, her eyebrows tenderly bowed as she watched him with concern. He hated her seeing him like this—broken, weak—like he'd felt for the last several months.

"I'm *perfect*." He took her hand and led her from the small room and they encountered Reid and Gage advancing at a fast walk down the hallway.

"We heard a scream." Reid's sharply angled jaw was set, his fists balled at his sides. Gage looked similar, minus the fists. His mouth wore a scowl, his gaze sweeping the area around them for looming danger.

"You okay?" Gage asked Sabrina.

"I didn't scream. That was Veronica."

"We're fine," Flynn said before amending, "Julian's nose is broken."

"Broken?" A fraction of a second passed before Reid's face split into an impressed smile. He clapped Flynn on the shoulder.

"Do *not* encourage him," Sabrina warned.

"So what now?" Gage asked at the same time more of Julian's groaning and Veronica's soothing echoed from the adjacent room.

"We're skipping the rest of the funeral," Flynn announced. "Who wants to go to Chaz's for fish and chips?"

"I do," Reid said, his British accent thickening. The man loved his fish and chips.

Gage, ever the cautious, practical friend, watched Flynn carefully. "You're sure this is what you want to do?"

Flynn thought of his father, angry, yelling. His gutting words about how if he wanted to become as great a man as his father, Flynn would have to first grow a pair. He thought of Emmons's bitter solitude after Mom had succumbed to cancer fifteen years ago. Emmons had suffered that same fate, only unlike Mom, he'd never woken up to what was really important. He'd taken his bitterness with him to the grave. Maybe that's why Flynn couldn't bear seeing his old man lowered into it.

Sabrina wrapped her hand around Flynn's and squeezed his fingers. "Whatever you need. We're here."

Reid and Gage nodded, concurring.

"I'm sure."

That was all it took.

They skirted the crowd patiently waiting for him to take his place as pallbearer. Moved past nameless relatives who had crawled out of the woodwork, and past one of Veronica's friends who asked him if he knew where she or Julian were.

"They're inside," he told her.

Never slowing his walk or letting go of Sabrina's hand, he opened the passenger side door for her while Gage and Reid climbed into the back. Then Flynn reversed out of the church's parking lot and drove straight to Chaz's.

Two

Six months later

At Monarch Consulting, Flynn brewed himself an espresso from the high-end machine, yet another perk—pun intended—of being in charge.

The break room had been his father's private retreat when he was alive and well, and he'd rarely shared the room. Not the case for Flynn. He'd opened up the executive break room to his closest friends, who shared the top floor his father had formerly hogged for himself.

Flynn didn't care who thought he was playing favorites. When he'd returned home from vacation and become president, he'd outfitted the upper floor with three new offices and placed his friends at his sides. They were a good visual reminder that Flynn wasn't running Monarch in a vacuum—or worse, a void.

It was his company now. He could do what he wanted. God knew Emmons had been doing it his way for years.

Monarch Consulting was a management consulting firm,

which was a fancy way of saying they helped other businesses improve their performance and grow. Monarch was dedicated to helping companies find new and better ways of doing things—an irony since Emmons had done things the same way for decades.

Gage Fleming's official title at Monarch was senior sales executive. He was in charge of the entire sales department, which was a perfect fit for his charm and likability. Reid was the IT guy, though they fancied up his nameplate to read Digital Marketing Analyst. Sabrina, with her fun-loving attitude and knack for being a social lubricant, was promoted to brand manager, where she oversaw social media factions as well as design work and rebranding.

Flynn stirred a packet of organic cane sugar into his espresso and thought about his best friends' support of his climb to the very top. They were the glue that kept him together.

"What's up, brother?" announced one of those best friends now. Flynn turned to find Gage strolling into the room. Gage wasn't his biological brother, but was worthy of the title nonetheless.

Oh, that I could choose.

Gage's hair had grown some since Flynn's father's funeral. Now that it was longer, the ends were curling and added a boyish charm to the *mountain* of charm Gage already possessed. Flynn didn't know anyone Gage didn't get along with, and vice versa. It made him an asset at work, and he provided a softer edge for Flynn whenever he needed it—which, lately, was often.

"Surprised you're still upright after the long weekend." Gage slapped Flynn's back.

The long weekend was to celebrate the finalization of Flynn and Veronica's divorce. It couldn't have come soon enough, but Flynn hadn't felt like celebrating. His divorce marked an epic failure that piled onto the other failures he'd been intimately acquainted with lately. In no way would Gage and Reid have let the momentous occasion pass by without acknowledgment.

Acknowledgment in this case meant going out and getting well and truly "pissed," as Reid had put it. And honestly, Flynn had had fun letting go and living in the moment, at least for a weekend.

"I always land on my feet," Flynn grumbled, still tired and, yeah, probably a little hungover from last night. He should've stopped drinking before midnight.

"Good morning, Fleming." Reid sauntered in next. "Morning, Parker." Reid had refused to leave his accent in London. He kept it fine-tuned for one essential reason: women loved it.

Where Flynn was mostly an insensitive, shortsighted, hard-to-love suit, Gage was friendly and well liked, and Reid…well, his other friend was a split between the two of them. Reid had charm in spades but also had a rough edge from a past he'd always been tight-lipped about.

Flynn figured he'd tell them when he was ready. At this rate probably when one of them was on his deathbed.

"Well, well, well, what have we here? Three of Seattle's saddest rich boys."

Sabrina strolled in with her signature walk, somehow expressing both childlike wonder and sophisticated capability. Her slim-fitting skirt, blouse and high-heeled shoes proved she was 100 percent woman. Sabrina had a fun-loving attitude but liked everything in its place. She was the only one who'd balked at the promotion that Flynn had had to talk her into. She put others ahead of herself often, which was so converse to who Veronica was it wasn't even funny.

Sabrina saw the world as a sunshiny bouquet of happiness even though Flynn had cold hard proof that it was a cesspool.

"Whoa." Sab's whiskey-smooth voice dipped as she took in Flynn. "You look like last night handed you your own backside." Her eyebrows met the frame of her glasses as she studied Gage and Reid. "You guys don't look that great either. Were you... Oh my gosh. It's final, isn't it? It's done?"

"He's single with a capital *S*," Reid confirmed.

Her smile was short-lived as she approached Flynn. "Are you okay?"

"I'm fine."

"Are you sure?"

That question right there was why he hadn't told her about the finalization of the divorce. He wanted to drink away his feelings on the topic, not discuss them.

Flynn sent a glance over her head to Reid and Gage.

Little help, guys?

"You wouldn't have wanted to accompany us even if we invited you," Gage said.

"What's that supposed to mean?" Her frown returned, but she aimed it at affable Gage, which was fun to watch. He finished stirring his own coffee and sent her a grim head shake.

"Darling." Reid looped an arm around her shoulders. "Don't make us say it."

"Ugh. Did you all pick up girls?" She asked everyone but her eyes tracked to Flynn and stayed there. "And why wasn't I invited? I'm an excellent wingwoman."

Flynn felt a zip of discomfort at the idea of Sabrina fixing him up with a woman—or being there while he trotted out his A game to impress one. He'd suffered a few crash-and-burns last night and was glad she wasn't there to witness them.

Sabrina pursed her lips in consideration. "Did the evening have anything to do with you three reaffirming your dumb pact?"

"It's not dumb," Flynn was the first to say. Family and marriage and happily ever after were ideas that he used to hold sacred. He'd seen the flip side of that coin. Broken promises and regret.

Divorce had changed him.

"You're single with us, love. Did you want in on the pact?" Reid smiled as he refilled his paper Starbucks cup.

"No, I do not. And I'm single by choice. You're single—" she poked Reid in the chest "—because you're a lemming."

"I'm to believe you're single by choice," Reid stated flatly. She wisely ignored the barb.

"A pact to not fall in love is juvenile and shortsighted."

"We can fall in love," Gage argued. "We agreed not to marry."

"Pathetic." She rolled her eyes and Flynn lost his patience.

"Sabrina." He dipped his voice to its most authoritative tone. "It's not a joke."

She craned her chin to take in all six feet of him and gave him a withering glare that would've shrunk a lesser man's balls.

"I *know* it's not a joke. But it's still pathetic."

She turned for the coffeemaker and Reid chuckled. "You have no effect on her, mate."

"Yeah, well, vice versa," Flynn said, but felt the untruth hiding behind his statement. Sabrina had enough of an effect on him that he treated her differently than he did Reid and Gage. As present as she was in his life, it'd always been impossible to slot her in as one of the "guys." And in a weird way he'd protected her when he'd excluded her from last night's shenanigans as well as the skiing weekend. Flynn was jaded to the nth degree. Sabrina wasn't. He needed her to stay positive and sunshiny. He needed her to be okay. For her own sake, sure, but also for his.

"Heartbreak isn't a myth," Reid called out to her as she walked for the door. "You'll see that someday."

"Morons." She strolled out but did so with a twitch in her walk and a smile on her face. Immune to all of them, evidently.

Three

Sabrina had lectured Flynn as much as she dared. She'd pushed him to the point of real anger—not the showy all-bark/no-bite thing he'd just done in "the Suit Café" as she liked to call their private break room, but real, shaking, red-faced anger. Which was why she recognized the sound of that booming timbre when she passed by a closed conference room door later the same afternoon.

Definitely, that was Flynn shouting a few choice words, and definitely, that was the voice of Mac Langley, a senior executive who had been hired on at the beginning by Emmons Parker himself.

She bristled as more swearing pierced the air. She'd seen a glimpse of the old Flynn when the four of them had fled the funeral to go to Chaz's for fish and chips and ice-cold beers. In that moment she'd realized how much she missed hanging out with him, and how his marriage to Veronica had been the beginning of her new, more distant BFF. In college Sabrina used to bake him cookies, do his laundry, make sure he was eating while studying.

She felt that instinct to take care of him anew. Maybe because Veronica was so classless, having tossed aside what she and Flynn had, or simply because Sabrina wanted Flynn to be happy again and their college years were when she remembered his being happiest.

Flynn loudly insulted Mac again and Sabrina winced. There'd be no putting that horse back into the barn. No man could call another man that and not pay the price. It'd take time to smooth over, and some distance. And with a man like Mac, the distance would have to be Tokyo to London.

The heavy wooden door did little to mute the noise, and as a result a few employees had gathered outside it—staring in slack-jawed bewilderment.

When the shouts ceased, a charge of electricity lingered like the stench from a burnt grilled cheese sandwich—like the tension couldn't be contained by the room and had crept out under the door.

She pasted a smile on her face and turned toward the gathering crowd—two gawping interns and Gage.

"Yikes." Gage smirked, sipped his coffee and eyed the interns. "Unless you want to be on the receiving end of more of that," he leaned in to say, "you might want to clear the corridor before they come out."

He kept his tone light and playful, adding a wink for the benefit of the two younger girls, and when he smiled they tittered and scooted off, their tones hushed.

"Do you have to charm everyone you come in contact with?"

"I wasn't charming them. I was being myself." He grinned. Gage was both boyish and likable. The thing was he wasn't lying. He *hadn't* been trying to charm them. Flirting came as naturally to him as breathing. Still, she doubted the wink-and-smile routine would silence the girls permanently. They would tell a friend or two or be overheard dishing in the employee lounge and then the entire company would know about Flynn's outburst. Damage control would take a miracle.

She didn't want anyone to think poorly of him, even though he'd been an ogre since he'd taken over the company. But couldn't they see he was hurting? He needed support, not criticism.

Gage came to stand next to her where he, too, watched the door. "Who's in there with him?"

"Mac. And, judging by the voices, a few other executives. I don't hear Reid."

He shook his head. "I passed by him in his office before doing a lap to check on the sales team."

A meeting where none of them had been included. Hmm. She wondered who had called it.

"Did something happen this weekend?" she asked as they faced the door. Maybe the bar night where many drinks were consumed prompted Flynn to admit his feelings...though, she doubted it.

"Drinks. More drinks. Reaffirmation that the pact was the right thing to do." Gage shrugged.

"Seriously how can you continue with that cockamamie idea?"

"You know no one says *cockamamie* any more, right?"

"Veronica is a hot mess, but you can't celebrate the end of her and Flynn's marriage like a...a..."

"Bachelor party?"

"Yes." She pointed at him in confirmation. "Like a bachelor party. Especially when you are celebrating being bachelors forever and ever, amen."

"Sabrina. If you want in on the pact, just yell."

"Pass." She rolled her eyes. Why did everyone keep offering her an "in" like she wanted to be a part of that? "I've never been married, but I've watched friends go through it. Divorce is devastating. And after losing his father, it'll be like another death he'll have to grieve. A weekend of shots isn't going to remedy it."

Over the last six months, she'd watched Flynn deal with his father's death. The grief had hovered in the anger stage for a while, before he'd seemed to lighten up. The day they did a champagne toast to their new offices, Flynn was all smiles. He stated how Monarch was going through a rebirth. There was a sincere speech during which Flynn thanked them for sticking with him, which simultaneously broke her heart and mended it at the same time. Now the optimistic Flynn was nowhere to be found. He'd looped around to the anger stage again and was stuck in the rut worn of his own making.

"He's busy." Gage palmed her shoulder supportively. "Running this place is stressful and he doesn't have the respect he deserves. Don't worry about his emotional state, Sab. He's doing what needs to be done. That's all."

But that wasn't "all" no matter how much denial Reid and Gage were in. She *knew* Flynn. Knew his moods and knew his values. Sure, they'd suffered a bit of distance since his marriage to Veronica, but Sabrina had still seen him day in and out at work. She'd shared countless meetings and lunches with him.

He used to be lighthearted and open and gentle. He used to be happy. Who he was now wasn't in the same stratosphere as happy. Though if she thought about it for longer than three seconds, she might admit that he hadn't been truly happy in years. Veronica, even when she hadn't been cheating on Flynn with his brother, wasn't an easygoing person. She had a way of sucking the oxygen from the room. As much as Flynn had scrambled to appease her, it was rare that she was contented.

Sabrina shook her head, as sickened now as she was then. Flynn deserved better.

"It's more than that," she told Gage.

"He's fine. Probably needs to get laid."

Sabrina recoiled, but not at Gage's choice of phrasing. Gage and Reid, along with Flynn, had been close friends since college. She was comfortable around them in and outside of work. No, what had her feeling *uncomfortable* was the idea of Flynn sleeping with someone else. She'd grown accustomed to his belonging to Veronica, but the thought of him with someone else...

"Gross."

He shrugged and then turned in the direction of the elevator.

What a pile of crap-male logic.

Flynn needed time and space to acclimate—time to *heal*—and the last thing he needed was to spend time with a nameless, faceless woman.

He'd spent years with a woman who had both a face and a name. Sabrina felt possessive of him at first, but quickly determined that wasn't fair. She'd never had a claim on him. As his best friend, sure, and that meant she supported him no matter what—that hadn't changed. She'd tell him exactly what she thought if he started entertaining the idea of taking home a random...*floozy* in the hopes of improving his mood.

As she was contemplating whether anyone still used the word *floozy*, the door opened. A swarm of suits filed out of the room. Most of them were the senior members of the staff, the men and women who had helped build Monarch back when Emmons had started the company with nothing more than a legal pad and a number two pencil. It was admirable that Emmons Parker had built a consulting business from scratch, and even more so that it'd become the top management consulting firm for not only Seattle but also for a great deal of the Pacific Northwest.

He'd demanded excellence from all of them, in particular Flynn, who had been strong-armed into the executive level within the firm. When Flynn graduated college, he'd landed Gage and Sabrina internships. Reid started a few years later, after an unsuccessful trip back home to London resulted in his admitting that he preferred living in America. Sabrina wasn't surprised. Reid was much more suited to Seattle than London. And the weather was similar.

She stepped out of the way of Mac, who was marching past her, propelled by the steam coming out of his ears. He wore an unstylish brown suit and his jowls hung over the tightly buttoned collar at his neck. His tie was tight and short, his arms ramrod stiff at his sides, and his hands were balled into ham-sized fists.

The rest of the executives who ran various departments of Monarch paraded out next, but no one appeared as incensed as Mac.

She offered a paper-thin smile at Belinda, Monarch's legal counsel. Belinda was smart and tough, but also a human being who cared, which made her one of Sabrina's favorite people.

"What's going on?" Sabrina whispered, following Belinda's lead away from the pack.

Belinda stopped and watched the rest of the crew wander off in various directions of the office before leveling with Sabrina in her honest, curt way. "You need to get Flynn out of here, Sabrina, or they're going to revolt."

"Oh-kay. I can…take him to lunch or something."

"Not for an hour. For a few weeks. A month. Long enough for him to remember what is important or they're going to abandon ship. Son of Emmons Parker or not, he doesn't have their support."

"I've never had their support," Flynn boomed from behind Belinda. To her credit, she didn't wilt or jerk in surprise. She simply turned and shook her head.

"You heard my suggestion," she told him with a pointed glance before leaving Flynn and Sabrina alone.

"What happened in there? You guys brought down the house."

"What *happened* is that they're blaming me for stock prices taking a dive. Like it's my fault Emmons died and made our investors twitchy."

He dragged a hand over his short, stylish brown hair and closed his eyes. Long lashes shadowed chiseled cheeks and a firm, angled jaw. If there was only one attribute Flynn had inherited from his father it was his staggering good looks. Emmons, even for an older guy, had been handsome...until he opened his mouth. Flynn wielded those strong Parker genes like a champ, wearing jeans and Ts or suits and ties and looking at home in either. He wore the latter now, a dark suit and smart pale blue shirt with a deeper blue tie. A line marred his brow—that was a more recent feature. He'd had it since he'd taken over Monarch and inherited the problems that came with it.

"They have to know that the company was declining as soon as the *Seattle Times* ran the article that announced your father was ailing," she told him. "That has nothing to do with you."

"They don't care, Sab." He turned on his heel and marched to the elevator. She followed since her office was on the same floor as his. He held the door for her when he saw her coming and she stepped in next to him as the elevator traveled up the three floors she had intended to walk so she could count them on her fitness tracker.

"Belinda said—"

"Mac is a horse's ass. He's been pissed off since I pulled my friends into the inner sanctum instead of him, and this quarter's numbers are the perfect excuse to summon the townsfolk to bring their pitchforks. Belinda wants me to run from him like a scared rabbit." He glowered at Sabrina. "Do I look like a rabbit to you?"

"No. You don't." She gripped his arm in an attempt to

connect with him, to break through the wall of anger he was behind. His features softened as his mouth went flat and a strange sort of awareness crackled in the air between them. An electric current ran the length of her arm and skimmed her form like a caress. Even her toes tingled inside her Christian Louboutin pumps.

She yanked her hand away, alarmed at the reaction. This was Flynn, *her best friend*. Whatever rogue reaction her body was having to him was…well, crazy.

She shook out her hand as if to clear the buzz of awareness from her body. "You'll have to tell me what's going on sooner or later."

He watched her carefully, his blue eyes revealing nothing. They were more gray today thanks to the color of his suit jacket. Handsome even when he was angry.

Veronica was an idiot.

A surge of anger replaced the tingles. Whenever she thought of his ex-wife's betrayal, Sabrina wanted to scream. He was too amazing a person to settle for someone who would discard him so carelessly.

"Flynn."

He sighed, which meant she'd won, and she had to fight not to smile. The elevator doors swept aside and he gestured for her to go ahead of him. "My office."

She led the way, walking into the glass-walled room and waiting for him to follow before she shut the door.

His assistant, Yasmine, was out sick today so Sabrina didn't bother shutting the blinds. The only other two people on this floor wouldn't heed a closed blind any more than she would. Like her, Gage and Reid had an all-access pass to everything Monarch and everything Flynn. Their loyalty to him ran as deeply and broadly as her own, which was why she pegged him with an honest question the moment he propped his hands on his waist and glared down at her.

"What is going on with you?"

Admittedly, her intervention was about six weeks too late. She'd assumed he'd bounce back any moment. A possibility that grew further and further away as the days passed.

"Meaning?"

Short of grabbing him by the shoulders and giving him a good shake, she didn't know how to reach him except to ask point-blank. "Meaning, what was the screaming about downstairs? What was it *really* about? I don't want some generic comment about how you and Mac don't see eye to eye."

"Nothing." His face pleated.

Deciding to wait him out, she straightened her back and folded her arms over her chest. She wasn't going to let him throw up a smokescreen and keep her out of this any longer.

"No one here believes I can do this job," he said.

"They're wrong."

"They want my father back. They want a ruthless, impersonal asshole to sit in this office and deliver their bonuses." Flynn sat down in his chair and spread his arms. "I'm filling the ruthless, impersonal asshole part of the request and they're not appeased. They're like…like an active volcano that needs a virgin sacrifice."

She lifted an eyebrow at the metaphor.

"Know anyone?" His lips twitched at his own joke.

She smiled and the tension in the room eased. "I'm sorry to say that my V-card was awarded to Bennie Todd our freshman year in college."

"Your first clue that was a mistake was that his name was *Bennie*."

"Yuck. We're not talking about him."

His eyes flickered playfully. The Flynn she knew and loved was still inside the corporate mannequin she was currently addressing. Thank God.

He'd always sworn he'd never turn into his father. And yet after his father's illness and subsequent death, after finding out Veronica had screwed him over, Flynn had devolved into a close simulation of Emmons Parker.

His face drawn, he stood and gestured for her to take his chair. "Have a seat. I want to show you something."

She sat in his plush, ergonomic chair and he leaned over her, the musky smell of him familiar and not at the same time. He'd been this close to her a million times, but this was the first time she noticed her heart rate ratcheting up while he casually tapped in the password on his laptop. What was with her today? Had it really been that long since she had male attention?

Yes, she thought glumly.

"Read this." He opened an email addressed from Mac and backed away, taking his manly scent—and her bizarre reaction to it—with him.

"They're threatening to leave," he said.

She read the subject of the email aloud. "Tender of resignation?"

"Yes. From our CFO, director of human resources and vice president. They're going to start a new company and take most of our office with them. Or at least that's the threat. If I agree to Belinda's suggestion and take an extended break, they'll stick around and give me a second chance."

"It's mutiny." She could hardly believe this many bigwigs at Monarch would agree to such an insane plan.

"To say the least. If we were to attempt to keep Monarch afloat after they left, I doubt we'd be able to stay open while we trained a new...everyone." He gestured his frustration with a sweep of his arm.

He was right. Hiring that many new executives would take months. Monarch would fold like a pizza box.

"I'm not backing down."

"What do they believe will change if you take an extended break?"

"They think I'm burned out and need to take some time to *reflect*." He said it like it was a swear word.

"Well…"

How to agree and not side against Flynn? That was the question…

"Is reflecting so bad? You didn't take bereavement after your father passed."

His face hardened. Even twenty-three years younger than his late father, Flynn was a picture-perfect match for dear old Dad.

The execs were used to the way things were, and when Flynn implemented new things—*good* things that the company needed—the change hadn't gone over well. Flynn was the future of Monarch and had always been more forward thinking than his father.

"It's a bluff," he said.

She wasn't so sure. Mac was powerful. Both in position and in his ability to convince his colleagues to go along with his scheme.

"Would a monthlong sabbatical be that bad?" She turned in her chair and met his gaze, which burned through her. Eyes she'd looked into on many occasions, and never failed to make her feel stable and like she mattered.

"If I leave for a month, God knows what those dinosaurs would do to the place." Flynn would never voluntarily abandon ship—even if it was for a break he was in desperate need of taking.

"Reid's here. Gage is here. They wouldn't let Mac ruin your company." And neither would she… But she wouldn't be here once she convinced Flynn to take a hiatus. Belinda had plainly told Sabrina to "get him out of here" and Sabrina wouldn't leave him to his own devices. Without work distracting him, she knew he'd be unpacking some hefty emotional baggage.

She refused to let him go through that alone.

Four

"So? Advice?" Sabrina raised her eyebrows at her younger brother, who lifted his frosted beer mug and shrugged one shoulder.

Luke had thick, dark hair like hers but was blessed with their mother's electric-green eyes. The jerk. The best Sabrina could hope for in that department was "greenish."

"Leave him alone?" He smirked. Two years her junior, Luke's twenty-eight was balanced by an even-keeled sense of humor and a huge brain. He was gifted and had embarrassed her a million times in the past by challenging some poor, hapless soul to a math contest he'd always win.

"Kidding." Luke gave her hand a playful tap. "He's been through hell, I'll give him that."

"He has. And that pact is ridiculous."

"Eh, I can't fault him for that."

Of course he couldn't. Luke was male and therefore incapable of being reasonable. "You're saying that because of Dawn."

Luke's eyes darted to one side and his jaw went taut

at the mention of his ex's name. "You're one to talk, Sab. Name the last guy you've been over the moon for besides your precious Flynn."

"I'm not in love with Flynn, moron. You've been trotting out that argument for over a decade now. We're friends and it works, and stop changing the subject."

In spite of the fact she kept noticing Flynn's looks, his smell and his overall presence at work. That was just... That was just... Well, okay, she didn't know what it was. But it would pass. It had to.

Remarkably, Luke let the argument go. With a sigh, he settled his beer mug—now empty—on the table between them and signaled the bartender that he'd like another. He waited until it was delivered to say what he had to say.

"Dawn's getting married."

"What? You guys broke up like three minutes ago!"

He shrugged.

"I'm sorry."

"I'm just saying Flynn's idea isn't a bad one. After Dawn, I barely want to date. I don't think at this rate we'll ever give Mom the grandchildren she's been crowing about."

Their mother, Sarah, was infamous for bringing up significant others and babies and how many of her close friends were becoming grandparents. Luke wasn't the only one banging the "Sabrina loves Flynn" drum. Sab had argued with her mother on several occasions—some of them in front of Flynn. Then he was married and her mother's pushing, thankfully, came to a halt.

"Now that his divorce is final, Mom's going to start up again." Sabrina rolled her eyes. Just what she needed. Someone stoking the flames of Flynn Awareness that had flickered to life.

"Better armor up. Or get pregnant." The comment earned her brother a slug in the biceps that hurt her hand more than it hurt his rock-hard arms. She shook out her fingers.

"Yikes. Are you lifting again?"

"Yes." He rolled up a T-shirt sleeve and showed off his guns. She couldn't resist a squeeze.

"Unbelievable."

"Come to the gym with me. First session's free." For all his brainpower, Luke had opted to become a fitness trainer, blowing the idea of "dumb jock" out of the water. It was pretty simple math. Women found him irresistible and booked countless sessions with him. He made a great living giving them his full attention.

"No thanks. I'll stick to my yoga and meditation." Her cell phone buzzed and she dug it from the bottom of her purse.

A text from Flynn read: Busy?

She keyed in a reply of: No. What's up?

Need you.

She stared at those two words, a dozen thoughts pinging through her head as her heart pattered out an SOS. She reminded herself not to be weird and typed in a reply.

Where are you?

Then her phone vanished from her hand.

"Hey!" she squawked as Luke held it out of reach.

"I knew it." He smirked. "This is a booty call, Sab."

"It is not." She swiped at the phone but he kept it away from her. Until she grabbed his ear and yanked.

"Ow! Are you serious?" Her brother rubbed his ear, affronted. "We're not ten years old any longer."

"Could've fooled me." She glared at him before reading Flynn's one-word reply. Home.

Not his old home, but the new one. Julian had been awarded the family estate and Flynn had been given Emmons Parker's Seattle penthouse. Forty-five hundred square feet of steel beams and glass, charcoal-gray floors and dark cabinetry built by the finest designers.

She pecked in her response—that she'd be there in ten minutes—bottomed out her sparkling water and stood, blowing her brother a kiss. "Later, Einstein."

"Booty call," he replied.

"Shut up."

"Be safe!" he called behind her, his laughter chasing her out the door.

At Flynn's building, she pulled into the private parking area where she used the code he'd given her and tucked her compact into the spare space next to his car. Inside, she took the elevator to the penthouse, again using a passcode to zoom to the uppermost floor. The building felt far too serious for him.

Or for who Flynn used to be, anyway. He was pretty serious nowadays.

His seriousness had tripled when he and Veronica were married. Sabrina didn't want to be unfair, but credit was due where it was due. He'd been a committed husband and now that Sabrina didn't have to play nice any longer, she'd admit that Veronica had kept Flynn running in circles. His ex-wife had wanted to be pleased at every turn. With jewelry, more money and bigger, better everything. The house they'd lived in on Main and Eastwood was a friggin' mansion and *still* Veronica had whined about it.

With that unsavory thought simmering in her veins, she stepped from the elevator and into his foyer, announcing herself as she walked in. Expectedly, her voice bounced off the high beams and rang from the glass windows. She opened her mouth to sing a song from *The Sound of Music* when she spotted Flynn walking down the slatted stairs.

"Don't you dare," he warned.

"Spoilsport." She blew out a breath without belting out a single note and then relinquished her purse and coat to the dining room table. A white block with white chairs and in the center, oh, look, a white bowl with some weird porcelain white orbs in it. She palmed one and tested its weight. "Your decorator has no personality."

"I didn't hire the decorator for her personality." Flynn glanced up from the iPad in his hand. "I hired the decorator to remove my father's personality."

She glanced around at the square black sofa and gray coffee tables. The gray rug. The white mantel over which hung a framed painting of a black smudge on a white background.

"Success," she agreed with a placid smile. "What'd you need me for? I was under the impression you were sad or drunk or having some sort of belated episode because of the divorce."

"What I am about to have is enough Chinese food to feed an army."

"What about Gage and Reid?"

"What about them?"

"Um." What she couldn't say was that she felt the out-of-place need for a buffer or two. "Wouldn't they suffice in helping you rid yourself of excess takeout?"

Setting aside the iPad, he looked down at her, his handsome smile dazzling. "I'd rather hang with you. I've felt lately like you've been on the outside for too long."

"The outside?"

"In the background." His mouth pulled down at the edges. "The four of us used to hang out more. Outside of work. And then…we didn't."

Sabrina's heart swelled. She'd missed him over the last

three years he'd been married, but accepted that marriage required attention. Still, it was nice to know that she mattered and that he'd missed her.

"Aw." She beamed at the compliment and patted his cheek, not thinking a thing of it. Until she became acutely aware of the warmth from his skin and the rough scrape of his facial hair as she swept her fingers away. She cleared her throat and reminded herself that Flynn was her friend and nothing more. "There, was that so hard?"

His smile returned. "Begging is unattractive."

An hour later, they sat at the dining room table, food containers, an iPad, laptop and a manila folder stuffed with reports between them. They'd eaten a little of everything before cracking open a few beers, and that's when Flynn brought out the work accoutrements.

Tonight reminded her of late-night study sessions when they were in college. She'd been reflecting on those days more often than before lately and on how simple life had been back then.

"It'll work," he concluded.

Chin resting on her hand, elbow on the table, she yawned. "I think you're cruel and should offer me a refill for making me work late on a Friday."

"I fed you." He frowned. "Do you want another drink?"

"Do you have Perrier?"

"Perrier is not a drink." But he turned for the fridge and came back with a bottle of sparkling water for her. He even went to the trouble of spinning off the top and then proffering a highball glass. "I'd appreciate your thoughts."

His hands landed on her shoulders, kneading the tired muscles. She was torn between moaning in pleasure and freezing in place. Luke really had gotten into her head with that "booty call" comment.

Flynn's hands left her shoulders and she shakily filled

her glass and took her time sipping the sparkling water before she told him what she thought—about his idea. "It won't work."

Even his frown was frowning.

"If there were ten of you working eighty hours a week, *maybe* you could make up for losing half your staff. As it stands, even if Gage and Reid and I double our workloads along with you, I don't see how Monarch would survive everyone walking out."

"So I should let them force *me* into walking out?"

"It's a *vacation*," she reminded him on a soft laugh. "You've heard of them, right? You take a few days or weeks to relax and do something that's not work."

"My father built this business from scratch. I don't see why I can't put my head down and plow forward and end up in a better position."

"The staff is resisting change. Maybe when you're not there—but your changes are still implemented—they'll come to see you're right. If they need to flex their muscles and try to put you in your place, it's not like they'll succeed. It's for show. You're still in charge."

"My father would have died before letting anyone tell him how to run his business. Including me."

"He *did* die, Flynn." She reached across the table to palm his forearm. She understood why Flynn was angry with Emmons. Flynn had tried to impart his ideas at Monarch but had always been shut down by his father. Now was Flynn's chance to shine and he was being shut down by his father's ilk. It was insulting.

Flynn had lost the jacket, loosened the tie, but left on the starched shirt. There was a time he'd have his sleeves rolled up and would've laughed and lounged through both the meal and the beer. They'd had plenty of after-hours staff meetings, just Sabrina, Flynn and the guys, and Flynn was usually a hum of excitement. Now, that hum was gone.

There wasn't any excitement, just rote habits. He was as cold as his current environment.

"You're *not* him, and you don't have to become him," she said. "Not for Mac or Belinda or anyone else who believes that Monarch can only be run the way Emmons ran it."

Flynn's mouth compressed into a silent line.

"I hate seeing you like this. I know you're sick to death of me lecturing you, but if you don't loosen your hold, you're going to have a breakdown. Or a heart attack. Or—"

"Get cancer?" he finished for her. "I'm thirty years old, Sabrina. Hardly in the market for the thing that's going to kill me."

She flinched. Imagining Flynn dead was a fast track to revisiting her dinner. She tried again with even more honesty.

"*I miss you.* The old you. The *you* that knew where work stopped and fun started. Now you're like…" She waved in his general direction. "…a robot."

His features didn't soften in the slightest.

"Remember when we used to stumble out of college parties or go to the pub for Saint Patrick's Day? Remember playing poker until all hours of the night?"

"I remember you losing and refusing to pay up."

"It was strip poker and I was the only girl there!"

"Reid's idea." He let loose another smile and it resembled one that was carefree. "I don't know why you balked. I'd seen you in your underwear before."

"Yes, but not…not them." Her cheeks warmed. Yes, Flynn had seen her in her underwear. In her dorm room when he'd come to wake her up, or when she was changing to go out to a party. But that was different somehow.

She palmed her cheek to hide her hectic coloring. "I miss those days. What happened to us?"

"We grew up. We started working." He reached for her

hand, his thumb skimming over hers as he watched her closely. "I'm sorry if you've felt shut out lately."

A lump of emotion tightened her throat and she nodded, blinking to keep from crying. She had felt left out, and had made peace with seeing him at work and the occasional after-work dinner, but that wasn't enough.

"We used to be inseparable."

"I remember." His secret smile was all for her and she reveled in it. No one was here to intrude or put him on the clock or demand he stop being himself.

"When's the last time you took the time to do something you love?"

"A while," he admitted.

"Same. I've been wanting to paint again and I haven't had the time." Her eyes went to the mantel and that sorry excuse for art he had hanging over it. "I'd like to replace that lifeless painting with a Sabrina Douglas original."

"Clown on a bicycle? Elephant balancing on a waffle cone?"

"That was my circus era and I'm over it. You certainly have enough space in this vault for me to spread out a canvas or two." She moved to tug her hand away but he held fast. His blue eyes were locked on hers when he squeezed her fingers.

"I'll think about it."

"That's all I ask."

For now.

Five

Flynn thought long and hard about what Sabrina said while he lay staring at the glass ceiling in his living room. The stars were bright, the sky a navy blue canvas. A canvas like Sabrina wanted to paint and hang over his fireplace.

From his position on the sofa, he turned his head and looked at the black-and-white painting that was as bland as Sabrina had hinted. His life—his entire life—could use some color. A color other than monotone neutrals or angry reds. A color like Sabrina. Splashy yellow or citrusy orange, he thought with a smile.

Tonight might have been the first time in months he'd stopped to evaluate any part of his existence. If he hadn't been gathering information for his lawyer for the divorce, he'd been making funeral arrangements for his father, or relocating to this apartment after first removing every single trace of Emmons Parker. Fat lot of good it did him to erase his father from the apartment when Flynn himself was morphing into a younger version of his old man.

He couldn't let it happen. *Wouldn't* let it happen. Sabrina was right. He used to make time to do the things he loved, rather than serve at the pleasure of a sixty-plus-hour week.

The last year had been a blur of takeout, reports and meetings. He pulled a hand over his stomach, and while he hadn't developed a gut in the slightest, his abs weren't as chiseled as they could've been. At last glance in the mirror, his eyes weren't as bright either. The dark circles were a result of restless sleep, and the shadow of scruff on his jaw was unkempt enough that he looked more homeless than stylish.

Sabrina's being here had been reminder enough of what he'd been missing—her presence. And now she was offering to take a hiatus with him to help him out.

After years of her doing things for him, the least he could do was listen to her. His plan to work around his execs' bailing wasn't foolproof. Somewhere in the back of his stubborn mind he'd known that all along. Sabrina was unflinchingly honest when she'd told him she missed him and who he used to be. Which meant he was on the fast track to turning into a bitter, iron-hard man like his father.

That glaring truth made deciding easier.

First thing Monday morning, Flynn would call a meeting with his three best friends. A strategy meeting. He could walk away if he knew the place wasn't eroding in his absence. And if he armed Gage and Reid with what they needed to keep Mac from overriding every implementation he'd put in place, then Flynn could actually relax.

The shiver of relief was foreign, but welcome. He'd tried running the company his father's way. It was time to try a different strategy—Sabrina's strategy. Flynn had lost sight of what was important.

It was time to get it back.

Monday morning at Monarch looked the same as it had last week. Flynn was pouring himself a cup of coffee when Gage walked in.

"Morning. Get yourself fired yet?"

"Not yet." Flynn leaned against the counter.

Reid sauntered in next. "Morning, gentlemen."

"Singleton." Flynn dipped his chin. Gage saluted.

"Do you ever have one of those really good dreams," Reid said as he rinsed his travel mug and set it in the drainer to drip dry, "where you're with a woman and you're so in tune with her that even the sunlight doesn't snap you out of it?" He moved to the espresso machine and started the process of creating his next cup while Flynn blinked at him in disbelief.

His best friend had read his mind.

"Just this morning," Flynn answered. "Except I woke up before I saw who it was."

"Perfect." Reid nodded in approval. "Bloody perfect. When you can't see who it is, all the better."

Flynn had spent the weekend sleeping on the sofa despite a brand-new $8,000 bed in the master bedroom. The vestiges of a vividly erotic dream loosened its hold the moment the sun crept over the horizon. He'd made a futile attempt to hang on with both hands, long enough to figure out who belonged to that husky voice murmuring not-so-sweet nothings into his ear.

"How far'd you get?" Reid asked. At Flynn's questioning glance, he added, "Were you actually laid in your dream or are you still blue-balled from it?"

"Not far enough," he mumbled. It cut off before the good part.

"Mate." Reid shook his head. "We need to get you a girl."

"He's right." Gage moved Reid's espresso aside to make his own. "You can't handle this much stress and not have sex. Stephenie has a friend, by the way."

"I thought you'd stopped seeing Stephenie." Reid leaned a hip on the counter, settling in next to Flynn.

"I did." Gage poured milk into the steel carafe for steaming. "She'd let me set up Flynn with her sister. Steph and I didn't end badly. We just ended."

"You ended it," Flynn guessed.

"I don't need *serious* to have a good time. And you, my friend—" Gage dipped his chin at Flynn "—are way too serious lately."

"So I'm told."

The room filled with the sound of the steamer frothing milk to a perfect foamy consistency. If Flynn needed a second to Sabrina's "serious" motion, he'd just heard it.

A hazy, golden image filtered through his memory, the sun at the mystery woman's back, a shadow blotting out her face. He closed his eyes and tried to see the woman with the sultry voice, but she faded much like early this morning. Odd. He'd never had such a lucid dream. God help him if that face belonged to Veronica. He didn't have that much time to dedicate to therapy.

"We're here for the meeting you called, Parker. Where are we doing it?" Gage asked him.

"Yeah." Reid straightened from his lean, a delicate espresso cup dwarfed in one hand. "And what's it about? Are you retiring to live off your millions?"

"Dad's millions were wrapped up in assets, not lying around in the bank."

"Bummer." Gage shook his head.

"You wouldn't quit if you had millions, would you?" Reid asked.

"I would." Gage shrugged. "I can find something else to do with my time."

"Like what?" Sabrina strolled in, her phone in hand. "Which one of you fine baristas is whipping me up a cappuccino?"

"Gage," Reid answered.

Gage retorted and Reid argued something back that

Flynn missed. Reason being was that he was staring in shock as the face from his dream crystallized.

The golden light receded as she leaned forward over him. He swept her mussed dark hair from her face with his fingers as her mouth dropped open in a cry of pleasure.

"What the *hell*?"

The coffee banter stopped abruptly and they all turned their attention on him.

"What the hell…what?" Sabrina tipped her head and sent her long hair—the same long, dark hair from his dream—sliding over one shoulder. Desire walloped Flynn like a two-by-four to the gut.

No.

No, no, no, he mentally reprimanded himself, but the rest of his body parts had other ideas.

His eyes took in her jewel-toned red dress and then fastened on the delicate gold chain sitting at the base of her throat. His ears delighted at her kittenish laugh in response to something Reid said. And the one part of him that absolutely should *not* be reacting to her stirred in interest as if waking from a deep, deep sleep.

"Aren't you jealous?" Reid asked. And because his arm was slung around Sabrina's neck, it took Flynn a second to clear the fuzz from his head. "Of our fancy coffees."

"Flynn should make my cappuccino, and then he can make himself one, too." Sabrina sashayed over to him, her skirt moving with her long legs, ending in a pair of pointy-toed black high heels. She took his mug from him and he stiffened. And he did mean *all* of him.

"What do you have in there?" The husk in her voice caused his mind to nosedive into the gutter. But she wasn't talking about what was going on in his pants, she was referring to his coffee mug. She sipped and then wrinkled her cute nose.

"Plain old drip. *Boh*-ring. Cappuccinos for everyone and

then we'll get started. Oh! We could have the meeting in here!" She carried the mug to the sink and dumped it. "I'd much rather sit over there than in that conference room."

"Over there" was a grouping of leather sofas and chairs. Flynn focused on the furniture, desperate to reroute his thoughts from the insane idea that Sabrina was anything other than his best friend. He'd already done her a disservice by benching her. She didn't need him sexualizing her on top of it.

But thinking of the words *on top* only served as a reminder of where she was in his dream. On top of *him*.

"Must've been the pizza." He said that aloud and earned some raised eyebrows from his two male friends. He forced a shaky smile and went to the espresso machine, hoping to busy his hands for a bit, too. "Cappuccinos all around."

Mugs empty, they lounged in the executive break room. Reid, leg crossed ankle-to-knee in one of the leather chairs, propped his grotesquely handsome head up with one hand, eyes narrowed in thought as Flynn continued listing the details that would need handling when—eventually—he extracted himself from Monarch as Sabrina had suggested. Gage sat across from him in the matching chair, his cell phone in hand as he typed notes into it. Sabrina had chosen the couch across from Flynn. She'd been scribbling notes in a fancy spiral-bound notebook she'd run to her office to fetch before they started.

Flynn had been glad for the break. Her leaving the room had given him a chance to settle his formerly unsettled self. By the time she'd returned, he was back to looking at her like a coworker and friend and not like a man who apparently needed to get laid more than he needed a third cappuccino.

"Understanding that spring is a busy season for us…" His mouth continued on autopilot, but his brain took a sharp left turn when Sabrina set aside her notebook and pen to slip off one shoe. She set the spiked heel on the ground and crossed her leg, massaging one arch with insistent fingers. He watched the movement, his eyes fastened on red fingernails, not too long, not too short. His own voice was an echo, and he hoped to God Reid and Gage weren't staring at him while he stared at Sabrina. Not that it mattered. Flynn wasn't capable of stopping.

She bent to slip her shoe on and the neck of her dress gapped, giving him an eyeful of the shadow between her breasts. The lost dream cannonballed back into his subconscious so hard he sucked in a breath midsentence and didn't recover right away.

Sabrina over him.

Sabrina's red mouth parted to say his name.

Sabrina's long hair covering her nipples and hiding them from view.

Were they pink? Peach? Dusky tan? Or—

"As soon as what?" Reid asked, leaning forward, his elbows on his knees and his attention on Flynn.

Flynn snapped his head around to face Reid, who thankfully wasn't wearing an *I Know What You Did Last Summer* smirk.

"Sorry. Where was I?"

"You said you figured you could take time off as soon as…"

As soon as I pull my head from my ass. Or, more accurately, Sabrina's cleavage.

"May. I can take off in May." What the hell was wrong with him? Maybe he was heading for a breakdown.

"May!" Sabrina yipped, her voice a high-pitched complaint rather than the soothing alto of his dream. "I'm not letting you wait until May. Hiatus starts *now*."

Her stern exclamation glanced off him like a butterfly's wing. He'd known her for a hundred years and had never wondered what color her nipples were. Did he notice she had boobs? Sure. Had he guessed what cup size she wore? Absolutely. Did he notice when other guys looked at her while she wore a bikini at the beach? You bet. But other than unwitting glimpses that were more male programming than intentional ogling, he'd never mentally stripped her down for his own pleasure.

She was his best friend. It'd never occurred to him to imagine the color of her nipples any more than he would imagine the color of Gage's.

Flynn had no earthly clue how he'd made the leap from sharing Chinese food with her on Friday to waking Monday with morning wood from a dream where she was stark naked and moaning his name.

Unless she'd been right about his not dealing with the emotional toll the last year had taken. His entire life had been in upheaval when he'd been handed the company. He'd been acting president, but there was a safety net in place—his father. After Emmons had passed, Flynn was on his own. He'd lost his mother at fifteen, his brother to betrayal and his father right around the same time. He had no one, save the three people in this room.

He couldn't let them down. Taking his mind and hands off the controls would have to come with some sort of reassurance—the reason for this meeting, or else Monarch Consulting would sink like the *Titanic*.

Flynn wiped his sweaty brow and attempted to regroup. Not a simple task since Sabrina spoke next, forcing him to look directly at her.

Six

"Are you insane?"

Even as she asked the question, she thought to herself that while Flynn wasn't insane, he certainly did look a little...unhinged. His gaze wouldn't settle in one place, bouncing from her face to Gage to Reid to his lap before going around again. Maybe he'd had too much coffee.

"May is two months away," Gage said. Sabrina was glad she wasn't the only one who'd noticed that.

"So?"

"*So*, it's not going to take *two months* for you to hand over our assignments." Gage set his phone aside and sat on the edge of the chair. "We're capable of doing what needs to be done."

"I emailed Rose my vacation hours this morning," Sabrina said of the HR manager. "We're taking off starting Monday."

"We?" Reid turned toward her. "Where are you going? And why are you at this meeting if you're not going to be here helping us battle the powers of evil?"

"I oversee design and social media and my teams are perfectly capable of handling my being away from the office. Plus, I already told them they can reach out if there's an emergency."

"You said you wanted to paint," Flynn said, his voice gruff.

"I do. I will."

"You lectured me nonstop Friday night about taking time away and doing something other than working and now you're promising your team you're available for an emergency? You said you'd paint me something for the mantel."

"You two went out on Friday? I wasn't invited." Reid frowned.

"Fine. I'll ignore my phone and email, too," she told Flynn before turning to the other two. "We ate Chinese in Flynn's personality-free apartment—"

"Penthouse," Flynn corrected.

"Sorry. His personality-free *penthouse*." She flashed him a smile. "Where I tried to explain to him that vacation is different from retirement."

"I still don't understand why we weren't invited." Reid tipped his chin at Gage. "Where were you on Friday, Fleming?"

"My sister's boyfriend dumped her so I was on ice cream duty. I couldn't have showed up anyway."

"Well, I could've." Reid folded his arms over his thick chest. His dark hair was slightly wavy, his jaw angled and stubborn. His mouth was full and his eyes were piercing blue. If he wasn't acting like a ten-year-old right now, she might admit he was stupidly attractive.

"This isn't about you, Reid." She sighed. "It's about Flynn and how he's different than he used to be. Admit it, he's not the guy you became best friends with. If you were married to him, you'd be in counseling right now."

"If I was married at all I'd be in counseling right now," Reid quipped.

Gage laughed, but sobered when Sabrina communicated via a patient expression that she could use backup. Thankfully he showed up for her.

"Sabrina has a point," Gage said. Flynn shot him a glare that plainly said he did *not* want to talk about it. "Hear me out. Since Veronica…uh, *left*…you haven't been yourself. I understand that she and Julian simultaneously stabbed you in the back and kicked you in the balls. I've tried to be here for you, buddy. And your dad dying was another blow. I know you believe you don't have to mourn him as long since you two never got along, but you do."

"Agreed," Reid interjected. "I hate to admit it, but Sab is right." He winked at her to let her know he was teasing. "Since the funeral, you've been behaving like Emmons back from the dead. Frankly, none of us want to work with the next generation of wanker."

"You want to try running this place?" Flynn practically yelled.

"Yes." Reid didn't so much as flinch. "While you, and evidently Sabrina, paint and ride horses bareback or live in a yurt or whatever she has planned for you."

"Things to Do When You're Twenty-Two," Sabrina announced proudly. Every pair of eyes swiveled to her in question. "That's what Flynn and I are doing. We're going to live like we did in college."

"In a cramped dorm that smells of old gym socks?" Gage asked. She ignored him.

"I'm going to help Flynn remember what life was like before we were given the keys to the city. Before there was a Veronica. Before any of us knew we'd be running the biggest consulting firm in the Pacific Northwest. Before I could afford a six-hundred-dollar pair of shoes." Flynn's gaze lingered on her shoes for a moment before it met her eyes. "When we used to share a car because we couldn't be bothered to own one separately.

"Back when Bennie took my virginity and Gage was engaged." She sent him a glance and he paled slightly at the mention. She focused on Reid. "Back when you were sleeping your way through half of campus."

"It was a service I provided. Girls back then didn't know what good sex was until they met me." He offered a cocky smile.

"You two were twin disasters back then, but Flynn and I… We were good." She smiled at her best friend and his features softened. "We were better than we are now with our expensive sports cars and our gourmet coffees and our bespoke clothing. We were better than the corporate drones we're turning into."

"I'm not a drone," Gage argued.

"Me neither. We take umbrage to that accusation." Reid straightened his shirtsleeve. "Though I do enjoy nice cuff links."

"I wouldn't go back to being engaged. That was a mistake." Gage's tone suggested he needed to state that for the record.

"Hear, hear," Reid agreed. "I had a lot of fun in college, but I have no interest in reliving my past."

"That's why you're not invited to our hiatus," Sabrina said, her tone implying the "duh" she didn't say. "You may be fine balancing work and play, but I, for one, am terrible at it. And so is Flynn. I need to paint and he needs to focus on something other than Monarch's well-being."

Stress showed in the lines on the sides of Flynn's eyes and the downturn of his mouth. Two more months of not dealing with his feelings and she feared she'd lose her momentum. He was saying yes to the hiatus, which was huge. It'd take only a nudge for him to agree to starting it on Monday.

"Flynn. You can trust Reid and Gage. Monarch won't implode if you walk away. You can start your hiatus on Monday. With me." She reached over and palmed his knee, noting that his nostrils flared when she did. The way he looked at her wasn't impatient or upset, but more...*aware*. It reminded her of the way she'd looked at him on Friday evening.

"I'll put it in my calendar." Gage lifted his phone, typing as he slowly spoke the words, "Flynn and Sabrina's sabba...ti...cal. There. Done." He showed them the screen. "Monday's Valentine's Day by the way."

"I know." Sabrina grinned. "Flynn and I are going out."

"On Valentine's Day?" Reid's voice was comically high. "That day should be treated tenderly. Every single man knows that occasion is a minefield. What are you going to do, love? Take him to a fancy couples' dinner and shag him afterward?"

Sabrina let out an uncomfortable laugh, looking to Flynn to laugh with her, but he looked as if a grenade had gone off in his general vicinity. His shoulders were hunched and his face was a mask of horror. So...possibly she misread his expression a moment ago.

"Thanks a lot." She let out a grunt. "I wouldn't be *that* bad to sleep with!"

Flynn rubbed his eyes with the heels of his hands.

"I'd happily sleep with you, Sab. I've been offering for years."

"No way." She rolled her eyes at Reid's offer. She couldn't imagine sleeping with, kissing or being romantically involved with Gage or Reid. She winked over at Gage, who smiled affably. They were like brothers.

Her gaze locked with Flynn's next and they had a brief staring contest. His slightly crazed expression was gone and now he simply watched her.

Flynn was...not like a brother.

But there was a deeper camaraderie between them that was worth resurrecting. And it'd be fun to go out on Valentine's Day with him. They could make new memories since neither of them had ever been single at the same time as the other.

She blinked as that thought took hold.

Until now.

"So now you're dating Flynn and we're still not calling it dating?"

Her brother, Luke, delivered doughnuts to her place on Saturday morning. One of which was a cruller that she tore in half and dunked into her coffee.

Mmm. Coffee and crullers.

"Hello?" Luke snapped his fingers in her face. "You and that doughnut are having a moment that's making me uncomfortable."

"You'll live." She tore off another bite and stuffed it into her mouth.

Her apartment was in the city not far from Flynn's, but the two residences were worlds apart. His, a penthouse and shrine to all things soulless, and hers an artsy loft filled with cozy accents. A red faux leather sofa sat on a patterned gold-and-red rug, a plaid blanket tossed over one arm. Framed art hung on the wall, one of them Sabrina's own: a whimsical painting of an owl sitting on a cat's head that always made her smile. Butter-yellow '50s-style chairs she'd reupholstered after salvaging them from a trash heap circled a scarred round kitchen table that she and Luke sat at now.

"Flynn lives in a barren wasteland of a penthouse, but the view is a million times better," she said, scowling out at the view of a nearby brick wall.

When she'd first rented her place, she'd fallen in love with the C-shape of the building and the ivy climbing the rust-red-and-brown bricked facade. Now, though, she'd like a view of the sunset. Or a sunrise. As it was, very little vitamin D streamed through her kitchen windows, and only for a few choice hours a day.

"That's most rich guys, isn't it?" Luke smirked.

"Oh, like you don't have aspirations to make millions."

"I do. Off my Instagram account. Eventually." He religiously posted at-the-gym selfies. Luke had rippling abs and a great smile and if she were to ask any female her opinion of him, she could guess the answer. Her girlfriends in college had labeled him "hot" even when he was younger, and his loyal league of followers contended that he was gorgeous.

"And when you make your millions, will you live on a top floor and invite me over for doughnuts?"

"No. I'll live on a few hundred acres and buy a llama."

"A llama." She hoisted one eyebrow.

He grinned. She shook her head. He was still *just Luke* to her, no matter what thousands of random women thought of him.

"Tell me about your Valentine's Day date with Flynn." He chose an éclair from the white cardboard box. She wiggled her fingers over a bear claw and then a powdered jelly before grabbing another cruller. She was a purist. Sue her.

"It's not a date. I mean, it is but it'd be the same as if I went out on V-day date with a girlfriend. Like Cammie."

"Mmm, Cammie." A quick lift of Luke's eyebrows paired with a devilish smile.

"*No.* We've been through this. You're not allowed to date my friends because it'd be weird and awkward and…no." Plus, Cammie moved to Chicago last year. Sabrina missed having a girlfriend close by.

"Flynn is dating you and he's my friend."

"We're *not* dating," she reiterated. "And he's not your friend. You know him. There's a difference."

Affronted, Luke pouted before taking a giant bite of the éclair.

"And we're not going to a cliché superfancy, elegant dinner. We're going to Pike Place Market and having breakfast, then hearing a cheesemonger speak about artisan cheeses, and then—"

"Did you just use the word *cheesemonger*?"

"—*and then* we're going to finish up with a trapeze show." The part she was most excited about.

Luke made a face.

"It'll be fun."

"It sounds lame."

She punched him in the arm but he was asking for it, delivered doughnuts or no.

"I thought you were supposed to be reliving your college years. The Market was built, what, a few years ago?"

"We're reliving the *spirit* of our college years."

"I'll give you this, Sabs." He stood to grab the coffeepot and refilled both their mugs. "Your date sounds positively *unromantic*. Fifty points to you. I guess Flynn is only a friend."

That rankled her, especially after she and Flynn had been exchanging some eye-locks and subtle touches that had felt, while not romantic, at least *sensual*. Rather than clue her brother in, or entertain the words *sensual* and *Flynn* in the same thought, she mumbled, "Right."

Seven

The rain fell on a cool fifty-degree day that the weather-man said felt more like thirty-seven degrees. No matter. Sabrina had convinced Flynn to start his hiatus Monday—today—and she was determined to both pry her best friend out of his shell and enjoy herself.

They started with breakfast, tucking into a small table for two near the window where they could watch the foot traffic pass by. She ordered a cappuccino and orange juice and a glass of water.

"Like you, I usually drink my breakfast," Flynn said after ordering coffee for himself. He could give her all the hell she wanted so long as he was here with her.

When their drinks arrived, she resumed her sermon from the ride over about how he needed time off. "It'll take you a while to get used to relaxing."

"I'm relaxed." His mouth pulled to the side in frustration and he lifted his steaming coffee mug to his lips.

"Yes. With your shoulders clinging to your earlobes and

that Grouchy Smurf expression on your face, you're very convincing."

He forcefully dropped his shoulders and eased his eyebrows from their home at the center of his forehead.

"It's okay to admit you have emotions to deal with. It's okay to talk about your father. Or Veronica and Julian—or either of them apart from the other."

"How can I talk about them apart from the other if they're never apart?"

Sabrina stirred her cappuccino before taking a warm, frothy sip. As carefully as if she were disarming a bomb, she asked a question that pained her to the core.

"Do you miss her?"

He took a breath and leaned on the table, his arms folded. Huddled close over the small table for two, he pegged her with honest blue eyes. "No. I don't."

That pause had made her nervous for a second. Her chest expanded as she took a deep breath of her own. Then she pulled her own shoulders out from under her ears. Sabrina was there for Flynn's engagement and the wedding and the aftermath. She knew what Flynn was like dating Veronica, being betrothed to Veronica and then married to her. Sabrina had watched the evolution—the *de*volution—of him throughout the process. It broke her heart to watch him be used up and discarded.

"I don't miss her either."

He returned her smirk with a soft smile of his own.

"She never liked me."

"She did so." His low baritone skittered along her nerve endings, that inconvenient awareness kicking up like dust in a windstorm.

"You don't have to lie to me now. It's not like she's sitting here. She tolerated me because you and I were friends and we share a birthday and because I'm too loyal to leave you."

"I wouldn't sweat it. She's clearly not stable since she's with Julian." He let out a small breath of a laugh and she clung to it. She'd love to hear Flynn laugh like he used to, big and bold. Watch how it crinkled his eyes. She loved so many aspects about him, but his laugh was at the top of her list.

"It's fitting to be out with you on Valentine's Day," she told him. "You might be the only guy in my life aside from Luke who I've cared about consistently."

"Never ruin a friendship with dating, right?"

"Right." She smiled but then it faded. "We were never tempted to date, were we?"

Mug lifted, he sent her a Reid-worthy wink. "Not until today."

"It recently occurred to me that we were always dating someone other than each other. Do you think that was why we never dated, or were we just too smart to get involved?"

"We weren't always dating other people. I had long stints of being single."

"Yes, but they never coincided with my stints of being single." She was right about this. She knew it. "Go through your list."

"My *list?*"

"The list of girls you dated from your college freshman year through now."

"How am I supposed to remember that?" He swiped his jaw, and his stubble made a scratchy sound on his palm, reminding her of when she touched his face last week. She shifted in her seat and shut out the strange observation.

"I need corroborated evidence."

"Who the hell's going to corroborate?"

"Me. I remember who we dated in college."

"Everyone?"

"Everyone."

"That is a useless amount of information to store in your noggin, Sab."

"Nevertheless it's there. Go. You can start with Anna Kelly."

"Anna Kelly does not count."

"You and I had first met. You were dating her and I was seeing Louis Watson."

"Good ole Louie."

"We went on that—"

"Disastrous double date," he filled in for her. "Louis didn't know better than to talk politics."

"She baited him! Anyway, so there was that. Then I broke up with Louis and started seeing Phillip."

"Cock."

"Cox."

"He was an idiot. Okay, let's see…that was when I was with Martha Bryant. For a few weeks and then another M. Melissa…something?"

"Murphy. Don't act like you don't remember her just because she was crazy."

"God, she so was."

"And you stayed with her for like, ever."

"Only for a few months. I had a weakness for crazy back then. And then I dated Janet Martinez."

Her name rolled off his tongue in a way that made Sabrina seasick. "She was gorgeous. What happened to her? Did she ever become a swimsuit model?"

"Yes."

"Lie!"

"Truth. She didn't land *Sports Illustrated*, but she was on the covers of a few health mags. She lives in Los Angeles. Or did the last time I saw her."

"When did you see her? You didn't tell me that." A misplaced pang of jealousy shot through her.

"She was in town randomly a few years ago and was considering hiring Monarch."

"For what?"

"She owns a company that makes surfboards."

"Wow. I didn't date anyone that interesting ever. Unless… Ray Bell."

"Puke. He was *not* interesting."

"He was!"

"You were too good for him."

"As were you for Janet," she shot back.

"Which was why I started dating Teresa."

"And after Ray dumped me, I dated Mark Walker for a long while."

"I thought he was the one."

"I thought Teresa was the one for you. She was smart, funny."

"And only dating me to get close to Reid."

"To his credit, he didn't take her up on it," Sabrina pointed out. "That's what friends should do. Reid's a good friend."

"He is." Flynn examined his coffee. "Wish I'd have seen Veronica coming. She blindsided me."

"True story." Sabrina had witnessed it firsthand. Flynn was fresh off a breakup with Teresa and smarting over it. Gage's engagement had ended so he was as sad a sack as Flynn. Reid was in charge of keeping them from moping and so he dragged them to a party one random Friday night and that's where Flynn met Veronica. She'd swept in and convinced him—and the rest of his friends—that she was the woman Flynn needed.

"I guess Julian didn't abide by the friend code."

"I guess not," she concurred sadly. Because it *was* sad. Devastatingly upsetting, actually. How could Veronica leave Flynn when her job was to love him more than she loved herself?

"I really hate her sometimes." Sabrina pressed her lips together, wanting to swallow the words she shouldn't have said.

They were true, though. She didn't hate Veronica only because of the cheating and leaving. Sabrina had felt that surge of bitterness toward the woman throughout Flynn's marriage for one simple reason: Veronica was selfish. As had now been proved.

"I'm sorry I said that."

"Don't be," Flynn said.

They were interrupted by the delivery of waffles and a refill of coffee for Flynn. A plate of bacon appeared, smoky and inviting, and he moved it to the center of the table like he always had. Sabrina never ordered bacon because it was unhealthy and, frankly, she felt sort of bad for the pigs. He suffered no such guilt and knew she would cave and have a bite or two. He always shared.

"Hate whomever you want." He pointed at her with a strip of bacon before taking a bite and blessedly changed the subject. "After all, I hated Craig."

"Craig Ross."

A minor blip to get her over Ray. It worked on the short term and then she realized he was a complete narcissist. She dumped him shortly after they started seeing each other.

"And there you have it," she stated. "I've been single most of the time you and Veronica were married. But this is the first time you have been single at the same time as me."

"But you've dated."

"Nothing serious."

"Meaning?" He paused, fork holding a bite of waffle midair, syrup drizzling onto the plate.

"Meaning…nothing serious."

"No permanent plans, you mean."

"No…other things, too." She dived into her own waffle.

"No sex?"

Okay, that was a little loud.

"Shh!" She and Flynn had talked about sex and dating plenty but now that his physical presence was *more* present than ever, she felt strangely shy about the topic.

He chuckled and ate his waffle, shaking his head as he cut another piece precisely along the squares.

"It's not funny. It was a choice."

"Aren't you going mad?"

"Are you?"

His pleasant smile faded and there was a brief, poignant moment where their eyes met and the rest of the dining room faded into the background. She counted her heartbeats—one, two, three—and then Flynn blinked and the moment was over.

"I'm failing at cheering you up," she said.

"No. I started it. I have no right to judge you for your choices, Douglas."

"Well. Thanks. I just…didn't want to be attached to the wrong guy again. Sex makes everything blurry."

"God. Dating." He made a face. "I'm not in the market—"

"Actually, you are *at* the Market."

His smile was a victory in itself.

"I'm not in the market," he repeated, "for a relationship or a date. Gage and Reid think sex is going to magically fix everything. But you're right. It won't."

That was a relief. She didn't want him to go find someone else either. It was too soon.

"Sex has a way of uncovering feelings you've been ignoring."

His blue eyes grew dark as he studied her.

"What do you mean?" he asked after a pregnant pause.

"In the same way alcohol acts as truth serum, sex makes you face facts. Like if the attraction wasn't actually there, and when you have sex it's dull. Or, on the flip side of that same coin, if there is a spark, sex heightens every sensation and it's incredible."

Flynn's cheeks went a ruddy, pinkish color. "Incredible?"

"Sometimes." She swallowed thickly. "Unless it's just me."

"It might be you," he muttered cryptically before grabbing another slice of bacon. "Help me eat this."

Sabrina's statement at breakfast followed Flynn around like a bad omen.

"Sex has a way of uncovering feelings you've been ignoring."

He'd like to believe that wasn't true, but it *felt* true. Right about now, watching her with an itchy, foreign sort of *need*, it felt really, really true.

"Stop grimacing," she whispered as the cheese tour continued.

Their group of eight dairy-delighted couples were eating their way through various artisanal cheeses and the tour wasn't half over yet. Their guide, head cheesemonger Cathy Bates—yes, that was her real name—had just served samples of blueberry-covered goat cheese. Sabrina must've assumed that was what turned his mood.

"Who can eat this much cheese? No one," he growled under his breath.

Sabrina shot him a feisty smile that was like a kick in the teeth. It rattled his brains around in his skull and his entire being gravitated closer to her. Until this morning, he'd never laid out their timelines and dating habits side by side. They'd never talked about how they were always overlapping each other with other people.

It was an odd thing to notice.

Why had Sabrina noticed?

He watched her as cheese samples were passed around but he couldn't detect by looking if she'd had the same sort of semierotic dream about him as he'd had about her, or if she was thinking of him in any way other than as her pal Flynn.

He'd never looked at her any differently until that dream. Sabrina Douglas was his best girl friend. Girl *space* friend. Not a woman he'd pursue sexually.

She hummed her pleasure and wiggled her hips while she ate a graham cracker topped with goat cheese, and Flynn felt a definite stir in his gut. For the first time in his life, sex wasn't off the table for him and Sabrina.

Which meant he needed his head examined.

Pairing with the confusing thoughts was a palpable relief that down south he was operating as usual. He'd worried after the one-two punch of losing his wife to his brother and his father to cancer he'd never be back to normal.

Now that he reconsidered, who cared that a mental wire had crossed and put Sab's face in his fantasies? He'd had weird dreams before and they hadn't changed the course of his life.

After the tasting, Sabrina chattered about her favorite cheeses and how she couldn't believe they didn't serve wine at the tour.

"What kind of establishment doesn't offer you wine with cheese?" she exclaimed as they strolled down the boardwalk. She was a few feet ahead of him yelling at the wind, her jeans and Converse sneakers paired with an army-green jacket that stopped at her waist. Which gave him a great view of her ass—another part of her he'd noticed before but not like he was noticing now.

Not helping matters was the fact that he didn't have to wonder what kind of underwear she wore beneath that tight denim. He *knew*.

No amount of trying to forget would erase the image of her wearing a black thong that perfectly split those cheeks into two bitable orbs.

"What do you think?" She spun and faced him, the wind kicking her hair forward, a few strands sticking to her lip gloss. He was walking forward when she stopped so he reached her in two steps. Before he thought it through, he swept those strands away from her sticky lip stuff, ran his fingers along her cheek and tipped her chin, his head a riot of bad ideas.

With a deep swallow, he called up ironclad Parker willpower and stopped touching his best friend. "I think you're right."

His voice was as rough as gravel.

"You're distracted. Are you thinking about work?"

"Yes," he lied through his teeth.

"You're going to have to let it go at some point. Give in to the urge." She drew out the word *urge*, perfectly pursing her lips and leaning forward with a playful twinkle in her eyes that would tempt any mortal man to sin.

And since Flynn was nothing less than mortal, he palmed the back of her head and pressed his mouth to hers.

Eight

What. Was. Happening?

A useless question since the answer was as plain as the tip of Flynn's nose on her face, because *Flynn Parker was kissing her.*

Her eyes were open in shock and she was using every one of her senses to rationalize this moment. But she couldn't. There was absolutely no way to sort out why his lips were on hers.

Time *slowed.*

She'd never imagined what his mouth would taste like, but now she knew. It was firm and sure with a hint of sweetness from the blueberry cheese they'd sampled. His kiss was delicious and confident. He held her as her knees softened and her eyelids slid shut. Sight lost, her body was a mangle of sensations as she became aware of every part of her touching every part of him.

His hand in her hair. His other hand on her hip beneath her coat, squeezing as he pulled her in tighter. The feel of his always-there scruff scraping her jaw. The low groan in his throat that reverberated in her belly and lower still...

She jerked her head back to separate their mouths, her eyes flying open. His mouth was still pursed, his lips shimmering a little from the gloss she'd transferred to them. She witnessed his every microexpression as it happened. His eyebrows ticked in the center, his mouth relaxed, and his eyes followed the hand that slid down her hair as he played with the strands between his fingers.

She opened her mouth to say something—to say anything—but no words came. Just an ineffectual breath of surprise. Unable to speak, or reason, or tame her now-overexcited female hormones, she waited for him to speak.

When he did she was more confused than ever.

"I don't want to go to the trapeze thing," he said.

"Oh-kay."

"What was between cheese and the trapeze?"

A slightly hysterical giggle burst from her. A release valve—not only was "cheese" and "trapeze" funny in the same sentence but Flynn grabbing her up and kissing the sense out of her was ridiculous.

Omigosh. I kissed Flynn Parker.

She touched her lips, reliving what seconds ago had her rising to her tiptoes—the kiss. A really great kiss.

"Shopping," she croaked when she was finally able to utter a coherent word.

"For what?"

"For...whatever." She shrugged, feeling awkward that they weren't talking about The Kiss. Feeling more awkward about standing here not bringing it up. "Um, Flynn?"

"I know." He pinched the bridge of his nose and while he collected himself she used the moment to check him out. Brown leather jacket, worn jeans, brown lace-up boots. He looked sturdy and capable and...now that she thought about it, pretty damn kissable, too. It was as if every subtle nuance she'd noticed about him over the last week had come into sharp focus. Flynn was still her best friend, but he was also freaking *hot*.

"What…was that?" she ventured, feeling like she should ask and that she shouldn't at the same time.

He raised an arm and dropped it helplessly, but no explanation came.

Tentatively, she touched his chest. This time when their eyes met a sizzle electrocuted the scant bit of air separating them.

"Let me guess. You're going to suggest we don't do that again," he murmured.

She became vaguely aware of the couples walking by, but since it was Valentine's Day none of them stopped to gawk at a man and woman standing in the center of the pier kissing.

"Why? Was it bad?" Her voice was accidentally sultry and airy. She wasn't *trying* to impress or woo him. It just sort of…happened. Maybe it was nerves.

"It wasn't bad for me." A muscle in his jaw twitched as he watched her mouth. Those blue eyes froze her in place when he demanded, "Why'd you ask? Was it bad for you?"

"It was different." That wasn't the best word for it, but it was the safest. "Not bad."

"Not bad. Okay." He raised his eyebrows and with them his voice. "Where do you want to shop?"

"We're just going to…"

"Shop. And since we're skipping the trapeze show, do something else."

"Like what?"

Like more kissing? a wanton part of her shouted with an exuberant round of applause.

"Whatever."

"Well, the show included dinner. I'm not sure where

we'll find reservations this late." She gave him a light shove when he didn't respond. "I've been wanting to see it."

"I've been wanting to check my work email. We can't always have what we want."

"You can't kiss me and then tell me I can't have nice things!" she said, unable to bank her smile.

His mouth spread into a slow grin. One filled with promise and wicked intentions, and one grin in particular she'd never, *ever* had aimed in her direction.

He was so attractive her brain skipped like a vinyl record.

"Fine. You win. You can have your show." He put his hand on her back and they walked to the nearest store side by side. His hand naturally fell away and she was left wondering if she could barter—no trapeze show in exchange for more kisses.

That'd be wrong, she quickly amended.

Right? she asked internally, but at the moment the rest of her had nothing to say.

"Sabrina *Douglas*?" Gage asked after Flynn told him what had happened last weekend.

"Do you know any other Sabrinas?" Flynn raised his beer glass and swallowed down some of the brew. Gage and Reid had wanted to go out, so here they were. *Out*. Chaz's, on the edge of downtown where they'd come on a zillion occasions, including when Flynn ditched his father's funeral. He shoved the memory aside. He had enough on his mind. Like making out with his best friend, who'd determined the kiss wasn't bad.

"*Our* Sabrina?" Reid asked, but he looked far less alarmed than Gage.

"Yes." Flynn set his glass down and stared into it.

The memory of pulling her to him and lighting her up with a kiss hadn't faded over the week. It was as crystal clear as if it'd happened seven seconds ago instead of seven days. He could still feel her mouth on his, her hip under his palm, the soft sigh of her breath tickling his lips. Her wide-eyed, startled expression was etched into his mind like the Ten Commandments into a stone tablet.

"Then what happened?" That was Gage, still sorting it out.

"Then we went shopping and watched a trapeze act. Then I dropped her off at home."

"And then you shagged," Reid filled in matter-of-factly.

"No. I dropped her off at home."

"And you made out in the doorway, tearing at each other's clothes regardless of passersby," Reid tried again.

"The kiss was a mistake," Flynn said patiently. "I knew it. She knew it. She stepped out of my car and walked to her building—"

"And then turned and begged you for one final kiss goodbye before she went up?" Reid appeared genuinely perplexed.

"Dude." Gage recoiled. "This isn't a choose-your-own adventure."

"It makes no sense, is all." Reid was still frowning in contemplation.

"Again, nothing happened," Flynn told them.

"You're truly incapable of enjoying yourself, do you realize that?" Reid leaned to one side to mutter to Gage, "It's worse than we thought."

"It sounds pretty bad already." Gage looked at Flynn. "What do you do now?"

"I haven't seen her since Valentine's Day, but we've been texting."

"You mean sexting," Reid corrected.

"What is the matter with you?" Flynn grumbled.

"You want the list in alphabetical order or in order of importance?" Gage chuckled.

Reid let the comment slide. "If you're not going to shag, then you need to fix it. Before something awful happens like she quits and we have to replace her. Sabrina isn't only your friend, you know. We all need her."

"She's not quitting. We're fine. It happened. I just didn't want there to be any awkwardness when we're inevitably in the office together again. So now you know. Don't make a big deal about it."

Reid snorted.

"I'm serious."

"You're the one who brought it up." Reid smiled at a passing waitress and she almost tripped over her own feet. He turned back to Flynn. "You tried to log in to your work email."

"How do you know that?" So, yeah, he'd attempted to check his work email three times. On the third try he was locked out for having the wrong password. A lightbulb glowed to life over his head. "You changed my password."

"You don't let me run your IT department for nothing." Good-looking and ridiculously smart shouldn't have been a combo that God allowed.

"I didn't agree to be shut out entirely."

"That was implied," Gage chimed in, the traitor.

"You're in sales. What do you know?"

"Sales brings in the money. I'm a direct link to Monarch's success. Don't be angry with me because you don't know how to relax."

"Refills?" the waitress who'd nearly stumbled stopped to ask, her eyes on Reid.

"Please, love," he responded, all British charm.

"And a round of tequila," Gage told her. She tore her eyes off Reid but her gaze lingered on Gage long enough that Flynn assessed a passing admiration. Then she turned to ask Flynn if he also needed a refill.

"I'm good," Flynn told her. "Word of advice, stay away

from him." He pointed to Reid, who promptly lost his smile, and then gestured to Gage. "And him."

Propping a hand on her hip, she faced Flynn, pushing out her chest. Her breasts threatened to overflow from her tight, V-neck shirt. Her blond hair was pinned into a sloppy bun, her figure curvy and attractive.

"So your friends would recommend I go out with you?"

"Incorrect, love," Reid piped up. "My pal Flynn is not the one for you."

"No? Why not?" she asked, flirting.

"He's far too serious for a girl like you. You look like someone who knows how to have fun."

"I do." She tipped her head toward Reid, mischief in her dark brown eyes.

"As do I."

"Hmm. I don't know." She turned back to Flynn. "I like serious sometimes. I'm Reba." She offered a hand and Flynn shook it. "Would you like to have a drink with me tonight, Serious Flynn? I'm off at eleven and I don't work until noon tomorrow. That gives me a space of thirteen open hours if you'd like to fill them."

She swiped her tongue along her lips and it took a count of ten while staring up at her, her hand in his grip, for Flynn to realize what Reba was offering. To sleep with him tonight after her shift and then to sleep in with him tomorrow.

"Sorry. I have plans." He dropped her hand and her smile fell. With a slightly embarrassed expression, she promised to return with their beers. Gage and Reid glared at him like they'd been personally offended.

"What gives?" Reid shook his head in disbelief. "She tied a bow on that offer."

"Nothing *gives*. I'm not interested."

"In her," Gage supplied.

"In anyone," Flynn growled.

"Except for Sabrina." Now Gage was smiling. He and

Reid exchanged glances and, as if the universe intuited that he needed another challenge, Flynn's cell phone picked that instant to buzz in his pocket. He studied the screen and the words on it before standing from his chair. "Thanks for the beer."

"What about your shot?" Reid asked.

"Give it to Reba."

"Who was the text from?" Gage asked, but he knew. And Reid had figured it out, too, if his shit-eating grin was anything to go by.

"It's Sabrina," Reid guessed. Correctly.

"Change my password back," Flynn told him.

"Not for another month."

"I mean it."

"What are you going to do, fire me?" he called after him.

"Tell Sabrina we said hi!" That was Gage.

Assholes.

Nine

Luke was out of town and her landlord was ignoring her calls. Sabrina had spent the last two days without clean water, even though various other units on her floor had plenty. She knew—she'd knocked on doors and asked. She'd been brushing her teeth and washing her face and other body parts at the sink using jugs of distilled water and washcloths, but this was getting ridiculous.

Desperate, she'd texted Flynn a mile-long message detailing how she really wanted to take a shower and cook something and how Luke was gone and her landlord was a neglectful jerk, and could she please, *please* come over for an hour. Just long enough to return to feeling human again.

Then she stared at the screen waiting for his response. According to the time on her phone she'd sent the text eight minutes ago.

Things had been fairly normal between them since Valentine's Day, she supposed. She'd checked in on him to make sure he wasn't working every day and then went about enjoying her vacation…sort of.

A stack of canvases leaned against an easel and her paints were lined up on the kitchen table like colorful little soldiers. But the canvases were as dry as her shower floor. Inspiration hadn't arrived with the downtime like it was supposed to, so instead of creating art, she'd been reading novels and cleaning her apartment. The place was sparkling, not a speck of dust to be found anywhere, and her to-be-read pile was in a reusable tote to be returned to Mrs. Abernathy across the hall. That woman loved her romance novels and had lent Sabrina a stack of them a while back. Until now, she hadn't taken time to read them.

She also learned that reading romance novels after a confusing kiss from her best friend meant her mind would slot *him* into the hero role in every book. So far Flynn had starred as the rakish Scot who fell for a married, time-traveling lass, a widower artist pining for his deceased wife's best friend and a ridiculously cocky NFL player who won over a type-A journalist.

No matter how the author portrayed the hero, dark hair, red hair, brown eyes or green, Sabrina gave every hero Flynn's full, firm lips and warm, broad hands. Each of them had his expressive blue eyes and permanent scruff and angled jaw. And when she arrived at the sex scenes— *hoo boy!* She knew what Flynn looked like with his shirt off, and wearing nothing but board shorts, but she'd never seen him *naked*.

Mercy, the authors were descriptive about *that part* of the hero. She'd allowed herself the luxury of attaching that talented member to the Flynn in her head. As a result, she'd had a week's worth of reading that had proved to be more sexually frustrating than relaxing. She needed to have sex with someone other than herself and soon. She didn't know what the equivalent of female blue balls was, but she had them.

Was it any wonder she'd reached out to Flynn after all she'd done was imagine him in every scenario?

It might be wrong, but it felt right.

Just like texting him had been right but felt *wrong*. She wished there was a way to retract the text, but there it sat. Unanswered. Maybe she could borrow Mrs. Abernathy's shower instead. That might be safer.

At the fifteen-minute mark without a response, she decided to let him off the hook. She was keying in the words *Never mind* when her phone rang in her hand. The photo on the screen was one of Flynn sitting at his desk, *GQ* posed as he leaned back in the leather chair. It was the day he'd moved to the office upstairs after his father left Monarch and announced that he was ill.

Flynn looked unhappy even lampooning for the camera like she'd asked. She'd hoped asking him to be silly with her for a second would improve his mood, but cheering him up had been an uphill climb ever since.

"Hi," she answered, and began to pace the room.

"I'm coming over. Pack what you need for the weekend. I'm going to have a chat with your landlord, but in the meantime, you're staying with me."

"Uh…" *What?* "No, that's okay. I just need a quick shower."

"Sabrina, I'm already pissed this has been going on so long and you haven't told me."

"I didn't want to bother you." Plus, she didn't know how to behave after he'd kissed her and then acted like he hadn't for the last week.

"See you in a few minutes." He disconnected and she quirked her mouth indecisively before turning for her dresser and pulling open the top drawer.

"No big deal," she reassured herself as she riffled through her undergarments, but when her fingertips encountered clingy satin and soft lace thongs, she bit down on her bottom lip. A surge of warmth slid through her like honey as a mashup of love scenes from the novels she'd read this week flickered in the forefront of her mind like a dirty movie. One that starred Flynn. She held up the silky red underwear.

Definitely this was a bad idea.

She dug deeper in the drawer and pulled out her sensible cotton bikini briefs. They came in a package of four: two navy blue, one red and one white. There. Harmless. She threw them on the bed and then bypassed the sexy bra, choosing the nude one instead. It was designed to be worn under T-shirts and not reveal her nipples, and if that wasn't the perfect choice for a platonic night or two spent at Flynn's she didn't know what was.

From there she chucked a few pairs of jeans, a dress and T-shirts as well as a nice blouse onto the bed. Shoes were last. Since she was wearing her trusty Converses, a pair of flats would do nicely with the dress or jeans. Plus, she wasn't going to be at Flynn's for long. A night or two, tops. She was sure her landlord would have the plumbing issue fixed soon, she thought with a spear of doubt.

She could admit that it wasn't the worst idea for her and Flynn to be around each other in person. They could tackle the issue of The Kiss head-on. It was totally possible he'd been caught up in the spirit of Valentine's Day at the Market. Maybe she had, as well. Maybe they'd both been swamped by a rogue wave of pheromones from the other happy couples walking the pier that day. That could've been what made him—

"Kiss me until I couldn't remember my own name." She shook her head and sighed. She sounded like one of Mrs. Abernathy's romance novels.

A sharp rap at her front door startled her and she let out a pathetic yelp.

Shaking off her tender nerves, she drew a breath before

facing Flynn for the first time since last Monday. He stood in her doorway, sexy as hell, and her gaze took it upon itself to hungrily rove over his jeans and sweater.

He looked like the same old Flynn, but different.

Because you know what he tastes like.

His blue eyes flashed with either an answering aware-ness or leftover angst about her plumbing situation. She couldn't tell which. She noticed he took a brief inventory of her jeans and long-sleeved shirt before ending at her sock-covered feet. From there he snapped his gaze to the bed covered in her clothes.

"I didn't know what to pack…" She didn't bother finishing that sentence, gesturing for him to come in while she dug a suitcase from the back of her closet. She started piling clothes into it while Flynn wandered around her studio, taking in the blank canvases on the floor.

"Not inspired?" His deep voice tickled down her spine like it had over the phone. Flynn had a deep baritone that was gruff and gentle at the same time.

Just like his mouth.

She was inspired all right, but not to paint.

"This is a bad idea," she blurted out, halfway into her packing. "You don't want me living with you even on the temporary. I'm messy and chatty and wake up in the middle of the night to eat ice cream."

"I have ice cream. I also have just shy of five thousand square feet going to waste. And plenty of clean water."

"But—"

"I didn't ask. Pack." He surveyed her art supplies. "You can bring this stuff, too. I think the easel will fit in the backseat."

"Don't be silly! It's only for a few days."

"Sab, you live in a building that was erected sometime around the fall of Rome. The plumbing issue could be bigger and deeper than you think."

The words *erected* and *bigger* and *deeper* paraded through her head like characters in a pornographic movie. He didn't mean any of them the way she was envisioning them, but she still had trouble meeting his stern gaze.

"Pack extra clothes in case. If you need more, you can pick them up later."

"Moving me in wasn't what you had in mind when you took a hiatus, I bet." She shoved more clothes into the suitcase.

"I didn't have a hiatus in mind. You're the one who made me do it." He bent and lifted the canvases.

"I haven't been able to paint, so don't bother with those."

"I haven't been able to relax, and watching you paint is relaxing. Will you at least try for the sake of my sanity?" His mouth quirked and again she had the irrational notion that she'd like to kiss that quirk right off his face.

"I'll try," she said, simultaneously talking about painting and not attacking him like a feral female predator.

"I'll run these to the car. Oh, and Sab?"

"Yes?"

"Remember those cookies you used to make? The ones with the M&M's?"

"Yes…"

"If you have the stuff to make those, bring it."

She smiled, remembering making him M&M cookies years ago. He'd devour at least a half a dozen the moment they came out of the oven. "I have the stuff."

"Good." With a final nod and not another word, he made the first trip down to his car with the canvases.

Sabrina resumed her packing, reminding herself that being tempted by Flynn and giving in to temptation didn't have to coincide.

"You've got this," she said aloud, but she wasn't sure she believed it.

Ten

Flynn set Sabrina up in a spare bedroom, one furnished with a dresser, night tables and a bedside lamp. The bed in there was new, like every bed in the penthouse. He'd be damned if he would sleep one more night in a bed he used to share with his cheating ex-wife.

After Veronica had confessed she'd been "seeing" Julian, which was a nice way to say "screwing" him, she'd stayed in the three-story behemoth that she and Flynn had bought together. Fine by him, since he'd never wanted to live there in the first place. At the time, he'd rented a small apartment downtown.

He felt as if he didn't belong anywhere. Not in his marital house overlooking a pond, not in this glass-and-steel shrine that reminded him of his father's cold presence, and though he'd loved his mother and the estate reminded him of her, he didn't feel as if he belonged there either. Just as well since the rose gardens had fallen to ruin when she died. How fitting that the place had been left to Julian.

It didn't surprise Flynn that Veronica had moved in immediately. She'd always crowed about how she wanted more space inside and out, and the estate, with its orchards and acreage and maid's quarters, would definitely tick both boxes.

And now he was moving Sabrina into his place without thinking about it for longer than thirty seconds.

Reason being he shouldn't *have to* think about it for longer than thirty seconds. She was his best friend and had been for years, and she needed a place to stay. The fact that he'd kissed her last week shouldn't matter.

It shouldn't, but it did.

He was determined to push past the bizarre urge to kiss her again, confident that once she was in his space, painting or baking M&M cookies, they'd snap back to the old *them*—the *them* that didn't look at each other like they wondered what the other looked like naked.

He pictured her naked and groaned. It was a stretch, but he clung to the idea that he could unring that bell. It wasn't looking good since the buzz reverberated off his balls every time he thought about her.

He dragged in the easel, Sabrina's suitcase and the last of the canvases tucked under one arm. She was unpacking the makings of cookies onto his countertop and clucked her tongue to reprimand him.

"I told you I'd help." She moved to take the canvases and he let her, then he leaned the easel against the wall.

"This is the last of it. Besides, you've helped plenty."

In the bedroom he rested her suitcase against two smaller totes. The suitcase was bright pink, one tote neon green, the other white with bright flowers, adding energy to the apartment's palette of neutrals. If Sabrina being here infused him with a similar energy, he wouldn't complain. He'd been living in black and white for far too long.

Until Valentine's Day, when she'd taken him to breakfast, on a cheese tour, and made him sit through a trapeze act he'd found fascinating rather than emasculating, he hadn't noticed just how long it'd been since he felt… well, *alive*.

His life had been a blur of Mondays, and he'd been working every day until he dropped. He'd been under the mistaken notion that if he kept moving forward he'd never have to think about Veronica or Julian or Emmons ever again.

"Bastards."

"Yikes. Are you talking to the luggage?" Sabrina asked from the doorway.

She'd tied on her Converses and slipped a denim jacket over her T-shirt. Her hair was pulled off her face partway, the length of the back draping over her shoulders. She was gorgeous. So stupidly, insanely gorgeous he wondered how he'd kept his hands off her for this long.

"I'm here if you need to talk." Her dark eyes studied him carefully.

"I don't need to talk." What he wanted was to not talk, preferably while her mouth occupied his.

"Okay." She patted him on the arm.

It was the first time she'd touched him since Monday and he wanted it to feel as pedestrian as any pat from any hand belonging to any random person. A certain member of his anatomy below his belt buckle had other ideas, kicking into third gear like it was trying to break free of his zipper to get to her.

"Are you too tired to bake cookies?" he asked, desperate for a subject change.

"Are you too tired to help?" She hoisted an eyebrow.

"Can I drink a beer while helping?"

"Hmm." She tapped her finger on lips he wanted on his more than a damn cookie. "I'll allow it."

With a wink that had him swallowing another groan, she led the way to the kitchen.

* * *

Sabrina dusted her hands on her jeans and set the last tray of M&M cookies on top of the stove. Flynn came jogging into the kitchen from the adjacent TV room to snag one.

"Those are piping—"

"Hot!" He blew out a steaming breath, a bite of cookie hovering on his tongue, and then needlessly repeated, "Hot."

"Yeah, I know."

He took another bite, his eyes closing as he chewed. He moaned almost sensually. She tried not to notice as she slid the spatula beneath each cookie and transferred them to the cooling rack—also brought from her apartment.

She hadn't baked him cookies for years and yet nothing about the scenario had changed.

She'd pull them out of the oven and he'd run in, eating one while simultaneously complaining they were "hot." Then he'd blow on the remaining half of the cookie in his hand before dropping it into his mouth with a moan of pleasure.

"Amazing." Over her shoulder, he reached for another. "So good."

The words were muttered into her ear and answering shivers tracked down her spine. Nothing had changed, and yet *everything* had changed.

She turned to warn him that the cookies were still as hot as before, and came nearly nose to nose with him.

It was like they were magnetized.

Cookie in hand, he didn't move when her breast brushed his shirt. She didn't back away and neither did he.

Someone should…

"Want a bite?" His nostrils flared as he took a slow perusal of her face.

"No thanks," she said quickly. "They're too…hot." That last word came out on a strangled whisper.

He backed up a step, broke the cookie in two and carefully blew on the halves. She watched his mouth, mesmerized by the sudden hold he had over her. The powerful, almost animal reaction she had to him. She wondered if it'd always been inevitable, but ignored. And if it had always been there, how had she ignored something so *explosive*? It was the difference between a warm burner on a stove versus a roaring bonfire throwing sparks into the air.

In this case, Flynn was the fire, and she was the wood, unable to keep from catching aflame whenever he touched her.

He offered half a cookie and she took it, brushing her fingers against his. They ate their halves, he in one big bite and she in three little ones. She jerked her gaze to the stove and back to him again.

"We should talk," he said.

"I agree."

"You first."

"Chicken."

"I'm not scared. I'm smart. Go."

She would've laughed if she didn't want him so damn much.

"When you kissed me on Valentine's Day, you opened Pandora's box. When I'm around you, it's all I think about."

Well, not *all*. She'd thought about a hell of a lot more than kissing him, but she wasn't going to reveal *that*.

"Agreed," he said. "And you have a suggestion?"

"I do."

"You're not going back to your apartment. That's final. Not until you have running water that's not the color of rust-stained pipes."

"I wasn't going to suggest that."

His head jerked as he studied her curiously.

She licked her lips, willing herself to say what she was thinking. There was a very big chance Flynn would refuse her, which would be bad for both her ego and their friendship.

If he agreed it could *also* be bad for their friendship.

Which was why she started with, "Promise me we'll always be friends because we've always been friends. It's not worth throwing away because of a weird wrinkle in the universe where we explored a possibly brief attraction for each other."

"Never," he agreed without hesitation. "I'd never let you go, Sab. You know that." His eyebrows were a pair of angry slashes.

"I know. I wanted to say it before I made a suggestion."

"Which is?"

"I think you should kiss me again."

He didn't react like she thought. He didn't recoil, nor did he lean forward. He stood motionless, watching her as carefully as a hunter approaching a skittish deer.

"I'm pretty sure that moment on the pier was a fluke," she continued. "And since we never *really* talked about it, and I was caught off guard, I thought if we tried it again we could finally put it behind us. Especially if this time there aren't any sparks."

"You felt sparks?" His question was an interested murmur as he closed the gap between them.

Yes.

"I...it's an expression." She pressed her lips together.

"And you think we should try again to make sure there are no...sparks." Seeming more comfortable with the idea than she was, he lifted a hand and slid his fingers into her hair. When those fingertips touched the back of her scalp, a shot of desire blasted through her limbs.

She swallowed thickly. "Then we can go back to...to... the way things were before."

"Friends without kissing."

"Friends without kissing."

His other hand moved to her hip, and his fingers were in her hair. She'd seen Flynn kiss other women before, but she'd never paid close attention. Now she couldn't *not* pay attention.

It was as if the world had tipped violently on its axis, putting her squarely in his personal space and sharpening her awareness to a fine point.

She heard his breathing speed up, felt his heart thudding under her hand when she placed her palm on his chest. His eyelids drew down as he tilted her head gently and moved his mouth closer to hers.

Instinctively, she did the same.

When their mouths met, it wasn't surprising or awkward. The kiss was tender and curious as he stroked her jaw with his thumb and moved his mouth over hers. He opened, encouraging her to do the same. She complied, accepting his tongue on hers.

And, *Oh, yes, please, God, don't stop.*

It was like someone plugged her into a power source. Her body vibrated with need as her mouth moved eagerly over his. She couldn't get enough of the new, unfamiliar taste. Their tongues kept rhythm without their trying. Stroke, in. Stroke, out. It was mind-numbingly *incredible*.

He moved his hand from her hip to her back and tightened his hold. Her thundering heartbeat echoed between her legs as blood thrummed in her ears.

Then he pulled away, his chest moving up and down beneath her fingers, his eyes a murky, dark ocean blue. His hips tilted forward of their own volition and that's when she felt it. The very determined ridge of his erection pressing into her belly.

Her mouth opened and closed once, then twice, but no

sounds emerged. He'd yet to let go of her and she'd yet to untangle herself from his hold.

There weren't sparks this time around, that was an honest-to-goodness forest fire. An atom bomb. The burning surface of a thousand suns.

She blinked, wanting to *I Dream of Jeannie* herself back into last week before her entire life turned into a friends-to-lovers romance, but her surroundings didn't so much as wiggle.

Which meant this was real.

She was attracted to Flynn. *For real.*

And given his physical reaction and the way he was leaning in for another taste of her lips, it seemed Flynn was just as attracted to her.

Eleven

A breath away from laying his lips on Sabrina's for another taste, the knob turned back and forth on the front door like someone was attempting to barge in.

"I know you're in there!" came a voice from the other side.

"Reid," Sabrina breathed against Flynn's lips.

"I don't hear anything," he murmured, regretting giving Reid the passcode to his penthouse floor.

She flashed him a brief smile, but he detected worry in her eyes. "I should…"

She backed away like he'd caught fire, and damn if he didn't feel like he had. That experimental revisit to the Valentine's Day kiss had proved her theory 100 percent wrong.

They were attracted to each other. Either by proximity or convenience, or Sab's pointing out that they were single for the first time at the same time. Didn't matter why.

Now that he'd had a taste, he wanted more.

"You got a girl in there or something?" Gage shouted through the door as the knob jiggled again.

Sabrina's wide-eyed panic would've been cute if Flynn wasn't so turned on his brain was barely functioning.

"I was out with them tonight. Apparently they didn't like that I left them unsupervised." Thumbing her bottom lip, he sent a final longing look at her mouth before letting her dash out of the kitchen. She checked her hair and face in the mirror in the living room and he had to smile when she wrinkled her nose, worried.

"I look like I've been making out," she whispered.

"Hell yeah, you do." He couldn't hide his pride any more than she could hide those warm, rosy cheeks or the flush on her neck. "Gimme a second. I'll kill them, we'll hide the bodies and then we'll return to what we were doing."

With a wink to Sabrina, Flynn jerked open the door and blocked the crack with his body. "What do you want?"

Reid held up a six-pack of beer with one bottle missing as Gage held up the missing bottle. "We thought you might want company."

"And we want to know what happened with Sab… rin…a…" Reid's voice trailed off as Flynn widened the gap in the doorway to reveal Sabrina standing in the center of his foyer.

"Hey, guys!" she chirped. "I made cookies. Just like the old days!"

Reid swore and Gage ducked his head to hide a laugh.

"Come in. It's just cookies." *And kissing.* But they'd officially shut down that last part.

"Hello, Sabrina," Reid said like he was addressing his arch nemesis. "Beer?"

"No thanks. I'm going to bed. I'm exhausted."

Reid grinned and Sabrina backtracked, making herself appear guiltier in the process.

"I'm staying here. Temporarily. I'm staying in the guest room. My pipes are leaking and I don't have clean water. Plus, I need a shower, so I'll do that. In the guest bathroom, obviously." An uncomfortable giggle. "Not anywhere near Flynn's bedroom. I mean, not that it would matter."

Flynn shook his head and she gave him an apologetic shrug. He was going to catch hell from his best friends the second she fled the room, which she did three seconds after ensuring the oven was off.

Once she was ensconced in her bedroom and the shower cranked on in the attached bath, Flynn grabbed one of Reid's beers and headed for the living room.

"Well, well…" Gage, who'd helped himself to a cookie, swaggered in with Reid on his heels. "Sabrina has leaky pipes and your suggestion was for her to move in with you?"

"What would you have done?" Flynn asked, tipping the bottle.

"Called a plumber?" Reid suggested before having a seat on the sofa.

"I'm going to do that tomorrow. As well as rip her landlord a new one for neglecting her needs."

"Seems like you're in charge of *her needs* now." Reid's eyebrows jumped.

"In the meantime," Flynn continued, ignoring Reid's accusation, "she needed a place to stay. I'd have offered you both the same if the situation were reversed."

"Except you didn't kiss us at the Market on Valentine's Day," Gage supplied.

"And I wouldn't have made you cookies." Reid took in the canvases stacked by the window. "She appears to be staying awhile."

"As long as she needs."

Flynn didn't owe either of them explanations. But a few in his and Sabrina's defense filled his throat. She was also his best friend, she needed him and he wanted her here. Since those sounded like excuses, he said nothing.

"We didn't come over here to bust your balls about Sabrina, believe it or not," Gage said.

"Why are you here?" Flynn asked.

"We have a work conundrum," Reid answered.

"You changed my email password to keep me away from work." Flynn narrowed his eyelids in suspicion. "And now you *want me* to work?"

Did they have any idea how epically off their timing was?

"Right." Reid pursed his lips for a full three seconds before admitting, "We have…an issue. A minor issue, but one that could use your…expertise."

They had Flynn's attention. He tracked to the chair in the living room and sat, elbows on his knees. He leaned in with interest. "Tell me."

She'd heard Reid and Gage leave sometime around 1:00 a.m. She'd fallen into bed right out of the shower, and was asleep seconds after her head hit the pillow. Which explained the crinkled hairdo she was currently trying to tame with a brush and smoothing spray in her private bathroom. Long plagued by insomnia, she'd hoped she was through that phase of her life but it'd started up again around the same time as Flynn and Veronica split.

Which she'd thought was a coincidence until recently.

She'd tossed and turned and watched out the window at the city lights and the insistent moon that wasn't looking to give up its coveted spot in the sky to the sun anytime soon. Finally, she'd given up and climbed out of bed—still in her long-sleeved shirt from earlier, and panties and socks. She'd forgotten to pack pajamas, a situation she would rectify in the morning.

Cracking her bedroom door the slightest bit, she peeked down the silent hallway in one direction and toward the staircase in the other before deciding to risk running downstairs in her underwear for the midnight snack she'd been craving since her eyes popped open.

The moment her toes touched the wood floors of the hallway, the door at the end swung aside and Flynn ambled out shirtless. He was rubbing his eyes and looking as groggy and sleep-deprived as she felt, but by her estimation he looked much better in that state.

Her eyes feasted on the strong column of his neck, the wide set of his chest and trim stomach tapering to a pair of distracting Vs delineating either side of his hips. His boxer briefs were black, snugly fitting thick thighs that led down to sturdy male bare feet. By the time her inventory was complete, he noticed her standing there and paused about a yard away.

"I couldn't sleep," she said.

He scanned her body much in the way she'd done his, pausing at her panties—utilitarian, but he didn't seem to have the slightest aversion to her red cotton bikini briefs.

"I had to sleep in the shirt I wore," she blurted out. "I forgot my pajamas. I'll pick up some tomorrow."

As she bumbled out those three clumsy sentences, he advanced, backing her to the threshold of her guest bedroom. He touched her arm, a soothing stroke while he watched her. "You can borrow one of my T-shirts."

Her throat made a clicking sound as she swallowed past a very dry tongue.

He stole a glance at her mouth before backing away and scrubbing his face with one palm instead of ravishing her where she stood.

Shame.

When he opened his mouth the words "Ice cream?" fell out, sending her brain for a loop.

"Um…"

"Ice cream or I kiss you again. Those are your options."

A nervous laugh tittered out. "Do you…have tea?"

He flashed a devilish smile that made her knees go gooey. "I have tea."

He strode down the stairs and she watched him, trying to decide if it was okay to follow him in only her underwear while she enjoyed the way he looked from behind.

In the end, she opted not to overthink it. The idea of slipping into a pair of skinny jeans when she was this comfortable was as abhorrent as the idea of putting on a bra. They were adults and Flynn was far from a stranger. So, they'd kissed. So what? That didn't mean he was going to shove her gruffly against a wall and feast on her neck and her nipples, while his hand moved insistently between her legs...

"Mercy," she muttered, her hand over her throat as she came to a halt in the middle of the staircase.

"I know. The wide slats throw you off at first," he called from his position behind the counter, reading her reaction incorrectly.

Her hand tightened on the railing as she completed her descent but not because she was afraid of falling. Flynn was a distracting sight, shirtless in his kitchen. She couldn't see his boxers behind the counter, so for all her imagination knew he could be completely nude. And didn't that introduce a fine visual? Especially after she'd felt the evidence of his arousal against her this evening.

They went about dishing out ice cream and preparing tea in a silent dance, both either too weary or too wary to speak. Once she had filled her cup with hot water and he'd topped his scoops off with chocolate chips, peanut butter and sliced almonds, they went to the living room, where they both angled for the same cushion on the sofa.

"Sorry." She felt weirdly shy—something she'd never been around him.

"Ladies first. You're the guest." He pulled a blanket from the trunk that served as a coffee table. "In case you're cold," he explained. "But if you're not, don't cover up on my account."

She playfully rolled her eyes, but there was a nip in the

air of his cavernous apartment. She pulled the blanket over her lap as she sat and folded her legs beneath her.

Cupping her mug in both hands, she inhaled the spicy cinnamon scent of the tea and hummed happily. Regardless of the kiss or them being nearly naked and in close proximity to each other, she was happy here with him. Flynn had a way of making her life brighter and her day better. It was good to have him back in any capacity.

"Gage and Reid came to debrief me," he said.

"They're not allowed to do that! I told them any emergencies were to go to the management team or me."

"They wouldn't take issues to the management team instead of me if their lives depended on it. You know that."

"I know. But I wanted you to have a real break. What's it been, a week?"

"You deserve a real break, too, Sab." His lingering gaze did a better job of warming her than the blanket. "Bethany in accounting is leaving for Washington Business Loans."

"No!" She liked Bethany. "Why?"

"Reid said her fiancé works there and Bethany would like to work with him. Reid and Gage suggested offering her a pay raise and an extra week's vacation not to leave, but they wanted to clear it with me first."

"Oh. I guess that's reasonable. But then why did they come over and ask in person?"

"My guess? They wanted to have beers and dig up dirt on you and me."

The phrase "you and me" made them sound like a *them*. An idea as foreign as everything else that'd happened this week.

"I didn't help," she admitted. "I was obviously nervous. I talked too much. Ran away too quickly."

Flynn palmed her knee and the heat of his touch infused her very being. "It's not your fault, Sab. I told them about the kiss last week. They suspected more than that had happened after you dashed off to the shower. Don't worry, I told them nothing."

"Well. I guess it's silly to pretend we're doing something wrong." That sentence was one she'd been testing out in her head and now that she'd said it out loud, it was sort of silly.

"If anything, what we're doing feels scarily right." He ate a spoonful of ice cream. "I'm not sure what that means, but I'm sure we should stop overanalyzing it."

"Have you been analyzing it?"

"No. But you have. I can see it in your eyes. I'll bet there's a completed pros/cons list in that brain of yours."

"Not true!"

He cocked his head patiently. And dammit if he wasn't right.

"*Fine*. But I call it a plus/minus list, just so you know."

"What's in my plus column?" He asked that like he couldn't think of a single reason why he'd be a plus.

"You're my best friend," she answered rather than recite his yummy physical attributes. "Ironically, that's item number one in your minus column, too."

Twelve

Okay, yes. He would hand it to Sabrina that this situation was a little…odd. Not their usual mode of operation and possibly a bad idea for the reason she'd placed at the top of both lists: they were best friends.

But there was something to say for the impulsiveness of the Valentine's Day kiss on the pier. And there was even more to say about the kiss in his kitchen that was as premeditated as they came.

"You're worrying about…*this* ruining our friendship?"

A strangled sound left her throat like she couldn't believe he'd asked that question. "Aren't you?"

"I'm not worried about anything. I was told to take a hiatus for the specific reason of not worrying about anything. Isn't that right?"

Her posture relaxed some, her legs moving slightly under the blanket. Her bare legs. Her long, smooth, bare legs.

He wanted to touch her, and not in a soothing way. Not in a consoling way.

He wanted to touch her in a sexual, turn-her-on, see-what-sounds-she-makes-when-she's-coming way. If she decided she'd have him, he'd take her upstairs before she could say the words *plus* or *minus*.

"What do you suggest we do, Flynn? Sit here and make out?"

"That's a good start."

Her delicate throat moved when she swallowed, her eyes flaring with desire.

Yeah, she wanted him, too. It was time she stopped denying it. He set his ice cream bowl aside and carefully took her hot tea from her hands.

"I wasn't done with that."

"You're done with that."

When he reached for the blanket, her hand stopped him. They were frozen in that stance, his hand on her blanket-covered thigh, her hand on his hand and their eyes locked in a battle that wasn't going to end with them going to separate bedrooms if he had anything to say about it.

"Do you want this?" He watched her weigh the options, jerking her gaze away from his and opening her mouth ineffectually before closing it again. "It's a simple question, Sabrina. Do you want this?"

"Yes—"

He didn't let her finish that sentence—finishing it for her by sealing his lips on hers in a deep, driving kiss as he tore the blanket from her lap. She caught his face with her palms, but leaned into him, opening her soft mouth and giving him a taste of what he hadn't gotten enough of earlier this evening.

He ran his hand over her knee to her outer thigh and then to her panties. They weren't the thong he'd expected, but he couldn't care less. She wasn't going to be wearing them long.

After gliding her fingertips over his jaw and his neck, she rerouted and grazed the light patch of chest hair over one nipple. He groaned into her mouth. She responded with a kittenish mewl before digging her blunt fingernails into his rib cage in an effort to draw him closer.

It was the encouragement he needed.

Shifting his weight so he wasn't crushing her, he flattened a palm on her back and pulled her to him. She came willingly, both hands on his abs as he switched their positions and reclined on his back.

With her on top, he held her thick hair away from her face and continued kissing her, the position reminding him of the erotic dream he'd had not so long ago. The strands of her hair tickled his cheeks and her breath came in fast little pants when he gave her a chance to catch it.

It felt good to feel good. It had been a long time for him. And according to her, a *really* long time since Sabrina had felt this good. He couldn't think of a single reason not to make love to her right here on this couch.

He wanted to bury the past year in the soft lemon scent of her skin and give in to the attraction that had rattled them both for the last week-plus. Maybe longer, if he was honest.

She sat up abruptly like she might shove him away, but instead she crisscrossed her arms, grabbed the hem of her shirt and whipped it over her head. Flynn had thought her legs were amazing. Sabrina's legs had nothing on her breasts. Her small shoulders lifted and he zeroed in on her nipples—dark peach and too tempting to resist. He stole a quick glance at her and grinned, and when she grinned back it was as good as permission.

Propped on his elbows, he wrapped one hand around her rib cage and took one beautiful breast deep into his mouth. He let go, teasing and tickling her nipple with his tongue. Her cute kittenish mewls from earlier were long gone. He was rewarded with the sultry moans of a woman at the pinnacle of pleasure. He couldn't allow her to reach the pinnacle yet. There was more to do.

Turning her so her back was to the couch, he gave himself more room to maneuver. He slipped his fingers past the edge of her red panties to stroke her folds. She was wet and she was warm and she was also willing to reciprocate.

While he worked over her other breast, his fingers moving at a hastened speed, she cupped his shaft and gave him a stroke. And another, and then one more, until he had to pull his lips from her body to let out a guttural groan.

"Flynn," came her desperate plea. "I need you."

"I need you, too." So bad he could hardly think. Ending the torture of foreplay, he swept her panties down her legs and paused long enough to strip off his briefs. Only then did he hesitate. There was a small matter of birth control to consider before they continued. "Condom. I have one upstairs."

She nodded hastily. "I'll come with you."

"Yeah," he said with a lopsided smile because damn, he was at ease right now. "That'd be best."

He snatched her hand and helped her up, leaving their dishes and scattered clothing where they lay. They darted up the stairs naked, but not before he gave her a playful swat and sent her ahead of him. He had to get a better look at that ass, and since she'd robbed him of the pleasure of a thong, he hadn't had the chance to admire it yet.

Sabrina naked was a beautiful sight.

Her bottom was heart-shaped, leading to a slim waist, strong back and small shoulders. Each and every inch of her was deliciously toned yet soft and touchable. And touching her was exactly what he intended to do.

At the back of the hallway, she entered his bedroom and turned around. His breath snagged. Not only were her dusky nipples perched on the tips of her breasts like gumdrops, but between her legs she was gloriously bare. He'd noticed when he touched her with his fingers, but seeing it nearly brought him to his knees.

She bit her bottom lip, white teeth scraping plump pink flesh and setting him off like a match to a fuse.

When he caught up to her, he wrapped her in his arms and cupped her bare butt with both hands, giving her cheeks a squeeze. They tumbled backward onto his king-size bed framed by a leather headboard.

She looked good on his deep charcoal-gray duvet and crisp white sheets beneath. The contrast of her dark hair spread over the white pillowcase made him glad he didn't have a drop of color in this room. Sabrina added her own. From her pink cheeks to her bright blue toenail polish.

He found a condom in the nightstand drawer and rolled it on, his hands shaking with anticipation. She must have noticed, because next she caught his wrist and smiled. Then she nodded, anxious to get to the next part—almost as anxious as he.

Positioned over her, he thrust his hips and entered her in one long, smooth stroke. She pressed her head into the pillow, lifting her chin and saying a word that would forever echo in the caverns of his mind.

"Yes."

It was damn nice to hear.

She felt like heaven. Holding him from within as reverently as she held him with her arms now. His throat tightened as he shoved away every thought aside of the woman beneath him. Which wasn't hard to do, since the physical act of making love to Sabrina Douglas was a singular experience.

If there was room for any other thoughts, he couldn't find it.

He rocked into her gently as they found their rhythm in the dark. Save the slice of moonlight painting a stripe on the bedding, the room was marked with shadows. He had no trouble making out the slope of her breasts or the luscious curve of her hips.

And when he had to close his eyes—when the gravity of what was happening between them was too much to bear—he still saw her naked form on the screen of his eyelids.

The vision stayed until he gave in to his powerful release, caught his breath and was finally able to open his eyes.

Thirteen

Light filtered in through slits in her eyelids, but that wasn't what woke Sabrina the next morning. It was the tickling sensation against her forearm that beckoned her toward the sun. When that tickling climbed higher up her arm, she shivered and popped her eyes open.

Goose bumps decorated her arm and the tickling sensation was courtesy of the tip of a dry paintbrush. Flynn dragged the brush over her collarbone and down over the top of her breasts. She was only slightly alarmed to find she was still naked.

The man currently painting her with shudders had made her shudder *plenty* last night before they fell asleep side by side in his very big bed. It'd been a long time since she'd had sex. The physical act of making love was amazing. Almost as amazing as the man she'd made love with.

Flynn's stubble shifted as his smile took over his face. He was a glorious sight. His messy hair was bathed in Seattle's morning sun. His blue eyes dipped to follow the path of the paintbrush down and over the crest of her breast.

She smiled, drugged by this stunning new facet of their relationship.

"You're dressed," she croaked, her morning voice in full effect. "No fair."

"I picked up coffee and croissants. Thought I'd wake you before you slept the day away. And before your coffee went cold."

"What time is it?"

"Little after eleven."

"Eleven!" She bolted upright in bed and looked around for a clock. Not finding one, she pressed a button on her phone. 11:14 a.m. "Wow. I never sleep this late."

His grin endured and she narrowed one eye.

"Don't be cocky."

"Hard not to be." He stood and slid the paintbrush into his back pocket. "Come on. Breakfast awaits."

She didn't know where he bought the croissants, but they were the best she'd ever tasted. Especially with strawberry jam and a healthy dollop of butter. The coffee was perfection, and she had the passing thought that this would be a splendid way to spend every morning.

"You seem to have settled into your hiatus okay," she teased.

"You had a lot to do with that." He slathered a croissant with jam and took a huge bite. After he swallowed, he added, "I thought you being here would help me relax, but I didn't expect you to help me relax that much."

An effervescent giggle tickled her throat. The low hum of a warning sounded in the back of her mind but she ignored it. She didn't want to consider what could've changed—what definitely *had* changed—since last night. "I think it's safe to say that neither of us expected that."

"Or expected it to be that great." His eyebrows jumped as he took another bite.

"It *was* great." Her eyebrows closed in as she turned

over that unexpected thought. "This is oddly comfortable. I guess it shouldn't be odd. It's not like we don't know each other. It's just that now we know each other…biblically."

That earned her a rough chuckle, a sound she loved to hear from her best friend no matter the situation. Only now that chuckle sent chills up and down her arms much like the paintbrush this morning. Sex had added a layer to their friendship that she wasn't done exploring.

"I talked to your landlord."

"And?"

"He bitched a lot about how he regretted buying the building, which he affectionately called a 'dump,' and then he mentioned that they've been looking into leaks in the apartments above you and below, but yours is the one they can't isolate."

"Lovely. I was so adamant about having that apartment in particular." She shook her head with a token amount of regret. At the time she hadn't been thinking about the lack of light coming in through the windows or the noise coming from overhead and on both sides of her since she was in the center of the C-shaped brick building. "I was too busy admiring the rough wood flooring and the open layout and the proximity to the elevator to think of much else."

"Doesn't look like you'll be going back to your own apartment anytime soon. I have plenty of space here." He watched her carefully, as if waiting for her to argue.

That alarm buzzed a little louder, warning her that things were changing—*had changed*, she mentally corrected. But how could she say no? She wanted to make Flynn happy, and herself, and sex with him had ticked both boxes with one overlapping checkmark. Her apartment had sprung a leak—so there was no sense in living like she was in a third-world country when she had Flynn's penthouse on loan. Plus, who was to say that they couldn't go back to normal after a sabbatical filled with great sex and plenty of Flynn's deep chuckles?

There. Now that she'd justified that, she felt like she could respond.

"You do have plenty of space." She shrugged. "I can't think of any reason to leave."

"Good. You should stay. We'll see if we can one-up last night." He waggled his eyebrows and a laugh burst from her lips. Who knew the secret to pulling Flynn from his shell was sex? Who knew they'd be so damn good at it?

His phone vibrated on the table next to him. He broke eye contact for a cursory glance at the screen.

"That better not be work," she warned.

"I don't work anymore."

"Very funny." She sipped her coffee. "Is there at least part of you that's enjoying the break? Besides us sharing a bedroom?" she added, figuring he would've added it for her.

"It still chaps my ass that most of Monarch's grand pooh-bahs would rather send me out the door than come into the twenty-first century with me."

"They're in love with the way things were, which is standard for most old companies. Monarch's stockholders were nervous when Emmons died and there wasn't anything you were going to be able to do to prevent that."

She'd vowed to table this conversation until after his hiatus but since he'd opened the discussion she no longer saw the point in holding her tongue.

"You are *not* your father. The changes you made when you took over were made *because* you're different from your father. I didn't like who you were changing into." She ignored his pleated brow and continued. "I wanted my Flynn back."

He watched her for a long beat. In a way Flynn was never hers, and yet he'd always belonged to her in some fashion. She didn't have the romantic part of his heart—even now.

Her smile came easily when she considered what a relief that was. Flynn's place was at her side. They could care about each other, blow each other's minds in bed and escape their entanglement unscathed. She had faith in both of them—and anyway, he'd already promised their friendship wouldn't change.

"I deserve that." His shoulders lifted and dropped in a sigh of surrender. "You've always looked out for me, Sabrina. Always."

He reached across the table and took her hand, gently holding her fingers, his eyes on his empty plate.

"I always will be." Just as she knew he'd be there for her.

Sabrina collected her pajamas and a few more changes of clothing from her apartment. Flynn had invited her to stay and she'd failed at reasoning her way out of it. Not that she should. They had always needed each other and now they needed each other in a different way, a physical way. She was more than happy to reap the rewards for the rest of their sabbatical.

"Rewards like an insanely hot, wealthy best friend who curls your toes in the evening and makes you laugh in the daytime."

Even though she was talking to herself and no one else was there, she hesitated to use the word *boyfriend* or the phrase "guy she was dating" because that wasn't who Flynn was. Not really.

"Then who is he?" she asked herself after collecting her mail. She walked to her bedroom dresser and plucked out a few shirts along with a few pairs of sexy underwear worthy of hot nights in the sack.

He was…

"Flynn."

That was enough explanation for her.

She hesitated packing pajamas before tossing a shorts

set onto the bed. The oft-ignored top shelf of her closet caught her eye, specifically the spines of her journals. It'd been a long time since she sat and sketched an idea for a painting, or wrote an entry.

A vision of her in a T-shirt, stroking the brush down the canvas, filled her with purpose, and when Flynn stepped into the picture and swept her hair aside to kiss her neck, a zing of excitement flitted through her.

She flipped through the journals in search of inspiration, finally settling on the one filled with sketches of birds. If Flynn's mantel needed anything, it was a breath of life. A bird on a perch watching over his lonely penthouse when she wasn't there sounded perfect. It made her sad to think of "the end," but before she could explore that thought further another journal toppled from the uppermost shelf and fell open.

She bent to retrieve it, smiling at her sloppy college handwriting and doodles in the margins. She'd written about places where she and Flynn—and Gage and Reid—had hung out back in their college years. Chaz's, which had been their hangout ever since, and the restaurant that served the best burger in town: Fresh Burger. Before veggie burgers were trending, they'd served up a black-bean and poblano pepper masterpiece that the guys sometimes chose over basic beef. She slapped the book shut, pleased with her finding. She had another idea for what she and Flynn could do together.

"Besides have sex," she reminded herself. Her mission during this hiatus was to guide Flynn back to his former self.

She packed the journals with the rest of her clothes into a bag and carried her things to the door. She'd just pulled out her front door key to lock up when a thick Chicago-accented voice behind her nearly scared her out of her skin.

"Your boyfriend called about the plumbing. You know

you can call me and talk to me directly. You don't have to send in the heavy." Her landlord had a thick dark mustache, a receding hairline and a particularly unpleasant demeanor.

"I *did* call you directly, Simon," she told him patiently. "You didn't return my calls. Also, Flynn is my best friend not my boyfriend."

He frowned and so did she. Clarifying that for herself was one thing, but there really wasn't any reason to do it for her landlord.

"I'm not sure when we're going to have it fixed." His dark eyes inventoried her tote bag and her person in a way that made her uncomfortable.

"Well, you have my number. And Flynn's. Flynn and I actually are dating, I don't know why I said we weren't."

Fortunately, Mrs. Abernathy picked that opportune moment to open her front door and save Sabrina from their potentially lecherous landlord.

"You and Flynn are dating! I am so excited!" Mrs. Abernathy rushed out of her apartment and into the hallway. She was wearing classy appliquéd blue jeans and a floral top. Her jewelry was gold and shiny, and her nails perfectly manicured. "Did the books help? Tell me the books helped. I believe that romance novels are magical. They bring people together."

Rightly sensing this wasn't a topic for him, Simon grumbled something about women that was likely sexist before hustling down the hall to ruin someone else's day.

"I enjoyed the books," Sabrina told Mrs. Abernathy. She didn't know if they'd helped but they definitely hadn't hurt.

"I knew you two would be good together. Every time you insisted that you and Flynn were just friends, I doubted it in my heart of hearts." She put her hand to the gold chain around her neck, and her fingers closed around the diamond dangling there. "My Reginald, when he was alive, was the most romantic man. Tell me your Flynn is romantic."

Sabrina's cheeks warmed when she thought about what they'd done together last night. Surely there was a PG-rated nugget she could share with her romance-loving neighbor.

"Well…he woke me up this morning by tickling me with a paintbrush. And he also went out and bought coffee and croissants for breakfast." She checked the hallway for Simon once more, but he'd already gone. She lowered her voice anyway when she continued. "And he called Simon and demanded he fix my plumbing issue."

"That's *very* romantic." Mrs. Abernathy's smile faded. "Except for the plumbing situation. Is that still going on?" She checked the hallway, too, before whispering, "I don't like that man."

"I don't think *anyone* likes that man." Sabrina wished her neighbor a good day before turning for the elevator.

As the doors swished shut, Mrs. Abernathy called, "Are you staying with Flynn, then?"

In the closing gap between the elevator doors, Sabrina smiled. "Yes. Yes, I am."

Fourteen

Fresh Burger's salsa fries were a thing of beauty.

Sabrina pulled out a hand-cut fry dripping in fresh pico de gallo, melty cheese and sour cream and groaned in ecstasy around a bite.

She swiped a napkin over her mouth. "If I eat another bite, I'll die."

"Back away from the fries, Douglas."

Watching her eat was fun. Watching her do *anything* was fun. Flynn's brain had been a minefield of what he'd do to her and what he'd like her to do to him the second the sun went down. For that, he needed her not to eat herself into a food coma. He swiped her plate out from in front of her and polished off her fries.

They left Fresh Burger and stepped into cold, spitting rain that was turning to snow—a typical February day in Seattle. Sabrina wrapped her arms around her middle and huddled closer. He held her against him while their steps lined up on the sidewalk. Nothing out of the usual for them, but now it felt different to have her in the cradle of his arms.

Protecting her, watching out for her—those ideas were nothing new. But wanting to please her on a carnal, sexual level? Whole new ballgame. Hell, he wasn't sure it was the same sport.

He'd had plenty of girlfriends and one wife, so he knew how relationships went. This one wasn't like those. It was a mashup of his favorite things: a best friend who was on his side plus an exciting new experience between the sheets. The difference in this relationship was that he wasn't trying to get to know Sabrina. He *knew* Sabrina.

He knew she loved peanut butter and hated olives. He knew she'd fallen off the stage in an eighth grade play and earned the nickname "Crash." He knew that as cool as she'd played it, Craig had broken her heart and she'd spent months wondering if she'd ever recover.

Since Flynn already knew those things about her, he could concentrate on learning other things. Like she had sensitive nipples, or that she slept with her mouth slightly open. That she murmured in her sleep and clung to him like a sloth on a tree limb.

"What are you smiling about? Is it funny that I'm cold?" she complained next to him.

"I'm not smiling because you're cold. Do you want to go home? Watch a movie? Paint?"

"I tried painting today. It didn't work."

"Not true. You took out the paint, but you didn't put a single line of color on that canvas. How am I supposed to replace the artwork over the mantel if you won't create one for me?"

"I'm out of practice," she said when they reached his car. He opened the door for her and she slid in. That halted the conversation until he climbed in next to her and started the engine.

Revving it a few times while he adjusted the heat, he said, "You can't put it off forever."

"Says the man who's supposed to be relaxing."

"Relaxing is boring."

"You spent most of the day on the laptop. Doing what? I know not checking your social media."

No, not that. He'd spent most of the day writing a fresh business plan. One that combined his ideas and his father's way of doing things. He wasn't sure how to blend the two approaches yet, but there had to be a way. Sad that their collaboration had to happen on the wrong side of the grave, but Flynn didn't have much choice. Sab had pointed out that he hadn't taken time off for bereavement. He supposed now was as good a time as any to mourn.

"I was writing for my mental health."

"Journaling?" Her lips pursed and her eyebrows went up.

"Kind of. And no, you can't read it."

"Understood. I have journals I wouldn't want you to read either. Even though I read you the one about Fresh Burger." She dug the journal and a pen out of her bag and drew a checkmark next to the entry. "It'd be cool to do some more of these things." She turned a page. "Do you have Jell-O?"

"Why? Are we going to fill an inflatable swimming pool with it and wrestle?" He shot her a grin.

"No! For Jell-O shots."

Ah, well. He tried.

"What about the time we repainted my dorm?" she asked as she flipped forward to another page. "Your place could use some color."

"The only painting you'll be doing is on canvas. You were the one who said you wanted to make art while you were off work."

Like he was open to halting the transformation into his old man and becoming more like his old self—he also wanted Sabrina to find her old self. She used to be confident; certain about what she wanted. Evidence of both her confidence and certainty made an appearance now and then, but not often enough. He'd hoped her going back to doing what she loved, painting, would unlock that door for her.

She was hell-bent on taking care of him, but what she didn't know was that he was returning the favor. He wasn't the only one in need of change in his life.

So was his best-friend-turned-lover.

Halfway into making their second batch of Jell-O shots, Sabrina was feeling darn pleased with herself for convincing Flynn to give it a try.

After their burger-and-coffee date, they stopped at a supermarket to procure what they needed to make strawberry and lime Jell-O shots. Flynn had a liquor cabinet that was well-stocked, though he hesitated slightly before allowing her to put the Cabo Wabo tequila into the lime Jell-O. He insisted it was better enjoyed straight. Good thing she was convincing.

Plastic containers stacked in his fridge to solidify, Flynn excused himself to the bathroom while she wiped down the countertops with damp paper towels. She lifted his phone to move it when it buzzed in her hand. A quick glance at the screen showed a message from Veronica. A second buzz followed—another message from her, as well.

Sabrina caught the words "so sorry" and "mistake" before she placed the phone facedown on the counter and stared at it like it was a live cobra.

It wasn't her fault she'd seen Veronica's name or accidentally read a word or two, but she would be culpable if she flipped the phone over to read the messages in their entirety.

And oh how she wanted to…

But.

She wouldn't.

She finished cleaning the kitchen and Flynn returned,

cracked open a beer and took a long pull. She waited for him to lift his cell phone and check the screen, but he didn't. Not even when she picked up hers.

"It's supposed to be partly sunny tomorrow." She showed him the cartoon sun and cloud on her cell phone's screen.

"Good day for you to paint," he said, taking another sip from his beer bottle.

She checked her personal email next, deleting a few newsletters from clothing stores before coming across an email from her mom. Her mother lived in Sacramento with Sabrina's stepfather and checked in once a week. She was a technical writer and considered any form of communication other than the written one superfluous. Sabrina was keying in a reply when she noticed Flynn finally reaching for his cell phone.

He gave the screen a cursory glance, frowned and then pocketed it.

It was on the tip of her tongue to ask "why the frown?" but she didn't. When he didn't offer any intel either, she returned her attention to her own phone. She finished the email to her mom and clicked Send, more than a little troubled that Flynn hadn't confided in her that Veronica was clearly trying to weasel her way back into his life.

"What do we do while the Jell-O sets?"

"You have to ask?" He plucked the phone from her hand and gripped her hips, pulling her against him. He dipped his head to kiss her and she wrapped her arms around his neck, enjoying the slow slide of their lips and tongues.

She fit against him like she was designed to be there, her breasts against his chest and her hips nestled against his. How had she never noticed that before? He slanted his head to deepen the kiss, and a low male groan vibrated off her rib cage.

Wait. That last vibration was his phone.

She pulled her lips from his when the buzz came from his pocket again. "Do you need to get that?"

"No." He rerouted them from the kitchen to the stairs, climbing with her while kissing her. Their lips pulled apart several times during the clumsy ascent, their laughter quelled by more kisses.

She shouldn't be jealous of Veronica, for goodness' sake. Veronica wasn't in Flynn's bed—Sabrina was.

"Your room or mine?" Her voice was a seductive purr.

"My bed is bigger." He kept walking her backward, his eyes burning hers and his mouth hovering close. "I have a plan for you and it's going to require a lot of room."

"Oh, really?"

"Probably. Are you a squirmer?"

"Why do you ask?"

"I have to taste you, Sabrina. I have to know."

Her mouth dropped open as a spot between her legs fluttered to life.

"Yeah?" He smirked.

Speechless, she nodded.

In his bedroom, he stood over her and the bed and slowly stripped her. The thin sweater and T-shirt she wore underneath went first. Then he thumbed open her jeans and slipped both hands into them, his palms molding her backside.

"Thong," he praised. "That's more like it."

"I packed some this time."

"Why didn't you before?"

"I… I'm not sure. I guess I was trying to stay in my friend role."

"You're still in the friend role, Sab. It's just that now there are added perks."

"Perks, huh?"

"Do you prefer bonuses?"

"No." She laughed with him as he yanked her jeans to

her feet. He helped her with her shoes and socks and then she stepped from the pant legs.

"Ready to feel good?" From his position on his knees, he looked up at her, his expression as sincere as his offer.

The moment she jerked her head up and down in the affirmative, he put a kiss just under her belly button before dragging his tongue along the waistband of her panties.

Pressing her knees together, she wiggled her hips. He was right. She was a squirmer.

He rolled the thong down to her thighs and she rested her hands on his shoulders when he prompted her to step out of them. Then he tossed them over his head and held her calf gingerly with one hand.

"Throw your leg over my shoulder," he instructed. She did, opening herself to him, her heart thundering as he took in her most private place. He did so approvingly before cupping her backside and leaning in for a slow, intentional taste. That's when her other knee buckled.

He held her to him like he was sampling the sweetest fruit and then feasted on her while she fought to hold herself upright and not dissolve.

When he finally took her over, she folded from the power of her orgasm, coming on a cry that could've woken the dead.

The next thing she knew she was on her back in his bed and his talented mouth was sampling her breasts. She held his head and writhed, sensitive from his earlier pampering. Her hips lifted and bumped against his jean-clad leg between her thighs.

"Please, Flynn." She fumbled with the stud on his jeans and cupped his erection. He drove forward into her hand, allowing her to massage him until she was holding several inches of hard steel.

Shoving his chest, she pushed him to his back and lifted his shirt, revealing abs and a happy trail of hair leading south. She reveled in the thought that it was her trail to follow down, *down* until she reached the promised land. She rolled his jeans and boxer briefs to his thighs and his erection sprang to life, very happy to see her indeed.

Before she gave it a second of thought, she lowered her head and licked him from base to tip.

His hips bucked, accompanying a feral growl. She opened wide and took him into her mouth, running her tongue along the ridge of his penis and slicking him again and again.

He guided her with his hand on the back of her head, his fingers twined in her hair. When she dared look up from her work, she saw the most exquisite combination of pleasure-pain on his face. His desperate need for her turned her on more than what he'd done to her earlier. She doubled her efforts, but he stopped her short, gentling her mouth off him and catching his breath.

He was a sight to behold, shirt rucked up over his bare chest, pants no farther down than his thighs. She liked this uncontrolled, unplanned disarray. It wasn't a way she'd ever experienced him. That there were still new ways for them to be together was exciting.

Before she became too smug, Flynn threw her for another loop.

"On your back or on your knees?" He gave her a wicked grin. "We're doing both, but I'll let you pick where we start."

Fifteen

"It never once occurred to you to have sex to scratch an itch?" Flynn asked.

They'd started with Sabrina on her knees, which thrilled him—he'd known she had confidence stocked away for emergencies—and then finished with him on top, her on her back. Her eyes had blazed into his as he'd thrust them into oblivion. They were very, very good at pleasing each other, that was for damn sure.

They were in his bed, sheets pulled haphazardly over their bodies. Between them, his right hand and her left were intertwined, his thumb moving over hers while they talked.

"Why is that so hard to believe?" she turned her head to ask.

He turned his head and shot her a dubious look. "You are a live firecracker and you dare ask me that question? What have you been doing to get by all this time?"

She rolled her eyes, but her smile widened. He'd flattered her. He liked flattering her. Almost as much as he liked having sex with her. Hell, that was a lie. He liked having sex with her more than anything.

"*I managed.* I haven't seen you taking any strangers home since you and Veronica split."

At the mention of his ex-wife, his mouth pulled into an upside-down U. The truth was, he hadn't wanted anyone after he'd found out Veronica was cheating on him. As emasculating as it was to learn she didn't love him anymore, that had compounded when he found out she'd been fucking Julian. He didn't know which one of them to hate more so he settled on hating both of them. The hate had faded, but the anger was still there. She'd texted him several times today in an attempt at the lamest apology on the planet, which had downgraded his anger to disgust. Though, it might've been more of a lateral move.

No doubt she'd grown tired of Julian the Artist. He looked good on paper—or canvas, as it were—but where real responsibility and presence were required, he was a no-show. Julian cared about Julian more than anyone. It probably shouldn't, but it gave Flynn a shot of satisfaction to know that Veronica was likely comparing the two brothers and noticing that even with his money and inheritance, Julian wasn't measuring up.

"She contacted me," he told Sabrina.

"I know."

Guilt shadowed her face. "I was cleaning the countertop and saw her name pop up on your phone. I didn't read the messages, though."

"She's sorry. Which I already knew."

"Didn't we all," Sabrina said, droll.

"I didn't run out and get laid after we split because I was heartsick and wounded." It was the most truth he'd admitted to anyone—himself included. "She was my world before we fell apart. I should've seen it coming—read the signs. I don't know how I missed it. Guess I was preoccupied with Monarch, which is a lame excuse." Veronica had always told him he couldn't focus on work and her at the same time. God knew he'd tried to satisfy her. Where she was concerned, filling her "needs" seemed to be a bottomless pit.

"Lame, but nonetheless true." Sabrina squeezed his fingers before letting go of his hand and rolling to face him. He stole a peek at her breasts, beautiful and plush resting one on top of the other. He had to force himself to look into her eyes while she talked. Something she'd noticed, given her saucy smile.

"Were you in love with her when you found out she'd been unfaithful? Or had you two been growing apart?"

"We'd been growing apart…like, I don't know, two ships drifting in the ocean. Wow, that is a bad metaphor."

"Horrible."

He allowed himself a small laugh. "We used to be in love. So in love we were stupid with it. We didn't eat or sleep, we just…" He bit his tongue rather than finish the sentence. Best friend or no, he doubted Sabrina would appreciate hearing about past *sexcapades* with his ex-wife. "We wanted to be together all the time. You know how it is."

"I don't, actually." Her eyes roamed the room, not landing on one spot in particular while she spoke. "The day we went through our list of exes, I was thinking about how sad my experience has been with relationships. I was enamored with a few, and smitten by one or two, but I never uttered the *L* word."

"Never?" He didn't like hearing that. Everyone should feel loved and love in return—at least once—even if it was misguided.

"No. I didn't think it would change what was between us for the better."

"And none of those guys expected you to be in love with

them? I would've thought Phillip might've been chirping those three words like a smitten lovebird."

"Oh, he did." Her laughter softened the hard knot in his chest that had been there for too long. "He knew I wasn't that into him, I think. Which hurt his feelings." She bit her lip like she was debating what to say next. "When we broke up, he said it was because he couldn't be second place any longer. He thought I was holding out for you. Wouldn't he have the last laugh if he saw us now? Sleeping together and living together."

Now, obviously, Flynn knew he and Sabrina had just had sex. Also, *obviously*, he was planning on having more sex while she, *yes*, lived here. But hearing that she was both sleeping with him and living with him stated in plain language sounded almost...ominous.

What would anyone say if they knew? If Gage and Reid knew the whole truth. If Veronica knew. If Julian knew...

"Yeah. Unbelievable," Flynn murmured, his mind on the fallout. Fallout he hadn't let himself consider before this moment. He'd been too preoccupied with enjoying himself for a change. It was nice not to play the role of Atlas bearing the weight of the world on his back.

After a long pause, he admitted something else he hadn't planned on saying aloud. "You deserve that, Sab. That stupid love. You deserve to feel it at least once."

"Yeah, maybe," she said, sounding contemplative.

Flynn didn't feel so much contemplative as wary. Sabrina *did* deserve to feel that kind of bone-deep love, but she wasn't going to find it with him. He was good for sex. He was a great friend, but the love part he was done with.

He wouldn't risk diving into the deep end again, not after he'd nearly drowned. It was safer on the shore, with her. It was also completely unfair to tie her up with whatever this was between them when he knew she deserved better.

He cared about her too much to let her go, and he cared too much to keep her. That thought darkened his mood and kept his eyes open and on the ceiling for the next hour while she slept in his arms.

It'd been so long since she'd had a paintbrush in her hand, Sabrina almost didn't know where to start. But once she was over the fear of the blank canvas and drew that first line of paint, she'd be fine.

Noise-canceling headphones over her ears, music piping through them, she danced as she painted those first simple strokes onto the canvas. By the time she'd shaded in the shape of the chickadee, a familiar, easy confidence flooded through her. She could do this. She'd done it dozens of times.

She painted the bird's delicate taupe and tan and white feathers and used a razor-thin brush to fill in his tiny pointed beak and delicate, spindly legs. She placed him on a tender branch and added a few spring buds and lush, green leaves, finishing off the painting by adding a pale blue background.

Pulling her headphones off, she stood back from the easel to admire her work. Still wet, and far from perfect, but the painting was all hers. Created from her imagination and brought to life through acrylics. It was exhilarating to think about what she was capable of with a few simple tools.

Once she'd been completely confident in her painting abilities. She'd endeavored to sell them, or show them at an art exhibit. She didn't let go of that dream all at once. It'd faded slowly. She'd put her brushes and acrylics in her closet, and then she'd tucked away her canvases, as well. She'd been distracted by life and friends and family—Flynn and Luke included—and there suddenly wasn't enough time or room for hobbies.

She frowned, wondering how many other loves she'd sidelined over the years.

"What is that? Sparrow?" Flynn jogged down the stairs wearing jeans and a T-shirt, a laundry hamper hooked under his arm.

"It's a chickadee." She smiled, amused by the sight of Flynn in the midst of doing laundry. "I'm assuming you're sending that out somewhere?"

"Yeah. I'm sending it to the washing machine," he said with a displeased frown.

"I did your laundry in college. You always hated it."

"Who the hell likes to do laundry?" He gave her a sideways smile. "You should feel reassured that I don't need you to do my laundry."

That was too close to "I don't need you" for her to feel reassured about anything. Her very identity was wrapped up in being needed by Flynn, and now wanted by Flynn... a thought she definitely wasn't going to explore deeper.

"I'm going to paint him a friend." She tilted her head to study the painting. "He seems lonely."

"Why? Do they mate for life or something?"

"No, actually." She'd researched them when she'd practiced drawing chickadees in her journal. Sadly, her sweet little bird wasn't a one-chick kind of guy. "They're socially monogamous."

"What the hell's that mean?"

"They're only together to procreate."

"Typical guy. Only there for the sex."

Her laugh was weak as that comment settled into her gut like a heavy stone. Sounded like her current situation with Flynn.

"If you have anything to throw in..." He tilted his head to indicate the laundry room before walking in that direction.

Sabrina's mind retreated back to his college dorm room.

To sitting next to him on his bed while he searched through a pile of clothes for a "cleanish" shirt. The memory was vivid and so welcome.

Remembering who they were to each other eased her nerves. She wasn't some convenient girl and he wasn't a random hot guy. This was Flynn. She knew him better than anyone.

She rinsed the paint off her palette and cleaned her brushes, considering something she had never considered before. What if they had real potential beyond best friends with benefits? What if they'd overlooked it for years? They could blame inconvenience since they'd been dating other people until now, or they could blame their friendship. They'd accepted their role as friends so completely, it hadn't occurred to them to take it to the next level.

But now that they had taken it to the next level, now that they had been naked together on more than one occasion—and she was looking forward to it again—was there more to them than just friends or just sex? And if there was a possibility to move into the next realm, was she brave enough to try?

Wide hands gripped her hips and she jumped, dropping her paintbrushes. They clattered into the stainless steel sink where she'd been cleaning them.

"Oh!" She spun to find Flynn looking pretty damn proud of himself. She gave him a playful shove. "I'm not sure I like this version of you."

He lowered his face until his mouth hovered over hers. "I don't believe you. I think you like this version of me just fine."

Unable to argue, she lifted her chin and placed a sweet kiss on his lips. Just a quick one. He didn't let her get away with quick, though, kissing her deeply and wrapping his arms around her waist. Lost in the pleasure of his mouth, she clung to his neck.

When they parted, she sighed happily, opening lazy eyelids. "We have plans later. We can't only paint and do laundry and make out in the kitchen."

"What plans?"

She trickled a fingertip down his neck and along the collar of his shirt, deciding to keep that surprise to herself. "You'll see. But first I'm going to have to do my hair and makeup—" he stole a kiss and hummed, a sound that thrilled her down to her toes "—and change out of these dirty clothes."

"Allow me to help." He yanked the paint-splattered, baggy T-shirt off her shoulder and kissed her skin. Sabrina's mind blanked of all other thought. Whenever Flynn put his lips on her, she wanted to climb him like a cat on a curtain.

"Oh, but it'd be much more fun if you let me do it," she purred, shaking off his hold. She backed out of the kitchen, lifting the edge of her T-shirt and revealing her stomach— teasing him and having a damn good time doing it. "I'll just throw these dirty clothes in the washer."

"You think this is going to work. You think I'll just follow you wherever you lead because you have no clothes on." But even as he spoke, he followed her every backward step toward the hallway.

She whipped the shirt over her head and tossed it to him. He caught it before it smacked him in the face and gave her the most delightful, reprimanding glare.

"Yup. I *do*." She rolled down the waistband of her sweatpants and turned, revealing the back of her black lace thong. She peeked over her shoulder to bat her lashes and found Flynn's gaze glued to her body. When that gaze ventured to her face, an inferno of heat bloomed in his eyes.

"You're right," he growled. He gave her a wicked grin, and then broke into a run. She yipped and giggled, dashing down the long hallway for the sanctuary of the laundry room. He caught her easily, before she was even halfway there, but she didn't put up even the weakest of fights.

Sixteen

At Chuck's comedy club, Sabrina pulled up to the valet. "We're here!"

"You're kidding."

"I'm completely serious. All of the kidding is done inside the building." She looked completely pleased with herself at his surprise. She should be. She'd surprised him, all right. Flynn climbed from the car, catching up to her as she handed the keys to the valet.

Chuck's was not a new establishment, but it was under new ownership. The club's facade was fresh and stylish rather than its former seedy dive-bar state.

"We came here, what, three or four times?" Flynn smiled at the memories. "I don't remember it ever looking this nice. When did they get a valet?"

"I know, right? I was flipping through one of my journals and there was an entry about us going to Chuck's one night when you were dating someone and I was dating someone else." She made a show of rolling her eyes. "Blah, blah, blah, details, details. Anyway, I checked to see if it was even open, and not only is Chuck's still open, but I found a coupon online for tickets tonight!"

There was an argument about her using coupons for comedy clubs on the tip of his tongue, but he'd digress. It was bad enough she insisted on surprising him and paying for this evening. He'd argued and argued and had finally given up. He'd buy her something to repay her—painting supplies maybe.

Since she'd had those brushes in hand, she'd been more focused on what brought her pleasure instead of trying to help him. She always did things for other people, but didn't do enough for herself. He was struck with the need to make her life easier, better.

He reached for her hand. Their fingers wove together as easily as if they'd been holding hands since the day they met. He'd touched Sabrina in the past, but never in an intentionally sexual or romantic way. Until the kiss happened.

The kiss that changed everything.

Earlier today they'd had feisty, playful, incredible sex against the wall in the laundry room, and then he'd added her discarded clothes to the washer. Through the clear glass lid he'd watched her shirt and pants mingle with his clothes, twist around each other in an almost…intimate way. Which was how holding her hand felt now. How had he never noticed that before?

Sabrina wore an A-line red dress that flared at the waist. Her knees were exposed, her high-heeled shoes tall and sexy as hell, and the simple gold chain at her throat was distracting to the nth degree. When she'd stepped out of the bedroom ready for their date he could think of nothing other than getting her out of the dress. If it was up to him, she'd keep on the shoes and the necklace. Something to look forward to tonight.

Their seats were at a table in the middle of the room rather than up front. He'd been heckled by comedians a time or two in the past when he'd had front row seats, so the middle was fine with him. The headliner was someone he'd never heard of, and Sabrina admitted she hadn't either. He ordered a beer and she ordered a cosmopolitan, and they made it through the opening act. Barely.

As they pity-clapped, he leaned over to whisper, "If that was any sign of what we can expect from the headliner, we should cut our losses and leave."

"Nope. We're here for the duration," she whispered back. "That's half the fun."

It came as no surprise that she could enjoy even bad comedy. Sabrina enjoyed *everything*. He took a sip of his lukewarm beer and mused that she'd probably found a redeeming quality in her watered-down drink. Her superpower was that she found joy everywhere. Even in a formerly seedy club where the tickets were overpriced and the acts should've hung up their jokes years ago.

That same knot that had loosened in his chest before loosened a bit more. He pulled in a deep breath and took her hand again, shaking his head in wonderment at how lucky he was to touch her this freely.

The headliner was introduced and Flynn decided that no matter what crap joke the guy trotted out, Flynn would enjoy the show because he was here with Sabrina. She was contagious in the best possible way—infecting the world with her positivity. That, he'd known for years. That she enjoyed sex and he enjoyed it with her was a surprise.

This sort of ease with a woman shouldn't be simple. Nothing was.

He applauded the opener, shutting out the thought that had the potential to ruin his optimism. Halfway through the guy's set, which was much funnier than his predecessor's, Flynn's phone buzzed and buzzed again. A third insistent buzz had him reaching into his pocket to check the screen.

As if he'd tempted fate by wondering how things could

be this simple, there sat Veronica's name on his phone. *Simple*, she was not.

He read through the texts, wanting to ignore them and brush her fears aside as Veronica being Veronica—dramatic and attention seeking. Except he couldn't. Even though he was 90 percent positive there wasn't a decent bone left in her body, there was in his.

Under his breath he muttered an expletive before leaning close to Sabrina's ear. He whispered that he had to step outside for a moment. When he stood, the target landed squarely on him and the comedian on stage ribbed him for getting up in the middle of his show.

Flynn amiably waved a hand as he exited the room, taking the insults in stride. Go figure. Outside the darkened club, he walked past the ticket counter and bar, forgoing a return text to call Veronica instead.

"Flynn, oh my God. Thank God you called." Her voice was frantic, hushed. Part of him suspected that the text messages were merely to get his attention, but she sounded legitimately frightened.

"What's the problem?" Other than a few veiled words about how his mother's estate was big and Julian was gone and she was hearing things, Veronica hadn't come out and said what she wanted.

"Julian is away at an art show in California and I'm stuck here in this massive house by myself." Her voice shook. "I wasn't sure if the sound I heard was someone breaking in, or if the house was settling."

In that house a break-in was pretty damned unlikely. The neighborhood was gated, and the house itself armed with a security system.

"It's a big house, and it's old. Probably the latter. What do you hear?"

"Cracking. Popping. I don't know." What she described didn't sound like a burglar to him.

"Can you come over and look around? I hate to ask, but…"

He sighed from the depths. She didn't sound frightened but inquisitive and a touch desperate. She wasn't afraid. She wanted to see him. And given the nature of the texts from earlier this week, which had revolved around her being sorry and saying that she missed him, this entire situation was damn fishy.

"Veronica, if you believe that someone is in the house you need to lock the bedroom door, call the police and wait for them to arrive. If I left now, I wouldn't arrive for at least forty minutes."

Silence stretched between them before she spoke again.

"I checked the camera system. And the alarm. Neither of those have tripped." She admitted it sheepishly, like she knew if she'd started the conversation that way she'd be talking to dead air. He cared about her well-being; he did *not* care for being manipulated.

"If you're afraid," he reiterated, "call and have an officer come to the house to take a look around."

"I just… I thought if you were here…we could talk."

"We don't have anything to talk about. Especially when Julian isn't there." Her texts had been hinting at some sort of resolution between them, which he didn't see the point of. He didn't love her and he didn't trust her. He cared about her, though, which she must've known or else she wouldn't have baited him into this call.

"Look, I'm on a date, so I'm going to go."

"Who are you on a date with?" she asked, sounding wounded.

He took a breath, debated telling her, then decided to tell her anyway. "Sabrina."

"I knew it." There was venom in her voice, and the ugly, petty tone compounded with her next comment. "You two have always had a thing for each other."

"We never had a *thing* for each other. I *had* a thing for you." He walked to the exit in case this call required him to raise his voice. "You exclusively. There was a time when you had a *thing* for me, too. Before you had a *thing* for Julian."

Pain seeped in without his permission, so he covered it with anger.

"Since Julian's your guy now, I suggest you call him in a panic."

"I was worried someone was in the house," she snapped.

"Well, the someone who will *not* be in that house to-night is me."

He ended the call, glaring down at his cell phone's dark screen.

"Everything okay?" Sabrina's tender voice asked from behind him. He turned to find her holding her clutch in both hands. "You were gone awhile so I closed our tab. We prob-ably shouldn't attempt to reenter that club given how much crap the comedian gave us both for leaving."

"You don't have to miss the show." He regretted his ex-wife snaring him in such an obvious way. "I shouldn't have taken the call, but her text sounded…" When he met Sabrina's gaze, he noted a dash of surprise.

"Her? You mean Veronica," she stated flatly.

"She's at Mom's estate and was afraid someone was breaking in. I told her to call the cops."

Concern bled into Sabrina's pretty features, magnified through the lenses of her black-framed glasses. "If you need to check on her…" She winced like she didn't want to con-tinue, but then she did anyway. "It might not be a bad idea to make sure she's safe."

God. Sabrina. So damn sweet. She hadn't liked Veron-ica before, and liked her less now that she and Flynn had divorced for the ugliest of reasons.

"You'd let me end our date to go to her?"

"If it would ease your mind, I would. And hers, I guess."
She quirked her mouth. "I want her to be okay. I just don't
want her to hurt you anymore."

Ah, hell. That got him.

He tucked his phone into his back pocket and grabbed
Sabrina and kissed her, losing himself in the pliant feel
of her lips and the comforting weight of her in his arms.
When they parted, he shook his head. In the midst of the
unluckiest time of his life, he was lucky to have her at his
side. "I'm sure Veronica's fine."

Sabrina must've heard the doubt in his voice. She pulled
her coat on and flipped her hair over the collar. "There's
only one way to be sure. We'll go check."

"We?"

"We. I'm coming with you."

Thirty-five minutes later, thanks to light traffic and Sabrina's lead foot, they arrived at his mother's estate. On the
way, Flynn had texted Veronica to let her know that Sabrina suggested they come by. He expected Veronica to tell
him never mind, or that a visit wasn't necessary, but she
didn't. Either she was playing a long game when it came
to winning him back, or she really did need to see a familiar face tonight.

After they'd been buzzed in at the gate, Flynn studied
the house, sitting regally in the center of a manicured lawn.
It looked the same as when he'd grown up here, save for the
missing rosebushes lining the property—his mother's passion. He hadn't missed this house when he'd moved out just
three years after she'd passed away. His father hadn't stayed
there either, moving to his downtown penthouse instead.
Flynn would drive by his childhood home on the rare occasion, but only to remember his mother. It always made him
think of her. It occurred to him for the first time that there
had been no reason for his father to keep the house, except

for a sentimental one. Flynn hadn't thought of his father as a "sentimental" man, but why else would Emmons have kept the house clean and the grass mowed all these years?

Flynn wasn't sure if he was more disturbed over the idea of his father's hidden feelings, or the fact that Flynn was here for the sole purpose of checking on his ex-wife.

Veronica opened the ornate etched glass, cherry-red front door.

"Sabrina." The greeting was a jerk of her chin. "I'm sure this is the last thing you wanted to do tonight."

Sabrina smiled patiently. "Pour me a glass of wine and I'll consider the trip worth it."

Veronica gestured for them to come in and Flynn followed Sabrina into his mother's house. The place had the same vibe as when his mother was alive: an improbably homey feel for an unbearably large home. That was his mom's doing. Everything about her had been approachable and comfortable even in the stuffy multiroomed estate where she'd passed.

"I'm going to poke around and make sure no one's hiding in any closets."

"Here. Take this." Veronica opened a drawer and pulled out a flashlight. "Check the closets. And under the beds."

Much as he didn't want to look at the bed Veronica slept in, he gave her a tight nod before consulting his date.

"You two going to be okay alone? Did you want to come with me?" he asked Sabrina.

Veronica pulled a bottle of white wine out of the fridge. "I can be amicable, you know."

Sabrina gave him a sultry wink that made him wish they were anywhere but here. "I'll let you battle the bad guys while Veronica and I have some Chardonnay."

"Fair enough." Sabrina could handle herself. She didn't need him hovering over her. With a nod of affirmation, he started down the first hallway and flipped on the lights.

Seventeen

Sabrina accepted a wineglass from Veronica and sipped the golden liquid. It was good. Expensive, she'd guess. Seemed like Veronica to demand only the best.

The square breakfast bar where Sabrina sat was positioned at the center of a huge kitchen. The stainless steel gas stove had eight burners and a tall decorative hood. There were roughly two million cabinets painted a regal buttercream with carved gold handles.

"This is a beautiful kitchen." It was the safest thing to say in this situation.

"For the amount of cooking done in it, it might as well be a bar." Veronica's smile was tolerant.

Sabrina honestly didn't mind that they were here, but she wasn't about to suggest Flynn come alone. Not that she thought anything would happen between him and his ex-wife, but Sabrina felt much better keeping an eye on Veronica.

"I always knew you liked him," Veronica said.

Sabrina had been waiting for the gloves to come off. She

didn't have a snappy comeback prepared, but she was less interested in being witty than being honest.

"He's been my best friend for a long time." *Predating you*, she wanted to tack on, but didn't. "We weren't planning on dating. It just kind of…happened."

"Uh-huh."

"It's true," she continued as if Veronica wasn't growing increasingly peeved about this conversation. "We went out on Valentine's Day as friends. I was trying to extract him from the office since he's been so stressed." *No thanks to you.* "It was his idea to kiss me on the pier."

The look on Veronica's face was priceless. Sabrina was half tempted to pull out her cell phone and snap a picture for posterity.

"I was the one who asked him to kiss me again. We didn't expect it to turn into more. Or at least *I* didn't. I was testing a theory." A theory that had since been proved false. The idea that Sabrina and Flynn could go back to just friends was as dated an idea as Pluto being a planet.

"I'm not sure there's anything long-term there for you," Veronica spat, "but you're certainly welcome to look."

Ouch. Gloves off, claws out.

"Oh, I'm looking. I don't want to *overlook* it. Life is about trying. We never know if things will work out or not until we try. I didn't expect your approval, and that's not why we're here." Sabrina purposely referred to herself and Flynn as *we*. "I didn't want you to spend the evening in fear."

Veronica took a healthy gulp of her wine before tipping the bottle and refilling her glass. "How big of you."

Sabrina had attempted to be polite, but apparently Veronica wasn't going to reciprocate. Sabrina refused to sit here and take it.

"While I totally disagree with you for cheating on Flynn, I don't begrudge you for following your heart. I do think you should have ended your marriage before you started an affair with your husband's brother, though."

Veronica gaped at her for a full five seconds before she managed, "How is that any of your business?"

"I'm here tonight at Flynn's side. That's how it's my business."

A condescending, but musical laugh bubbled from Veronica's throat. "Oh, I see. You think this little rebound he's having with you is going to last."

Sabrina couldn't help flinching. She didn't like the word *rebound*. The word itself hinted that their affair was temporary and meaningless. What Sabrina and Flynn had was layered and complex.

"I disagree." Not her strongest argument, but there it was.

Veronica's brow bent in pity. "I'm sure you're building castles in the sky about how you two are going to be married, have babies and live a wonderful, long life together, but, Sabrina…" She sighed. "Woman to woman, I'll level with you. He's not cut out for it."

"I'm not building anything except for one day on top of the last. But I'm not going to waste time worrying and wondering about an expiration date."

"He's not working now, right? I called the office earlier this week to talk to him and Reid said that Flynn was on hiatus. Are you on hiatus with him?"

Thrown by the line of questioning, it took Sabrina a second to regroup. "I—I took my vacation at the same time as him, yes."

"And how long are you two *lovebirds* off work together?"

She ignored the sinister smile and answered Veronica straight. "We go back around Saint Patrick's Day."

"A bit of advice—think of this as your honeymoon stage. Right now, you're with Vacation Flynn. I remember him from Tahiti and that month we spent in Italy." Her gaze softened as if she was remembering the things they'd done together on those vacations.

Sabrina tried not to imagine the details, but her stomach tossed.

"Anyway." Veronica snapped out of her reverie. "Vacation Flynn is very different from Workaholic Flynn. When your fun, albeit temporary, traipse down romance lane comes to an end, don't be surprised if it coincides with the day he returns to the office. You'll see what I mean soon enough. He can't balance a relationship and a bottom line."

Anger bubbled up from the depths. Sabrina hated being talked down to, or having her future predicted for her. Especially by this woman.

Plus, a part of her begrudgingly admitted, what Veronica was saying felt too close to the truth. Hadn't Sabrina already witnessed Flynn's inability to balance their friendship with the demands of Monarch? But a larger part of her didn't want to believe Veronica was right, and that was the part of her that spoke next.

"Are you blaming your divorce on Flynn's work ethic? He had a massive company to run, and his father was terminally ill." And Veronica had been the one cracking the whip. She was more than happy to let him work his ass off so she could buy more, have more and look like she *was* more.

"The erosion of our marriage didn't start with my affair with Julian," Veronica said, surprising the hell out of Sabrina by using the word *affair*. "Our marriage has been falling apart for years."

"*Had*," Sabrina corrected. Veronica was getting to her. As much as she'd sworn to herself that she was Switzerland when she stepped through these doors, either the wine or Flynn's ex-wife's sour attitude was beginning to loosen her tongue.

"*Had* been falling apart," Veronica amended. "A marriage can't sustain cheating. But make no mistake, it was Flynn who cheated first. With Monarch."

"Oh, give me a break! You can't come at me with the 'his job is his mistress' argument."

"Half the company is threatening to leave, and Legal begged you to remove him from the building."

An exaggeration, but that wasn't the point. "How do you know that?"

"I have friends there, too, Sabrina. I also know that he's rapidly morphing into Emmons Parker. You knew that man. He was horrible. Death literally could not have come for a better candidate. And when Flynn is at work, mired in numbers and focused on success, he's exactly like him."

Sabrina paused, her brain stuck on how unflinchingly *true* that assessment was. And if Veronica was right about that, was she also right about Flynn being unable to maintain a relationship?

No.

Sabrina refused to believe it. She couldn't refute the relationship part, but she could argue Veronica's other point.

Sabrina pushed to standing. "Flynn is a caring, generous, amazing person. Whatever combination of Emmons and his mother he ended up being, he has the best of both of them."

"Honey, you are in for a rude awakening."

"No, *honey*—" the words dripped off Sabrina's tongue "—I'm already *awake*."

They stared each other down, Sabrina with her heart pounding so hard she was sure Veronica could hear it. Veronica's smile was evil, as if she began each morning polishing the skulls of her enemies.

"All clear." Flynn entered the kitchen, flipped the flashlight end over end and set it on the countertop. "How are things going in here?"

Sabrina tore her eyes off Flynn's ex-wife and speared him with a glare.

"Everything's peachy, dear," Veronica cooed. "I was just warning Sabrina about what she can expect if you two attempt to stand the test of time."

"So, that went well."

It was a lame attempt to lighten the stifling air in the car. Flynn had been debating what to say and when to say it since they'd walked out of his mother's home. He knew better than to let Sabrina drive, especially when he noticed her hands shaking as she pulled on her coat. He'd made the excuse that she'd had a glass of wine and shouldn't drive, but that wasn't the real reason he took her keys.

She'd been sitting in the passenger seat, her arms folded over her waist, watching out the window since he'd reversed out of the estate's driveway.

"Sab…"

"I was trying not to hate her. But I do. I hate her."

"You don't hate anybody." He leaned back in the seat, settling in for the easy drive home on a virtually traffic-free road. "Veronica is not worth hating. Trust me. I tried for months and my only reward was heartburn."

Sabrina said nothing.

"You wanna tell me what she said that frosted you?"

"She insinuated that I've been in the wings for years waiting for her to screw up so I could swoop in and steal you away!" The words burst from her like soda from a shaken can. Like she'd been wanting to say that for a while. It hurt him that she was hurting, especially because he knew it wasn't true. What had happened between them since the kiss on Valentine's Day had been as unexpected as it was incredible.

"We both know that's not true." He lifted her hand to kiss her fingers. When Sabrina spoke again, her voice wasn't as angry as before.

"She went on and on about what a horrible person you

were. Which is also *not* true, by the way." She apologized by squeezing his thigh, which didn't do much for him in the apology department, but gave him plenty of other ideas. "She wants you back, which I'm sure you figured out since you have the texts to prove it."

"I don't know what she's doing." He was suddenly tired. Too damn tired for this conversation. He'd rather have it sometime around, oh, never. Never would be good.

"Well, *I do*. Julian's probably behaving like a total flake and she realizes that he can't sustain her high-maintenance needs. She's regretting losing you, her sugar daddy." Another thigh pat accompanied an apology. "I'm sorry. I'm not trying to insult you. You're not a horrible person. And I don't think of you as a sugar daddy."

"I know you don't," he said on the end of a chuckle. Could she be any cuter trying to protect both his feelings and his ego? "Veronica was trying to ruffle your feathers. From where I sit, they look pretty ruffled." He took one hand off the steering wheel to run his fingers through her hair. "I like you ruffled. It's hot."

"You *cannot* be flirting with me right now."

"No? You don't think?" He shot her a lightning-quick smile, pleased when she smiled back. It was the first time he'd seen a real smile since they'd left the comedy club. That was his fault. It was his fault for running off to take care of Veronica when his focus should've been on Sabrina. "You planned a great night and I bailed. I should've ignored her texts."

"No," she admitted on a breezy sigh, "you shouldn't have. If you *weren't* the kind of guy to run to the aid of a woman in need, I wouldn't be friends with you. You did the right thing. It's my fault. I forgot how heinous a person she was when I suggested we go over there."

It felt good to laugh off the evening, so he allowed himself another chuckle at her comment. "I promise to make it up to you."

"Deal."

"Home okay with you?"

"Home sounds good."

Home did sound good. And her coming home with him sounded even better.

Eighteen

Sabrina insisted on baking M&M cookies when they returned to his penthouse. While she measured the flour and sugar, Flynn considered how the last week-plus had been a blur of domestic activity.

He'd checked on the status of her apartment's plumbing—progress, but no solution yet. She seemed content to stay here with him and he wasn't in a hurry for her to leave. She'd been painting almost every day in between trying out a few new recipes his stomach was enjoying.

She'd nibbled at the freshly baked cookies, and he'd wolfed down half a dozen while stretched out on the couch and watching the rain. He finally stopped itching to check his email so he'd kicked back to read a spy novel instead of a business book—something he hadn't done in ages.

His entire adult life had been about bettering himself and gaining knowledge of his father's company. Flynn had assumed Mac, or someone like him, would be put in charge of Monarch if and when the impervious Emmons Parker passed on. Though Flynn had always known it was a possibility the company could fall to him, it seemed unlikely. Now that he had what he'd always wanted, it'd come at a price he wouldn't have paid—his father's death. Reconciling grief over a man who was hard to love hadn't been easy, and unbelievably, inheriting ownership of a company he loved had been harder.

Being owner/president of Monarch was and wasn't what he'd expected. Flynn knew that taking over would be hard work, knew that stepping into his father's shoes would rankle Mac's back hair, but what Flynn hadn't counted on was to turn into his father in the process. Before this hiatus, he'd scarcely been able to tell the difference between them.

Thank God for Sabrina for tirelessly pointing out he was changing—even when he hadn't wanted to hear it. He'd felt that gratitude for her tenfold tonight, while she'd lain on the couch next to him, her feet propped on one of his thighs, her eyes fastened to a book. That same book now sat on the kitchen counter as she poured a few inches of Sambuca into two glasses. She'd insisted on a nightcap, and he'd agreed. It was rounding midnight, but he wasn't the least bit tired.

"Do you have coffee beans?"

"There." He pointed to a cabinet.

She dropped three into each snifter, saying for each one, "Health. Wealth. And happiness."

She turned around to present his glass of warmed licorice liqueur, but his hands were full at the moment. Of the book she'd been reading.

"What are you doing?" Her mouth dropped into a stunned O, her voice outlined with worry. "Close that book immediately and take your drink."

"Why?" He edged around the long end of the counter, putting them on opposite sides of it. "Something juicy in here?"

"No." But her pink cheeks begged to differ.

He opened to where she'd slotted her bookmark, skimmed a few sentences and hit gold. He grinned at her.

"Flynn." It was a plea he ignored.

"'His mouth was as intoxicating as any liquor, but a thousand times more potent,'" he read.

"That's out of context." She came around the counter but he walked backward as he continued reading from another section.

"'He replied to her complaint by sliding warm fingers over her bare back, and then snicking the zipper of her dress down over her backside.'"

"Flynn, please." Her giggle was a nervous one. "Please don't read that."

"Why not? It's a hell of a lot more interesting than what I was reading earlier." He let her catch up to him and snatch the book from his hand. She hugged it to her chest, hiding the cover from him. "Anything in there you want to try?"

He thought she would protest. Her cheeks were rosy as her teeth stabbed her bottom lip in what he assumed was indecision. Hooking a finger in the belt loop of her jeans, he tugged her to him, enjoying the plush softness of her breasts against his chest.

"Is my mouth intoxicating, Sabrina?" He nipped her bottom lip.

"You're making fun of me." She shoved his chest.

"I'm not. I promise I'll try anything in that book."

Her eyebrow rose even as her cheeks stained a darker shade of pink. "Promise?"

He trusted her not to find a section where the hero was kicked in the balls. He raised a hand and took the oath. "I swear."

"In that case." She flipped through the book, back and then forward, before relocating her bookmark and handing it over.

He scanned the page quickly and smiled over the cover

before tossing the book onto the couch. "I had no idea you liked that sort of thing."

She shrugged one shoulder, adorable and tempting. He couldn't refuse her.

Bending at the waist, he threw her over his shoulder and started up the stairs. Her laughter warmed every part of him and chased away the chill from the wet, rainy night. He set her on her feet at the door of his bedroom.

Then he kissed her, skimming one hand under her shirt and tracing his fingertips over her bare belly. Her breaths shortened as he kissed and tongued her neck. He moved his hand higher, higher still until he reached her nipple, thumbing the tender bud. When she gasped, he caught it with his mouth, their tongues battling as he drank in her flavor. He used his other hand to cradle the back of her head as he walked her toward the bed.

He took off her shirt and soaked in the sight of her gorgeous breasts before lowering his mouth to sample each one. And when her fingernails raked over his scalp, his jeans grew uncomfortably tight.

"I don't remember what came next in the book," he murmured in between kisses.

"You're doing great."

He smiled against her skin, and her belly contracted with her laughter. Rising to capture her lips with his, he stole a kiss before undressing her further and pushing her to her back.

He liked her like this, naked and sighing his name. With Sabrina he lived in the present rather than in the future—where work trials awaited—or in the past—where the people he loved the most had betrayed him.

There was only the feel of her heated mouth on his neck, and the way they moved together.

She was the perfect distraction, but a part of him insisted that she was much more than that. A part he ignored since he couldn't imagine a scenario where they could live happily ever after. No one did. Of that he was certain.

He cast aside the thoughts as he thrust into her, making love to her in the lazy rhythm he set, and doing his level best to match the fantasy that'd been brewing in her head.

"Hmm." Her limbs vibrated pleasantly from her last powerful orgasm, one that'd had her shouting Flynn's name as she clutched his shoulders and ran stripes down his back.

She smoothed her fingers over the raised skin on his back and winced. "Sorry for the scratches."

"No." He lifted his head from where it'd been resting on her chest—he'd worked hard—and speared her with an intense blue-flamed glare. "Never apologize for sex injuries. Those are bragging rights."

Her cheeks paled.

"Not that I'd brag." He gently slipped free of her body and climbed out of bed. "I don't kiss and tell, Douglas," he called over his shoulder as he padded to the bathroom.

When he stepped back into his bedroom she admired the full view of him naked. The rounded shoulders, muscled limbs, narrow waist and hips. He truly was a work of art.

"Are we going to tell?" she asked. "Eventually?"

His brow crimped.

"We'll be back to work soon. Reid and Gage already assume you and I have done more than kiss. Other people will probably notice that we act differently around each other." How could they not? She doubted she'd be able to keep a flirty smile under wraps or resist standing close to him, or touching him. "Come to think of it, HR might ask us to disclose our relationship."

She'd been enjoying herself and their break together, but reality was creeping closer. Their relationship had changed—drastically—and while her original goal was to help Flynn remember who he used to be, she had to wonder if there was more at stake.

Sabrina needed Flynn's friendship. He was a constant, made her day better. Made her *life* better. He made her feel valued. *Important.* She saw now how badly she'd needed his attention after being sidelined during his marriage.

If sex risked their friendship, well…that wasn't an option.

"Let me worry about HR." He kissed the space between her eyebrows and climbed into bed.

Veronica had warned Sabrina that this was a rebound. As much as Sabrina hated to admit it, there was a large part of her that wondered if Flynn's ex was right.

If there was one outcome Sabrina refused to accept after their brief affair, it was losing Flynn entirely. She'd not risk their friendship for the sake of sex—no matter how much she was enjoying herself.

Under the blankets, Sabrina snuggled with Flynn and squeezed her eyes closed. He wrapped his big body around hers, an arm over her middle. She pressed one of his hands beneath her cheek—her mind spinning.

She'd never imagined Flynn being hers. He'd always seemed meant for someone else. Now she wasn't sure if her hesitancy was a premonition or worry that'd she'd potentially ruined what they had.

She'd moved from the girl at his side to the girl he was *inside*, and the shift was significant. Veronica had been wrong about Sabrina envisioning her future with Flynn or imagining what their kids or wedding would look like. But Sabrina *was* planning some sort of future with him if she was wondering how they'd handle being around each other at work.

But why?

Because you love him, her mind accused.

Of course she loved him. He'd been her best friend since college.

You're in love *with him.*

No I'm not, she argued silently. A chill streaked down her spine despite Flynn, the human heater, blanketing her back. She wasn't *in love* with him. She cared about him. She loved him as a friend.

It's more than that. Think about it. You can't wait to open your eyes and find him next to you every morning. You go to bed next to him every night, dreading the end of this break. You've been silently hoping your apartment's plumbing is never fixed so you can live here for good.

Fear joined the chill in her body and she shivered. She'd never been in love before and certainly hadn't planned on falling in love with Flynn. And because she knew him as well—*better*—than herself she also knew the last thing Flynn wanted was for her to be in love with him. After Veronica he'd sworn off love permanently, and who could blame him?

Which was why he slept with you.

Sabrina wasn't clingy. She was familiar. She made him M&M cookies. Everything he wanted in a friend with all the benefits of a lover.

The word *rebound* danced around her head like a demented performer.

She was in love with Flynn Parker. Her best friend.

Your lover.

He was also the last man on earth she should give her heart to.

So she wouldn't.

They'd abandoned their snifters of Sambuca on the kitchen counter to indulge in a different sort of nightcap, but she could use that drink now.

She eased out from under Flynn's arm—his low snore signifying he wouldn't wake anytime soon. Feeling around in the dark, she found her thong and pulled it on before snagging the first T-shirt she found—his. It took more rooting around blindly before she found her own. It felt wrong to slip into his clothes after her personal revelation.

She walked down the stairs as silent as a soft-pawed cat and grabbed one of the snifters before curling into a ball on the couch. Blanket over her legs, she listened to the rain pound and watched as it streaked the windows and muddied the ambient city lights.

She'd fallen in love with him and she could fall back out. It was as simple as that. How hard could it be? She'd been his best friend for over a decade and his lover for only a few weeks. For the remainder of this hiatus, she'd find a way to separate her feelings of friend love and true love.

For both their sakes.

That would hurt, but she was a strong woman. She would get through this. They both would. Nothing would ruin their friendship together, especially a bout of great sex they could chalk up to timing and proximity.

She sipped her liquor and studied the three coffee beans in the pale light from the city lights outside.

Health, wealth and happiness.

Two out of three wasn't bad.

Nineteen

Sabrina and Flynn had been back at Monarch for a little over a week. There was plenty to do, so at first she barely had time to think about anything other than her burgeoning email inbox.

Last week the landlord had called her to let her know the plumbing had finally been fixed in her apartment. In addition to a hectic work pace, she'd been cleaning up the plumber's mess and unpacking.

She didn't enjoy having the space to herself as much as she'd anticipated.

She'd focused on laundry and preparing meals and definitely did *not* read any of the new romance novels Mrs. Abernathy had dropped off. Sabrina had also dodged a few questions from her well-meaning, prying neighbor about whether or not she and Flynn were in love. Mrs. Abernathy took Sabrina's silence as confirmation, rather than assuming the relationship had imploded.

Not that Flynn *knew* things had imploded. Sabrina hadn't exactly stated anything for the record.

Since they'd returned to work, the distance between them had come naturally. Flynn was doubly busy after his month off, staying at the office some nights until eight or nine.

She'd told herself that this was a good thing—that it was her chance to slot him back into the friend zone where he belonged. They could write off the last four weeks as a fling, and go back to normal.

Instead, she'd thought about how Veronica was right about Flynn's new love being Monarch Consulting. Why did that hurt so much when she'd done exactly what she'd set out to do? Flynn was no longer stomping around like an angry ogre and the senior execs at the company were more accepting of him. Everything was back to normal.

Except for her.

She'd tasked herself with reversing the mistake of falling for him, but her heart wasn't cooperating. Every night she lay in bed alone, her mind on Flynn and the way his mouth tasted. Missing the comfort of his body, big and warm and wrapped protectively around hers, or hearing his light snore in the middle of the night whenever her eyes snapped open and her mind was full…

"Hey." Flynn's low rumble brought her head up from her laptop. He stood in her doorway, dressed in an expensive suit with a silver-blue tie bisecting a crisp gray shirt. His jacket was buttoned, his shoes were shiny and he was the most delicious vision she'd seen all day.

There used to be a time she could look at him and think, "Hey, there's my friend, Flynn." Now she looked at him and thought about touching him and being close to him. Touching him and watching the raw heat flare in his eyes. Which made working directly across from him and keeping her hands to herself pure, unadulterated torture.

"What's up?" She was aiming for casual, but the greeting sounded forced.

"Finally managed to poke my head out of the water. I thought Reid and Gage were supposed to handle my email, but I came back to about a million of them. Lazy bastards."

That made her smile. "Yeah, nobody took care of mine while I was gone either."

A heated smolder lit his eyes that was 100 percent intriguing and 1,000 percent out of place at work. He ducked his chin and stepped deeper into her office. "I've missed you."

Her heart hammered against her ribs as she anticipated what he would say next. Would he ask her out? Invite her over? And how was she going to say no if he did?

How could she possibly say anything but yes when what she wanted was to be with him more than her next breath? Not only tonight, but the night after that and the one that followed...

Definitely, she was terrible at breaking up with him.

"How's the plumbing?" he asked. "I'm talking about your apartment, not your person."

"Har, har. I see that your sense of humor hasn't improved."

"Well, you can't expect a month off to work miracles."

"Thanks to you, my apartment is perfect." *Except that you're not in it with me.*

Those were the kinds of thoughts she shouldn't be having about him and yet they boomeranged back no matter how hard she threw them.

Last night she'd sat down to add a female partner to the chickadee painting, her mind on Flynn and their conversation about those philandering little birds that were together only for the sex.

What a metaphor for how things had ended up. She couldn't look at the chubby, charming, whimsical birds without thinking of what she'd lost.

Except Flynn wasn't looking at her like he'd lost anything. Or like he wanted to change anything. More proof came in what he said next.

"What do you say we carve out some time for each other?" His eyebrows lifted in the slightest way, his sculpted lips pursed temptingly. "Tonight?"

"Tonight?" Her brain jerked to life and provided a handy excuse that happened to be true. "Sorry. Can't. Luke is coming over. I've been ignoring him lately, so I promised to cook him dinner. You know my brother. He rarely indulges in any food outside of his gym rat diet, so when he's ready for a cheat day, he calls me."

"Later this week, then."

She didn't say anything to that since it wasn't a question.

He lingered at her desk, running his eyes down the royal blue dress she was wearing. "I'd like to get you out of that dress. Sure you can't reschedule with your brother?"

Never had an offer been so tempting and terrifying at the same time. She could say yes and blow off dinner with Luke. Then she and Flynn could have wine, and make love on the couch or the bed. He could carry her up the stairs or they could walk up hand in hand, side by side. An entire choose-your-own-adventure scenario unfurled itself like a red carpet leading to a night of absolute indulgence.

Out of her dress and into his arms sounded perfect, but that wouldn't help her fall out of love with him.

"Rain check," she muttered, but couldn't help adding, "I can always wear this dress again."

He leaned over her desk, coming closer, closer until his lips nearly brushed hers. Then he turned his head and pretended to study the screen of her laptop, his minty breath wafting over her cheek when he said, "I like the sound of that."

A thin breath came out in a puff when he straightened and walked out of her office. She'd made the wrong decision for her heart, but she'd made the right decision for their future. As much as she wanted to believe that they were meant to be, she had an uneasy feeling that they *weren't*. Their fun new pastime would soon grow old and wither on the vine.

She refused to let that happen—to risk losing him completely when having him forever as a friend was well within reach. There was time to put Jack back in the box. To corral the loose horse into the barn. To cork the genie's bottle...

Horrible metaphors aside, she was going to make this right.

Their friendship deserved no less.

"So let me get this straight. You're not dating Flynn, but you're trying to think of a way to break it off with him?"

Luke lounged on her sofa, scrolling through his cell phone. She'd spilled her guts at dinner and told him everything. Well, *almost* everything. He was still her brother and she would never be comfortable sharing sex stories with him.

"How can you say we're not dating?" she called from the kitchen as she rinsed the dishes and loaded the dishwasher. "I lived with him! We shared a bed. That's dating."

Luke winced when she said the word *bed*. He set his phone aside and shoved a pillow under his head, regarding her patiently.

Dish towel in hand, she stepped into the living room and collapsed into a chair. "What? Tell me."

"It sounds like you went on some dates. That's dating. The other stuff... I don't know what the hell that is. Not dating."

"Of course it's dating. What else could it be? It's more than a hookup."

"Have you at least admitted to yourself that you're in love with Flynn Parker?"

She let out a sigh of defeat. "Yes. I have."

"Any reason in particular you're not sharing this news with him?"

"If you had a girl as a best friend for nearly half your life, would you want her to profess her love for you when you knew it wouldn't last?"

"First off," he said, pushing himself into a seated position, "I would never have a girl who was a friend for that long without attempting to get into her pants."

She frowned. "That's unsettling."

"It's also true. Second." Luke held up two fingers. "How do you know he thinks it won't last?"

"Because of the pact. The bachelor pact. Or whatever they call it."

"That's stupid."

She used to agree, but now she wasn't so sure. "He didn't reinstate it lightly. Which makes me the biggest rebound of all rebounds."

"He'd better not think of you as a rebound or I'll kick his ass myself."

She didn't know if Flynn felt that way, but it was good to know Luke had her back.

"I don't want to see you hurt, Sab."

"I don't want to see myself hurt either." Back in the kitchen, she scrubbed the counter with a damp cloth and continued her thought from earlier. "Which is why I'm trying to wrap this up while I have a scrap of dignity left. Yes, the dates went well. Yes, we had a great time while I lived with him. Yes, it was the best sex of my life—"

Luke groaned.

"Sorry. But you see my point, right? I can't top that off with an *I-love-you*. I've made up my mind to go back to being friends with Flynn. Just friends. When I make up my mind about something, you know I do it."

"I know." Luke walked over to her, bending his head to look down at her. Funny, she remembered when he was shorter than her. He'd been a pain in her butt then, and not one of her closest confidants. "Are you sure this is how you want to play it?"

She wasn't, but there was no other graceful way out of it. "I'm afraid if I wait too long Flynn will have to give me a speech explaining how temporary we were."

"Okay." Luke sounded resigned as he went to the fridge and pulled out a bottle of beer. "Let's make a plan for you to pull the trigger before he can."

Hope filled her chest. "Thank you, Luke!"

Her excitement about making a plan mingled with pain in the region of her lovesick heart, but she ignored it.

This was the best solution—the only solution. Soon enough she'd be on the other side, Flynn back where he belonged, her heart having accepted that he wasn't theirs for keeps.

The sooner she let him know they were through, the sooner she would heal.

She hoped.

Twenty

It was like ripping off a Band-Aid. That was the comparison Luke made last night.

He'd suggested she text Flynn, but there was no way Sabrina could break the news via a text. She and Flynn were too good of friends to have an important conversation via text message. Besides, she knew him. He would've shown up at her apartment and demanded she explain herself.

She entered the executive conference room with her fresh cup of coffee to meet with Flynn, Reid and Gage. As much as she wanted to tell Flynn her decision sooner than later, now wasn't the time for a private conversation.

"Thanks for joining us," Reid said with a smile.

"I was stuck on a conference call the three of you insisted I make." She narrowed her eyes at them in reprimand, but when her gaze hit Flynn's, she rerouted. She couldn't look him in the eyes with a whopper of an announcement sitting on the tip of her tongue.

"Gage, you called this meeting. We're here." Flynn set aside his iPad, thereby giving Gage the floor.

"Now that Mac and company have retracted their threats to leave Monarch and take their friends with them," Gage started, "we need to massively increase sales. A huge boom in profits means bonuses all around, which makes Flynn look good, my sales department look good and Monarch look good. If we're growing and Mac threatens to leave again, chances are he won't have many followers. If any."

"I'm all for growth." Flynn's eyes narrowed. "I feel like there's more."

"There is. I'm bringing in an expert. Someone who can aid me with coaching my team. I don't love the idea of handing this to someone else, but I can't handle my work-load and training and expect to do both efficiently. I found a guy who comes highly recommended. I read about him in Forbes and then stumbled across his website. He's incredibly selective about the jobs he takes, but several profitable Fortune 500 companies are on his client list."

"Who is this wizard?" Reid asked.

"His name's Andy Payne. He's made of smoke, and somewhat of a legend. He's also virtually unreachable. I couldn't get him on the phone so I settled for a discussion with his secretary."

"Sounds mysterious," Reid said. "If he'd be open to shar-ing that he's working for us, we could use the media curi-osity. Flynn?"

To Sabrina's surprise, Flynn turned to her. "You've been quiet."

"I've heard of Andy Payne. His website isn't much more than a black screen with his name on it. If we share that we're working with him across our social media channels, it might not even matter how much we improve sales. His involvement alone would be enough to gain stockholders' support." She looked at Gage. "It's smart."

"Thanks." Gage smiled.

"Okay then." Flynn nodded. "How much is this guy going to cost us?"

Sabrina shut down her laptop for the day and glanced at the clock. The digital read was 5:05, which meant the lower floors had already packed up to enjoy a rare day of sunshine.

Flynn's assistant, Yasmine, had already left, Gage and Reid were at their desks, and who knew how long they'd be here. They usually didn't stick around as long as Flynn, but if she waited for them to leave she might be sitting here another hour-plus.

She was tempted to chicken out and leave without talking to him at all until he looked up from his computer as if he'd felt her eyes on him. Once his mouth slid into a wolfish smile, she knew she didn't have a choice.

"Now or never," she whispered to herself as she strode across the office. His door was open but she rapped on the door frame anyway.

"Sabrina." The way he said her name sent a warm thrill through her. One that harkened back to long kisses and their bodies pressed together as they explored and learned new things about each other. She had the willpower of a monk and the hardheadedness of a Douglas. She could do this.

She *had* to.

"Do you have a minute?" she asked, pleased when her voice came out steady. "I wanted to talk to you about something."

"Of course." He didn't look the slightest bit worried. Not even when she shut the door behind her and sat across from him in a chair on the opposite side of the desk.

"It's about the pact."

"The pact?"

"Yes. The pact you reinstated with Gage and Reid about never getting married."

"I know what the pact is, Sab." He didn't look worried but he definitely looked unhappy. Maybe she was on the right track here. Maybe Flynn *was* worrying about the future as much as she was and didn't want to ruin their friendship with more complications.

"In college I thought the pact was a stupid excuse for your horndog behavior."

His mouth eased into a half smile.

"When you met Veronica, you threw it out because you knew it was a stupid excuse. But I was unfair to call it stupid this time around, Flynn. You're only trying to protect yourself. And I respect that."

"Okay…" He was frowning again, probably waiting for her to arrive at a point.

"Even though I've never been in love before—" *a tiny lie* "—I expect to fall someday. I envision walking down the aisle in a big, white dress. I may not want it now, but I will."

He shifted in his seat, nervous like she was going to propose to him then and there. She wasn't, of course, but last night she'd intentionally tried to imagine a groom at the end of the aisle waiting for her, and guess who she pictured?

Flynn.

"I'm getting married someday, Flynn. And you're not."

She let the comment hang, watching his face as he understood that she wasn't asking him for more, but less.

"While being with you in a new way has been fun, it's time to move on. We arrived in good places—you're back to yourself and I'm painting again…" Kind of. She didn't feel much like painting now. "I don't know if you want a pair of chickadees over your mantel, but the painting's yours if you want it."

She didn't want it. She related too much to the female

who had been foolish enough to fall in love with an emotionally unavailable bachelor.

Flynn's brow dented in anger, but still he said nothing.

"So. That's it, I guess. We just go back to the way things were before…you know. We'll pretend this never happened." She stood in an attempt at a quick getaway.

"Where the hell are you going?" Flynn stood and pointed at her recently vacated chair. "Sit down."

She propped her hands on her hips in protest. "I will not. That's all I had to say."

"Well, I haven't said a damn thing."

"There's nothing for you to say!"

"Oh, trust me. There's plenty to say." He flattened his hands on the desk and gave her a dark glare.

She folded her arms over her chest to prevent her heart from lurching toward him.

"Are you breaking up with me?" he asked.

"Are we…dating?" Her voice shook.

"You bet your beautiful ass we're dating. What would you call what we've been doing for the last two or three weeks?"

"Having fun." She gave him a sheepish shrug. "Having a fling."

"A fling." He spat the words.

"A really fun fling," she concluded.

"Listen to me very carefully."

She glared, attempting to match his ferocity, and leaned over his desk, her fingers pressing into it. "I'm listening."

"Good. I don't want you to miss a single word."

Twenty-One

Flynn's thunderous mood only grew darker as the evening grew later. The moment last week in his office when Sabrina confronted him still banged in his head like a gong, vibrating from every limb and causing his fingertips to tingle.

Granted, he hadn't handled it well. He'd told her under no circumstances was she dumping him on his ass when they were just getting started.

That hadn't gone over well, and if he hadn't been simultaneously pissed off and hurt by her suggestion to stop seeing him, he could've predicted as much. It seemed they'd both succeeded during their break from the office. Sabrina stopped his metamorphosis into his father and he'd convinced her to put herself first.

She didn't want him. Not anymore, anyway.

He made himself respect her decision. Even when she left crying and told him she always cried when she was angry and not to read too much into it.

After the explosion in his office, Reid and Gage barged

in to offer their two cents, a.k.a., find out what the hell had happened.

Flynn hadn't told them everything, so they were probably still confused about why Sabrina left crying and never came back. They blamed him, and since he'd behaved like a horse's ass, he didn't blame them for blaming him. He'd digressed to pre-Valentine's Day Flynn, and felt every inch the corporate piranha he used to be. He wore a dark suit, a darker outlook, and palpable anger wafted off him like strong cologne.

How the hell else was he supposed to feel when Sabrina had come into his office, looking beautiful and sexy, and then broke up with him? He'd been yearning for her so badly, he could scarcely get her out of his head and she'd been ruminating on the best way to let him down easy.

She'd called what they had a fling.

What a load of crap.

She'd emailed him the morning after their argument telling him she was taking a "leave of absence," without an end date. He'd been sure she'd come to her senses in a day or two.

Unfortunately, the week had passed as slowly as the ice caps melting, and her office remained empty and dark. There was a lack of sunshine in Seattle, and he blamed that on her, as well. Even when Seattle wasn't sunny, which was almost always, Sabrina brought her own light with her.

It wasn't only that he missed her, or that he'd been forced to outsource some of their marketing for the time being, it was that she was…gone.

Gone from the office, gone from his bed. Gone from his *life*. Her absence was like a shadow stretched over his soul.

Waiting for her to come to her senses was taking a lot longer than he'd thought.

He rubbed grainy eyes and shut his laptop, considering what to do next. At that moment Gage darkened his office door.

"Did you call her yet or what?" Gage sat in the guest chair, looking tired from the long day. The workload that hadn't been outsourced had fallen to Gage and Reid.

"I have not."

"Reid and I tossed a coin to find out which one of us was going to come in here and ask the question we promised not to ask you."

Flynn pressed his lips together. Saying nothing was the safest response. As expected, Gage didn't let him get away with it.

"More than hanky-panky went on in your apartment, didn't it?" He lifted one eyebrow and paired it with a smug smile. "You guys rushed in, expected a little slap and tickle, and ended up falling flat on your faces."

Before Flynn could decide how loud to yell, Reid stepped into the room.

"What our fine cohort is trying to say is that you two kids accidentally fell in love with each other, and neither of you have admitted it."

Flynn blinked at his friend, unsure what to make of his assessment. It wasn't as if Reid went around accusing people of falling in love. He'd sooner die than bring up the topic of love at all.

"We're not blind." Gage tilted his head slightly and admitted, "Okay, we were blind for a while. But after that outburst between you and Sabrina in your office—"

"And the fact that she left crying and hasn't returned," Reid interjected.

"We caught on."

Reid sat in the chair next to Gage and they each pinned Flynn with questioning expressions. No, not questioning. *Expectant.* And what the hell was Flynn supposed to say?

He'd been accused of falling in love with his best friend.

The same best friend who'd come into his office on this day last week and told him she didn't want anything to do with him. What would either of them say if they knew that the month he'd spent with Sabrina had been the best one of his life? What would his buddies say if they knew the truth—that he'd never experienced sex the way he'd experienced it with Sabrina?

With her, sex was more than the physical act. She towed him in, heart and soul. Blood and bones. He'd been 100 percent present with her, and then she threw him away. Walked out!

He'd told her if she really believed that what they had was a "fling," she could march her ass out of his office for good. He knew damn well what they had wasn't just sex or convenience. The dream he'd had about her was a prediction. Some part of his mind had known that she belonged in his arms and in his bed.

He never counted on her cutting him off at the knees. He missed her. He wanted her back. And yet he cared for her too much to demand more than she was willing to give.

"She told me she was getting married someday," he told Gage and Reid. They both blanched at that confession. "That's right, boys. She made sure to tell me she was getting married and since I made a pact never to be married, she didn't want to lead me on."

"She wouldn't ask you to give up the pact," Reid said with a disbelieving laugh.

"Wouldn't she?" Flynn asked. He didn't know the answer to that. "We only had a month together. What the hell am I supposed to say when she tells me she's getting married someday and I have a pact not to so we may as well wrap up whatever fling we were having? She called it a fling, by the way. A fucking *fling*."

"Was it?" Gage asked, his face drawn.

"Hell no it wasn't a fling!" Flynn boomed. "And if she's

too hardheaded, or too dense or whatever other adjective you'd like to assign her, to realize that what we had was something special, then...then..."

"She doesn't deserve you?" Reid filled in with a smirk.

"Shut up." Flynn glowered.

"You know, we can sit here all day and wait, or you can admit how you feel about her now." Gage crossed one leg, resting his ankle on his knee. He propped his elbow on the arm of the chair and did a good job of appearing as if he *could* sit there all day.

"Yep, and after you admit it to us—" Reid made a show of stretching and lacing his fingers behind his head "—then you can go tell her."

"Tell her what?" Flynn asked, his blood pressure rising.

"You tell us." Gage lifted his eyebrows in challenge.

"We can order in," Reid said to Gage. "I haven't had Indian in a while."

"Great idea. Amar's has the best naan."

"Wrong. Gulzar's is much better."

"Hey," Flynn growled. "Remember me? What the hell do you two want me to say?" He stepped out from behind his desk to pace.

Hands in his hair, he continued complaining, mostly about how he should fire both of them if this was the support he could expect from his other two best friends.

"What am I supposed to do? Go to her and tell her I have no idea what we had, but it's not worth throwing out?"

"I think you're going to have to do better than that," Gage said and Reid nodded.

"What, then? Tell her she was special and I didn't want her to leave?"

"Warmer," Reid said.

"You want me to tell her..." Flynn sighed, his anger and frustration melting away. Could he say it aloud? Could he tell his two boneheaded friends the truth that he'd been avoiding since the first time he'd made love to Sabrina? "Tell her I'm in love with her and that she belongs with me?"

"By God, he said it." Reid grinned.

"Shit." Flynn sat on the corner of his desk, the weight of that admission stifling. Too stifling to remain standing.

"And then she'll admit she loves you, too," Gage said.

"Weren't you listening? She ended *us* in this very office."

"She's scared of losing you," Gage told him. "She cut things off before you could so that the two of you could remain friends."

"I wasn't going to cut things off! And if that's true, why isn't she here, huh?" Flynn gestured to her empty office. "Wouldn't my *friend* be here still?"

"Not if you told her to bugger off," Reid said.

"I ran your situation by Drew," Gage said. "She agreed you need to tell her."

"I highly doubt your sister has any insight into Sabrina." Reid snorted and Gage turned on him, glaring. "I only mean because she hasn't been around. I haven't seen Drew in an age."

"This isn't about Drew." Gage let his glare linger on Reid a moment before snapping his attention back to Flynn. "Tell Sabrina you love her. Kiss and make up."

"We hereby release you from the pact," Reid announced. "But Gage and I are still in it." He shot an elbow into Gage's arm. "Right?"

"I have no plans on matrimony. So, yes."

Flynn's head spun. "No one said anything about marriage."

That he was in love with Sabrina was a massive leap for his head and heart to make.

"Either let her go or allow yourself to be open to it. She walked in here to tell you that she's marrying someday. So if it's not going to be you, you should let her off the hook." Gage was clearly in lecture mode.

"You two should've married years ago." Reid stood as if his business was concluded here. "You've always belonged to Sabrina and vice versa. She won't look at me sideways and I've been flirting with her for years. If she's managed to keep from sleeping with me, there must be something stopping her. In this case—" Reid leveled Flynn with a look "—you."

Gage stood, too. "He's right. Go get her. Marry her. Either that or we quit. We never wanted to work for Emmons Parker, and if you don't show some favor to your neglected heart you're going to end up just like him."

"Filthy rich and hopelessly lonely," Reid summarized.

Then they walked out of his office, yammering about eating naan at Gulzar's.

Without inviting Flynn to join them.

Twenty-Two

Sabrina had spent her third straight morning in a row at the gym with Luke. She was sad and upset and punishing herself. There was no other logical reason on this planet to do burpees.

Her body took the doled-out sets like a trooper, but that wasn't really why she was working out so much. She was paying penance for believing for a single second that she could fall out of love with Flynn.

As Luke had told her this morning, "I knew that wouldn't work."

She'd slugged him in the arm and asked him why he'd let her do it, but he'd only shook his head and said, "Like you'd listen to me anyway."

Unfortunately, he was right. Her stubborn nature had shown up at the wrong time—outshining her positive, Pollyanna attitude and leading her astray.

And when Flynn had demanded she keep seeing him, she'd dug in her heels and fought out of principle. He couldn't tell her what to do, not when she was trying to stop loving him. Turns out she didn't have to stop loving him, since Flynn probably hated her for leaving Monarch high and dry.

Okay, fine, he probably didn't *hate* her. But he'd let her leave and that felt like the same thing.

She'd ended what they had so that they could be friends, but she'd lost him altogether. Couldn't he see she was trying to help both of them?

"By keeping your feelings to yourself," she grumbled as she hooked her purse on her shoulder.

Gage had asked her to meet him at Brewdog's for a cup of coffee. The hip café was a block from her house. She'd told him no but then he'd begged, saying he had a work problem that only she could solve. "The outsourcing Flynn hired, Sab, they're a nightmare. Don't leave me hanging. This project is too important."

Outsourcing that was her fault because she'd walked out without notice. She'd felt too guilty to say no again. Besides, she would like to go back to work eventually. After however long a cooling period she and Flynn needed before they rekindled their friendship.

They *had to* rekindle their friendship. Living without him in her life was miserable. Monarch Consulting had given her a sense of meaning and purpose. She wasn't so stubborn that she didn't recognize that Flynn was a very big part of that. He was important to her, and she'd just have to woman up, convince her heart to accept that he wouldn't fall in love with her back, and move on.

She could do it. She just hadn't figured out how yet.

Outside, the spring rain fell in a light drizzle, but she didn't bother with an umbrella since she'd worn her contacts instead of her glasses. She was as grumpy about the weather as she was about agreeing to help Gage. On the steam of her own bad attitude, she stepped into Brewdog's and nearly plowed into a man picking up his coffees at the counter.

"Sorry." She moved aside, but then her gaze softened on the most handsome face she'd ever seen.

Flynn's.

His jaw clenched, a muscle ticking in one cheek.

"I'm…meeting Gage?" But even as she said it, she doubted Gage was here. This moment had setup written all over it.

"So am I." Flynn's eyes narrowed in suspicion. "He called two minutes ago, asking me to grab his coffee for him since he was running late. I'm supposed to meet him—"

"At the table by the plant," they said at the same time.

"Does one of those cups contain a salted caramel concoction?" she asked of her favorite indulgence.

"I knew that sounded off when he ordered it." Flynn handed her one of the cups and they walked to the corner table by the plant, which was currently occupied by a British guy in sunglasses pretending to read a newspaper.

"*Et tu*, Reid?" she asked.

He lowered the paper and feigned shock. "What are you two doing here? No matter. You can have my table. I was just leaving."

"Convenient," she muttered.

Reid stood and kissed her forehead. "Miss you, Sab."

That was sweet. The jerk.

She watched him leave and then she and Flynn sat across from each other, her stiffly, with her purse in her lap.

"You feel nothing for him when he pulls that charming shtick?" Flynn asked.

"For Reid? I feel… I don't know. I feel like that's just Reid."

"No butterflies?" Flynn asked. Weirdly.

"No." Reid Singleton was good-looking and all, but just…no.

They sipped their coffees and sat in silence for a few lingering seconds. The café was filled with the din of chatter and the sounds of steaming milk and the clattering of cups and spoons.

Someone had to end this standoff. That's why Gage and Reid had set them up. They wanted reconciliation, and had probably convinced Flynn to talk her into coming back to work. She never should've walked out on them. Plus, she really did want her job back...

Determined to eat her crow while it was still warm, she would be the first to apologize. "Flynn—"

"I'm in love with you."

Every word she was going to say next flew out of her head. His expression was desperate, pained. Because he regretted saying it, or because he wasn't sure if she loved him, too?

"It's inconvenient and the timing is completely wrong and I'm not sure if you feel the same way, but I'm in love with you and I miss you like crazy."

Her heart beat double time, the joy in it hardly able to be contained. Flynn was in love with her!

He lowered his voice. "I don't want the painting."

Well. That was an odd segue.

"The birds. The birds who only want each other for sex," he explained a little too loudly. "That's not what I want. That's not what I ever wanted. And when I was finally brave enough to take the leap, I did it with the wrong person."

"Me?"

"No," he practically shouted. "Veronica."

She wasn't going to deny the punch of relief she felt hearing his ex-wife's name.

"She screwed me over and I was sure the universe was trying to show me that my original plan never to marry was the right call all along. If we hadn't married so quickly, we would've ended years ago."

"You...would've?"

"She knew it. I knew it. Neither of us came out and admitted we were unhappy. It doesn't forgive what she did, but I understand why she left." His eyes dashed away before finding Sabrina's again. "I haven't thought about getting married again. Only about avoiding the pain of having my wife leave me. She was supposed to love me. She didn't do a very good job of it."

Sabrina opened her mouth to agree, but Flynn spoke first.

"You do." He reached over the table, palm up, and she slipped her hand into his. It felt inexplicably good to touch him. To have him here. To listen to the words tumbling out of his mouth like a rockslide he was powerless to stop. "You love me better than anyone ever has, Sabrina Douglas. You show it in every small gesture, and in every action. Even the one that led you to come and tell me that we were through. I'm sorry it took me this long to pull my head out of my ass."

"Me, too," she whispered, tears stinging her nose. She blinked her damp eyes, Flynn going momentarily blurry as she swallowed down her tears.

"You, too, meaning you're also sorry it took me so long to pull my head out of my ass, or..."

He waited, eyebrows raised, and then she realized that she hadn't told him the most important news of all.

"I'm in love with you, too. And you're right. I do a very good job of loving you. The only time I didn't do a good job was when I walked away. But I never stopped loving you, Flynn."

"God, am I glad to hear you say that."

His smile was the most welcoming sight she'd seen in over a week.

"I'm not saying you have to marry me now or...ever, honestly," he told her. "I'm saying that if you try this thing with me and you start imagining the guy at the end of the aisle and see my face—"

"I already do."

"Yeah?"

"Yeah. Which is nuts." She let out a nervous laugh. "That's nuts, right?"

"I don't know anymore." His sideways smile was filled with chagrin. She loved it. She loved him. "We don't have to decide that now, but you do have to decide something."

"Which is?" She couldn't wait to hear what he said next considering his every confession had been better than the last.

"You have to come back to Monarch," he said so seriously that a few banked tears squeezed from the corners of her eyes.

She sniffled and swiped them away. "Done."

"And you have to be mine. Not like the chickadees, Sabrina. Like…whatever species of bird mates for life. Paint that kind of bird—two of them—and I'll hang that painting over my mantel."

"The only species I know that mates for life is black vultures." She wrinkled her nose.

"How the hell do you know that?"

"I went through a macabre phase in my angsty teenage years."

"Yikes," he said, on the end of a deep chuckle.

"Oddly enough, a pair of black vultures is fitting for your apartment," she teased.

He squeezed her hand, but instead of teasing her back, he said, "So are you. You belong there with me. I used to think I was good by myself. That I liked my space and having things easy, simple. But since you walked into my black and white penthouse, you changed all that. You've been too far away during the years Veronica and I were married. Then you came back and brought color into my life, Sab.

And you brought love—real love. The patient, kind type of love they talk about in wedding vows. I've known for a while there's been something missing in my life. I used to think it was success or money. But all along, it was you. You're what's been missing in my life. I'm tired of missing you. I don't want to miss you again. Not ever."

As he gave the speech, an earnest expression on his face, his hand held hers tightly. The words were stacked on top of one another like he was trying to say them all at once.

She had to make sure she understood what he was saying. There'd been too many moments lately where she and Flynn had been vague. They'd paid the ultimate price—losing each other. She wouldn't risk him again.

"Just to be crystal clear," she said, "you want me to work with you. And…live with you? Maybe marry you in the future?"

"Yes, yes and hell yes. You're my vulture, Sabrina." He winked. "Plus, I was absolved from the bachelor pact."

"You were?"

"Yep. These two weird guys I know don't want me in it. They'd rather us be together."

Okay, she was giving Reid and Gage huge hugs the next time she saw them.

"They said I've always been yours. I thought about that a lot this past week. Over the years you and I have known each other, no matter who we were with at the time, we stuck together. You and I have never strayed. I've always been yours, but you've also always been mine."

The truth of his words resonated deep in her soul. She, too, thought of the years they'd spent in each other's company. The easy way they could talk and pass the time together. Of course it'd always been Flynn. Who else would it have been?

"I've always known the right place for you was by my

side," she told him. "I never dreamed you'd be more than a friend."

"Then it's a good thing I kissed you on the pier on Valentine's Day."

A thrill ran through her as she remembered the first contact with his lips. How surprised she was to explore another side of him. Who knew it could get better, then worse, and then better than before?

"I'm taking the rest of the day off." He stood and pulled her to her feet.

She lifted a hand to his forehead, checking for a fever. "A half day? Are you sure you're not sick?"

"Lovesick." He lowered his lips for a soft, way-too-brief kiss and then handed over her coffee cup.

"Besides, we have a lot to do. Pack up your apartment, hire movers—"

"Redecorate your colorless apartment."

"You'll bring the color, Sab."

Yes, she would.

Outside of the café, Flynn paused under the awning as the rain went from a drizzle to a borderline downpour. Fat drops splattered the sidewalks as people ran for the shelter of the coffee shop and other surrounding stores.

"Do you think we've been in love with each other this entire time but we're only just now realizing it?" he asked.

"It doesn't matter."

"How could it not matter?"

"Because you were a different you before this exact moment. And I was a different me. It never would've worked out if we'd attempted it before we did."

He pulled her in with one arm, careful not to spill their coffees as he leaned down to nuzzle her nose. "I love you."

Her smile was unstoppable. "I love you, too. I don't know how to not be in love with you, so I may as well stick around."

"That's the spirit." He looked out at the pouring rain. "Nice day for a walk."

"The perfect day for a walk," she agreed.

His arm around her neck, they stepped out from under the awning, allowing the rain to drench them as they meandered down the sidewalk. "Plus, no one else makes me M&M cookies."

"The foundation of every strong relationship," she said.

"That and sex in the laundry room."

"Or on the couch."

"Or the balcony."

She blinked up at him, the rain soaking her cheeks. "We didn't have sex on the balcony."

"Not yet. I read a balcony sex scene in the romance novel you left at my penthouse. I think we should try it."

"You read a romance novel?"

"I have a lot to learn."

"Seems like you've learned a lot already." She gripped his shirt and tugged him close. "Now kiss me in the rain. It'll make the perfect ending."

Flynn dipped his mouth to hers and drank her in, the cool rainwater causing their lips to slip. He held her tightly, making good on his promise never to let her go. Rain or shine, apparently.

When they parted, his blue eyes locked on hers, his arms still holding her. Then a genuine, perfect grin lit his face. "Say it."

"Say what?"

"The ending."

"Oh, right." She cleared her throat and announced, "And they lived happily ever after."

* * * * *